The baby was born in early March, on a wild wet afternoon. The wind lashed the rain against the windows of her room, while inside by the fire the fierce pangs of her body did their work.

At dusk the wind died down and the rain ceased and into the candlelit quiet Susannah saw her child emerge, a tiny creature covered with the greasy coating of birth. She saw her father bend over to cut the cord, heard the first cry, growing in force.

'A boy – a healthy little boy!' It did not sound like her father's voice, but was somehow harsh and muffled at once. Susannah saw that there were tears in his eyes, though he would not look directly at her, but simply turned to take the child and hand him to her.

Then he suddenly leaned over and kissed her and she looked up and saw that he was smiling through his tears. 'God knows I wouldn't have chosen it to be this way. But I thank Him all the same . . . What will you call him?'

'Daniel.' She said. 'He'll need all the courage I can give him.'

DISORDERED
LAND

Helen Cannam

WARNER BOOKS

A *Warner* Book

First published in Great Britain
in 1995 by Little, Brown and Company
This edition published by Warner Books in 1997

A CIP catalogue record for this book
is available from the British Library.

ISBN 0 7515 0537 4

Typeset by M Rules
Printed and bound in Great Britain by
Clays Ltd, St Ives plc

Warner Books
A division of
Little, Brown and Company (UK)
Brettenham House
Lancaster Place
London WC2E 7EN

For my brothers Tim and Hugh,
with love.

SCOTLAND

• Dunbar
Edinburgh •
• Berwick

• Tynemouth
• Carlisle   • Newcastle
             • Durham

                        • Scarborough

             • York
Bradford •   • Leeds • Hull
• Preston
             • Pontefract

• Chester
    • Nantwich
       Newark •
    • Shrewsbury • Nottingham

         Leicester •
    • Worcester   ENGLAND

IRELAND   • Northampton
Drogheda •   Colchester •

Dublin •   • Gloucester
                         • Oxford
            Abingdon • • Brentford
WALES   • Bristol   London
Clonmel • Wexford • Newbury • • Reading

Belfast •

            Taunton •

       Exeter • Lyme •
Fowey • Plymouth

PEOPLE IN THE STORY

All the main characters are listed below, except those rarely mentioned and those born in the course of the book. Those marked with an asterisk had some existence in history.

The Blackheugh Connection

Ludovick, Lord Milburn
Rob Robson, his servant
Lady Katherine Milburn, his mother (formerly Dillon, née O'Neill)
Charles, his twin brother
Shane O'Neill, his cousin
Master Hedley, his steward

Soldiers in Ludovick's troop

Tot Charlton
Toby Milburn
Doll, Toby's woman
Will Dodd
Barty Robson
Jack Robson
Simon Milburn
Arthur Hoskins
Davy Pugh
Goodwife Pugh, Davy's mother
Lieutenant Haynes
Father Young, chaplain

At court

*King Charles the First
*Henrietta Maria, his wife
*Charles-Louis, his nephew, Elector Palatine of the Rhine
*Thomas Wentworth, Earl of Strafford
*William Laud, Archbishop of Canterbury
*George, Lord Digby
Lady Selina Blackwood

Royalist soldiers

*William Cavendish, Earl of Newcastle
Harry Middleton
Captain Percy

*George Goring
*Prince Rupert, brother of the
  Elector Palatine
*Prince Maurice, his younger
  brother
*Daniel O'Neill
*Sir Henry Gage
*Sir John Byron
*James Graham, Earl of
  Montrose

In Ireland

*James Butler, Marquis of
  Ormonde, devoted Royalist
*Owen Roe O'Neill, Confederate
  Irish leader
*Hugh O'Neill, another
  confederate leader

The Widehope Connection

Sir Ralph Liddell
Elizabeth, his wife
Dorothy, Cuthbert and Mark, his
  three eldest children
John Bolam, their neighbour
*Anthony Pearson, another
  neighbour

The Thornside Connection

Richard Metcalfe of Thornside
  Hall
Dame Alice, his mother
Anne, his sister
Henry Greatorex, her husband
Reverend Nathaniel Johnson,
  vicar of Thornside
Jeremiah, his brother, also a
  minister

Barbara Chaytor, a Royalist
  heiress
Doctor Matthew Fawcett
Susannah, his daughter
Margaret and John, their
  servants
Margery Nelson, town midwife
Nan Bestwick, town whore
Mary Wetherald
Jane, her daughter
Nicholas Lobley, music master
John Alderson, farmer
Jane, his wife
Anthony Dowthwaite, farmer
Ellinor, his wife
John, his brother, Roundhead
  soldier

In York

Judith Moorhouse, sister to
  Matthew Fawcett
Molly, her servant
Doctor Baty

In London

Abel Reynolds, saddler
Cecily, his wife
Esther, his daughter
Walter Barras, his apprentice
*John Lilburne, rebel

Members of Parliament in
opposition to the King

*Sir Henry Vane the younger
*Earl of Essex
*Earl of Manchester (formerly
  Lord Mandeville)

*John Pym
*Denzil Holles
*Oliver Cromwell
*John Hampden
*William Strode
*Sir Arthur Hazelrigg
*Ferdinando, Lord Fairfax
*Sir John Hotham and his son

Parliamentarian soldiers

*Sir Thomas Fairfax, son of
    Lord Fairfax
*Anne, his wife
*Mary (Moll), their daughter
*John Lambert
*Sir William Waller
*Colonel Edward Massey
*Major-General Browne

*Colonel John Okey
*Colonel Graves
*Major-General Philip Skippon
*Robert Lilburne, brother to
    John
*Cornet George Joyce
Amias Stephens, former brewer's
    apprentice
Roger Tyler, cloth merchant's son
Corporal Samuel Revol
Will Harper
Will Betterton, of Fairfax's foot
Poll, his wife
John Sawyer

Quakers

*James Nayler, former soldier
*George Fox, weaver

1640

CHAPTER ONE

'Tynemouth Castle,' said Rob. 'We're there.'

Ludovick, on deck beside him, peered into the grey dawn mist. He could just make out the looming shape of the castle on its rock, the priory church behind. Twelve years since he had last seen them . . . He shivered – but then it was cold, so early on this last day of April 1640.

'Not long now,' Rob added. He had a foolish grin on his face. By this evening, all being well, they should reach Blackheugh. 'No land like it,' Rob went on, 'Northumberland. And Tynedale's the best part of it. You can keep Flanders – and France – and anywhere else you care to mention. Just give me Northumberland. Home.'

'I never knew you minded so much.' Ludovick's tone was casual, but he kept his eyes on his companion's face.

'Minded what?'

'Being away.'

'Oh, I didn't. Never gave it a thought, most of the time. But, by, it's good to be back, all the same!'

There was a little silence, as the ship slowly edged towards the mouth of the Tyne. Ludovick peered again into the mist, watching. Then he said sharply, 'Looks as if there's a welcome party.'

A small boat was just visible, coming towards them from the direction of the Castle. Shouts echoed over the water, the words muffled. 'Maybe we're embarking here, not at Shields,' suggested Rob.

Ludovick shook his head. 'No, it's my guess it's Customs.'

'Oh God, that's all we need!' Rob glanced up at the spread of sail behind them. 'Maybe the captain'll put about, give them the slip.'

'What, with no wind worth speaking of and all the guns of Tynemouth trained on us? He'd be a fool. Someone must have tipped them off. They'll be watching every move we make. No, we'll just have to brazen it out.'

'It's all right for us.'

'Aye.' Ludovick knew Rob was thinking of the only other passenger, the self-styled merchant from Flanders, at present, presumably, still asleep below deck.

When the Customs men boarded the ship, the merchant looked calm enough, though bewildered, as would any man who understood little English and did not quite know why he had been so suddenly roused from sleep.

The men searched the ship with exemplary thoroughness, and all the passenger baggage too, but found nothing incriminating. Then they took the passengers ashore, to the Customs House at Tynemouth, allowing the Captain to sail on up the Tyne in search of his cargo of coal. By now it was mid-morning. 'So much for getting home tonight,' muttered Rob.

They were all three examined at great length, the merchant first of all. He clung to his story, babbling away in frightened Flemish or incomprehensible broken English when the questions became most pressing. Forced to turn out his pockets, he laid a rosary among the other objects on the table before him, but a Fleming could not be arrested simply for being a Catholic; as a subject of the King of Spain, he probably had little choice in the matter. His papers must have borne out his story better than Ludovick had feared they might, for after an hour the officers gave up on him.

'Now, you two. You're travelling together?'

Ludovick handed over their papers, which the man took an uncomfortably long time to read. Their contact in Antwerp had done his work well – the signature of the then Secretary of State, Sir John Coke, giving permission last summer for three years' travel, was excellently done. But one could never be sure. 'You're Ludovick Milburn, and this is your servant, Robert Robson. My Lord Milburn, I should say.' The officer removed his hat and got to his feet, making a slight, reluctant bow.

'That's why I'm here,' said Ludovick. 'My father has died.'

'A notorious Papist . . . But that was last year, I recall. You took your time coming home, my lord. What was your lordship doing overseas?' The officer returned his attention to the papers. 'For your health, this says.' He studied the young man's face. It had little natural colour, but looked healthy enough. 'Your lordship doesn't look sick to me.'

'I'm not. The cure worked.'

The officer tried a different approach. 'We found a sword in your lordship's baggage, along with a carbine. Perhaps your lordship would be so good as to account for them.'

Ludovick considered his reply with care. The penal laws against Catholics were an unpredictable area. Since King Charles, while still Prince of Wales, had married the Catholic Princess Henrietta Maria of France, the laws had often fallen into virtual disuse, but now and then public pressure would force their sudden harsh revival. Ludovick had no idea whether or not they were in such a period now. He did know, however, both that it was illegal for Catholics to carry arms, and that an heir to a Catholic father, sent abroad for his education, was liable to lose all rights to his inheritance. His own father, in favour at court, had bought exemption from the laws, but how far that went Ludovick did not know, and in any case he was not his father. 'I carry the sword for my own safety. I've been travelling in lands at war.'

'For the good of your lordship's health!'

'To reach the waters at Baden one must pass through troubled areas. Then there are brigands and—'

'Yes, yes. But your lordship is now in England. I must ask that your lordship take the oath of allegiance.'

The oath that confirmed not only loyalty to the King, but also denied the worldly authority of the Pope: it was a notorious trap for scrupulous Catholics. Ludovick hesitated. He seemed to feel a hand on his shoulder, at once warning and encouraging. He knew exactly what it meant, what was hoped for; but he had no intention of giving way. He shrugged, as if to throw off an unwanted restraint, and then he drew a deep breath and, trying to sound casual, said, 'Of course.'

He took the oath, with his fingers crossed below the table, and Rob took it too, presumably with similar mental reservations. After that, to their great relief, all three passengers were allowed to go.

By now it was well into the afternoon. They went together to an inn to find something to eat and, while they sat at table in a quiet corner, the Flemish merchant leaned across and said, in an undertone but in perfect English, 'You'll not get to Tynedale today. The lady of the house where I'm going will offer you hospitality until morning.'

She was almost effusively welcoming, though she reserved her most lavish attentions for the merchant, who had several aliases but whose real name was Father John Bullen. Her hospitality was not without its uncomfortable side. Over supper she scarcely stopped talking about her fears for the future: fears of the Scots army gathered on the border, so near to her house in the suburbs of Newcastle; fears of what dangers and discomforts warfare might bring; fears, worst of all, of what might happen if the Scots allied themselves firmly with like-minded Protestants in England and sought to impose their intolerant rule on their sister kingdom. 'Then we shall find ourselves in such a plight, we shall wish we had the worst of the penal days back again, to give us relief.'

'My daughter, trust in God to keep you safe,' Father Bullen said soothingly. 'And be sure that if the worst happens then you will be given the strength to bear it.'

The next morning early Father Bullen celebrated mass for the household in the simple attic chapel (easily converted to a mere lumber room); after which Ludovick and Rob hired horses and set out on the last stage of their journey.

'I thought you weren't going to take that oath, yesterday,' Rob said, with a shudder in his voice, as they followed the line of the Pictish wall westward from Newcastle.

'Well, I did.'

'What I thought was, Master Charles wouldn't have done.'

'I know.' Ludovick had felt it yesterday, at that moment of choice. 'Not everyone takes such a strict line as the Jesuits.' His twin was not yet a Jesuit, not even a priest, but if all went as he hoped that was his ultimate goal.

It was the first of May, and in many of the villages through which they passed maypoles had been set up, and men and women in their Sunday best, decked – like the maypoles – with flowers and ribbons, were dancing round them to the lively screeching of fiddles. The air was full of the sounds of music and laughter. Trees and hedgerows were coming into leaf, sharply green in the clear northern light against a landscape also greening and covered with violets and primroses, cowslips and daisies and dandelions. Even the stinking squalor of the colliery settlements, through which they passed at first, was softened by the spring sunlight and the holiday celebrations.

There was, Ludovick thought, something odd about it all,

something he could not quite lay his finger on. And then it came to him: there were no signs of war here, no convoys of wagons, well guarded, carrying supplies of food or cash, no burnt-out villages and frightened people, no sound of guns. Women looked round in mere curiosity as they passed; children played without fear. In the fields crops sent green shoots into a brown earth untrampled by the hooves of passing cavalry. In gardens, neat rows of vegetables had been planted, in the clear expectation that no thieving army would prevent their growing. A tranquil land, untouched by disharmony, with not a soldier in sight. 'You wouldn't think it was in the same universe,' he said.

Rob looked round, clearly puzzled. 'As what?'

'Flanders.'

'No, you're right.'

They both had in their minds memories of the past five years: of endless marches through a landscape scarred by war; of sieges and sacked towns, burning buildings, drunken soldiers greedy for loot; of men and women and children tortured and raped and muti-lated – a world in which it felt sometimes as if all humanity had been reduced to savagery. It was hard now in the clear northern light of this May morning to believe that such horrors were still tak-ing place just a few miles away across the sea. It was hard even to believe that the peace of this land might ever be threatened. If their host of last night was afraid, it did not seem that anyone else was.

They did see one small troop of soldiers, after they turned along the North Tyne river. They were closer to the border here, so per-haps it was to be expected. But the men were as much in holiday mood as the rest of the population. They had dismounted on the river-bank in the sunshine and were eating and drinking and dicing, with much noisy talk and laughter. Most of them had neither uni-form nor armour of any kind, and their weapons, flung on the grass, were an odd assortment of antique swords, farm implements and even bows and arrows; there were few guns. They seemed quite unconcerned to see two strange men riding purposefully past them, though to be on the safe side Ludovick paused to explain his errand to their officer, who turned out to have known his father slightly. They were borderers too, the officer told them, recruited to meet the threat from the Scots, their natural enemy. They looked forward to a fight, but were by no means sure they would get one.

Beyond the village of Wark, the country grew wilder, and in the air was a smell that caught in Ludovick's nostrils, bringing a rush of memory: peat smoke. It was years since he had smelled it, not since childhood. But what now came into his thoughts, obliterating the sunny half-remembered landscape, was not Tynedale, but another, earlier place, when he was just an infant . . . Peat smoke and the smell of reeds and dung and damp thatch, the sound of rain; a darkness that was external only, for there was warmth, and arms about him, and safety, there by the glowing peats. It was a memory without definition or detail, yet shot through with a quite disproportionate intensity of feeling . . . Warmth and safety; and an aching, eternal sense of loss.

'Home,' said Rob beside him, with a note of rapture in his voice. Ludovick was brought sharply back from that elusive memory of what had indeed been home – if he could give any place that name – to the wild land into which they were riding, the place where Rob had been born and grown up, where his ancestors had lived for centuries, from the very dawn of time perhaps. So too had Ludovick's ancestors, on his father's side. But they made no call to his heart; he felt no sense of being rooted here. He saw Rob glance at him, as if suddenly recalling that for him there could be no rapture in this return. Did he too remember the day of their leaving?

They forded the river at Bellingham, a poor little town with a few better stone houses and a fortress-like church. There, bordered with primroses and violets and the faded remnants of ribbons hung as offerings on nearby branches, was Cuddy's well, sacred to St Cuthbert, where once, on Ash Wednesday – *the better the day the better the deed* – he had called down an ineffectual curse upon his father, with all the solemn passion of a desperate child.

Along the winding track, the river on their left, then a turn to the right through oak trees . . . His heart was thudding, so that he could scarcely breathe. Up a little, a bend in the track, and there it was: Blackheugh.

There was the tower, solid, dark, somehow smaller than he expected. In his memory it was a vast edifice, like Tynemouth Castle on its rock. This was soft grey stone, only one part of a range of buildings, merging well into the fine modern house his father had constructed on its eastern side. That, on the other hand, was larger than he remembered, but then his father had been constantly building, driven by his vision of a mansion worthy of the Barony he had acquired, the dynasty he was to establish. Strange that he should have left the tower standing . . . Or perhaps not strange at all. So simple and unimpressive a building, that tower; yet Ludovick remembered its sombreness, the dreadful haunted darkness, splashed with blood and fear.

Almost, for a moment, he wanted to swing his horse round and ride away, as far as flesh and blood could take him. Then he felt again that steadying sensation, like a touch on his shoulder, though no human hand touched him, no voice spoke. Only the feeling was there, strengthening him to face what must be faced. This time he did not reject it, but allowed himself to accept what it offered.

'Here we are,' he said, his voice only a little shaky. They had reached the front of the house and servants in black and scarlet livery hurried to take their horses and grasp the baggage, bowing, calling him 'my lord', as if they had been doing it all their lives. Not quite knowing what he was doing, too full of dark and confused emotions for clear thought, Ludovick dismounted and then found himself stepping towards the doorway, with its carved hawk badge over the stone arch. There stood the gaunt figure of his father's steward, bowing very low, the other servants – fifty or sixty in all – ranged behind him in descending order of superiority, the men bareheaded, all bowing and curtseying in a wave as he passed them, like flowers in a border swept by the wind. Beyond them in the depths of the hall waited a slight woman in black with untidy greying hair and a pale face. Suddenly shaking uncontrollably, Ludovick took off his hat and went to her and knelt on the flagged floor at her feet.

'I ask for your blessing, mother.'

CHAPTER TWO

In London there were maypoles too, for the holiday. But within a few days the dancing was at an end and the city apprentices, in more serious mood, had found other, graver, work to do. King Charles had just dissolved his first parliament for eleven years, after less than four weeks of its sitting; it was said that the Archbishop of Canterbury had urged him to it.

Walter Barras, saddler's apprentice, was there with the other lads as they marched across London Bridge and through the streets of Southwark to St George's Fields, where a great throng of the young and the unemployed was gathering, full of noise and rage.

This morning, as for days now, they had woken to find placards posted on every convenient surface – walls, doorposts, pillars – urging the people of London to rise for their freedom, in support of the Parliament, against the Bishops. 'John Lilburne, he'll be behind them,' many of the apprentices had said, echoing Esther's words of two days ago. Today, she had said to Walter, 'You give him a cheer on your way past the Fleet.' Crossing the stinking Fleet river the apprentices had done just that, chanting Lilburne's name like a rallying cry so that he might hear them from his prison and be heartened. Walter's voice was loudest of all: 'John Lilburne! John Lilburne!' In his mind all the time there had been the picture of the young Durham man as he had last seen him two years ago, stooped in the pillory in New Palace Yard at the end of his agonising journey from the Fleet prison to Westminster, whipped all the way at the cart's tail. Bloody, exhausted, yet he had talked, on and on though his voice grew hoarse, his eloquent denunciation of the malice of bishops pouring over the listening crowd, until his captors savagely gagged him.

'He talks like you do, the same accent,' Esther had said that day, as she and Walter had walked back to her father's workshop in Holborn, fired with indignation. Walter had known that was not quite true. If he still had any of his childhood accent left to him – and he thought there was little enough after ten years in London – it bore only a surface resemblance to that of the Durham gentleman. Tynedale was a long way from the Bishopric, its accent softer, more lilting, closer to that of the Scots a short distance away across the border. But to London ears one north-east accent was doubtless much like another, and he could excuse Esther any inaccuracy, any fault even, which this was not. Besides, to be compared even in the slightest degree with the heroic John Lilburne made him hold his head high with pride.

On St George's Fields, a stocky young seaman – out of work, like so many of his fellows – was beating a drum to call the neighbourhood to join them. Around him, voices chanted for the downfall of Papists and Spaniards and bishops. In every corner of the field there were wild speeches and prayers and songs, a noisy, chaotic chorus of anger, growing and spreading until at last, after an hour or so, it found a focus. A single voice rose high and clear and harsh above the din. 'Let's hunt the fox – let's get Laud!'

There was a massive, united roar of rage, and then the entire crowd turned as one man and streamed west towards Lambeth Palace; city apprentices, seamen and dockers and glovers and tanners, and Walter too, howling for the downfall of William Laud, hated Archbishop of Canterbury, who in the court of Star Chamber had so savagely condemned John Lilburne, just for refusing to swear an oath.

Laud must have had his spies watching events that morning, for by the time the apprentices reached Lambeth he had long gone. By then, too, the London militia – the Trained Bands – had been ordered out by the King to suppress the riot. Walter, like all but a few, escaped arrest and slipped quietly home. He felt obscurely humiliated, like a huntsman cheated of the kill.

His master, Abel Reynolds, listened quietly to his subdued account of events and then declared, with sober confidence, 'The day of the Lord will surely come.'

Esther, on the other hand, gave him the sweetest of looks from under her long dark lashes, but it was only later, when her father's back was turned, that she said with soft concern, 'You're hurt,

Walter!' He felt her hand touch his cheek and then saw it come
away smeared with blood.

'I didn't know,' he said, but when she took out her embroidered
handkerchief and wiped the wound – no more than a graze – he
wished it had been something much worse, so that she might have
been impressed by his courage and loved him the more.

The clamour of the streets outside the inn had kept Sir Ralph Liddell
awake for much of the night, but by the time he came downstairs, at
dawn the next morning, everything seemed to have returned to normal – that is, noisy but peaceable. He had a little time to wait until
his hired coach was ready for him, so he settled down in the parlour
to a good breakfast of mutton collops, eggs and ale. The inn was
busy, but a snatch of conversation from two men at the further side
of the room suddenly caught his attention. 'I'll write as soon as I get
to Thornside . . .' He looked up, and saw that the speaker was a
young man, tall and strongly made, with soft fair hair and a warm
complexion, dressed much like any other gentleman about to set out
upon a journey. His companion was older and more soberly dressed,
a servant perhaps. Soon afterwards, the young man parted from the
other and passed near Sir Ralph, who called to him, 'Pardon me, sir,
for my curiosity, but did I hear you speak of Thornside?'

'Indeed yes, sir,' said the young man, a little warily. 'That's where
I'm bound.'

'Thornside, in the North Riding of Yorkshire?'

'In Wensleydale, yes.' He grinned, which gave him a boyish look.
'Where else?'

'Then we're bound for the same destination.' Sir Ralph was aware
that in disclosing his intentions so freely to a complete stranger he
was taking something of a risk; but not much of one, he felt. The
young man had a pleasant, open face and an agreeable manner.

'Indeed, sir?' he said now. 'That is a coincidence.' It was, for
Thornside was a small market town of no great significance, except
to its inhabitants. There could be few people in London who had
even heard of it. 'I live there,' the young man went on. 'In fact, I
have the honour to represent it in Parliament.' He spoke with a certain pride which Sir Ralph found touching.

'Then you must be Master Richard Metcalfe!'

'Indeed, yes.' He pulled up a stool. 'Do you mind if I sit here, sir?
Whom have I the honour—?'

'Sir Ralph Liddell of Widehope in the Bishopric. Where I'm bound, but intending to call on my old friend Doctor Matthew Fawcett on the way.'

The young man paused to remove his hat and exchange a bow with Sir Ralph –'Your servant, sir' – colouring meanwhile with ingenuous pleasure. 'I know Doctor Fawcett well! But if I may ask, how do you come to know him?'

'I'm kin to his wife. As a child I lived with her family.'

Sitting down, Richard assumed an expression of suitable solemnity. 'I never knew her. But I know he cherishes her memory.'

'She was the best of women, like a second mother to me. Her death was a most terrible blow, made the worse perhaps because Doctor Fawcett felt he should have been able to prevent it. But God willed otherwise. At least she gave him Susannah.' Sir Ralph shook his head in the way one does when absorbed in pleasant reflection. 'A lovely young creature. She will break a few hearts one day.'

Richard could bring to mind only a silent, gawky young girl, a little intimidating, for she was said to be learned. 'I have no very recent acquaintance with her. I have been away from home a good deal. But Doctor Fawcett often sups with us at the Hall.' He beamed, as if suddenly realising the joyful implications of this unexpected meeting. 'My dear sir, this is indeed a pleasure!'

'Tell me then, how do you intend to travel? By coach?'

'No, they are saddling a horse for me.'

'Then I beg you to countermand the order and accept a place in my coach. They should have it ready soon. I plan to make use of it as far as York, and then ride from there.'

'That is most kind, sir. It would be a pleasure.'

And so the two men found themselves an hour later side by side in the hired coach as it lumbered its way through the streets towards the city gates, already feeling as if they had known one another all their lives.

'I've been in London on business,' said Sir Ralph, in answer to a question from Richard.

'Successfully completed, sir, I hope,' said the young man.

'Very much so.' Then Ralph added, a little warily, 'It has to do with my plans for my daughter's marriage.' He did not go on to explain the nature of his business, or even to enlarge upon his satisfaction at its success. He did not quite know why not. There was nothing secret about it and he liked this young man, and they had a friend in common. But he could not quite rid himself of a very faint feeling of shame, which detracted a little, even in this moment of triumph, from his pleasure at his success.

It was all Elizabeth's fault. He had assured her that whatever happened Dorothy would be allowed the final say in the matter. He was an indulgent father. Elizabeth was a good wife too, the very best, and he valued her approval, but in this he knew he did not have it. 'All you want is revenge,' she had said, when he had at last insisted that she explain her persistent look of disapproval. 'You say you're doing what's best for Dorothy, but you know that's not true.'

'It will be a most advantageous match, one such as any girl could hope for.'

'Not if he's like his father.'

'If he's like his father then I'll milk him for all he's worth and send him packing, and, of course, there'll be no wedding. It's as simple as that.'

'I never knew you were a vindictive man,' Elizabeth had said, and had then refused to discuss the matter further, on the grounds that he clearly had no intention of listening to what she had to say, still less of acting upon it.

Sir Ralph was quite sure he was not vindictive, but it had seemed too good an opportunity to miss: the sudden, unexpected death of Randal, Lord Milburn, just ten months before his heir came of age. Someone had to manage the Blackheugh estates until the boy reached his majority and that fortunate someone would have the right, not only to a good financial return for his pains, but also to find a bride of his choosing for the heir. Sir Ralph was himself sufficiently well-to-do to be able to grease the appropriate palms about the Royal Court of Wards, and patient enough to persist through the long weeks and months of waiting for a decision and for the heir to be found. Now he had his reward and an opportunity to regain, with interest, the lands that the late Lord Milburn had so ruthlessly filched from him, by means of dubious legal proceedings, all those years ago: five profitable coal mines bordering the Tyne, with prospects for considerable improvement, three good farms and a mill. He was only doing what any good father would do, providing for his wife and babes as best he could.

He realised suddenly that Richard was speaking to him, and put his own unease out of his mind. 'It is, in part, a marriage that takes me home,' the young man was saying. 'I should have had to go home soon, even had Parliament not been dissolved. My sister is to be married.'

'A younger sister?'

'Yes, sir, by six years – my only sister, so we have always meant much to one another. I shall be grieved to lose her. But I couldn't wish a better bridegroom for her. He is my dearest friend.'

'The foundation of all human happiness, a good marriage,' said Sir Ralph.

Richard agreed, a little uncomfortably, for it reminded him that there was another marriage that ought to be occupying his attention: his own. He was twenty-five and the owner of considerable estates, which must be provided with an heir. But so far none of the eligible ladies suggested to him by his widowed mother had tempted him. 'You are too particular,' Dame Alice Metcalfe had told him, more than once. 'You can't expect perfection in this life.' Yet still he refused to accept second best, all the while aware that time was running out.

'Troubled times,' said Sir Ralph, as they glimpsed a group of young men on a street corner, gathered in angry talk before a poster. 'And where there's trouble there's John Lilburne, somewhere about – or so I begin to believe.'

'Certainly he seems to have influence, sir, even from his prison cell. But then he has justice on his side.'

'Maybe. He was always a firebrand, even in childhood.' Ralph smiled at Richard's look of surprise. 'The Lilburne lands run close to mine,' he explained. 'But of course our troubles go deeper than young Lilburne's sufferings. I suppose with the dissolving of Parliament we are now further than ever from their solution. His Majesty will be hard pressed to raise troops against the Scots without the necessary funds.'

'Perhaps, sir,' said Richard, aware that he might be treading on dangerous ground; one had to be so careful these days, 'His Majesty – or those who advise him – should have considered that, before so provoking our northern brethren.' He waited, a little anxiously, for an outburst of disagreement from Sir Ralph. He had taken a liking to the man, and in any case to offend him would be a poor way to recompense him for his kindness. But, good-natured though he was, Richard had never shrunk from controversy where matters of principle were concerned.

'In that I must agree with you,' said Sir Ralph, to his relief. 'The whole thing has been sadly mismanaged. We all know the Scots are fanatical in their religion. To tamper with it was to rouse the lion. Better to have let it sleep and allow Scots and English to differ.'

The danger was not after all safely passed. Richard even felt a surge of indignation at so unprincipled a view. 'Ah, but in that I cannot agree!' he returned vehemently. 'Religion can never be a matter of indifference! That is to say that the truth is open to argument. No, sir, the fault in this business lies rather with the servants of His Majesty – the Archbishop, supremely, and my Lord of Strafford too – those who wish to turn the Church away from the reformed path, in Scotland as in England. Surely in matters of religion it is the Scots who have the right of it, and we who should rather look to them for an example?'

'Ah, now, if you're going to argue for Presbyterianism, then you'll lose me. But then, I admit I'm no theologian. So long as we're not under the heel of either Pope or Presbyterian Assembly, then I'm content to take whatever seems the most peaceable path – which, I fear, is not the one His Majesty or my Lord Archbishop have chosen. In that at least we're agreed. However, it's one thing for the Scots to oppose their King in council or Parliament. It's quite another to raise an army against him. That army must be defeated, with all speed. Yet the doing of it – that's going to be the difficult part. We made a poor enough fist of it last year.'

'It will not be done, sir. Parliament is dissolved, the King has not the means to raise fresh troops, *ergo* the Scots must be given what they require, or they will march into England.'

'If you lived a little further north,' said Sir Ralph, 'you would not look on that prospect so philosophically.'

'Perhaps not,' Richard admitted. He paused a moment, then asked, 'You had heard that my Lord Strafford has been seeking troops in Ireland?'

At that Ralph shook his head, all gravity. On the subject of the Earl of Strafford, Lord Deputy of Ireland and previously a much-hated President of the Council of the North, they could agree. 'I heard he was trying his luck with Spain, which is much the same thing. To bring a Papist army in to crush Presbyterian Scots – that would be to fan the flames indeed.'

'Please God it won't come to that, sir.'

'To which I'll say *Amen*, and trust that good sense will prevail before it's too late.' He sounded as if, on the whole, he rather thought it would. He glanced out of the window. 'Ah, Gray's Inn! When we get to this point I know we're well on our way.'

That night the apprentices were on the streets again, rushing in force to Newgate gaol, where they beat down the doors and freed the handful of men arrested at Lambeth, now awaiting trial.

Their triumph was soon over. The King simply ordered more trained bands from outside London to suppress the disorder and recapture the escaped men. Among those later brought before the courts was the young seaman who had banged the drum on St George's Fields. He was tortured first, to make him name his accomplices in conspiracy against the State. He admitted nothing, but he was found guilty all the same, of high treason, along with a number of others, including a lad of nineteen, one Thomas Benstead. Walter was given leave to go and see them die, part of a massive indignant crowd, and then he came home to pour out his anger to his master and the other two apprentices; and to Esther, though for once she was not uppermost in his thoughts.

'You know what Tom Benstead did?' Walter demanded, tears of rage in his eyes, his voice hoarse with grief. 'He took a crowbar to the Archbishop's door. High treason that is, to break a door!' He raised his fists heavenward. 'Dear God, how much longer must your people suffer!'

His master laid a hand on his shoulder; it was, for him, a rare gesture of affection. Though he had given Walter almost everything that mattered to him in life, from the first moment he took him into his home, he was a severe and undemonstrative man and Walter had never been shown any favours. 'Not long, Walter Barras, not long now. The signs are there. The Scots are on the border. Godly men are working for the Lord's coming. Thou heard the preacher on Sunday: *There shall be a time of trouble, such as never was*. But also, *at that time Thy people shall be delivered, every one that shall be found written in the book*.

'But for now,' he added, looking round at the sombre faces of the young men gathered about him, 'we have a living to make. Let's get back to work shall we?'

CHAPTER THREE

Ludovick Milburn reined in his horse beside the solitary pine that crowned the slope above Blackheugh and gazed out over the valley, through which the North Tyne looped its shining eastward way from its source at Deadwater on the Scottish border towards its junction with the South Tyne, several miles away near the Pictish wall.

Immediately below him, on a swelling mound above the level river pasture, stood the house and its surrounding buildings, fringed by ancient oak woods. All the land this side of the river was Blackheugh land, almost as far as he could see; his land. Yet he knew now how small a fraction of his inheritance this was, a tiny part of the vast wealth accumulated by his father over the years, by means of judicious marriages, shrewd purchase, the ending of ancient – and unprofitable – forms of land tenure, and years of careful, calculated use of the law courts.

'A great man, your lordship's father, God rest his soul,' his steward had said, with irritating frequency, as he laid before the young heir document after document proving his title to this property or that, so many of them that his head had begun to spin. Ludovick had been relieved when, after the first few days, Master Hedley had given up trying to explain title deeds and rent rolls to him and taken him on a tour of his estates. He had not until then realised how very extensive they were, that they reached in tongues and fingers and great swathes not only through a large part of Northumberland, but into Durham and Cumberland and even, at one point, the North Riding of Yorkshire. They had ridden for many miles, staying overnight at this mansion or that former abbey, guests of a reluctant tenant or received with flurried deference by servants used to the late Baron's exacting standards. There was land, like this at Blackheugh, good for sheep but little else, but also with moors rich in game; there was pasture; there were forests with deer; there were cornfields; there were farms and mills; above all there were coal mines and lead mines, producing rich yields to pay for the exquisite luxuries with which the first Baron had signalled his importance to the world.

It was not until yesterday that the two of them, steward and master, had come back to Blackheugh itself, the house that had been designed as an island of civilisation in the wilderness of Tynedale, still scarcely tamed after centuries of border warfare. Back, too, to the mother Ludovick had only lately begun to know at all.

He pulled off his right glove and looked down at the gold ring he wore, set with a dark red stone cut with the family seal of a hawk: the badge of the Milburns of Blackheugh, his father's ring. His mother had given it to him on the night of his return, and he had put it on, slowly, fighting a sense of reluctance, because he must, because it was now his, the symbol of his inheritance and the power that went with it. Yet he had felt for hours afterwards as if it seared his flesh, infecting him with some poison from his father's malign spirit. If it had not been his mother who gave it to him, he might even have refused it.

Once it was on his finger, Ludovick had sat looking at it for a long time, much as he was doing now, except that then a chaos of painful feelings had been churning inside him. His mother had said nothing, but he had realised at last that she was watching him with the blue eyes that were an infinitely wearied version of his own.

'Would he have been proud of me, do you think?' he had asked, his voice suddenly sharp and ironic in the stillness.

She had not answered at once. Then she had said, with the soft lilt she had always kept, 'He was never proud of anyone but himself.'

'No.' The past had begun to drag him down again, shutting her out. Then, unexpectedly, he saw in her face a silent echo of his own memory of humiliation and contempt. 'Why did he marry you?' The question had burst out before the thought was fully formed in his mind, and at once he had wished desperately that he had not put it. *What had you to offer, I can see nothing* was unspoken in the question, though it was not what he had meant at all, but something much more complicated.

Lady Milburn smiled, very faintly, without warmth. 'It is well known wild Irish women give birth like animals. I had three sons by my first marriage, to prove it – three sons in four years. Two wives, he'd had, and no living child. Great wealth, a title, but never an heir to leave it to.'

'So he married you.' A vessel to carry the heir he so desperately wanted. How galling it must have been for him when the long-awaited child resembled, not the father's grace and splendour, but the earthen clay of the vessel! Ludovick had realised then how little he knew his mother. She had always been a silent, subdued woman, often pregnant though never again bearing a living child. 'I need Irish air to bear a healthy babe,' he had overheard her say once to his father, and had been surprised to detect a faint note of opposition. For the most part she rarely spoke and kept always in the background, making no comment, no protest, no observation on anything her husband said or did.

Emboldened by this moment of unwonted intimacy into further probing of a kind no son ought to direct towards his mother, Ludovick had said, 'But you were a widow. You could choose.' He had tried to imagine her, Lady Katherine Dillon, still very young, visiting her kin in the Low Countries, where Lord Milburn, passing through to take the waters, had met her again, grown to adulthood.

'He was handsome, and wealthy. His sister had been my dearest friend when we were at school together.'

Ludovick had studied her again, during the silence that followed, trying to imagine something of the life of which he had known so little. This woman who had once carried him in her body was a stranger to him still, after nearly twenty-one years, though he could see in her so much that, physically, had gone to make him what he was. Yet his father had played some part in forming him too, that was inescapable. His father, whose only sister . . . That was one other thing he wanted to ask, longed to know, but could not bring himself to put into words. What had she been like, his father's sister, as a girl in the Flemish convent where young Katherine O'Neill had been her schoolfellow and confidante? Had there been any wildness in her, any strangeness, to hint at what was to come? Had there been fierce swings of mood, sudden black pits of melancholy or horror of a kind he knew only too well, into which she would fall for days at a time, not knowing how to claw her way out?

Instead, he had said at last, 'You know I served with my cousin Shane in Flanders?'

There had been a momentary blankness on his mother's face, before she had suddenly smiled. 'He was always John when I knew him. Not that I can blame him for favouring the Irish form; he has no cause to love the English . . . Yes, I heard he was in Flanders, under Hugh O'Neill, was it not? I wondered if you would meet. There is nothing for him in Ireland any more, I suppose, not once they took Ballinary from my brother.' There had been a reflective silence, into which for Ludovick came that sharp evocative recollection of peat smoke and damp and warmth, and its concomitant sense of longing.

'Have you had news of him? Of my uncle, I mean?'

'He rubs along, after a fashion. He's well enough, but bitter. He was loyal, after all. Yet this is how they repay him! He had no legal title to Ballinary, they said – no legal title, when his forebears have lived there for centuries!'

'Shane thinks the Irish should look to the Scots for an example.'

'There's a Scotsman at Ballinary now.'

'Not in that. But the way they made a Covenant, for the defence of their religion and their liberties.'

'They are Protestants, so they can be sure of friends in England. The Irish have none, nor ever have had. They will have fewer still if the Scots get their way now.'

'There are some Irish have been welcomed at court. Besides, if you're strong enough then you don't need friends.'

His mother had shaken her head. 'I don't know.' Then she had changed the subject. 'Tell me, do you think one day Charles will come here as chaplain?'

It was a dream that had begun to form itself in Ludovick's mind, since he learned that Blackheugh's chaplain, once their tutor, had left long ago, following some disagreement with his father. He had begun to talk of what he knew of Charles's plans, bringing his brother into the room with them to chase the last shadows from it.

They had not gone for good, of course; the sense of his father's presence was too strong for that. It had returned to him in force as he toured his estates and saw for himself all that his father had achieved, for good or ill. He knew that the misery of so many of his father's tenants, struggling against neglect and ever-rising rents, was as much his father's handiwork as the fashionable splendour of Blackheugh itself.

Once, he had declared his intention to change something, to Master Hedley's clear disapproval. In the steward's eyes, nothing the late Baron had done could be in any way improved upon, still less questioned. But habits of deference had been bred deep in him by Ludovick's father. He had veiled his sense of outrage and said tentatively, 'If I may venture to remind your lordship that until you come of age, strictly speaking . . .'

'There's not three months to wait.' Ludovick had dismissed the hinted objection with a wave of the hand. 'I suppose my mother has the guardianship?'

'It has not yet been officially confirmed,' Master Hedley had said, 'and there was another party interested. But the days are gone when wardships were commonly sold outside the family. However, I would respectfully urge your lordship not to make any hasty decisions. You are – forgive me, my lord – you are young and you have little experience of the world. Your late father always had plans that you should spend some time at the Inns of Court. Your lordship's absence of course made that impossible. A great pity that it was not done, in my opinion. A knowledge of the law is invaluable for one in your position. You would not have such an inheritance as this had your father not been thoroughly versed in legal matters.'

'That,' said Ludovick, 'I can well believe.' He had seen Master Hedley give him a speculative look, as if puzzled and uneasy at the sharp note in his voice.

He had resolved then that as soon as he came of age he would set to work, piece by piece, to undo all the things his father had done, opposing him in death as he had never ultimately been able to do in life.

But he recognised that to know what he wanted to do was one thing, to do it would be quite another. The moment he had returned to Blackheugh, the atmosphere of the place had closed about him as if he were a child again, stifling him, and he knew he would have to fight his way through it before he could shake off its shackles of memory and habit. He had returned to his past, and things long forgotten had come rushing back to him, together with other things he would have liked to forget, but had never quite been able to put from his mind. More than once he had been tempted to leave it all behind and return to the Spanish service, where there had been nothing to remind him of Blackheugh or his father.

Yet he was young and strong and no longer a child, and his father was dead. He pulled his glove on again, covering the ring, and turned his horse's head and urged her down the hill towards the house. He had scarcely drawn rein in the stable yard when Master Hedley came running breathlessly to his side. 'My lord, I came in search of you. I have been with your lordship's mother. It is a most unfortunate matter—'

Ludovick went with him to the great chamber, where his mother sat by the fire. It was obvious that she had been crying, though she said nothing. The steward cleared his throat. 'If I may be permitted to explain—?' Lady Milburn nodded, so he went on, 'It would seem, my lord, that the wardship has not gone as we anticipated, as indeed anyone would have anticipated.' He too seemed unable to speak any more.

Ludovick broke impatiently into the long pause. 'You mean my mother has not been appointed guardian?'

'I fear not, my lord.'

'Who then? There are no other living kin that I know of. Except my uncle in Ireland, and my cousin Shane.' But that would surely not have set his mother weeping.

'They are Irish, Ludovick. Would they give the wardship of a precious English lord to a mere Irishman, still less a woman? Not even your own mother, God help us!' There was hurt and anger equally balanced in her outburst.

The steward waved a paper in front of Ludovick, with a broken seal dangling from it. 'This letter, my lord – to inform us in such terms! I had heard he was suing for the wardship, but I had no fear. Why should I? No one would have thought—! Sir Ralph Liddell of all people, one with every reason to do you wrong! I ask myself how it could ever have been permitted. After all the service your late father did for his Majesty the King, to reward it so. He is not even of your lordship's rank, a gentleman merely. It is, if I may say so, an insult.'

Ludovick took the letter, which simply stated, in bald terms that were just within the bounds of courtesy, that the writer had been appointed guardian of the heir and his estates and would be calling upon his ward in three days' time. 'That's tomorrow,' said Ludovick at last. 'Who is this man?'

'Sir Ralph Liddell had occasion more than once to enter into dispute with your late father, my lord. I fear he will not have your lordship's interests at heart.' And Master Hedley explained at some length the details of a particularly unpleasant court case, where the late Lord Milburn's influence had won advantages that seemed, on the face of it, contrary to common justice, though there was no trace of disapproval in the steward's manner as he told the tale.

Ludovick almost found himself warming to the thought of his new guardian; but not for long. After all, the man was unlikely to feel much more kindly towards the new Lord Milburn than the old, and was only too probably seeking some advantage for himself in the present business. 'Can he do much harm in three months?' He was vaguely aware that the Royal Court of Wards gave considerable powers to a guardian, which did not matter at all when that guardian was a trusted member of the family, with the ward's interests at heart. But in this case—

'A very great deal, I fear, my lord,' said the steward. 'Sometimes conditions are laid down, which must be met before an estate can be discharged from the wardship – over and above the customary financial dues, that is. I do know that Sir Ralph Liddell is not a Catholic. That fact may, I suppose, have carried some weight with the Court of Wards. He is said to have been responsible for the apostasy of several of his Catholic kinsfolk, entrusted in childhood to his care.'

'I am not a child.'

'Indeed no, but . . . We shall see. That is not all, however – you realise he has the power to arrange your lordship's marriage?'

That was probably the threat that had been furthest from Ludovick's mind. 'Do you think that's what he wants?'

'There is, I believe, a daughter . . .' The steward sighed. 'It is a great pity that the young lady your father had in mind for you is not still living. Alas, his lordship's own sudden tragic demise made it impossible for him to arrange another match. Though I fear even that could have been overthrown, had it not been brought to fruition. It is a matter of great regret that your lordship did not return home years ago as your father always intended – indeed, that you went overseas at all. You would otherwise have been safely married by now. How his late lordship would have bewailed the fate that may yet befall you!'

Ludovick could not imagine his father bewailing anything, but that he would have been enraged by it was the one cheering aspect of the present situation.

CHAPTER FOUR

There were salads, infinitely varied and decorative, boiled and roast meats, pasties and pies, three kinds of broth and a whole kid with a pudding in its belly. There was fish in abundance, boiled and soused, with lobsters and prawns and crabs. There was partridge and pheasant and swan and venison, and dishes of oysters and anchovies. There were custards and jellies and tarts. There were peas and artichokes and just a taste of that rare delicacy, the potato. There was claret and sack and muscadine, all set off with fine white damask and silver and glass. While the wedding guests ate and talked, a consort of viols played softly, though no one listened.

Behind the mounds of food on the long table in the great hall, Richard Metcalfe sat at his sister's left hand, taking the place at her wedding feast that would have been their father's, had he not died twelve years before. Now and then, he glanced round at her, as if to seek reassurance. Anne was looking unusually pretty today, in white satin and gold, with her fair hair – by nature straight and silky like his own – crimped into curls and crowned with flowers. Her face was flushed and, more to the point, she looked radiantly happy. Yet in church this morning Richard had thought her rather pale and solemn. He had feared she was not after all content with her marriage.

From his own point of view, it was everything that could be desired, and he had done all he could to promote it. Henry Greatorex was not only a good match in a worldly sense, and a kind and godly man, but he had also been Richard's closest friend ever since they were at Cambridge together. In bed last night (everyone had to share a bed in this overcrowded house) Henry had confided in Richard, more warmly than ever before, how happy he was to have won the hand of a woman who was the feminine counterpart of his dear friend, and would be loved the more for her brother's sake. It was only this morning that Richard had suddenly found himself wondering whether his sister shared their happiness. Anne was a dutiful girl, and what her mother and her brother thought was best for her she would invariably do, without complaint. Now, he turned to speak to her, anxious to study her face and read its expression. But before he could say anything to attract her attention, she had looked away from him to smile at the brown-haired young man on her other side, who reached out to take her hand and gaze at her as if she were the loveliest creature in the room. Richard felt not relief, but envy. Would he ever know a happiness like this? More than once, he had wished that Henry had a sister, whom he could make his wife; or he had until his return from London, when, on his first Sunday back at Thornside church, he had realised he wanted something quite different.

He tried not to look further along the table, away to his left, but his thoughts were there before his eyes had followed them, to the grave figure in pale blue silk, sitting quietly among the other women – among them, but not of them, with their whispers and giggles and sly glances at the men. Just a little lace edged her coif, from which soft tendrils of dark hair fell about the pure lovely oval of her face. No, his sister was not the loveliest woman in the room, whatever her bridegroom clearly thought. Richard wondered how it could have happened in so short a time, that Susannah Fawcett had grown from an awkward girl to a woman, and one so beautiful that the moment Richard had set eyes on her, walking out of the church into the sunlight, it was as if the world for an age stood still? 'She will break some hearts before she's done,' so Sir Ralph Liddell had said in London, to Richard's surprise. Yet within a matter of days he had known that she held his heart in her hands, to break or cherish as she chose.

Susannah's father, Doctor Matthew Fawcett, was also thinking of his daughter, though his eyes were on the bride. For the first time in his life he was making himself imagine Susannah in that seat, presiding over her own wedding feast, and it was an unsettling picture. What had put it in his mind was something his wife's kinsman Sir Ralph had said to him as they sat late by the fire one night during his recent visit, talking companionably of old times and new hopes. 'I suppose you'll be wanting a husband for Susannah before long,' Ralph had said, and it had been all Matthew could do not to cry out in protest. Yet she was twenty, an age at which many women were not only married but mothers, and Ralph had made him see only too clearly that the day must inevitably come when he would be asked to relinquish her to the care of another man. But he had no intention of seeking a bridegroom for her, as most fathers did, as Ralph had hinted he was soon to do for his Dorothy, who was five years younger than Susannah. Matthew was not such a fool as to give her up unnecessarily. Let her make her choice if she must, and let him only pray that it would be a wise one (as it would, for was she not wiser than any woman he knew?) and (less certain) that it would not result in her moving to the other side of the world – or even a few difficult miles from Thornside.

With some relief, the doctor pushed the unwelcome thought away and turned to listen to the bridegroom, who was, once again, enlarging with enthusiasm on the advantages of the land to which he would shortly take his bride – not quite the other side of the world, but far enough, in all truth. Thank goodness Anne Metcalfe was not Susannah!

'You should see the way they live, like hogs,' Henry Greatorex was saying, leaning across the table towards the shy, sombre figure of Sir Thomas Fairfax, distant cousin of the Metcalfes, who had evidently asked him some question about his property. 'All in one room, reeds on the floor for seating, bedding, everything. Animals and humans all in together, with no more modesty than the beasts in the field, and little more sense either. Most of them with not a word of English, and Papists to the last man and woman and child, of course.'

'Surely even in Ireland there are laws against their superstitious practices!' put in the Reverend Nathaniel Johnson, vicar of Thornside. 'And are they not well supplied with godly, preaching ministers?'

'Not as well supplied as one would wish, sir,' admitted Henry. 'But in any case, I fear they're past teaching. Lewd, quarrelsome, as truly savage as the native peoples of the Americas.'

'Then why choose t-to live among them?' asked Tom Fairfax, reasonably enough, Matthew thought.

'Ah, but we shall not be among them.' Henry smiled again at his bride. 'Most of the wild Irish have been removed from our part of

Ulster, a just reward for rebellion. Many of our neighbours will be good Scotsmen. My immediate neighbour came over from Fife ten years ago. You should see what he's made of his land – a transformation in the time he's been there. No, we planters are the hope of Ireland. What need is there to go to Massachussetts to find a new world, when we can have the shaping of one so short a distance away?'

Richard caught some of his friend's excitement, and felt a sharp pang of envy. For him there could be no such great enterprise as Henry and Anne were about to embark upon. Yet even here in his home country Papism was rife, and he had already begun to do what he could to build in Thornside a godly bastion against its corrupt influence. As patron of the living of Thornside, he had been able to instal Nathaniel Johnson in the parish, when the old vicar had died, two years ago. Master Johnson had been expelled from his previous parish in East Anglia for refusing to make his flock kneel for communion. On his arrival at Thornside he had swiftly banished from its ancient church every trace of superstitious decoration, and had set to work with equal thoroughness on the more daunting task of reforming his parishioners. He was a ferociously effective preacher.

Yet it was not enough, Richard knew that. Nor even was the influence he himself had as a justice of the peace for the district; nor as head of his household at Thornside Hall. For he was single still, with no like-minded wife to share his hopes and fears, to help and support him in his life's work and even, sometimes, against his formidable mother. It was not simply his sister's great task that Richard envied. It was also the fact that she would do it in partnership with the man she loved.

But he was nearer than he had been to the attainment of his goal, for at least he knew now what woman he hoped to make his wife. He knew, because he had made discreet enquiries, that Mistress Fawcett was not only beautiful and infinitely desirable, but godly too, and the heiress to a respectable property; such a wife as even his mother might have chosen for him, though he had not yet mentioned his preference to Dame Alice, who had been absorbed with the details of her daughter's wedding. Today, Richard resolved, he would try to find some time to be alone with Mistress Fawcett – or as alone as one could be in such a gathering – and begin his wooing of her.

Much later, the remains of the feast were cleared away and the musicians struck up a vigorous dance tune. Richard had not wanted any dancing, having been convinced by the vicar that it was a pastime likely to lead to all kinds of lascivious behaviour. But Anne loved to dance and their mother had insisted that the guests would think it a poor wedding otherwise, so Richard had been overruled. Going in search of Mistress Fawcett, he was gratified to find that she seemed to share his scruples, for she was standing in a quieter corner of the room talking to his cousin Tom Fairfax, who, being in mourning for his grandfather, was not dancing either. Richard was soon struck by Mistress Fawcett's masculine grasp of recent national events and her decisiveness in expressing her opinions on them. In spite of her sex, young though she was, she showed a rare understanding of the most profound subjects. He knew that many people would have seen that as a fault, but for him it was a relief. After years away in the exclusively masculine worlds of Cambridge and Gray's Inn and, lately, the House of Commons, he had little experience of the kind of light trivial talk that women were supposed to enjoy.

'So long as the Scots are in arms, then the friends of true religion will be heard,' Susannah said at one point. 'We saw last year that the King has not the power to defeat them.'

Richard glanced at his cousin. 'You surely cannot let that pass, Tom.'

Tom's smile instantly sweetened his dark face. 'It's t-true, I fear. We've been so long at peace that we've forgotten the art of war – if you can call last year's sad escapade war.'

'Then you will wish that this present trouble may be settled without a fight, whatever Mistress Fawcett's hopes.'

'You misunderstand me, sir,' Susannah intervened. 'I do not hope for war. I believe only that His Majesty, knowing how things stand, must make an early peace on terms that will be to the advantage of the godly cause.'

'Please God you're right,' said Tom. 'All I ask is to live in quietness with my family at Nun Appleton. As I was t-telling your good father just now,' he added to Susannah, 'the height of my ambition is to grow the finest roses in Yorkshire.'

Richard smiled. 'Yet I heard you took to soldiering as naturally as I would have hated it. With that "Sir" to your name to prove it.' Tom's knighthood had been conferred on him last year by a grateful

King Charles, when the army gathered for the short-lived and igno-minious invasion of Scotland had been dispersed.

'I was one of the few with any experience at all,' said Tom, who had briefly served with the Dutch forces in the Low Countries. 'Against the rest I must have shone. It's t-true I once had thoughts of a military career, but I was young and hotblooded then.'

'And so old and grave now!' Richard teased him. Secretly he thought that Tom, who was only three years his senior, had aged a good deal since they last met three years ago, at Tom's wedding to Anne Vere, daughter of his former commanding officer. But then his health had always been uncertain.

Tom grinned. 'An old grave married man, who wishes only to stay at home with his wife.'

So small an ambition, yet not an ignoble one. Again, Richard glimpsed the happiness that might be his. He glanced at Susannah, to see if she felt the force of it too, but her expression gave no hint that she did. Then he realised that Tom was still speaking. '. . . In all seriousness, I promised Anne I would try and be home t-tonight.' So Richard had, reluctantly, to go and see his cousin on his way.

By the early evening, many of the wedding guests had drunk a good deal and the celebrations were becoming increasingly noisy. Susannah stood below the gallery in the great hall watching the hectic dancing figures with a sense of disapproval. They looked, she thought, much as the devils in hell must look: dark cavorting shapes lit by the uncertain flames of torches and candles, which leaped and cowered to the rhythms of the music. She was surprised that in this most godly of households such things should be coun-tenanced, even apparently encouraged. Dame Alice was still in her chair by the hearth, giving the tacit approval of her presence to the proceedings, and now and then Susannah glimpsed the bride and groom among the dancers, as wild as any of them. She could not see Master Richard anywhere, which was perhaps a point in his favour; except that, as host at the feast, he bore ultimate responsibility for it.

'You see the vanity of all this,' said someone beside her, and she looked round to see the Reverend Nathaniel Johnson, evidently making his way towards the outer door – shaking the dust of the place from his feet, she thought, and then wondered that he did not first stand up and rebuke the company for its unseemly behaviour.

'I think it a pity so solemn a thing as a marriage should be an occasion for such wantonness,' Susannah said. As one of those who had felt God's assurance that she was among the Elect, she approved of Master Johnson. The vicar was as concerned for the morals of his parishioners as he was inspiring in the pulpit, indefatigable in visiting backsliders and sinners to remonstrate and pray with them in a way that had already had a conspicuous effect. There was much less open misbehaviour in the streets of Thornside than there had been before he came.

'I fear it is not what our good Dame Alice would wish either; or Master Richard, for that matter, or the bride and groom. But where unregenerate youth is allowed its head, then this is what happens.' The vicar glanced once more at the dancers. 'But I must not linger. It grows late. Goodnight, mistress.'

She watched him walk away, apparently evading a situation he disliked but felt unable to change. Of course, the Metcalfes were Thornside's most prominent family, and also his patrons. To speak publicly against them in their own house would be difficult for him. Very likely, he would instead have a word in private at some suitable moment. Yet she was disappointed in him.

The noise in the room grew louder, no longer just singing and laughter, but shrieks and shouts. Susannah saw a group of women gather together and then rush through the dancers, and emerge a little after with the bride, flushed and laughing, dragged between them. Then they lifted her up and bore her towards the stairs. 'To bed! To bed!' they were chanting, while some of them called lewd jokes. Somewhere behind her, the young men had seized her bridegroom and were carrying him up the stairs after her. Once up there, Susannah knew, the young couple would be undressed and then bedded together, with more laughter and bawdy jokes and all the accompanying rituals of the wedding night.

Susannah wondered that Anne Metcalfe, an apparently modest young woman, could bear it. This was not how she herself would wish to embark on the duties of the married state; but then she had no intention of marrying, ever. She could not imagine that any man would be able to offer her a more congenial companionship than did her father – and what other enticements could marriage afford? Children? She had no desire at all to be a mother. She had seen so many go through that bloody torment, an annual event in the lives of countless women, which at best led only to years of drudgery, at worst to an agonising death; like her own mother's, in giving birth to her.

She stood among the older and more sober women, watching the antics of their juniors, hearing their laughter and shrieks, wondering – not for the first time – if she had anything in common with them at all, except her womanly shape and the regular monthly bleeding that brought her a day or two of irritating belly cramps, but which otherwise she tried to ignore. She had no liking for the trivial things with which so many women occupied their time: domestic details, food and clothes and trinkets, gossip about neighbours or the doings of their children.

'You next then, Mistress Fawcett?' some silly woman standing near her said cheerfully. Susannah smiled, saying nothing. Even Sir Ralph, that dear family friend, had made the same assumption, that she would marry sooner or later, and probably (given the beauty on which he had commented so approvingly) sooner. Why was it that marriage seemed the only possible end for women, the only desirable one? Perhaps it was, for most women, with their minds full of nothing very much, weak and foolish and emotional as they were, in need of protection. But she knew she was not as other women. She was Susannah Fawcett, Doctor Fawcett's daughter, called by God to a life very different from the common lot of womankind.

She realised that there was someone at her elbow, and he must have heard what had been said to her, for he suddenly took her hand and said, 'I wish you would be next, Mistress Fawcett. I want you for my wife.'

It was Richard, red-faced and clearly a little drunk. Susannah was utterly astonished. Of all the things he might have said, this was the last she had expected. They had, after all, scarcely exchanged two words in all their lives until today. It was almost as if her previous thoughts had conjured him up to torment her. She was silent for some time, trying to take in what he had said and to make sense of it. She heard herself say, 'I think not, sir.' Then, in case that sounded abrupt and harsh, she added, 'But I thank you for the honour you do me in asking.' Then she disengaged her hand.

Richard looked as if he did not quite know what to do next, as if he had not expected so immediate a rejection; or, perhaps, as if he had not intended to make the proposal at all, so suddenly, without any preliminaries. Susannah was about to turn away, when he stammered, 'I spoke too hastily. Forgive me. Let me call on you. Let us be friends.' Implied was: then you will change your mind.

She would not, she knew, but she took his words at their face value and simply said, 'Certainly, let us be friends, sir.' Then, as calmly as possible, she walked away, in search of her father.

They left the Hall soon afterwards, she and her father together. It was growing dark, late on this May evening, but there was still enough light for her to see a couple in the shadows under the trees behind the house, shamelessly engaged in the savage act of coition, like animals, all reason, all decency put aside, the girl yielding eagerly to the man's violent act of possession. Susannah shuddered and wondered – not for the first time – how it was that godly men and women, like her parents, like Richard's sister and brother-in-law in their new marriage bed, could ever bring themselves to conceive children.

Out on the road, away from the trees, her father suddenly said, 'Hmm, Susannah – did Master Richard speak to you today?'

She knew from his tone that he meant more than just ordinary talk. 'He'd drunk too deep, I think. He spoke a little wildly . . . Why, what did he say to you?'

'He asked if he might pay his addresses to you.'

'And you said?' She held her breath, waiting for his answer. It was too dark to see his expression.

'Hmm. That I would not influence you in any way. That it was for you to say. That he must have a care, for a jewel is not won with base coinage.'

Susannah smiled to herself. 'I told him he must be content with friendship,' she said. She could feel his relief.

'As you say, he had drunk too deep,' said Matthew Fawcett, happily. 'I was a little surprised at it.'

Once back in their substantial house looking across the lane to Thornside churchyard, Susannah and her father did not at once say prayers and go to bed, though their servants, Margaret and John, had already retired. Instead, Susannah lit candles and drew chairs to the fire, and then for a time read quietly to her father, in the original Latin, from their favourite book, *De Motu Cordis*, Doctor William Harvey's stimulating and controversial proof of the circulation of the blood.

CHAPTER FIVE

Sir Ralph Liddell had ridden to Blackheugh through the spring rain with a picture in his mind of a tall, fair, handsome man whose pale eyes, somehow empty of all feeling, had never failed to make the hairs rise on the back of his neck.

He had been admitted to the great chamber and there saw at its far side a slight figure in black velvet seated by the ornate hearth, his face shaded by the plumes of a wide-brimmed beaver hat. His ward had made no move to welcome or to greet him, so Sir Ralph had taken off his own hat and bowed and then made his way uncomfortably across the expanse of empty floor. Only then as the young man raised blue eyes to look at him had he known for certain that – for all his cool manner, his air of disdain – the new Lord Milburn was nothing like his father. Sir Ralph had even found himself reminded suddenly of his second son Mark in one of his occasional moods of sullen rebellion.

As for Ludovick, he saw a square-shouldered, tawny-bearded man in his thirties, with an unexpected kindliness about his face, marked as it was with laughter lines and a mouth that looked as if only with a great effort could it be forced into its present stern expression.

For them both, prepared to dislike if not to hate, it was a disconcerting meeting. The terms of the wardship were enough to reinforce every prejudice on Ludovick's side, for they insisted on Lord Milburn's conformity to the Church of England as a condition of coming into his inheritance, as well as the expected betrothal to Sir Ralph's daughter. 'If only my Lord Cottington were not Master of the Court of Wards,' the steward had lamented, as soon as Sir

Ralph, having set the terms before them, was out of earshot. 'He had occasion to be offended once, long ago, at some supposed insult by his late lordship. Yet when his lordship's service to the King's majesty is considered – many hundreds of pounds, in gifts and loans, when His Majesty had most need and few would come to his aid. Perhaps if your lordship were to attend upon His Majesty, at court . . .'

Rob Robson's advice, when, later, Ludovick poured out his indignation to his servant, had been rather more blunt, at least as far as the matter of the marriage was concerned. 'First see if you've a fancy to the lass. Time enough then to give Sir Ralph some cause to take against you. I don't suppose he'll press the marriage until he's sure you'll do for his daughter.' As for the question of religion, Rob had pointed out that a certain measure of outward conformity might be sufficient to content his guardian, attendance once or twice a year at the parish church, for example.

The difficulty was that, in spite of his anger, in spite of his sense that he was being used, in spite of his frustration at the restraint upon his freedom that the whole business brought, Ludovick could not wholly dislike Sir Ralph. In other circumstances, he would most certainly have liked him. Even as it was, he would sometimes find himself forgetting what stood between them and responding to Sir Ralph's warmth and enthusiasm. His guardian had a lively curiosity about everything around him, which, Ludovick soon realised, had nothing to do with the man's concern to extract what he could from the Milburn estates, but was as natural to him as breathing. Ludovick found it both endearing and infectious. Forced, if only in his own interests, to make some show of common courtesy, he went through the motions of entertaining his guardian with hunting and hawking and, in the evenings, music, which he found was Sir Ralph's greatest passion, as it was his. Then, engaged in some activity that had no connection with the wardship, he would always, before long, find himself lowering his guard and starting to enjoy himself.

He discovered that his guardian's curiosity even extended to himself, and it was expressed with such kindly interest that he could almost have believed it stemmed, not from any ulterior motive, but simply from affection for him. Once or twice – when he had drunk a little too deeply at the dinner table, or late at night, after they had been playing music or singing – he found himself confiding in Sir Ralph as he had never before confided in anyone but his brother Charles or Rob. He told his guardian how, on leaving school in France, he had fled, with Rob's connivance, to join the Spanish forces in Flanders, alongside his Irish cousins. 'I don't suppose your father took kindly to that,' Sir Ralph had murmured.

'He didn't know. If he had, he'd have had me brought home somehow.' A shudder had run through him then, almost imperceptibly, though Ralph had seen it. 'Charles knew, but no one else.'

'So that's why no one could find you last year,' the older man said. 'There was some muttering in London about it. An heir to a Catholic estate overseas for years together – didn't look good. The conformity clause helped there,' he added, and then, before Ludovick could wonder if he might perhaps have some reason to be grateful to his guardian, quickly went on, 'Tell me, what do you know of Spanish music? Do their musicians compose only for the church?'

A few days later, Ludovick went with him to County Durham, to make the acquaintance of his family. Widehope Hall was a pleasant modern mansion set in meadow and parkland on the banks of the little River Gaunless not far from Bishop Auckland, in the southwestern corner of the Bishopric. There was nothing in its appearance to indicate that its owner's prosperity was largely based on coal. The pits he owned were nearly all several miles away, along the Tyne and in the east of the county, though there were a few near at hand. Yet it was clear that he wanted for nothing. There was none of the splendour of Blackheugh, but simply every comfort that a large family could require and no sign that their numbers stretched their father's resources in any way.

For there were a great many Liddells, a dozen at least, Ludovick thought. The clamour of the household broke over his bewildered head the moment he and Sir Ralph stepped into the house, to be greeted by children joyfully running from all sides to welcome their father. They were well-brought-up children, and they all made some attempt at kneeling for his blessing – even the small toddler in long skirts – before competing for his embrace, which was given with an effusive warmth that made Ludovick look away, feeling uncomfortable. Rather to his relief, the younger ones were soon despatched to the nursery with their nursemaid and the adults were accompanied to the light and comfortably furnished parlour by the three older children, Cuthbert and Mark, who were fourteen and twelve, and, of course, their sister Dorothy, who was fifteen.

Ludovick tried to avoid meeting her eyes, while making furtive glances in her direction. She was no beauty, that was certain. But then she was not ill-favoured either. She had her father's tawny hair and brown eyes, a healthy complexion and a boyish thinness of figure that might well improve with maturity. From the way she too avoided looking at him, keeping her head bent as much as possible, Ludovick concluded that either she was painfully shy or she knew perfectly well what was planned for her. If so, it was as uncomfortable a situation for her as it was for him and she was to be pitied.

Supper was made easier than it might have been by Dorothy's brothers, who, learning that Ludovick had seen active military service (it seemed to be a matter of indifference to them which side he'd fought for), questioned him eagerly about his experiences and seemed well on the way to turning him into some kind of hero. Afterwards Sir Ralph ordered that viols and recorders and lutes be brought out. At the end of a lively evening, Ludovick sang an old Spanish lament he had learned in Flanders, his sweet tenor pouring the desolate notes into the room above a stark accompaniment on the lute. He was too absorbed in the music to notice how still everyone had become, but at the end he looked up and saw Dorothy watching him with adoration in her eyes, her face glowing so that she looked almost pretty. He thought perhaps she might do quite well for him after all.

'He's not like his father,' said Elizabeth Liddell with relief as Ralph climbed into bed beside her that night. 'For a start, he looks as though he has some feelings.'

'I told you I was doing the best for her,' said Ralph.

'We shall see.' She was silent for a time, reflecting on the evening. 'If I were unkind I would say he plays more like a music master than a gentleman.'

'I can forgive him that small fault. Besides, he plays from the heart. I can think of no music master who could have made me weep like that. What a voice!'

'That's what I'm afraid of. Did you see Dorothy's face? I don't want her fixing her affections before we're sure.'

'She's a good girl,' said Ralph comfortably. 'She'll accept what's best for her.'

'Sometimes, my love,' said his wife with exasperation, 'you can be very stupid.' Then she added, 'I don't think it's just Dorothy who's dazzled. Someone just has to play you a pretty tune and he has you in the palm of his hand.'

Ralph sighed. 'What I would give to be able to play what I hear in my head, or my heart! I envy him that.'

Later, he was just dropping off to sleep, when Elizabeth said in the neutral tone he knew only too well, 'I'm pregnant again.' He tried to make her see that it was a matter not for regret but for rejoicing.

The days at Widehope were as ordered as those at Blackheugh, bounded by the household prayers that began and ended them and punctuated by meals and the children's lessons. Yet life there was nothing at all like anything Ludovick had ever experienced before. He found it at once bewildering and intoxicating. There was something magical about this place where the family outnumbered the servants and every single member seemed to care about every other one. He longed, desperately, to be a part of it, longed to give in to the sense of welcome and acceptance, which he knew must be an illusion, though sometimes he allowed it to break through his guard and close around him. Then he would remind himself what was the basis of the relationship between himself and Sir Ralph, and how it must always put a barrier between him and this lively, loving, laughing family. Were they not simply trying by their apparent kindness to make the nauseous potion less offensive for him to swallow?

One evening, having observed him for some days, Rob said, 'What's up, lad? Do you not fancy the lass, then?'

'No – no, I like her well enough.' Ludovick could say nothing more, not knowing where to begin. If only, he thought, it was a simple matter of whether or not he favoured Dorothy Liddell as his bride. As it was, he felt tossed this way and that by a confusion of emotions he could not disentangle.

The worst thing of all was to feel he had no choice, that he could do nothing to change things. On the surface, of course, there was a choice, of sorts. He could do what was asked of him, or give up all hope of coming fully into his inheritance and return to the Spanish service. It had been hard enough for him to come back to England at all. In the end, he had done so largely because Charles had persuaded him that it was his duty to care for their mother and to take full responsibility for the great property that God had entrusted to him, if only by trying in some way to make reparation for the wrongs his father had done. They had neither of them thought for a moment of the Royal Court of Wards.

Now he was here he had no wish to give it all up so soon, but sometimes that seemed the only honourable course. Master Hedley's suggestion that he should go and plead his case at court was, he felt, beyond him. He had no experience at all of the combination of intrigue and flattery that he imagined would be required of him. Besides, he did not even know if that was what he wanted. He did not know what he wanted, except that he wished that everything might somehow be different.

He might have found it easier if he had known what Charles thought he should do. Again and again he tried to send the questions out over the miles that separated them, hoping for some answer; but none came. Perhaps they were too far apart. Only once before, twelve years ago, had they ever been separated by so great a distance, and then it had come close to destroying him. He had thought it would be different this time, now they were adults and their father was dead, but he was no longer sure. It frightened him to think that they might at last be parted as completely as most other human beings would have been in their position. He felt as if he were wandering alone in a dense fog, which cut him off from all those around him, so that he could neither call for their help nor see which way to go.

It was not until haytime, well into July, that Sir Ralph realised that matters were not going as smoothly as he had hoped. The summer had been so wet that, more than usual, every hand was needed at the mowing. The moment the sun shone they were all out there, the entire Liddell household – servants, children, parents – and a large number of their friends and neighbours too. Ludovick, who had never mowed hay before, worked with a will, though mostly in silence, without joining in the songs, which was unlike him.

Then, when they stopped to eat at midday, he drank too much, picked a quarrel with young John Bolam, son of their neighbour, and, when Dorothy tried to make peace between them, was so sharp with her that she burst into tears. After that he stormed off to the stables, saddled up his horse and rode to Bishop Auckland, where he found an alehouse and got so drunk that Rob, who knew these black moods of old, had to have him carried back unconscious to Widehope. He did not appear next day until well into the afternoon, to be met on the hayfield by Sir Ralph, who said quietly, 'A word, my lord, if you will,' and led the way in silence to his study. 'What's all this about then?' he asked, once they were there.

'I don't know what you mean,' returned Ludovick, wishing that he were tall enough to look his guardian full in the eye, on the level.

He was taken aback when Sir Ralph went on, with a note of real kindliness, 'Is it that you don't want this match?'

'I've no choice, have I?' Ludovick retorted.

Sir Ralph frowned, clearly troubled. 'I'm not sure I've been quite fair to you. I have to admit we've come to like you, more than I expected. In fact, I can think of no one I'd rather have as a son. What's more, Dorothy likes you. I have a right to force it on you, as we both know. However, if you're set against it, then I'll think again.'

Ludovick heard himself say, 'I'm not set against it, at least, not . . .'

'I'm glad to hear it.' Ralph studied the young man's face for a time, then said, 'I tell you what, my lord: we'll put off the formalities for a bit, the marriage itself, that is. Give you time to get used to the idea. You've not long been back in England after all. You need time to settle in at home, at the very least. If you agree to the betrothal, the rest can wait, until you feel ready. A year or two, if need be. As for the matter of conformity, I'm prepared to take steps to free the estate from wardship without it. So long as you conform before you're married, that will serve.'

Ludovick looked up at him, fighting the proffered warmth and affection, which he so deeply mistrusted. 'I shall never turn Protestant,' he said. 'Not though Hell freezes over.'

'My concern is that you shouldn't get yourself hauled before Quarter Sessions on a recusancy charge, that's all. I don't want my daughter's happiness threatened by a constant burden of fines. They can ruin a man, you know.'

'It would take more than the odd fine to bring Blackheugh down.'

'Maybe, but the way the times are, the laws are going to press harder than ever on Papists, I'd say. That's not all of it, though. As a Justice, I should certainly have made you come to church while you've been here. I thought about it, but felt best to let it go for now. That said, I'm certain that were you to do so you'd sharp find it would have its effect on you. Then there's Dorothy. I've seen what the influence of a good Protestant wife can do.'

'What if it went the other way, and Dorothy turned Catholic?' He had noted the adoring look in her eyes. Married to a husband she worshipped, what could be more natural than that a wife should follow his religion?

'Oh, she's been carefully raised. I would wager she's proof against any Popish blandishments. I'm not without experience in these matters, you know. After all, my dear wife's parents were Catholics, though they died too soon to influence her. But her older brother was as obstinate a Papist as you could find, until he was well into adulthood. Yet thanks to his wife he is now as staunch a member of the Church of England as I am. I do remember too,' he went on, with a certain amount of caution, 'that even your late father was not averse to conforming, when it suited him.'

'I am not my father.'

That brought a smile from Sir Ralph. 'So I'd observed.' He laid a hand on Ludovick's shoulder and shook it gently. 'Let's leave it at that, shall we, my boy? Now, have you eaten anything today? I for one don't find it easy to keep a good humour on an empty stomach – especially when there's an army drumming in my head from the night before.'

The legal formalities of the betrothal were settled within the next few days and sealed with a chaste kiss planted by Ludovick on the lips of his future bride, who blushed and trembled and was not able to speak coherently for some time afterwards. That rather dry ceremony was followed by a family feast, though no more public celebrations. The most tangible outcome of the negotiations was that the property taken from Sir Ralph by Ludovick's father was returned to him, not as part of the future bridal settlement, but immediately, in full and without conditions; and in spite of objections from Master Hedley.

A few days later the older members of the Liddell family went with Ludovick to Blackheugh, where they were to take part in the festivities that would mark his twenty-first birthday at the end of July.

His late father's chill, ungenerous ghost seemed to draw back at their coming. His mother came to life as he had never imagined she could, and there was a new light and warmth about the house that made Ludovick believe it might one day be a place of real happiness. It all seemed more than a little unreal and he was quite sure it would not last, but he allowed himself to begin to enjoy what was in his reach, before it should be snatched away.

Dorothy, emboldened by her acknowledged future position as mistress of Blackheugh, demanded a full tour of the house, lingering a long time before the family portraits in the long gallery. There was a huge canvas showing the late Baron with his young sons, mounted as if for the hunting field. 'I didn't know you had a brother, my lord!' she said.

'We are twins, mistress,' Ludovick told her.

'Then how can your lordship be sure you are the heir?' She looked as if she saw a possible threat to her future splendour.

'I'm the elder by half an hour. If you look, mistress, you can see we're easily told apart.' His eyes stayed on the painting, as if it gave him pleasure to look at the boy with the red-gold hair who stood by his elder twin's stirrup.

'Where is he now, my lord?'

'In Flanders, mistress. Training to be a priest.'

Her eyes widened, and she gave a little shiver at the thought of attaching herself to a family containing so dangerous a member. 'Do you think I shall ever meet him?'

'Who can say, mistress? I hope so.' He wished again that he knew what Charles thought of this heretic bride of his.

Dorothy moved on to the next portrait, of a slender fair young woman in the stiff farthingale and large ruff of thirty years ago. 'My aunt Frances,' said Ludovick. 'My father's sister.'

'She looks very sad, my lord. What became of her?'

'She's dead.' The abruptness of his tone warned her not to question him further, for she had already discovered that at times his temper was not wholly predictable.

Later, when they had studied portraits of his father's first two short-lived and childless wives, Dorothy said, 'There are no portraits of your mother,' and he was surprised, because he had never realised it before.

He had left the tower until last, hoping that the imminence of dinner would give him an excuse to leave it for another day – which with luck might never come. But Dorothy would not be put off. 'Is it true, what they say, my lord,' she asked eagerly, as they halted by the tower door, 'that it's haunted?'

There was a pause before he answered. 'It's said to be.'

'Have you ever seen anything?' She faltered a little at the look on his face.

'The servants won't go into it,' was all he would say. 'Let's go to dinner, mistress.'

'Oh no, please, my lord, let me see inside! It's broad daylight. Surely nothing can harm us?' She sounded excited, but not frightened, except in the pleasurable manner of someone who had never really known any cause for fear in her life.

He had no more excuses, so he opened the door and they went in, and she fell immediately silent, looking round in awe. Just a room, and a spiral stair; ordinary enough, yet all at once he was a child again, eight years old and drenched with terror. His limbs felt frozen, useless, like limbs in a nightmare. Somehow, furtively, he managed to make the sign of the cross. Then he forced himself on, up the stairs. Another room, large and airy; another stair. In the next room they came to, lit by a long narrow window, she said, 'What is it – that haunts this place?' He wondered if she knew she was whispering.

'A redcap,' he said, and then realised she expected an explanation. 'He waits here, for blood. To keep his cap red. He has long talons and red eyes.' He laughed a little shakily, as if reassuring her that it was all ridiculous; after all, said like that, baldly, it did sound ridiculous, and inadequate too, bearing no relation to the thing in his mind. Dorothy reached out to push open an inner door. 'My aunt died in there,' he said. 'She went mad and hanged herself.'

Dorothy turned to look at him with horror in her eyes, and then she shivered. 'Let's go, my lord. I don't like it here.' With relief he led her away, putting an arm about her as they descended the stair.

Once outside the tower door, he quickly released her, though conscious that she looked at him with regret. They walked together, saying nothing, towards the parlour where dinner was served, though when they were nearly there, Dorothy said hesitantly, 'My lord, have you ever – well . . .?'

He halted, his thoughts still shadowed by the tower, wondering what she meant. She looked very pink.

'I wondered . . . Young gentlemen, nobles I should say – they . . .' She bent her head, and Ludovick, beginning, with a sense of awakening from nightmare, to guess in what area her questions were wandering, slid a finger under her chin to tilt her head back so he could look into her eyes. He could see that she was breathing very quickly.

'Come now, Mistress Dorothy, what are you asking?'

'I just wondered – have you ever loved?' Her face turned a fiery, uncomfortable red, and, suddenly light-hearted and reckless with relief, he had an irresistible urge both to laugh and to kiss her wide pink mouth, which he yielded to, though lightly in both cases. Then he said, 'That's no question to ask your betrothed, my mistress.' At which she concluded, rather miserably, that the answer was in the affirmative, and the woman in question was not herself.

Ludovick had no intention of telling her anything about the fickle Flemish girl, a little older than himself, who had seemed to open the gates of Paradise to him, only to kick him rudely out of the way when a handsome Spanish officer came by. She had been his first girl and he had thought for some time afterwards that his heart was broken. But either it had mended more quickly than he had feared or he had learned to defend it better, he was not sure which. There had been no one else who had come near to touching it, and he had no intention that anyone ever would.

The coming of age of the heir of Blackheugh was marked in full traditional style, with feasting for family and tenants alike, going on for days, no expense spared. When it was over, Elizabeth Liddell returned to Widehope with her children, urged on her way by Sir Ralph, who was made increasingly anxious by rumours of an imminent Scottish invasion. 'I'd sooner you were as far from the border as can be,' he said, when his wife suggested they might stay a little longer. He remained behind to attend to the formalities of freeing the estate from wardship.

In the intervals allowed him between sessions with his steward and his guardian, signing documents and discussing the details of the exorbitant payments due to the Court of Wards and other officials, Ludovick rode about the estate getting to know those who depended upon him and listening to their grievances. There was little left by now of the loyalty once felt by Blackheugh tenants for their landlord, even on the part of those who shared his name. The first Baron had made sure of that, by ending the old system of land tenure, based on military service against the Scots, and replacing it with a ruthlessly modern rent-based system, which had brought many of the tenants to poverty. Where he could, Ludovick put things right, often with Sir Ralph supporting him against the objections of Master Hedley, who thought he was in danger of letting all his property and power slip through his fingers by the kind of weakness that would have appalled his father.

On the twentieth of August the main force of the Scots army crossed the Tweed into England and began to march steadily south. Sir Ralph left Blackheugh the next day, parting affectionately with his future son-in-law, no longer his ward. 'Take care, my boy,' he said. 'I don't want my lass a widow before she's a wife.'

The next day Ludovick too rode south, with a handful of men at his back, mounted on sturdy ponies and armed with whatever ancient and rusting weapons they could lay their hands on at such short notice. There were representatives of all four Tynedale Names riding with him, two Milburns and a Dodd, a Charlton and three Robsons, of whom, of course, Rob was one. Knowing of his military experience, they had asked Ludovick to lead them, for, whatever their feelings towards his father, they were Tynedale men with a long-nurtured hatred for the traditional enemy. They were all Catholics too, and Ludovick would have liked to have had Mass said before they set out, as was always done in Flanders before they undertook any military enterprise. But there was no priest at Blackheugh and none at present in any of the many Catholic households in the area. Their prayers had to be private ones; but his at least were lightened by a renewed sense of his brother's presence.

They reached the Pictish wall and then turned to follow it in an easterly direction, making for Newcastle, towards which the King was marching, with all the forces he could muster under the generalship of the Earl of Strafford. Leading his little troop of men to battle, Ludovick had a strong sense that he had come to the end of a dream. War, which had been his life for so many years, had caught up with him again. There was something oddly comforting about its uncomplicated familiarity.

A week later Ludovick's troop was just a small part of a panic-stricken, undisciplined rabble fleeing through County Durham before the advancing Scots. The Blackheugh men had reached the royal army just in time for the brief inglorious battle at Newburn, when the entire English force on the south bank of the Tyne had fled before the pounding of the Scots artillery from the northern side. Now, behind them, Newcastle was already in enemy occupation, and with them went a flood of frightened refugees, carrying what belongings they could on carts or horses or just on their backs. As they were swept along in the mêlée, Rob said, 'This land's been too long at peace. They've gone soft. No stomach for war.'

Like Rob, Ludovick had been dismayed at the quality of the army with which they had found themselves at Newburn. For the most part, the soldiers had been scarcely trained and without discipline, men conscripted largely because they had not the wit to get out of it, so Rob suggested. The officers were gentlemen or courtiers with no military experience at all, apart from one or two who, like Ludovick, had served overseas. One such officer, knowing they were Catholics, as he was, had warned them to keep that fact quiet. 'Some of the men won't serve under us,' he had said. 'I guess most of them would sooner kill Catholics than Scots, given the chance.'

Remembering the man's words, Ludovick replied to Rob, 'There's no stomach for this war, at least. I suppose now the King will make peace, on Scottish terms.'

'Worse luck for us,' was Rob's comment.

1641

CHAPTER SIX

It was May again, that time of exuberant merrymaking and youthful high spirits; the time when London apprentices had leisure for protest and riot. This year it was also a time of fear, from the Palace of Whitehall to the brothels of Bankside – fear of Papist plots and Irish risings, fear of Spanish or French invasion, or, simply, that the King would call in his idle army to impose his will.

On this first Sunday after Easter, Catholic courtiers were deprived of the customary mass in the Queen's chapel because the royal family was preoccupied with the private wedding celebrations of the child Princess Mary to the Prince of Orange. In such circumstances, it would be natural for those of their religion to make their way discreetly to the chapels of the Catholic embassies, as Londoners, long exasperated by their immunity from the penal laws, knew well. Last Sunday – Easter Day – the crowd had broken into the Spanish embassy, disrupting the idolatrous worship in progress there. This week the embassy was shuttered, its doors barred, with no visible sign of life. Walter Barras and his fellow apprentices, fired by the sermons heard this morning in the best preaching churches of London, went to watch and wait in the street outside the embassy, shouting their anger with all the force of their lungs.

Near Walter, someone struck up a psalm, and soon it spread like fire through heather, catching him up too, the grand solemn tune and words loud enough to reach the ears of the Papists lurking in their hardness of heart behind the solid walls.

> *Consume them in thy wrath, O Lord,*
> *That nought of them remain:*
> *That men may know throughout the world*
> *That Jacob's God doth reign . . .*

Wonderful words, Walter thought them, strong, angry, righteous words, fit for the times, like every word in the wonderful book that had been his delight and inspiration since he first had his eyes opened. From that moment those holy words had become a light to guide his path, a light that had led him out of the darkness in which his poor blind parents had raised him, knowing no better. He, more than anyone in the crowd that Sunday morning, knew what dark twisted superstition lurked in the hearts of the damned souls who worshipped their idolatrous God behind the blank embassy walls. He knew they were there, knew that they must hear the singing, but it was frustrating all the same that there was no sign of their presence, the windows blank, no curtain stirring, no shutter opened, nothing to show what went on in there or who was present at it.

'Round the back – they'll be round the back,' someone said, and Walter was one of the small group who set off at once, into the quiet where the psalm was only a distant inspiration.

They were just in time. A carriage had that moment come to a halt in the yard behind the embassy, and another was rolling up beside it, while a servant hurried towards the building with word of their arrival. Walter and his friends gathered round the coaches, hammering on their painted doors, setting them rocking, jeering at the ineffectual cursing of the coachman, whose whip flailed the air, well clear of their raised hands and angry faces. The horses stamped and pulled at the reins, threatening flight.

Someone gave a shout and they saw, stepping from the embassy doorway, a small group of ladies and gentlemen. Walter could smell them from here, the effeminate vanity of their perfume catching in his nostrils. He hated them, in their silks and satins and velvets and furs, dressed as no modest man or woman should dress, as if half-undressed, their clothing exposing here the sleeve of a chemise, there a shirt sleeve, or with the flimsiest, most transparent layer of linen and lace covering breast and shoulders. Against all decency, men as well as women wore their hair in elaborate lovelocks, often decorated with ribbons or pearls, while earrings dangled from their ears. They were as corrupt and perverted as the faith they served, and as dangerous to the health and safety of England and all those of her people who – like Walter himself – longed for her to walk in the right path.

'Consume them in thy wrath, O Lord!' he roared with the rest of them.

First through the door, accompanied by anxious, attentive servants, led by the hand by an affected young man in black satin and silver lace, came a blonde lady dressed in yellow silk. The crowd surged forward. 'Idolatress! Whore!' Walter shouted.

Suddenly there were servants everywhere, pouring from the building to push against the crowd, struggling to clear a way to the coaches. A clamorous, bilingual scuffle spread and grew, Spanish oaths competing with righteous English rage. Walter bent to pick up a stone, aiming it at the lady's escort, who was edging his way along the narrow path that was being cleared, all the while talking lightly to his companion, as if he neither heard nor saw the angry jeering crowd, as if they were as mere dust to his feet.

Someone darted from the crowd and caught Walter's arm. 'Oh no you don't, damn you!'

Walter struggled to try and wrench himself free – the man had a ferocious grip. Then the words reached him, not in their meaning but in their accent.

Suddenly he knew that face looking into his: small, lined, tanned like leather; bright dark eyes. He did not know where he had seen it before, but seen it he had, long ago. The noise faded in his ears, his companions dwindled into mist. He looked down at the man's livery: black, brightened only by the scarlet badge on the shoulder, a hawk. He felt sick. 'Blackheugh! You're from Blackheugh.' . . . *A child peering round a stable door, helpless and terrified, raw flesh, and blood* . . . It was for a moment as if the blinding light of salvation had never struck his heart and swept him up to certainty; as if he had returned to the old darkness.

Somehow the stone was twisted from his grip, but he scarcely noticed.

'Then you'll know Blackheugh men give no quarter.'

'I know you – I know your face.' It was not this yard he was in, hazy with London smoke, but that other yard, wide and windswept, lit by a cold northern light.

'You'll know me again, I promise you, if you last this day: Rob Robson.'

He remembered. Robson . . . Robson, Dodd, Charlton and, of course, Milburn – the Graynes of Tynedale, the Names, to whom a Barras was an outsider, a broken man. For one of his own Name, a Tynedale man would shed the last drop of his blood, commit the foulest deed. But let a Barras fall and he would pass by on the other side, unseeing and uncaring. 'You were a groom, with my dad . . .'

'Your dad?'

'Jack Barras. Remember him? Friend he called you, but not a finger did you lift for him when he needed you.'

'No one stood up to my Lord Milburn, not if he'd any care for his own skin. Maybe you don't know that. You were just a lad.'

'You remember, then?'

'Aye. I remember . . . But that's no cause to hoy stones at his lordship. He was no less a bairn than you in those days.'

'Who—?' He followed Rob's gaze to the satin-clad young man, who by now had somehow reached the first coach and was handing the lady into it. Just another Papist courtier, he had thought him. 'Is that—?'

'Aye, the new Lord Milburn.'

'I didn't know he was dead.' He felt suddenly cheated, as if the first Baron's death had left him, for ever, with unfinished business. 'Just about my age he was,' he said bitterly, his eyes on the young man. 'A pampered brat with never a thought for what he did.' He watched the bowing figure as it flourished a plumed hat with a graceful gesture, extending a perfectly proportioned leg. 'Look at him – effeminate Papist bastard! You're a fool, Rob Robson. Follow him, and you're bound for Hell, as sure as night follows day. It's not too late, you know—'

'Oh, it is, Walter Barras, far too late.' Rob released Walter's wrist. 'What of you then? Done well for yourself have you?' His eyes took in the sober but serviceable clothes; the look of health and vigour; the brown hair cropped short, in the way that had lately become fashionable among London apprentices, anxious to distance themselves from the lovelocked vanity of courtiers.

Walter seemed to come to himself. He was back in London, the past firmly behind him, in the darkness where it belonged. 'The Lord in his mercy sought me out, unworthy as I am,' he told Rob, with the quiet confidence of utter certainty; for indeed He had, on a bitter winter day in Newcastle, in the person of the Reverend John Reynolds, who had plucked the child Walter, starving in body

and soul, from a doorstep and sent him to be apprenticed to his saddler brother in London, paying all that was required. There Abel
Reynolds had cared for the orphan's bodily needs, but, more than
that, he had taught Walter to read and write and put within his
reach the Bible, which was to bring light into his darkness of soul.
If there had been time, if there had not been this hubbub about
them, Walter would have told Rob all about it.

As it was, Rob did not seem impressed. 'I see,' he said, with a hint
of irony. 'Nice for you, that. Tell me, then, if we're bound for Hell
anyway, why bother with us? Don't tell me the Lord isn't strong
enough to do his own work.'

'The Lord makes use of His Elect to do His will. He has—'

Into his declaration of faith broke the voice of the spoilt child
grown to manhood, calling Rob; who said tauntingly, 'See you in
Hell, Walter Barras, one day!' and left him standing where he was,
feeling strange and unsettled. Walter watched him shut the coach
door on his master and swing himself up to the seat beside the
coachman, and then the coach lumbered forward, forcing a way
through the crowd. Walter wished there had been more of his own
kind there in the yard, to do some real damage.

Rob decided not to mention the chance meeting to Ludovick.
Walter Barras was not the only one for whom it might waken dark
memories, better left buried.

Richard Metcalfe, walking to the House of Commons the next
morning, saw the ominous sight of workshop yards silent and
deserted, shop windows barred, the spaces before them empty of
the usual displays of goods. For all that, the streets were busy
enough, not with customers, but with masters and apprentices hurrying purposefully towards Westminster. 'I fear their lordships are
in for a warm reception.'

Richard looked round to see his cousin Tom's father waiting for
him by the gates of Old Palace Yard. As Ferdinando, Lord Fairfax
bore a Scottish title, making him ineligible for the Lords, he had
been able to stand for election to the Commons as a member for
Yorkshire. Richard doffed his hat and the two men bowed to one
another before falling into step together.

The yard was seething with an angry crowd, larger than any
Richard had ever seen, its numbers still growing though there was
already scarcely room to pass through. He recognised the slight

figure leading the shouting from a flight of steps, his hoarse voice carrying through the din. They had all seen him often enough, outside Parliament or Whitehall or wherever there seemed cause for an outburst of anger, ever since last November when he had been released from prison. 'Lilburne's there again,' he said.

As they went on their way they could hear him clearly, 'Justice for Strafford or we pull the King himself from Whitehall!' The cheers almost drowned the words, but he simply shouted louder.

'I fear if he's not careful he'll find himself back in prison,' commented Lord Fairfax.

Richard's feelings towards the young man were mixed. In prison, Lilburne had been a martyr to the cause of liberty and true religion. Out of it, he seemed sometimes like the simple troublemaker that Sir Ralph Liddell had clearly thought him. There must after all be some order and respect for authority if things were not to fall apart.

Yet, 'If I cannot like his methods, sir, I believe he has cause to be angry,' said Richard, at which Lord Fairfax murmured his agreement. They were both impatient for an end to the Strafford business, which had dragged on since November, when the King's minister had been arrested. Until that was settled it was hard to continue with everything else that had to be done, and God knew how much business there was requiring the attention of Parliament.

This Parliament had been called simply to agree the terms of a peace treaty with the Scots, still occupying the northern counties, and to vote the means of paying them off; that, at least, had been the King's intention. Many of the members of Parliament had seen an opportunity – the only one they might have, before it was too late – to remedy the abuses under which they had all suffered for so long. The first essential step, of course, had been to remove the two men who, in the King's name, had been the chief minds behind the abuses: Thomas Wentworth, Earl of Strafford and William Laud, Archbishop of Canterbury. They had to act quickly, for hanging over the Parliament all along had been the fear of dissolution, the fate that had so abruptly ended their hopes this time last year. Though Richard thought they were safe so long as the Scots were still on English soil.

'Have you good news of your family?' Tom's father asked, when they had crossed New Palace Yard and reached the relative calm of Westminster Hall, bustling with activity though it was.

'My sister is well and happy, and with child,' Richard told him. She was also very pressing that her brother should come and visit them, something he looked forward to doing when this Parliament ended. 'Have you heard lately from Tom, sir? In his last letter he said they had been troubled by a rabble of idle soldiers – English soldiers.'

'I fear that is not over yet, nor will be, I suppose, until the army's disbanded. Which cannot come too soon for Tom.'

While the Scots army remained in England, so too did the English army raised to oppose it, stationed restlessly in the north with nothing to do but glower across the river Tees at the Scots, and live as best it could off the land, pay being sadly in arrears.

'I thought he might wish he were here with us, but he writes that he has no heart for affairs of state.'

'Tom is too straightforward for Parliament,' agreed his father. 'Or so I've often thought.'

They paused then to greet two other Yorkshire members, who had come to join them: Sir John Hotham, member for Beverley, and his son, who stood for Scarborough. The two older men walked ahead, the two younger behind them, towards the passage leading to the Commons chamber.

'You heard what happened yesterday?' the younger Hotham asked Richard, with a note of excitement in his voice.

'You mean the royal marriage?'

'No, not that . . .' Before he could explain, Lord Fairfax looked round.

'I heard that the Elector Palatine refused to grace it with his presence.'

The King's nephew Charles Louis, exiled and impoverished claimant to his dead father's lands in the Rhineland Palatinate, had timed his arrival at court to cause the maximum embarrassment to his uncle, maintaining that he had been promised the hand of the Princess Mary, before ever William of Orange had been thought of.

'He has cause, I suppose,' said Richard. 'The King has done little enough for his sister's family.'

Staunchly Protestant victims of the Catholic powers of Europe, the King's sister Elizabeth, once Queen of Bohemia, and her numerous family, had long been a cause championed – in vain for the most part – by patriotic Englishmen.

'It's clear though, isn't it?' said Lord Fairfax. 'The Elector has debts; the Dutch can supply His Majesty with money and arms – may already have done so, for all we know.'

The younger Hotham at last managed to break in, 'Never mind the Elector Palatine!' Then, recollecting his manners, 'Forgive me, sir. But did you not hear that the King sent soldiers to take over the Tower?'

The Tower of London, where the Earl of Strafford was held, was – or had been – governed by Lord Newport, one of the Earl's fiercest enemies.

There was a moment of shocked silence, before Richard said, 'I heard some rumour about armed men, but not that.'

'It's clear enough,' said young Hotham. 'He knows no one in Parliament will save Strafford, so he reckons to help him escape instead.'

'And that once done, what is there to stop him leading the army against us?' demanded Richard, thoroughly alarmed. He reflected that, though it might be helpful to Parliament to have the Scots keeping pressure on the King from the northern counties, it was not helpful to have the undisciplined remnant of the English army lying in readiness for the use of any adventurer who chose to lead it in support of the King.

They took their seats on benches already filling with members. Richard wondered if he imagined it, or if there really was something unusual in the air, tension and expectancy, even fear. He looked out for the men he was beginning to know and admire most – aside from the Yorkshire group, among whom, of course, he was proud to find himself. First and foremost, there was John Pym from Somerset, who saw things so clearly and spoke of them with such ordered passion, and whose speech soon after Parliament opened had seemed to put into words everything Richard had long been feeling, about the dangers they faced; in his opinion, Pym was the greatest figure of this Parliament, by a long way.

Then there was the ungainly, red-faced, scruffy member for Cambridge, one Oliver Cromwell, who, about the same time, had spoken fiercely for the release of John Lilburne; and Denzil Holles and William Strode from the West Country, who had both suffered years of imprisonment for opposing the King; and John Hampden, the courageous Buckinghamshire squire who three years before had questioned the legality of the King's imposition of the ship money tax, brought in without Parliamentary approval, and had fought the matter in court, and won. They were all mature men who, over the years, since the nearly-forgotten Parliaments of the 1620s, had gone on striving valiantly and apparently without hope against the King's encroachments on their liberties. Now newcomers like Richard, who had been children when they began their struggle, shared their hopes and looked eagerly to them for leadership and example.

Then there was the man taking his seat on the bench in front of him, turning to greet him as he did so. Sir Henry Vane, member for Hull and son of the King's Secretary of State, had recently played a notable part in the case against Strafford, by supplying evidence, from his father's notes of council meetings, to show that Strafford had suggested bringing an Irish Papist army into England to suppress its liberties. Much of an age – at twenty-eight Vane was the elder by two years – he and Richard had soon found that they had a good deal in common. Vane was also a close friend of John Pym, which in Richard's eyes simply added to his already considerable charm.

Now, Richard leaned forward. 'Have you heard, sir, about the attempt on the Tower. Do you know if there's any truth in it?'

'Oh, it's true,' said Vane grimly. 'Though, God be praised, it failed. For now.'

'Then we shall hear of it today.'

'Assuredly.' Prayers intervened, occupying their attention for some time. Afterwards, there was an expectant silence as the clerk cleared his throat to begin on the day's business. Richard knew that every thought must be on the threat that hung over them.

'A bill for regulating the trade of wiredrawing . . .'

It was a moment or two before his mind registered the banality of it. Then he heard the laughter growing about him and joined in himself, relief from tension making the whole thing seem so much more humorous than it was. From that moment, it seemed to Richard, God took control of their counsels. In their shared laughter all that happened afterwards was somehow made possible. Fear, tension, a sense of common experience, found a voice, though it was late in the afternoon before the culmination came.

Pym and Holles and the disreputable yet likeable Henry Marten, all spoke, moving the House towards the point where it seemed that the only possible course was to unite in a great oath, which would hold them together against the threats that faced them. Somehow, from nothing, the words were shaped, read, voted on; Richard was among the first to rise to his feet and swear the oath, immediately following Lord Fairfax.

'*I, Richard Metcalfe, do, in the presence of God, promise vow and protest to maintain and defend, as far as lawfully I may with my life, power and estate, the true reformed Protestant religion expressed in the doctrine of the Church of England, against all Popery and popish innovation within this realm . . . I will maintain and defend His Majesty's royal person and estate, as also the power and privilege of Parliaments, the lawful rights and liberties of the subjects, and every person that shall make this Protestation . . .*'

Later, leaving the Chamber in the company of Sir Henry Vane, Richard tried to express something of the emotions that had moved him that day. 'Did you not feel it, sir, that the Lord was with us?' he asked quietly.

Vane gave his oblique, charming smile. 'I felt it, my friend. It is a covenant as holy as any the Scots swore.'

Dorothy Liddell was bored beyond words. She wished desperately that her father, Sir Ralph, had not thought Widehope too dangerous for his children in these troubled times. After all, there had been no more fighting once the Scots had occupied Newcastle and the Bishopric, and even to have lived in a house in which Scottish soldiers were forcibly quartered must have been less trying on her spirits than this enforced exile.

It was not that she had nothing to do, for the Fawcett household at Thornside, to which she had been sent, had insufficient servants (in her opinion), which left rather more for the womenfolk to do than was usual at Widehope; and Mistress Susannah Fawcett seemed somehow to escape a good deal of it, by being constantly absent on the claim that some sick person needed her. Margaret Boulton, the gaunt servant who ruled the domestic portion of the house, was kindly enough in her brusque way, but she was not one for idle talk. In fact idleness of any kind was frowned upon in this place, and that included music and singing (except of psalms, with which the lengthy twice-daily household prayers began and ended), light chatter and generally doing nothing in particular, whether pleasurably or otherwise. Dorothy strongly suspected that even laughter was not permitted. Certainly she could not remember anyone laughing since she came to Thornside.

It would have been different if Cuthbert and Mark had been with her, but they had been sent away to school in York; or any of the little ones, but they had been distributed among other friends and relatives well out of reach of the occupying armies. As it was, she was lonely as well as bored, seeing no one outside the Fawcett household, except when she accompanied Margaret or John or their mistress to market, and to church on Sunday. Even the church was relentlessly austere, quite unlike the beautiful and familiar building at home. Mistress Fawcett told her that it had once been shamefully embellished with idolatrous wall paintings and stained glass windows, but now the walls were whitewashed and the glass was inoffensively clear. Dorothy's father had no liking for Popish trappings either, and was a firm critic of Archbishop Laud's innovations to the Church of England, but she thought even Sir Ralph would have felt this was going too far.

She knew that Doctor Fawcett was one of her father's oldest and dearest friends and that Sir Ralph hoped, even expected, that Dorothy would come to love and admire the beautiful Susannah, who was, he implied, the pattern of virtuous girlhood. 'She'll be good company for you,' he had said, and she had believed it, at least until she reached Thornside and met Mistress Fawcett. Dorothy supposed, grudgingly, that she was beautiful, in a cold sort of way, and her welcome had been courteous and kindly enough, but it was certainly not that of a bosom friend. In fact it quickly became obvious to her that Mistress Fawcett thought her childish and silly.

This morning Doctor Fawcett had been called out early to a difficult labour, and his daughter had gone with him, riding immodestly astride a sturdy pony in a manner that would certainly have shocked Sir Ralph, Dorothy thought, wishing her father could have been there to see it. What was worse in her eyes was that even in so undignified a posture and dressed in sober working clothes remarkable only for their spotless neatness, Susannah still did not lose that look of remote and untouchable beauty. On the other hand, Dorothy was able to console herself with the discovery she had made yesterday. Susannah had happened to come in just as she was dressing, and had lectured her on the folly of wearing stays. Dorothy was not sure if Susannah regarded them as vain and worldly, or as bad for the health. But after that she had studied

Mistress Fawcett closely and had been maliciously gratified to observe that her waist was rather thicker than was desirable.

Left to her own devices, Dorothy helped Margaret in the dairy for some time, and mended a sheet that in any but this frugal household would have been consigned to use as rags. After that, she wandered in the walled garden, laid out mostly with vegetables and fruit trees and a great many herbs, though there were also, brilliantly in bloom, beds of tulips, a strange new flower that was Doctor Fawcett's passion. She walked round and round in the grey morning, imagining how it would be if her betrothed should suddenly appear, climbing the wall with lithe, effortless grace to jump down and walk at her side, there to declaim in impassioned tones that he could no longer bear to be without her. But in the end even the power of her imagination could not keep out the cold and she grew tired of the quiet and went inside and up to her room.

She took out paper and quills and ink and sat down to write to her betrothed, the thought of him the only thing that could cheer her. But writing to him was not very easy. She longed to tell him all about her boredom and her loneliness, but she sensed that would not be quite what a young girl ought to write to her future husband, who would want his wife to be dutiful and patient and obedient to the wishes of those in authority over her. Besides, she had to enclose the letter with one to her father, since the betrothal was not yet public knowledge. He would then send it on to Lord Milburn, who was at present in London – and, of course, her father would have every right to read it first, should he so choose. She knew Sir Ralph admired Mistress Fawcett and would think the failing was all on her part.

My lord, she began in her careful script, and then paused. What could she say now? *Every moment that we are parted is a torment to me*? No, perhaps not. She liked the sound of it in a way, but the more sensible side of her thought it overstated the case somewhat. It was boredom rather than separation that really tormented her, though of course the company of her beloved would be the best possible remedy for that. But even to put it in those rather more modest terms would, she suspected, be forward in the extreme. Besides, she did not want to give him the impression that she wished their marriage to take place with precipitate speed. She looked forward to it, of course, but at the moment she was inclined rather to prolong the period of courtship, which she found very pleasurable, at least when they were together. Marriage was a rather more serious and frightening prospect, the worst part of which would be leaving the beloved familiarity of Widehope.

She dipped the quill once more in the ink and added, *I do greatly hope that your lordship is in good health.* She pictured him in good health: soft dark curls about his fair face, blue eyes looking into hers. She felt a strange uneasy sensation somewhere deep inside her, and gave a little shiver of excitement. She closed her eyes and thought of how he had kissed her, two or three times, though in her imagination the kisses were much more prolonged. That, however, made her feel really uncomfortable, so she forced her attention back to her letter.

I find myself here in a very godly sober family, she went on. And then, conscious of a certain amount of insincerity: *Indeed, I truly believe that I am not good enough for such company. Mistress Fawcett is very virtuous, though I think has too much learning to please a husband.* That, she thought, was verging on cattiness, but she suppressed a sudden frightened urge to scratch it out. Even her father might agree with it, she suspected. Certainly there were a great many things about Mistress Fawcett that were not at all like the pattern of womanhood held up to her from her earliest years. She had longed to be able to boast to the older girl about her future marriage to a fine, titled young man of great wealth. That would show that she was not after all so contemptible a person, and certainly no longer a mere child. It might even have put the other girl's perfect nose out of joint, just a little. But of course she must say nothing, though she let fall one or two obscure hints. Unfortunately, Mistress Fawcett only seemed to look on her more contemptuously than ever after that, as if she thought it foolish to be impressed by such worldly matters. She was indeed very godly, was Mistress Fawcett.

Here, there is great hope for the fall of my Lord of Strafford, and for Parliament to bring about a reform of the many abuses that have grown up with the times. We do hear too that His Grace of Canterbury is confined to the Tower. Would he think that unsuitable matter for a young girl's letter? Her father did not encourage political talk among women, but the Fawcetts seemed to have no such scruples. For the most part it bored her intensely, when she understood it at all, but she had to fill the page somehow. *I hope only that Parliament will find a way with all speed to rid my home country of the invader, so that we may live in peace*. Writing that, she suddenly found her eyes full of tears. *My lord, I have never lodged away from home in my life till now, and I find it hard*. Well, if her father didn't like that, it was too bad. To mollify him, she added, truthfully enough, *I do sorely miss my dear father and mother*. And then she decided she had said quite enough, and ended carefully, *But I do assure you that I am in good health and remain your lordship's most humble servant, D. Liddell*.

By the time he reached the House of Lords on Tuesday morning, Ludovick had finished reading Sir Ralph's ebullient, affectionate letter. There was no time now to begin on Dorothy's, which had been enclosed with it. He put it in his pocket to read later.

The peers' coaches had great difficulty making a way through the mob howling for Strafford's blood. When his vehicle finally came to a halt, Ludovick took a deep breath before stepping out into the press of people, one hand on the hilt of his sword, Rob aggressively watchful at his back. He was becoming uncomfortably used to these encounters with the vociferous London population.

It had been something of a shock the first time he had emerged from the enclosed, artificial world of the court to the smoky, stinking, hostile streets of the capital. His life since returning to England seemed to have become disjointed, full of different parts that did not quite fit together, at odds with one another. There had been that brief interlude divided between Blackheugh and Widehope, when he had thought that, after the years of war, the peaceful occupations of a country landowner were about to swallow him up and even to offer him the possibility of an unfamiliar happiness. Then war had caught up with him, even in this ordered and apparently peaceful land, only to end as abruptly as it had begun. Still technically an army officer, he had answered the summons to York, where last September the King had called the peers to a Great Council. There Ludovick had his first experience of the court.

'We welcome you for your father's s-sake,' the King had said, when Ludovick had first knelt to kiss his hand. 'We remember him as our right loyal and trusty s-servant.'

Ludovick had not much cared to be welcomed in those terms, but he had been surprised how many people seemed to have regarded his father with respect. Of course, when at court, the Late Lord Milburn had intended to please, and when he set out to do something he had generally succeeded. He could, when it suited him, conjure up a remote and chilly impression of charm. It was only his neighbours, his tenants and his family, and those who had crossed him in some way, who had a very different recollection of him.

In a way Ludovick could see why his father would have seemed made for King Charles's court, with its tasteful splendour and its grave, shy monarch with his love of fine paintings and good music and his irreproachable private life. It was a strange enclosed world in which he lived with his vivacious wife and the courtiers who, in their discreetly savage jostling for favour, seemed, here in London, to be a different species from the loudly critical members of Parliament meeting so short a distance away; though of course many of the courtiers also sat in Lords or Commons.

The ending of the Great Council had not, as he had anticipated, returned Ludovick to the routine of drilling the small troop of which he was captain. A new Parliament had been called, which had necessitated his taking his seat in the House of Lords. He had not expected to be long in London. No Parliament had ever lasted more than a month or two at most.

But now, four months later, Parliament was still sitting and showed every intention of resisting dissolution. What was more, Ludovick no longer had any position in the army, for, once Parliament opened, all Catholic officers had been promptly cashiered. That had been something of a shock, though now he was surprised that it should have been. He had been foolish to think that what he found at court told him anything about the country at large. At court, Catholicism was not only practised openly, it was even a matter of high fashion, at least in the brilliant circle about Queen Henrietta Maria, who, with the help of her chaplains, actively strove for conversions. Among her converts, indeed, was a younger brother of Lord Mandeville, staunch Puritan heir to the Earl of Manchester and friend of John Pym. Since there were also a fair number of Catholics in Parliament – particularly in the Lords – Ludovick had foolishly begun to believe that England had undergone a dramatic transformation and become tolerant.

One after another events had shown him how wrong he was. First, there had been the loss of his commission. Then, in January, he had been astonished by the virulence of the outburst when the King had dared to reprieve an elderly Jesuit priest, condemned to death by due process of law. It was a long time since any priest had actually been put to death, whatever the law said, but in the present angry climate there was no mood for clemency. In the end, Father Goodman had nobly refused the King's reprieve, after which, in spite of the fury of the city and the Commons, the Lords had not dared to be so harsh as to condemn him, to Ludovick's relief.

Now, it was the Earl of Strafford who might face the scaffold, and after him Archbishop Laud. The trial for treason of the King's chief minister had begun in March and had not gone well, or not at least from the point of view of those who wanted to see the downfall of the hated minister. In Ludovick's opinion the whole business had nothing whatsoever to do with justice. Observing the trial, he knew that he was watching the murder of a man, a killing as premeditated as any act of village vengeance. It was not that he cared greatly what became of Strafford. He knew too much of the wrongs the Lord Deputy had committed in Ireland to have any warm feelings for him, though it was not those wrongs for which he was on trial. On the contrary, the most heinous crime he was said to have committed was to have offered the King the use of an Irish Papist army against his English subjects. That, and to have striven deliberately to subvert the fundamental laws of England and, by his evil counsel, to set King and Commons at odds with one another.

The proceedings had dragged on, with Strafford, sick and exhausted though he clearly was, defending himself with a skill and eloquence that had surprised many and had clearly alarmed the men in the Commons who sought his death. At last in exasperation they had abandoned the trial altogether and brought in a Bill of Attainder. The bill had already passed the Commons, with ease. Today it would come before the Lords. Once passed there, only the King's prerogative could save his minister.

It was, to Ludovick, inconceivable that the King would allow Strafford to die, whatever the result of the vote. Even in the present heated atmosphere – especially in that atmosphere – to condemn his most loyal servant would be a deplorable, unthinkable demonstration of weakness. Once do that, and the gates would be open for the wilder spirits in Parliament to feel they could do exactly as they pleased; which, if nothing else, would certainly mean law after law against Catholics. Ludovick remembered an unpleasant incident last autumn, when that loathsome man John Pym had suggested in the Commons that all Catholics should wear a conspicuous badge to mark them out, as Ludovick had heard Jews in

Venice were obliged to do. Pym had found few supporters for his measure, but he was not alone in the virulence of his anti-Catholicism.

On his way into the Chamber, Ludovick met two Catholic peers coming out. 'The Commons are to send up a bill this afternoon,' one of them said, when he expressed surprise that they should be leaving before the day's business had even begun. 'They want us all to subscribe to the oath they concocted yesterday. You'd be wise to leave while you can.'

'I'll take my chance on its not passing,' said Ludovick. But when, early in the afternoon, the words of what they were calling the Protestation were read to an enthusiastic House, he knew his colleagues had been right. It had been drawn up with care and it was, unequivocally, an oath that no Catholic could possibly take, even with his fingers crossed and his mind disengaged.

Pleading sickness, he slipped out of the Chamber while the house was voting whether to take the oath. Outside, the crowd was waiting for him. He had to use his sword to clear a way, and even then reached his coach with his cloak torn. He thought, ruefully, that there was no need for Catholics to wear a badge, when they were obviously so well known already. Once his coach was safely on its way (it took some time), he said to Rob, who was sitting inside with him, rubbing a bruised cheek, 'One thing's certain: there'll be no Catholic lords voting to save my Lord Strafford.'

Back in his house in fashionable St Martin's Lane, Ludovick settled down to read Dorothy's letter, glad of a distraction from the sourness of the times. Its tone amused him. He strongly suspected that by sending her to stay in a 'sober and godly' household, her father had hoped to reinforce her defences against Papism, but it seemed to Ludovick that it was well on the way to making her feel the attractions of a less austere faith. He began to look more hopefully on his prospect of eventually winning her over to Catholicism, should they ever be married.

He almost sat down to write a reply to her at once, going so far as to reach for pen and paper, but when it came to the point he wrote to her father instead. Writing to Dorothy was not at all easy, though he had dutifully done so, as often as he felt he ought. He had no experience of children, and she was still very much a child, and trying to think what to write to her only made him realise how little he knew her. He would have to enclose something for her with the letter to her father, so he decided that tomorrow he would buy her a pair of embroidered gloves and send them with a tenderly worded note. Meanwhile, he settled down to give Sir Ralph a detailed account of the most recent proceedings of the Parliament from which, as a Durham man, he was excluded. It was one of his bitterest complaints that the Bishop of Durham, sitting in the Lords, was felt to be representation enough for the county. Now that there was a move to exclude all Bishops from the Lords, that might change, of course.

I fear the matter of the Brotherly Assistance has still not been brought to its conclusion, Ludovick wrote, having first commiserated with his former guardian for the continuing financial exactions of the Scottish army, which supported itself by heavily taxing the inhabitants of the occupied counties. The Brotherly Assistance was the sum that was to be paid to rid England altogether of the enemy.

Once the concerns closest to Sir Ralph were dealt with, he moved on to what had happened today. *It is clear now that the King alone has power to save my Lord of Strafford*, he wrote, *as he surely will* . . .

It was a relief after that to conclude with the subject of music. He had recently met the King's musician-in-ordinary, William Lawes, who had composed several fine consorts for viols, the sheet music for which Ludovick intended to copy out as soon as he had time and send to Sir Ralph, so that he could practise them. Then, as soon as the Scots had gone and everything had returned to normal and they could gather in peace at Widehope again as they had last summer, they would play them together. And, thought Ludovick as he signed his name at the end, perhaps I shall be married. There was still the religious barrier of course; less than ever could he imagine himself agreeing to conform. On the other hand, as the days went by and his connections with the Liddell family increased (if only at long distance), he wanted more and more to make sure of his place in it.

After that, with his head full of Dorothy, Ludovick went to take supper with Lady Selina Blackwood. A Catholic a few years older than he was, she was married, but her Protestant husband, who had a minor post at court, was said to be impotent and did not seem to mind who kept her entertained at night, so long as she was discreet. As she was beautiful, charming, sang and danced exquisitely and appeared to have no particularly deep feelings for anyone but herself, Ludovick was happy to enjoy the distraction she offered.

Tonight, however, he found he was not easily distracted. The day's events, the letter from Dorothy, all had unsettled him. After supper and a mildly pleasurable hour or two in Selina's bed, he lay beside her and found himself wondering what it would be like to lie with a virgin, and if Dorothy's evident adoration of him would be enough to light the mutual passion, which, at present, seemed very far away. 'What if you were a virgin,' he said suddenly, 'how would you wish me to seduce you?' It was a long time since Selina had been a virgin, but she entered eagerly into the spirit of the device, as she thought it, and showed him, at some considerable length, precisely what she would want him to do.

That brought him to sleepiness at last, from which he was roughly jolted by a soft, idly spoken remark: 'You know one thing I find I like about you, my dear? Eight months we've been together and there have been no awkward consequences. I've never yet found any certain means of preventing conception. A man who can satisfy a woman without getting her big-bellied is to be cherished.'

Ludovick was shocked into silence by what he realised she was saying. Her fingers continued to run lightly over his body, but they no longer stirred any excitement in him at all. He knew she had several children, left in the country with a nurse and acknowledged – however reluctantly – by the husband who had fathered none of them. He thought now of other women he had lain with: Maria in Flanders, who had borne him no child but had conceived almost at once by the lover who had displaced him. There were others too, and . . . No, he could think of none who had ever been made pregnant by him. Not that he had ever wanted it, but now he felt suddenly depressed, as if it made him less of a man. He had never thought of it before, but he realised that to give pleasure was not enough, by itself. It occurred to him then that Sir Ralph would certainly not think it enough, on his daughter's behalf.

He had meant to stay all night with Selina but after that he felt the need of air and solitude, and left her. Out in the streets he found solitude enough at this late hour, but the stinking, smoky atmosphere of London seeped into his lungs, making him cough; they said it had been even worse before the Scots' occupation of Newcastle cut off supplies of coal from the capital. For the first time that he could remember his thoughts went longingly to Blackheugh, or rather to the border hills and the clear sweet cold Tynedale air. There was no clear air in London.

Back at Milburn House he fended off Rob's discreet but anxious questioning and sent him to bed. Then he played savagely on the bass viol for a long time, filling the house with the melancholy harshness of its sound. Not long before dawn it suddenly occurred to him that if he was not able to produce an heir, then it did not matter if he never married at all. He did not find the thought consoling, nor the additional reflection that it would then be a matter of concern only to himself if he were to give up his entire estate and return to Flanders.

Unable to shake off his darkening mood, he set out to get very drunk indeed.

Two days later a thin House of Lords, in which no Catholic was present, voted for Strafford's death. The Bill of Attainder went at once to the King for the royal assent.

On the Sunday, the embassies were left in peace and the crowds thronged instead to Whitehall, where the King deliberated over the bill. They were calling now not only for the deaths of Strafford and Laud, but of the Queen too. Only with difficulty were they kept from breaking in to the Palace.

On Monday, the King gave his assent to two bills. One prevented the dissolution of Parliament without the joint agreement of King, Lords and Commons. The other condemned the Earl of Strafford to death.

Two days later Strafford went to the block on Tower Hill, receiving a last blessing from his friend Archbishop Laud, who watched from the Tower as he passed. It was rumoured that one of the last things he said was, 'Put not your trust in princes.'

1642

CHAPTER SEVEN

Richard Metcalfe knew that the first of November 1641 would be burned into his memory for ever. There had been rumours for days beforehand, even weeks, that something was brewing, but it had still come suddenly, like a thunderbolt.

Until then everything had been going well, or so it had seemed to Richard. The royal prerogative courts used for such tyrannical purposes by Laud and Strafford had been abolished, Star Chamber, the Council of the North, all of them. The Scots had been paid off at last and gone home, and – better still – the troublesome, worrying armies in England and Ireland had been disbanded. One by one Lords and Commons had taken from the King's hands the dangerous tools of his power, much as a parent takes from a beloved but too adventurous child the sharp implements with which he might harm himself and those around him, putting them aside until he reaches sufficient maturity to be trusted with them again. There was some unease at the King's absence from the capital, on a visit to Scotland that some feared would afford an opportunity for further intrigues against Parliament, but by the autumn their fears had lessened. More recently, those who thought as Richard did had been concerned with forcing godly reformation on the Church of England. Once that was done, then Parliament could be dissolved and they could all go home.

The end of October came and the House had resumed after its brief recess, a little reluctantly because warmer weather had brought an outbreak of plague to the capital, not yet ended. Richard, who had returned briefly to Thornside hoping to further his wooing of Susannah but had found her extraordinarily elusive, was glad to be back in London, with something useful to do.

And then, on that first day of November, the entire Privy Council had come to a suddenly silent House of Commons and stood bareheaded while Lord Keeper Littleton reported that they had just that day received news that the wild Irish in Ulster had risen in savage force against the English who had settled there.

Sitting motionless in that stunned House, Richard had heard the news with a horror beyond words. 'Anne!' was his first thought. 'Oh my sister!' And Henry, his dear friend; and their infant son and the new baby recently conceived; their rich and fruitful lands, their happiness, seemingly so secure . . . He had feared for them then, but, as the days and weeks passed and more detailed reports came in, his anguish grew. There were dreadful, appalling tales, tales that would have been beyond belief, ought to have been beyond belief, except that they were reported on impeccable authority by those who had been there; tales of burning homes and slaughtered men and women and children, of rapes and looting and crimes even more unspeakable.

He woke each day (when he had slept at all, that was) to a hope that these next few hours might at last bring a letter from Anne or Henry, assuring him they were safe. After all, he told himself, it was little more than two months since Anne had last written, a happy unconcerned letter full of domestic details. Admittedly, between them they generally wrote more often than that, but by no means always. They might simply be very preoccupied with domestic or farm duties. Anne might simply be a little unwell, as he believed women often were in the early months of pregnancy.

But the days passed, and the weeks, and still no word came, and Richard could no longer rationalise the lack of news. It was agony, knowing nothing, hearing nothing. They had not heard anything at Thornside either, for his mother drily, without comment, reported the absence of letters. *We have no late news of Anne*, she would say, never once mentioning the reason why this was something to be feared.

As autumn turned to winter, the rising spread from Ulster to Ireland's other provinces, gathering support daily, not only from the native Irish but also from many of the old Norman-Irish families. Distraught refugees began to reach England, each bringing his or her own tale of suffering to add to the oppressive weight of what they already knew. News-sheets, luridly illustrated, gave each story the widest coverage. It was whispered that the King himself was behind the rising. Sir Phelim O'Neill, its leader, claimed to have the royal commission in his hand, so the whispers said, and two of the rising's leaders, captured and tortured in Dublin, confessed to royal support. It was more than whispered that, once they had taken Dublin, the Irish would sweep across the sea, where English Catholics would swiftly flock to join them. Every day people braced themselves for the first news of a landing and watched their Catholic neighbours for signs of hidden stores of arms or unusual comings and goings.

The King – belatedly, Richard thought – condemned the rebels, and asked his Parliament for funds to raise an army to assist the forces already trying to suppress the rising. Richard's colleagues were eager for its suppression too, but few of them trusted the King to use an army simply for that purpose. What could be easier for a monarch not yet wholeheartedly accepting of the advice of his loyal Parliament, but to march his army instead against that Parliament? Evidence was just emerging that a number of senior army officers – one of them, significantly, a Major Daniel O'Neill, with a brother now among the Irish rebels – had plotted only last summer to use military force against Parliament. That army had now been disbanded, but there were still many individuals about the King, and even some in the country at large, who thought Parliament had overreached itself and who might be willing to use any new force for their own ends. The county militias were the one dangerous tool still in the King's hands, so Sir Arthur Hazelrigg, member for Leicestershire, brought forward a measure to put them under parliamentary control. Unfortunately, to be fully effective the measure would need the royal assent.

Meanwhile other business could not wholly be laid aside, though Richard no longer went eagerly each day to the House, his mind fixed on his great purpose. All the time, fear for his sister and her family gnawed at him, casting its shadow over every hour of every day and every night. He voted, however, for the Grand Remonstrance, which in one exhaustive document listed all the abuses suffered during the King's reign: innovations in religion, toleration of Catholics, unjust seizing of men's property by means of illegal taxation; and demanded redress. It was passed, though only by a small majority and after long and heated argument. At the end of November, the King returned from Scotland to the warm welcome of his capital, and the Remonstrance was set before him. He said only that he would answer it when he was ready. Within a month he had installed his own loyal garrison in the Tower, under a man he trusted.

Christmas in London was noisy with anti-Popish riots, fuelled by unemployment and cold and hunger. When Parliament resumed they heard evidence that the Queen had encouraged the Irish rising. They knew already that she had been the mind behind many other plots, before and since. In secret, plans were made for her impeachment. 'If the King hears, he'll take steps against us,' Richard said to Tom's father.

'Pym knows that,' said Lord Fairfax, and Richard knew he was right. He wondered if anyone else felt, as he did, that they were walking on eggs.

On the third of January the Attorney-General, Sir Edward Herbert, came to the Lords on the King's behalf and charged six men with High Treason: Lord Mandeville, John Pym, John Hampden, Denzil Holles, Sir Arthur Hazelrigg, William Strode. The Lords set up a committee to look into the legality of what the Attorney-General had done.

The next afternoon the blow fell. That was another day Richard would not easily forget: the commotion growing outside the doors of the Commons Chamber, the clatter of marching feet on stone coming steadily nearer just as the five accused members, forewarned, slipped away by river to safety; the doors flung wide and the King's small figure stepping briskly into the Chamber, bareheaded, with the Elector Palatine just behind him. All of them then removing their hats, rising to their feet. As the King moved towards the speaker's chair, Richard had glanced at the doors and saw the Earl of Roxburgh propping them open, so that everyone in the Commons should note the jostling mass of armed men waiting outside. Richard remembered how his heart had thudded.

Then, watching King Charles's grave bearded face, he had seen the King glance, swiftly, to the place by the bar of the house where John Pym usually sat, and then away again. Something showed in his eyes, though what it was Richard could not be quite sure.

The King had come to a halt before Speaker Lenthall. 'Master Speaker, I must for a time make bold with your chair.' The Speaker had stepped aside and the King took his place. Carefully then, in short phrases, without any hint of his customary stammer, he had explained why he was there. He was heard in silence, no one moving. After a time he turned to the Speaker again. 'Is Master Pym here?' There was still no reply, so he went through the other names, with marked impatience. His dark eyes, very hard and bright, swept the Chamber, seeking this face or that, warning of severe displeasure. 'Well, Master Speaker?'

Lenthall, visibly trembling, fell to his knees before his monarch. 'May it please your Majesty, I have neither eyes to see nor tongue to speak in this place, but as the House is pleased to direct me, whose servant I am here.'

Another little silence, while the whole House seemed to hold its collective breath. The only sound was the murmur and clatter of the soldiers beyond the doors. Then the King said, 'It's no matter. I think my eyes are as good as another's.' The royal eyes swept the Chamber again, and then the King rose to his feet. 'I see that all my birds have flown,' he said. Then, steadily, with all possible dignity, he walked again the whole length of the Chamber, between the standing lines of his Commons and away from them, the doors clanging shut behind him. Richard, like everyone else, had seen the rage on his face, and the bitter realisation that he had been humiliated. He had shivered, suddenly struck by the enormity of so offending a King.

A few days later the royal family fled from a hostile capital to the relative security of Windsor Castle, where it was rumoured that the King was gathering an army to march against Parliament. Then the Queen went to Holland, ostensibly to accompany Princess Mary to her new husband, in fact, many thought, to raise arms and money on behalf of King Charles. Parliament swiftly took measures to secure ports and town garrisons, and sent deputations to the King, who by now was beginning to move steadily north, urging him to put his name to the Militia Bill. King Charles refused in the strongest terms, and they knew that without his authority many of the county officials responsible for the militia would not obey them. However, in other things they could act. With the monarch safely out of the way, they began to send imprisoned Catholic priests to their deaths, to the noisy satisfaction of the Londoners.

There was still no word from Anne or Henry, though the flood of atrocity stories continued to grow and Richard did not know whether his appalling nightmares were worse than the grisly imaginings that tormented his waking hours. He saw his friend murdered, his sister raped and cut in pieces, his infant nephew's small helpless body spitted on a long knife.

The trickle of refugees became a torrent: terrified, destitute wretches who clogged country roads and city streets, begging for succour – which, because of the enormity of what had happened, they were speedily given.

Funds poured in to help them, and also for the scheme Parliament had brought forward to equip a military force adequate to the task of suppressing the rebels. As an incentive to generous giving, investors in the scheme were promised land confiscated from all those native Irish still in possession of it, once the rebellion was at an end. Members looked forward to an Ireland purged of Papists and wild Irishmen, settled in peace with godly planters, as had already been done in many places, but not soon enough, nor with sufficient thoroughness, for otherwise this thing could not have happened.

In mid-March the King reached York, summoning his loyal servants to join him there. He would, he said, place himself at the head of an army to go to Ireland and suppress the rebellion. Those members of Parliament who had been dismayed by their colleagues' treatment of him left the hostile atmosphere of London and went to York. In April, the King arrived in state to secure the great seaport and arsenal of Hull, but at the gates was refused admission by Sir John Hotham, whom Parliament had sent to govern the town. Tom Fairfax wrote to Richard full of concern for the slump in the wool trade that was causing such hardship to the West Riding, where he lived, and speaking of his hope that in these hard times any differences might swiftly be patched up, since they could only make life harder still for landowners and clothiers alike. In the angry, quarrelsome atmosphere of London, it seemed to Richard like a vain hope. Some of his colleagues were already beginning to talk of the possibility of armed conflict, not this time between English and Scots or English and Irish, but between King and Parliament. Yet part of him could not quite believe such a thing would be allowed to happen.

It was late in that confused and troubled spring that an outraged Commons learned of intercepted letters proving beyond any doubt that Lord Milburn, absent from the Lords for some months now, had been organising the supply of arms to the rebels in Ireland. On the day that news broke, Richard received a message from his mother, and went home at once.

A few days earlier, around suppertime, one of Doctor Fawcett's wealthy patients, wife of a substantial farmer near Countersett, had suddenly sent for him. His regular patients were almost all among the gentry, since few others could afford the services of a physician of his reputation – though he was always ready to attend the deserving poor free of charge, or give his time unstintingly when an epidemic struck. On this occasion, however, he was confined to bed with a slight fever, so Susannah went in his place to attend to Mistress Dinsdale's sudden attack of pain about the heart. 'Hmm. Very likely you'll find she's eaten too good a dinner,' advised Matthew Fawcett. 'She's never been one for moderation. But she'll keep you a long time. Take John with you. It'll be a dark night after so wet a day.'

Susannah's father was right in every respect. There was nothing wrong with Mistress Dinsdale's heart, though the woman was not easily convinced. 'It was Doctor Fawcett I asked for,' she complained, 'not a chit of a girl.' But Susannah persuaded her to remove her stays, go to bed and take an infusion of wormwood; and then sat with her until she admitted to feeling better.

By the time Susannah left the house, their servant John Piggott riding ahead with a lantern, the short June night was at its darkest point, intensified by the chilly rain. They made their way up the track from the farm to the long straight Roman road that ran in a north-easterly direction along the ridge. Then, heads bent against the rain, they followed the road steeply down into the dale.

They had gone only a short way when a sound, very faint in the wind, caught Susannah's attention. She thought at first it was an animal of some kind – there were sheep grazing on the fell – and drew rein, in case the creature was in trouble. Then the noise came again, a low moan, and she realised it was a human sound. It came from somewhere to her right, close to a twisted, windblown thorn whose shape she could just make out, rising against a stone wall. 'Bring the lantern, John,' she called. She dismounted, and John brought the lantern and held it high over her.

Huddled in the nook between the tree and the wall lay what looked at first glance like a bundle of rags, from which rose an

unpleasant animal smell. John lowered the lantern, and they made
out a woman, skeletally thin, her head bent over something held in
her arms. Against her breast a small face, still and waxen as a doll's,
gleamed in the light. 'Some beggar's whore, mistress,' said John.
'With her bastard.'

Susannah thought it likely he was right. In general she had little
time for beggars, most of whom she regarded as feckless creatures
more in need of correction than charity. But in these dark times, the
news from Ireland being what it was, things were no longer so simple. Besides, feckless or not, something was clearly amiss with the
woman and her child.

She made John lower the lantern still more, and its brightness
must have disturbed the woman, for she opened her eyes. Even in
the faint light, Susannah recognised terror, utter naked terror, not
just in the woman's face, but in every line of her body. The frightened mouth moved, but no words came. Susannah reached out a
hand and laid it on the woman's flinching shoulder. 'We shan't
harm you,' she said very gently. 'Tell me where you're hurt.'

The woman tried again to say something, though the formless
words ended in a moan. It was then, suddenly, shockingly, that
Susannah knew who she was.

How she knew, she had no clear idea, for there was nothing in
the stinking, degraded figure to suggest the fresh young bride of
two years before; nothing to remind her that this was Anne
Greatorex, who had once been Anne Metcalfe, dancing her way to
her marriage bed. Now, the woman struggled to speak again, and
this time Susannah caught the words: 'I can't walk any more.'

There seemed to Susannah such an unimaginable effort in those
words; they spoke of long terrible hours, days, months of struggle,
all the way from Ireland to this windswept place so near her home,
where her strength had at last deserted her. Susannah had a sense of
terrors beyond imagining, of unspeakable horrors. 'We'll get you
home, mistress,' she said. Then, to John, 'It's Mistress Anne, from
the Hall.' As she bent over the woman again, she heard John's horrified exclamation. The lantern light wavered for a moment, before
it steadied.

As quickly and gently as she could, she examined both mother
and child. She could see no obvious signs of wounds or other hurt,
and the child was – thank God – still living, though he was unconscious and his pulse was faint and uneven. She thought they were

both suffering from hunger and cold and exhaustion rather than any other more specific ailment, but she knew quite well that those things could be as deadly as any wound. She took off her own cloak and wrapped it about them, and then put John's on top of it, and then they set about lifting them both on to her pony. It was not easy, for Anne would not give up the child, so they had to be raised together. For all their emaciation, they were both big-boned, which made them heavy to lift, especially when it had to be done so as not to hurt them any further. Worse, Anne's understanding seemed clouded, so that she would suddenly forget where she was or what was happening to her, and cry out in terror.

But at last mother and child were safely installed. Susannah held them in place while John led the horses, and they set out, down the hill, across the river at the bridge, up the further slope and east towards the Hall.

It was an achingly slow journey, and at the end of it they found the Hall in darkness. It took some time to wake the servants, but, once done, the whole rambling edifice came suddenly alive with light and bustle and anxious cries. They carried Anne and the child up to her old room, and got them both to bed. Anne still refused to be parted from the child, though Susannah wheedled and pleaded: 'For his sake. He needs help!' In the end, dosed with laudanum – a new drug, opium dissolved in alcohol, which by good fortune Susannah had in her bag – Anne fell asleep, and Susannah was able to prize little Philip from her arms. She examined him carefully, removed his filthy rags, washed him and dressed him in clean linen and then laid him, well-wrapped, by his mother. She was troubled by his listlessness and his pallor. He still seemed scarcely conscious, and had no interest in eating. 'I think Mistress Anne will recover, madam, God willing,' Susannah said to Dame Alice. 'It's the little one I'm troubled about – he's very sick. I'll speak to my father and then come again in the morning.'

When she had gone, Dame Alice went to her room to write to her son, summoning him home.

Richard reached home the morning after they knew at last that little Philip was out of danger. 'Mistress Fawcett has been admirable,' Dame Alice told her son, as she greeted him at the door. 'We have never once felt the lack of her father.'

Richard was shocked beyond words by his sister's wasted

appearance. 'She looks very much better now,' his mother told him. 'But she says so little. We still don't know what happened. Of course, she's had no room in her thoughts for anyone but Philip.'

Then Susannah came to make her daily visit, and revealed to Richard quite another person from the remote, cool young woman he so painfully worshipped. It was as if, in tending the sick mother and child, Matthew Fawcett's daughter somehow came alive. Her voice soft, her small strong hands infinitely kind, her beautiful eyes watchful for any little hint as to what was needed, she was wholly absorbed in what she did. He found himself forgetting all about his sister and simply watching the woman who tended her.

And then he was jolted suddenly out of his absorption, for it was during the course of that visit that Anne at last found the strength and the courage to tell her story. It came in broken, whispered, panicky phrases, slowly at first and then with increasing force. All the time she talked, Richard stood by the door and Susannah sat holding Anne's hand and listening, as if she knew that there could be no healing until the story was over.

They had come at night, a great mob of armed rebels, surprising them at supper, without any warning. Henry had tried to resist, but they had quickly overpowered and disarmed him and then they had stripped them, Henry, Anne (who was five months pregnant) and even little Philip, and turned them out into the bitter frosty night, while behind them the house they had worked so hard to make into a home was put to the torch. In the cold, without shelter or food, their plight had been dreadful. Henry, hurt in the attack, had fallen gravely ill and died, in a ditch where, soon afterwards, Anne miscarried of her child. Her only wish then, sick as she was, had been to get Philip to safety before she lost him too. An Irishwoman, less savage than most of her kind, had taken pity on them and given them clothes to cover themselves, but the rebels were sweeping that way and she dared not do more. They had wandered for days, weeks even – it was all a blur now in Anne's memory, for she had been ill with fever some of the time and always hungry and cold and afraid. At last they had reached Dublin, which was crammed with refugees as desperate as themselves, and there she had been so ill they thought she would not live. Philip too had been ailing, so that when Anne recovered her wits she wanted only to make her way back to Thornside. Not really knowing what she was doing, she did not think to send a message or ask for help, except what she needed to get on a boat bound for England, and that had taken some time, for there were so many who wanted to leave. She remembered very little of the journey after that.

Near the end of her account, Anne grew drowsy; her voice slowed, her eyelids drooped, she faltered and even stopped once or twice, but it was not until the last word had been spoken that she fell asleep at last.

Once she had finished, Susannah bent once more over both mother and child, and then turned to follow Richard out of the room. Outside, on the stairs, she halted. All the softness had gone from her face. Her expression was harsh, her grey eyes brilliant. 'May God's judgement be swift on those who did this thing!' she cried.

'Amen to that,' Richard said, and suddenly wanted to kiss her. There would have been nothing out of the ordinary, on another occasion, in a kiss between friends, by way of public greeting; but they were not in public and he knew that his impulse had nothing to do with friendship. He went with her to the door and watched her walk briskly away into the night.

CHAPTER EIGHT

Two days before his twenty-third birthday Ludovick Milburn rode to Widehope knowing that by the time he returned to Blackheugh he would have made Dorothy Liddell his wife. It was a relief to have come to a decision.

The past was put firmly behind him. He preferred not to think of those long weeks last year when he had been cast into such despair by a woman's spitefulness, for such he now saw it to be. He had no wish to have anything more to do with Selina, ever again. It was ridiculous to think that at his age a thing of that kind could be decisively known. A part of him was ashamed that he should have been so cast down by it; another part was secretly frightened to remember what black pit of melancholy he had fallen into, how long it had taken him to emerge from it.

But he had emerged, to return to the Lords after the recess, helped by the peers' belated insistence that their Catholic colleagues should be able to refuse the religious clause of the Protestation. The concession had come too late to save Strafford, but it was a cheering indication that the Lords did not much care for Commons bullying of their members. Ludovick had set out to ally himself with his fellow Catholics, so that together they might oppose measures put forward by the wilder spirits in the lower House.

He had stayed on even after the Irish rebellion broke out, trying to urge the making of peace with the rebels, or at least moderation in repressing them. But he was not much of an orator and he knew he made no impression at all on a House fed daily with tales of unimaginable atrocities, which even he had not the means or knowledge to deny. Many Catholics, terrified by the anger against them in the streets, had left London, or barricaded themselves in their houses. Ludovick no longer ventured out without an escort of at least six armed men. On the day the London mob smashed all his windows and beat up a footman who unwisely remonstrated with them, his mother's anguished plea for help had reached him. He had already decided it was time to leave; the letter simply confirmed his decision.

Alone at Blackheugh except for the increasingly hostile servants, Lady Milburn had found that in these times there was no kindness left for any Irishwoman, even one who had lived in England for twenty-five years. Small acts of furtive viciousness aimed at herself, her pet dog, her horses, had turned her nearly hysterical with fear. Ludovick's return did little to calm her and in December, in spite of the bitter weather, he had at last been persuaded to make arrangements for her to sail discreetly overseas. In February he learned that she was safely in Flanders, where she had spent some happy hours with Charles at St Omer before going on to Antwerp, there to enter a convent.

The news had been brought to Ludovick, in person and without warning, by his cousin Shane O'Neill, on leave from the Spanish service to pay a visit to his ailing father in Ireland. That, at least, was his excuse, though whatever the truth behind it he had not dared to travel openly or under his own name. Once he had reassured Ludovick about his mother, the cousins had spent most of the night in earnest discussion, before Shane left early the following morning. A few weeks later he had written from Ireland, giving a long account of what he found there. Ludovick knew he was with the rebels, and that the time had come for him to put what they had agreed into effect, by means of coded letters and discreet visits to men with suitable contacts overseas, followed by the handing over of large amounts of cash.

That matter was all entirely secret, and would remain so. He told himself, as he had told Shane, that if he had been free he would have gone to Ireland at once, to fight alongside his cousins and his Dillon half-brothers, his mother's sons by her first marriage, who had joined them. Yet he was glad he was not free, that he had responsibilities and duties to keep him in England. For the first time in his life he wanted more than anything else to settle down. It was then that he decided that he would marry Dorothy as soon as possible. Some business had required his attention at one of his more remote properties, but now he was about to take the final steps. So long as war did not intervene.

He could not forget young Harry Middleton, exulting yesterday at the prospect of fighting for the King. Eldest son of one of his tenants, in whose Swaledale house Ludovick had been staying, Harry had been quite sure there was going to be a war. Harry's father, more sober than his son, had shared his view, though with misgivings. Until then Ludovick had discounted the possibility. Clearly the King had to regain his lost authority, but a decisive show of strength was, he had thought, all that was necessary. To take arms against an anointed King, however strong the forces he brought against them, was a step even the hotheads in the Commons must shrink from.

Now he was no longer sure. All he knew was that it was the more urgent that he should be married. Then he would get his wife with child – as he was now sure he would – so that, if war came, he could play his part wholeheartedly, without regret, knowing that Blackheugh had an heir. Sir Ralph could be trusted to care for his interests, if anything were to happen to him.

He had spent two days with the Middletons, not because they were his tenants, but because they were devout Catholics who harboured a priest, with whom he had arrangements to make. He did not tell the priest of the grave sin that he intended, deliberately, knowingly, to commit, though as he rode to Widehope he sent out a plea for Charles's understanding. Once at Widehope he would take the last necessary step towards marriage and go with Sir Ralph and his family to Sunday worship at the parish church, as many times as the law required. Then, once Dorothy was his wife, he would take her to Swaledale, where he would do whatever penance was required of him, so that he and Dorothy might then be married again, before God, in a Catholic ceremony. He told himself that it was, surely, excusable to attend heretic worship if in the end it should win a soul for the Church. For he was quite sure he would win Dorothy. His only concern was to stay on good terms with her family in spite of it.

It was good to arrive at Widehope without doubts, sure of his welcome. He left Rob to see to the horses and ran up the steps to the front door. It opened, for Sir Ralph had as usual been watching for him, though Dorothy was not with him this time. Ludovick reached out for the customary embrace, and was startled when Sir

Ralph stepped aside, avoiding his extended arms. 'To my study, my lord,' he said, with astonishing curtness.

Puzzled, not quite sure that he was reading the signs correctly, Ludovick followed him to his study. Usually children ran from every corner when he arrived, and Lady Elizabeth would come to add her not-quite-motherly welcome. Today, the house remained silent, but for the distant sound of childish laughter from the garden.

Sir Ralph held the door open for him to pass through and then closed it behind them. Ludovick turned to look at him and was alarmed by the severity of his expression. Quite clearly something very unpleasant had happened. 'Mistress Dorothy—?' he began, almost afraid to ask.

He wondered if Sir Ralph had heard him, for he said only, 'I want the truth, every word of it, about this business. I know that sometimes men's deeds are misread, their words misreported. It could be that there has been some mistake.'

Ludovick had no idea what he was talking about. 'What are you asking, sir?' Someone had told Sir Ralph something to his discredit; that much seemed clear. 'What have you heard?'

'Have you, at any time, had any communication with the rebels in Ireland, any of them?'

How could Ralph possibly know about that? 'I have cousins in Ireland,' said Ludovick, with careful evasion. 'I write to them from time to time, and they to me.'

'Don't prevaricate. I'm not talking about family gossip, as you well know.'

'I don't know. I have no idea what you're talking about.' Or he hoped he had no idea . . .

'Do you take me for a fool? Perhaps you do, perhaps indeed I am, to have been so taken in.' For a moment there was a terrible sadness in Sir Ralph's expression. Then the severity returned, and with it a sharp impatience. 'This Bill of Attainder they've brought before Parliament, against you—'

'What!' Ludovick knew he had gone white, felt the room spin about him. He grasped the back of the nearest chair.

'You didn't know? You must know!'

'I – I have not been home for some days. I've heard no news.'

Ralph took him by the elbow and steered him round the chair. 'You'd better sit down.' He sounded concerned and kindly, which restored Ludovick's calmness a little.

'What am I accused of?' he asked after a moment.

'High treason, of course.' Then, as if reading an indictment: 'That you did offer comfort and succour to the barbarous rebels in Ireland, by means of supplying them with arms.' Ralph stood over him, clearly seeing a glimmer of hope. 'It's not true then?'

Ludovick did not think to seize the opportunity of denying it. 'How did they know?'

'Dear God in Heaven, it is true! They stopped someone at some port, Sunderland, I think, with letters. Arms from Spain, that's what he was negotiating for, on your behalf.'

So all those elaborate arrangements had been wasted. But the first consignment had got there, he knew that, because Shane had written . . .

Sir Ralph was struggling again, not to accept the enormity of it, pleading in spite of all that he had heard for a denial. 'My boy, if you tell me on your honour that there is no truth in these stories, I'll believe you and stand by you, whatever happens. I give you my word on it.'

'I can't tell you that.'

There was a horrible, painful silence, while the two men looked at one another, striving for some kind of understanding, wanting it desperately, but knowing, on both sides, that it was beyond their reach. 'How could you?' Ralph asked at last, in a near whisper.

'They are my own kin. We were born in Ireland, Charles and I, reared by an Irish foster mother. Her language was the first I spoke – all I spoke, until I came to England. I was happy there.' He fell silent again, conscious that his words seemed somehow to be falling into a void.

'That can be no excuse. You owe allegiance to the lawful governments of these islands. Those men are rebels, kin or no.'

Ludovick stood up. 'Their lands stolen from them, forced into exile, their religion threatened – what allegiance do you owe to those who do that to you? Besides, the Scots were rebels too, but you didn't condemn the English who colluded with them.'

Ralph opened his mouth and then closed it again, saying nothing. Ludovick gave a bitter little smile. 'But they're not savages, like the wild Irish. That's what you were going to say, wasn't it?'

'Don't try and put me in the wrong! God knows there's reason enough to call those men savages, after what has been done. Even you must have heard the stories.'

'Oh yes, I've heard them. A sick old man dragged from his bed to watch his house burn, then hanged by the ruin, his wife beside him. Soldiers strung out in a long line, burning everything before them – trees, houses, crops, beasts, human beings. So the people run from their houses to hide in the furze on a hilltop, all of them, men and women and little children, and the soldiers ring the hill so no one can escape and set light to the furze and all are burned, every one.'

He saw that even Sir Ralph, used to atrocity stories, blenched at that. 'Then how in God's name can you think of sending arms to men such as these?'

'Because the soldiers were English, sir, and the men and women and children those wild Irish you so despise. You know what an English officer was heard to say, to justify the slaughter of children? "Nits will make lice." A poetic conceit, that, don't you think?'

Ralph exploded with indignation. 'No English soldiers would behave so, even to wild —'

'Oh, but they did, without any possible doubt they did! That sick old man was my uncle, my mother's brother, a harmless old man who never said a harsh word against the English, God knows why not. My cousin came home all unwitting and found what the soldiers had done. And those men and women and children on the hilltop – one of them was my foster mother. They'd burned her cabin, but I suppose it grieved them she was not in it at the time, for they stalked her with the rest until they'd finished the work.' *That old memory, the sweet smell of peat smoke and damp thatch, wiped out in the space of one letter by the stench of burning flesh.* Tears sprang to his eyes, rose in his throat. 'Jesu, what would you have me do? Turn my back and say this is not my fight?'

He saw uncertainty in Ralph's face, a struggle of some kind taking place. When the older man spoke again the note of confident indignation had gone. 'When great wrongs are done, people are made cruel,' he suggested, though he did not sound sure.

'Nothing so evil was done by the Irish. Oh, I've heard the stories, but you ask the people who were there, even the people who've fled to England. You'll hear of the odd murder perhaps, I admit it, but mostly they were just turned from their homes, nothing worse.'

'To be turned from your home in the dead of winter, stripped of everything, that is tantamount to murder.'

'I rather think my uncle and my aunt and my foster mother might have been happy to take their chance with that kind of murder,' said Ludovick.

There was a long silence. Sir Ralph went to the window and stood looking out on the green and sunlit garden, the children playing. Was he seeing instead the blazing furze, hearing the screams of the burning innocents, as Ludovick had done so often these past weeks?

If he was, he did not let it finally unsettle him, for when he turned back to face the younger man his expression had regained most of its old severity. 'My lord, there can be no defence for what you have done, not in the end. I regret it. I thought well of you. But there it is. You must see, I am sure, that from henceforth all communication must be at an end between your lordship and every member of my family.'

So that was it. All so suddenly ended, as if it had never been. Ludovick searched for some appropriate reply, but could not think what to say. It had happened so quickly and he had not yet fully taken any of it in. Before he could speak again, Sir Ralph said, 'Your lordship will leave at once, if you please.'

Another painful silence. Then: 'As you wish, sir. I bid you good day.' He turned and began to walk towards the door, mechanically. He heard Ralph speak again.

'If I were you I'd sharp go overseas, before they come for you.'

So something remained; but Ludovick did not trust himself to look round to discover what was on Sir Ralph's face, or to thank him for his concern.

He dragged Rob from the kitchen, where he had settled to his supper, and they set out on the first stage of the journey back to Blackheugh. He supposed that was where he should go, while it was still his, until he decided what to do. As they rode, he told Rob, in a briskly bitter tone, what had happened. 'Aye,' said Rob, 'I heard the talk in the kitchen. A Bill of Attainder. Do you suppose it'll get through?'

'Oh, it'll get through.' They had condemned Strafford on much slighter grounds, and Strafford had friends in Parliament. He would have none.

Rob looked at him thoughtfully, as if trying to imagine what it must feel like to discover without any warning that sentence of death had been passed upon you, that your title and property were forfeit, that even if you evaded capture you would have ceased to have any legal existence. 'Will you go to Ireland?'

It was the obvious course perhaps, but it was too soon yet to make any plans. All he could think at the moment was that he should have known it was all too good to last. It had to come to an end somehow, sooner or later.

When the door had slammed behind Ludovick, Sir Ralph stood for a long time at the window, waiting until the sound of hooves on the drive told him that the young man had gone. Then, bewildered and angry and miserable all at once, he went to break the news to Dorothy.

At prayers that evening, from which Dorothy was excused, he announced to his assembled family that my Lord Milburn had committed an unpardonable offence and henceforth had no further existence, as far as the entire Liddell family was concerned. His name was not ever to be mentioned again by any of them. After that he did not pray, as he did most days, for God's vengeance on the bloody rebels in Ireland. Instead he simply asked for God's mercy on all his people.

Later, he said to Elizabeth, 'Well, there's one good thing. It wasn't made public, so no one knows anything's changed.'

'Dorothy knows,' Elizabeth reminded him.

'Oh, she's young, she'll get over it,' Ralph said airily; but he was ashamed, though he would not admit it. Nor would he admit out loud that Elizabeth, with her persistent misgivings, had been right all along.

He could not sleep that night for the sound of his daughter weeping.

The news had reached Blackheugh before them. Something had changed, subtly, even in the manner of the servants towards their master. The steward sought an early interview with Ludovick and said, with chilly disapproval, 'Even had your lordship avoided attainder, I could not have continued long to serve your lordship, in the circumstances. Your father would never have done such a thing. So to misuse your inheritance – I have to say, my lord, that it most deeply grieves and offends me!'

This from the man who had admired and approved the ruthless and often barely legal devices of the first Baron! Ludovick would have been amused, except that he found little to amuse him in his present situation.

It took him a week to decide what to do, though he knew even that small delay was risky. Parliament had few friends in this strongly Catholic region, and the Bill of Attainder – it had been speedily passed, as he had expected – did not have the royal assent, but he doubted if anyone would rush to prevent his arrest, if it should come to that.

What made it harder to come to a decision was that he could not take in the fact that Blackheugh was lost to him. Harder still, in this week when he was looking his last upon it, Tynedale had never seemed so beautiful.

He had always thought it too wild, too harsh of climate for beauty. Yet, day after day, as he rode over the hills trying to make his choice, there would be larks singing high in the blue air, and curlews calling, and a breeze blowing soft from the south-west, sweet with the perfumes of bracken and peat and new grasses. This was beauty, he thought, this and the winding blue river below him, the rushing burns whose sound filled his ears, the wide lovely hills; this was where, after years of wandering, he had begun at last to put down tenuous roots. He wanted to stay, because it was his, because there was work for him here.

He supposed he could take to the hills as a fugitive, hiding out in the wilder places as his lawless ancestors had sometimes done, with the option of falling on his sword if they should track him down. But he could see little point in such a course.

That everything should be snatched from him like this enraged and grieved him. He did not in the least regret what he had done. He would do it again today, without a second thought. But he wished passionately that he had somehow taken more care, that he had not been found out.

There was no point in looking back. All that remained now was to decide what he should do next – and do very soon, before it was too late and the last choice, of life itself, should be taken from him.

He did not ask, this time, what Charles would have done in his place. He knew that Charles was happy, for he felt it in his blood; a happiness that had nothing to do with animal contentment, but was a matter of pursuing a goal towards which every part of body and mind and spirit strove in harmony. Charles would know that his twin was in trouble of some kind, and would pray for him. That was the best and only help he could give. Ludovick had to make his choice alone, and live with its consequences.

The obvious, the logical course was to go to Ireland. It was Ireland's struggle that had brought him to this pass. Why not take the last step and commit himself entirely to her cause, in which he believed so firmly, and to which every instinct, every tie, called him?

But he saw now, what he had somehow failed to see before, that if Parliament was not put in its place, then there could be no peace in Ireland, for the militant Protestants in the Commons and the Lords – helped, most probably, by their Scottish friends – would stop at nothing to destroy every lingering trace of the old Ireland. What it came down to, he suddenly saw, was that Ireland's only hope lay with the King; not the King as he had lately been, forced to make concession after concession to his Parliament, but the King as he ought to be, ruling according to his own unconstrained will, for the good of his people.

The King had condemned the rebellious Irish, but only belatedly and in vague terms. It was certain that he did not share the violent anti-Catholicism of so many of his subjects. It was likely that, untrammelled by Parliament, he would feel able to allow his Irish subjects to worship as they pleased, which was the chief demand of the rebels.

But if the King was to reassert his authority in full, then he needed armed assistance, because there was now no other way to dissolve Parliament without its consent. It was believed that he would accept assistance from any quarter – even from the rebel Irish, if need be. In which case, he would surely accept it from a man condemned by Parliament under a Bill of Attainder that did not have his assent – or not yet, at least.

Leaving Ireland aside, putting everything in the starkest, most personal terms, Ludovick saw that, if Parliament won, then he lost estates, life, everything. If the King won, there was a chance that he might escape death and even regain something of what he had lost – not Dorothy, not her father's friendship, but something.

There was, in the end, no choice at all.

'I'm going to Newcastle, to offer myself for the King's service,' he said that night, as Rob pulled off his boots.

Rob sat back on his heels and looked up at him. 'Aye, well, my lord, I suppose it makes some sort of sense.' In June the Earl of

Newcastle had been sent by the King to govern the town which
gave him his title, from which base he had begun to issue commissions in the King's name. 'You don't fear they'll just hand you over
to Parliament?'

'I doubt it. The King needs every friend he can win to his side.'
He grinned. 'Besides, as Master Hedley so sagely observed this afternoon, His Majesty could be said to be my debtor, considering all my
father lent him that never was repaid.'

'He knows you're going then?'

'Master Hedley? Oh yes. I think he could almost be said to have
given me his blessing. At least, he's promised to stay on here until
things are decided either way. He's to get together what funds he can
for me to take with me – to put the King still further in my debt, I
suppose. Or perhaps Master Hedley thinks money can buy anything, even life itself.' He was silent for a moment, frowning; then
he said, 'You're to be well provided for, I've seen to that.'

'I don't follow.'

'Enough to live in comfort to the end of your days – and may they
be long and happy.' His voice had grown a little husky, and it was
that as much as anything that made Rob realise what was implied.

'You don't think I'd stay here?'

'I'd not ask any man to share my fate, uncertain as it is.'

'I've served you since your schooldays, my lord. I'll not desert
you now.'

'You owe me no duty any more.'

'I wasn't talking of duty.' There was a silence, while they looked
at one another. Then, fending off emotion, Rob said lightly, 'You
know how it is with bad habits. Hard to break, that's the trouble.'
And they both laughed, a little shakily.

When Ludovick left for Newcastle, Rob was not the only one to ride
with him. The Blackheugh men who had followed him to Newburn
came too, eager for the action they had missed before, and the
chance of pay and plunder.

Less than a month later, Ludovick and Rob were once more in
Tynemouth, trying to find someone to take them to Flanders, from
where they intended to sail for Ireland.

'I'm ready enough to serve the King,' Ludovick had said. 'But I'm
damned if I'll serve as a common trooper under some ignorant
gentleman who knows not the first thing about soldiering.'

The Earl of Newcastle had not handed him over to Parliament, but neither had he received him with any warmth. He had made it clear, with his elaborate and lofty courtesy, that he regretted that the King's extremity required him to accept the services of a man of Lord Milburn's reputation. Scrupulous for his royal master's Protestant credentials, he had claimed that he had no authority to issue commissions to Catholics. Since he knew of a number of Catholics with commissions, Ludovick was not mollified. For a time he had stayed in the city, trying to persuade the Earl to change his mind, or hoping that he might simply realise that it was in his interests to issue commissions to the most able men, regardless of their religion. But the Earl was no soldier himself and seemed unable to see the point. It became clear that the only way Ludovick was going to be allowed to bear arms for the King was as a common soldier, and that he was not prepared to do. 'I'm going to Ireland,' he had told Rob brusquely last night. They had left the other Blackheugh men debating whether to remain in Newcastle or simply to go home, and set out at once for Tynemouth.

But though Tynemouth was in Royalist hands, the navy was commanded by the Earl of Warwick, who had declared for Parliament, which meant that enemy ships patrolled the coasts, especially close to any port garrisoned for the King. Only the boldest seamen were willing to risk putting to sea with Royalists on board.

It was late in the day, bitterly cold and already dark, and Ludovick had just finished an argument with a fisherman who clearly had no intention of taking them anywhere in his boat, no matter what inducements he was offered. As they turned, gloomily, to go and find lodgings for the night, Rob suddenly looked out to sea and said, 'Someone's got through. Maybe they'd get out again too, with us on board.'

They could hear the creak of oars, a good many oars, and were just able to make out some sort of dark shape – or shapes – moving towards the shore. A little after, a boat, or perhaps two, scraped to rest on the sand some yards away. Then came low voices, the sound of feet on the beach; and a large white poodle, very wet, came running out of the darkness and shook itself vigorously, all over Rob and Ludovick. It then stood still, stared at them, and began to bark with great energy.

A voice called: 'Boy!' The dog quietened and trotted obediently back towards the speaker. Another voice called, 'Who goes there? For King or Parliament?'

'The King,' called Ludovick, resisting the temptation to say, 'Neither.'

A little after, a man came into range of the lantern Rob held. He was sturdy, fair, red-complexioned, and had a pistol cocked in his hand. 'Give us proof!' Then, his gaze sharpening, 'By God, it's . . . Well, by all that's wonderful! Ludovick Milburn!'

'Dan O'Neill! What are you doing here?'

Daniel O'Neill was a distant kinsman of Lady Milburn, though a Protestant, having been raised largely at court. Ludovick and he had last met at Newburn, where O'Neill had been taken prisoner by the Scots. Last winter, he had been charged with high treason by Parliament for his part in the army plot, but had escaped overseas.

'I'd a mind to make myself useful.' Then, briskly, 'Tell me, where's the King to be found?'

'At Nottingham, when last I heard.'

The other men had reached them, and Daniel O'Neill turned to the nearest, whose hand was on the head of the white dog. He was a very tall young man, about Ludovick's own age, and strikingly handsome, but his eyes looked over-large and dark in his pale face, and he was clearly shivering: all the marks, Ludovick thought sympathetically, of recent seasickness. 'Your highness,' said O'Neill, 'we've the good fortune to fall in with a cousin of mine, my Lord Milburn. He served as a lieutenant at Breda when we were there – but inside the city, at the wrong end of our guns. He says His Majesty is at Nottingham.' Then, to Ludovick, 'Are you with my Lord Newcastle?'

Ludovick hesitated. He could hear the boats already putting to sea again. The tall man said, in a strongly accented voice, 'We have urgent need of good horses. Can you direct us where we may find them?'

'We must get to the King,' added Daniel O'Neill, 'with all speed.'

They walked up the beach towards the town, Ludovick leading the way. The dog ran ahead, then trotted back towards them, then stopped to examine some interesting smell or other, before chasing after them again. 'Their highnesses Prince Rupert and Prince Maurice are come to offer their service to their uncle,' O'Neill explained as they went. Ludovick looked round at the tall young man and his companion, who was not quite so tall and rather more heavily built. He knew who they were then: the younger brothers of the self-seeking Elector Palatine, both of them soldiers of considerable experience. The other members of the party, perhaps a dozen in all, were unknown to him. 'You didn't say,' Daniel was asking again, 'are you with my Lord Newcastle?'

'He won't have Catholic officers,' said Ludovick shortly.

'More fool him,' said Daniel. 'Come with us then. His Highness will speak for you to His Majesty.' He looked round at Prince Rupert. 'Is that not so, sir?'

'If you vouch for him, Dan,' said the Prince, who seemed to be feeling better with every step he took, at an increasing pace, away from the sea. He grinned suddenly, then bent to pick up a piece of driftwood, which he threw into the darkness for his dog to fetch. 'You can worship Baal for all I care, so long as you're a competent soldier.'

Once they had seen the travellers on their way, Ludovick and Rob returned to Newcastle, gathered the Blackheugh men, who were ready enough to go with them; and, as soon as it grew light, set out for Nottingham.

CHAPTER NINE

Towards the middle of August, Matthew Fawcett received a letter from Sir Ralph Liddell which was quite unlike his old friend's usual cheerful communications. True, it had been a worrying time for the family at Widehope, one way and another. Young Cuthbert had briefly been a student at Cambridge, but his father, anxious about the imminence of war, had ordered him home, to his sullen resentment. Mark, the second son, once more a pupil at the Grammar School at Bishop Auckland, which he had been attending before the Scottish invasion, was in frequent trouble with his master for idleness and insubordination. Worse, Dorothy had been quite seriously ill, though she was now somewhat recovered and they hoped the worst was over. 'He doesn't say what her symptoms are,' Matthew observed, pausing in his reading. He was entertaining Susannah with the letter while she stood at the bench in the still-room, vigorously pounding together elecampane root and dried mallow flowers with a pestle and mortar. An astringent aroma filled the room. 'I should have thought he'd want my opinion.'

For no particular reason Susannah recalled a rather trying conversation with Dorothy one day last year, when the girl had hinted darkly that there was some great love in her life. Perhaps, she thought, there had been an unsuitable secret love affair, now discovered and quite properly brought to an end. Not that she had any reason to suppose that was it, but Dorothy seemed to her the kind of foolish girl who would work herself into a frenzy over some man she scarcely knew. At the time Susannah had found herself wondering how so level-headed a man as Sir Ralph could have produced such a light-minded daughter; but then most women were like that, and Dorothy at least had the excuse of being very young. 'Perhaps she's so much better he felt no need of it,' said Susannah.

Her father read on, and it became clear that more than all the family troubles – which, with such a large family, were not unusual in themselves – it was the horrible inevitability of the slide into war that most depressed Sir Ralph.

Obedient to the King's Commission of Array, he was busily occupied in mustering the Bishopric's reluctant militia, but with a heavy heart. *I see both right and wrong on each side*, he wrote, *and whichever camp I choose I shall find myself at odds with my friends in the other. Indeed, I'm sometimes of the opinion that I cannot in conscience give my allegiance to either side, excepting only that to take up arms against the King's Majesty must be a course against all peace and order. Yet I know that you do not think it so, and I have ever valued your opinion.* But at the end a resurgence of his old optimism broke through the gloom. *It may be that once both sides stand on the verge of war, seeing in the enemy the faces of their friends, they will know what they have done and recoil from taking up arms against brother Englishmen. Surely, obstinacy and blindness cannot be proof against the sorrows of war?*

'Hmm,' said Matthew, unimpressed. 'The King's obstinacy is proof against any power in heaven or earth, as far as I can tell. Why would we have come this far otherwise?'

'I thought it was his evil counsellors that were at fault,' said Susannah slyly. That the King himself was in error was something she had never heard openly admitted before, though it seemed obvious to her that if a man gave heed to evil counsellors then he must at the very least be guilty of culpable weakness.

'Of course. Let him listen to the counsel of his good Parliament, and he may be as obstinate as he pleases, for there will be no harm in it.'

Susannah tipped the ground herbs into a bottle, added honey thinned with alcohol, stoppered the bottle, began to shake it vigorously. 'But will he listen without being made Parliament's prisoner?'

'Susannah!' Her father looked halfway between shock and amusement. 'No one intends any harm to the King's person.'

'No – unless he finds himself at the wrong end of a Parliamentary carbine.'

'And would you fire the shot, if you held that carbine?' He watched her in fascination, never having guessed that such extreme opinions lurked beneath his daughter's cool exterior.

'For what he has permitted to happen in Ireland, and in this land too; for what he has done. Yes, I would. If it were in battle and could not be settled any other way, that is.'

Her father stood up. 'Hmm. I should keep that opinion to yourself if I were you. Some would think it smells of sacrilege.' He took the bottle from her and examined it. 'Is this for old Mistress Johnson?' The minister's mother, who had lately come to live with her son, suffered from a persistent cough.

'Yes. I shall take it to her this afternoon.'

'Be sure she understands the instructions. I went over them with her, but she has a mind as full of holes as a beggar's breeches, poor soul. Will you call afterwards at the Hall?'

Susannah, irritated, evaded the question. 'Were you not there this morning?'

'You know how matters are. I think there is no bodily weakness, but she would scarcely talk to me. She insists on seeing you. No one but you can do her good.' He smiled gently. 'I can see I shall have to look to my reputation, or they'll all be asking for the lady doctor in my place.'

Susannah laughed and teasingly reassured him, but later, on her way to the vicarage, she thought, 'Why should they not? If I were a man, then this would be no matter for laughter, but in deadly earnest. My father might be proud, he might be jealous, but he would not laugh. Yet I know as much as any medical student, more than many.' She was sure of that, for once her father had received a visit from one such, son of an old friend, and his combination of ignorance and arrogance had appalled them both. She knew she had certain inborn – God given – skills, refined and developed by means of a single-minded pursuit of knowledge, both practical and theoretical, which had been the focus of her life for almost as long as she could remember. Yet if she were to use her gifts as her father used his, she would be looked on, at best, as some kind of village wise-woman, imbued with benign but semi-magical powers; at worst, as a witch. No woman could ever hope for the kind of respect and recognition that the most incompetent male physician enjoyed as a matter of course. By law, no woman could even practise as a humble surgeon or apothecary, still less apply for admission to the Royal College of Physicians, as so many men had done over the years, only to inflict untold suffering on their patients in the name of medicine. Yet now male physicians were even becoming practised in midwifery, the one sphere where formerly only women had practised, and no one seemed to think anything of it.

Susannah spent some time at the vicarage, giving careful instructions to the old woman as to when and how to take the medicine, and also to her harassed daughter-in-law, who might be expected to remember them. Young Mistress Johnson broke off the lesson she was giving to her five children and strove, through the clamour of exuberant young voices, to take in what Susannah said to her.

'I'll see she does what you say,' she said at last, and then went with Susannah to the door, where she lingered for some time, clearly glad of a break from her duties. She talked of her husband's continuing difficulties with Nan Bestwick, a Thornside woman lately condemned to yet another whipping for giving birth to the latest of many bastards. Since secular punishment seemed to have no effect, Master Johnson had been trying by persuasion to bring her to a proper sense of her sin – or at least to some kind of outward conformity, her example to the young and impressionable being so undesirable. 'If she would only wed one of the fathers – but she says she will not bind herself to any master. Can you imagine such disregard of all decency! If she would only go into service in some godly household, but then she makes too good a living . . . Well! If she must slake her lust, then she should do it in marriage, which is after all meant as a defence against sin. You will forgive my candour. I mean no reflection on you, of course. The Lord has shown His hand in the purity of your life, but I know that He will also send you a virtuous and godly husband in His own good time. Meanwhile, at least you still have your good father to guide you.'

Susannah took her leave politely, suppressing her irritation. She approved of the Johnsons, but though the minister clearly recognised in Susannah one of the Elect, an ally in his daily struggle against the Devil, he was also much given, like his wife, to hinting that it was high time she was married. In fact, lately, almost everyone about her seemed to be of the same view, as if marriage could be the only possible goal of her life. She absolved her father from that suspicion; he behaved towards her exactly as he had always done. Only once in his life had he mentioned marriage to her, after Richard's impulsive – and not yet repeated – proposal at his sister's wedding. She knew he had no wish at all for her to marry.

From the vicarage she went to call on Anne Greatorex at the Hall. Richard's sister had recovered quite well from her ordeal, on the surface at least, though she had become immensely protective – over protective – of her small son, who had so narrowly escaped death. She was also overpoweringly grateful to Susannah for her care of them. Often she would clasp Susannah's hands in hers and gaze into her face, saying with a catch in her voice, 'There's healing in those hands, Susannah; the Lord has given you a great gift.'

It might be true, though Susannah thought her mind had as much to do with her ability to heal as the skill of her hands – though of course both were God-given. In any case she was a little embarrassed by the whole business.

Today, Anne came to welcome her with an effusive kiss, after which Susannah tried to bring things down to a practical level. 'Are you sleeping better now, mistress?'

Anne shook her head. 'If I sleep at all, I wake after just a short time. Then sometimes I think Philip has gone. I have to put out my arms and hold him, just to be sure.' She sat with her eyes on Susannah's face, stroking and stroking the silky fair hair of the little boy at her side.

'He should be out in the sunshine on this fine day,' Susannah said gently. The child looked pale, which was hardly surprising since he scarcely ever went out, except when going to church with his mother. This summer's wet, cold weather had not helped, of course.

She saw Anne's eyes fill with tears. 'How can I let him out of my sight? You know how dangerous the times are become.'

'It's not war yet. Certainly we have seen none of it here.'

'But it is almost on us. Even Richard is certain of it now. He says they have set up a Committee of Safety in London to manage the daily business of the army. The Earl of Essex is appointed Lord General and they all took an oath in Parliament, to live and die with him, to strive for the safety of the King's person and the defence of both Houses of Parliament. And he is to come home, Richard, I mean. He thinks they will give Lord Fairfax command in Yorkshire. If they do, he will serve under him, with Tom.'

Susannah digested the news in silence. It was hardly surprising, in the circumstances, but it suddenly brought home to her that war was about to reach even into the remoteness of Thornside. She felt odd, thinking of it; at once excited, curious and a very little apprehensive. She could see that Anne had no such mixed feelings.

With her experiences in Ireland still all too fresh in her memory, she was terrified. 'They say the King's to bring over Irish rebels to fight for him. He is arming Papists, openly. They say Lord Milburn is with him, the one who sent arms to Ireland – despite being under sentence of death by order of Parliament.'

Susannah found it hard to believe that even King Charles would accept such an unsavoury ally, openly and before hostilities had officially begun. 'That may not be true.'

She could see that Anne was not reassured. 'I tell you what is true, though. You know the Middletons, from Ivelet? Their eldest son is at York, I heard.'

'That's just one man among many. I think you'll find most people simply want to be left in peace. Even Papists.'

'That's all I want,' said Anne, her voice rough with misery. 'Why does Richard have to think of fighting? He could perfectly well stay out of it. He has his Parliamentary duties. Why does he not stay in London?'

'Because he will do what is honourable, you know that. You would not really have him otherwise, now would you?' Susannah was simply offering the obvious consolation, but she realised almost at once that Anne had read something more into her words, and she wished them unsaid.

'No. Nor I think would you. You know his merits. That is a comfort, to know I have a friend who can recognise the virtues of my brother.' Implied was the unspoken conclusion: *and will one day marry him, if all goes well.* Anne had confided some time ago that Richard had admitted his hopes to her, and she had then set herself to give Susannah every encouragement.

'I think it would be good for you and Philip both if you were to take the air for half an hour or so,' said Susannah, firmly changing the subject.

'If you will come with us, just in case Philip should feel faint.'

Susannah thought it most unlikely that the child would feel anything but liberated to be outside and able to run and walk in a normal manner, but she agreed without argument. Whatever her personal feelings, it was what her patient needed; except that there was really no need for Anne to consider herself a patient any longer.

They set out sedately across the garden, towards the gate that led into the fields sloping down to the river. Mother and child were rather over-wrapped in capes and hoods and petticoats – at not quite two, the small boy was not yet breeched, still wearing the infant gowns common to all children of his age. Anne was anxious to tether him with leading reins, but Susannah insisted he should be allowed to run free, which he soon did, not far, but darting out from his mother's side and running back to her again, chuckling merrily in a way that made Anne laugh and cry at once, and often stop to sweep him up in a fierce anxious hug. A little further, and she had begun to lose some of her anxiety, seeing how happy her child was and how the colour had begun to brighten his face; there was even some colour in her own. 'Don't you wish for a little one of your own, like my Philip?' Anne asked after a while.

Susannah looked at the child and felt none of the maternal urges Anne clearly expected her to feel. She saw, not a delightful infant to shower with cooings and kisses, but a small creature who had been saved from imminent death by her skill – or, rather, by God's mercy working through her. She took pleasure in his childish energy, his sturdy limbs, his look of alertness and intelligence, as she did in those of any human being in good health, particularly when she bore some responsibility for it; but that was all.

'If I were cumbered with children,' she said, suddenly recalling the din in the vicarage this morning, 'I wouldn't be free to do the work God has for me.'

Anne spoke with all the force of her love for her brother, and her admiration for Susannah. 'Oh, but it is God's work, to care for a husband and children and all those of your household. What better work is there for a woman? As for those healing hands of yours, are they not made to be used as my mother has always used hers, to care for the sick and needy among her husband's tenants? You are especially gifted for that work.'

Susannah had occasionally met Dame Alice in the house of one or other of her father's patients, dispensing nourishing food and simple remedies from her stillroom. On the whole she did no harm (less indeed than many qualified physicians, as Susannah well knew, having a low opinion of any but her father and one or two others), but neither did she do much good, except, Susannah supposed, to her own self-esteem. To be reduced to administering nourishment and good advice to the poor, in the intervals between managing household and children – no, that was not the purpose for which she had spent hours of her life reading works in Latin and

English and French, talking over everything with her father, thirstily learning all she could from him, observing, reflecting, discussing, as she accompanied him to sick-beds and women in labour and children injured in accidents, or watched him conduct a post-mortem on a deceased patient, trying to understand what had gone wrong, always seeking ways to bring healing. 'This is my life,' she began, but Anne suddenly seized her arm, her eyes on some point far away in the direction of the river.

'Look!' Susannah followed her gaze. Her hearing too had caught something at that moment: horses' hooves, thudding over the grass. The watery sunlight drew sudden occasional flashes of brilliance out of the dark shapes emerging into view from a small wood that sheltered the eastern edge of the furthest meadow. She shaded her eyes, watching. Horsemen of some kind, the light picking out the shiny detail of bridle or stirrups.

'Soldiers!' Anne's voice was stifled with terror. 'They're soldiers!' She ran to the child, who thought it a game and tottered away from her, laughing. 'Philip!' she screamed. She caught him in her arms and he, halfway between rage at being thwarted and fright at his mother's panic, began to yell at the top of his voice.

Susannah, still gazing into the distance, was ready to dismiss Anne's verdict, but the figures were moving nearer, taking shape, and she saw there were about a dozen of them, the light shining not just on their horses' harness but also on some kind of armour, helmet or breastplate perhaps, worn by some of the riders. 'Friends of your brother's, perhaps,' she said, while she wondered how likely that was. 'Let's get back to the house.'

Anne, greyish-white and trembling, looked close to collapse. She would not give up the child, so Susannah supported them both while trying to propel her companion towards the garden gate. They were some distance from it, and the horses were steadily coming their way. She was still trying to tell herself that they were simply friends of Richard's, but her heart was beating a little uncomfortably, and not just from the exertion. 'Foolish,' she thought severely. 'What is there to fear?'

She heard a shout from behind her, and another, then whooping, cheerful enough, but not reassuring. She doubted very much if any of Richard's friends would greet two women who might be his kin with such a noise. Anne whimpered and stumbled, almost falling. Susannah was relieved when one of the servants ran from the house to meet them, quickly coming to support Anne on the other side, steering her through the gate. 'I saw them,' he said. 'Don't like the look of them.'

Susannah did not waste time looking round again, though Anne kept glancing fearfully over her shoulder. Soon, the horses were through the gate too, hooves churning up the grassy paths.

By the time they had crossed the garden, Anne was sobbing and shaking and could only with great difficulty be got into the house. There were other servants at the door, and Dame Alice too, coming to help her inside. About to follow, Susannah glanced round; and found herself looking up into the face of a fair and very young man on a big brown horse. He was grinning, but not pleasantly, and he had a pistol cocked in his hand. Behind him other young men sat making appreciative comments. Anne screamed, again and again, the noise growing fainter as they dragged her further into the house. Susannah stayed where she was, very still and straight and cold, looking at the young men. Now that she could see them face to face she no longer felt in the least bit afraid, simply very angry. 'Have you nought better to do than frighten women and children?' she demanded sharply.

There was a chorus of hoots from behind the first rider, but he merely tucked his pistol in his belt and swung himself out of the saddle. 'Aye, mistress, that I have.' He waved a paper in front of her nose, too close for her to see what was written on it. 'The King's commission. I have authority to take what arms I can from this nest of Roundheads for his Majesty's service.' Then he unsheathed his sword. Susannah saw that the blade was rusty, though a recent attempt had been made to polish it.

There was some kind of confused movement behind her. Out of the corner of her eye she saw Dame Alice come into view at her side. 'Harry Middleton!' said the old woman. 'It is Harry Middleton, isn't it?'

'Captain Middleton,' the young man corrected her, though Susannah thought he looked just a little less sure of himself. Dame Alice was a formidable woman and he was very young. 'In the King's service.' There were enthusiastic yells from his companions.

'If you take what is my son's without his authority then you are Robber Middleton and do the King's service no credit,' said Dame Alice staunchly. Susannah wondered if she was wise to say anything that could be taken to show that Richard was absent. On the other hand, they probably knew that already. 'In any event, we have no arms here.'

The young man glanced round at his company. 'Come, lads, let's take a look. Never trust the word of a Roundhead.'

Dame Alice, Susannah at her side, stood firm. Face to face with her, eyes level (Dame Alice was a tall woman), the young man wavered. He even stepped back a pace, his sword point falling to the ground. But his friends behind him were nudging one another, jeering, making comments in not-quite-undertones, mimicking the old woman's words '. . . do the King's service no credit . . . Mercy me, we have no arms!' One of them joined his fingertips and closed his eyes and intoned a mocking, high-pitched version of a Puritan at prayer, 'Oh Lord of Hosts send a thunderbolt upon these sons of Belial!' Their loud laughter restored young Middleton's boldness. He pushed his way roughly between the two women and into the house, his companions at his heels, all but two who stayed with the horses. By now, fortunately, Anne had been taken upstairs, out of sight, though the wailing of the child could still be heard in the distance.

There was nothing much anyone could do against a dozen armed men. Richard's bailiff, who was the only man at the hall who could handle a gun with ease, was somewhere out on the fells and would not be back until after dark. There were arms in the house, but not many and they were held in the Hall's small locked armoury, adjacent to the stables. In fact, three of the Royalists, breaking away earlier from their companions, had already ridden into the yard and threatened the stable lad into telling them where it was. By the time Harry Middleton reached them they had broken down the door and, whooping joyously, had begun to carry its contents out to their saddle bags.

'If I were a man—!' Dame Alice muttered under her breath. 'If only I had a pistol, or knew how to fire one!'

But she had not, and there was nothing they could do. The only sensible course was to endure the intrusion in patience, trying not to enrage the young men or to draw unwonted attention on themselves, and hoping it ended quickly.

The Royalists went through the house from top to bottom, mostly doing little more than glance into each room, terrifying servants and sending Anne into a full fit of hysteria, which it took all Susannah's patience and a strong sleeping draught to calm. The intruders came at last to the cellar where they found Richard's carefully hoarded barrels of claret and sack. For some time afterwards the noise of shouts and laughter and drunken singing came from the cellar. When they eventually emerged they had considerable difficulty getting up the stairs, and one of them tripped on the top step and fell flat on his face and had to be dragged to his feet by his giggling companions, who then lurched their way, leaning on one another, along the passage to the yard. It was even more of a performance mounting their horses, which caused one of the kitchen maids, diverted by the whole business now she knew there was nothing to fear, to stifle a giggle. She was rebuked for it later by Dame Alice, who was not at all amused.

When they had gone, taking with them all the best horses, Richard's mother said to Susannah, 'What did they mean, calling us Roundheads? Is that some new kind of insult?'

'I think it's to do with the London apprentices, madam,' Susannah said, having gathered something of the kind from one of Sir Ralph's letters – though where he'd heard of it he had no idea. 'The most zealous among them have taken lately to wearing their hair cropped short. A reproach to lovelocks, or some such thing.'

'Impertinent drunken louts,' said Dame Alice; by which she did not mean the crop-haired apprentices. 'What name do they have for the Royalists then? Rogues? It would fit.'

'Cavaliers, some call them – because they are like *caballeros*, Spanish horsemen, cruel and unmannerly.' That had come from Nathaniel Johnson, whose brother Jeremiah was a preacher in London.

'Very apt, if what we have seen today is any guide. Though Harry Middleton always was wild. God help us if that's what the King's army's made of.' She cast an approving eye over Susannah. 'I commend your courage. You remained remarkably cool.'

'I was not alone in that, madam,' said Susannah with a faint smile.

'Ah, but an old woman like me has little to fear. You are young and comely.' It was an extravagant compliment from someone generally so restrained. 'However, unpleasant though it may have been, it could have been worse.' They were standing at the top of the stairs, not far from the door of the bedroom where Anne was now asleep. Dame Alice glanced towards it. 'I fear this will undo all the good the past few quiet weeks have done.'

'Time will heal her,' said Susannah, who in fact had little patience with Anne's fearfulness. Physically she had made a full recovery and in Susannah's opinion all that she needed now was a little self-control; but she did not say so. Her father had expressed rather more sympathy and urged her to continue to humour Richard's sister. 'After what she's been through she needs more than medicine to bring healing,' he had said. That now prompted Susannah to suggest a different approach. 'Madam, has the minister talked with her? His words might calm her.'

Dame Alice sighed. 'She heard him, but it seemed to make little difference. However, I shall ask him to call again. Something must be done.'

They heard later that Henry Middleton had been in the dale for two days before reaching Thornside, recruiting others to join him on the way. From the Hall the young men had ridden on to the town, though by then they had been too drunk to do more than sit on their horses outside the vicarage, jeering and shouting very rude songs. Nathaniel Johnson had countered by leading his entire family in the loud singing of psalms in an attempt to drown the unseemly noise. Next day, he paid a stern ministerial visit to the town's wheelwright, whose two sons, passing by at the time, had joined in the mockery. No other houses in the area had been attacked, probably because most of the landowners in the dale were either outright supporters of the King, or neutral but Catholic.

Richard came home at the end of August and was appalled at the danger that had faced them all in his absence. He said as much to Susannah when he called to see her soon after his return. 'You might have been killed, or . . .' He shuddered, as if the alternative was even more unbearable to contemplate.

'They were just idle young men too full of their own importance,' said Susannah, with contempt rather than tolerance. 'Once they have real fighting to face they'll not be so free with their bluster and blasphemy.'

'Certainly not if I face them across the battlefield,' said Richard grimly.

'Then, sir, you expect to see action soon?'

'I don't know, mistress. I still pray it won't come to that. But what I shall certainly do is ensure that if those reprobates come to Thornside again, they will be received as hotly as they deserve. My mother has already learned to load and fire a pistol with the best of them. As soon as I'm easy in my mind about my family, I'm to Nun Appleton, to confer with cousin Tom Fairfax.' His expression became, if anything, more grim. 'We hear that the King was advised to arrest Tom, and his father, for fear they should take arms against him.'

'As they will, I suppose.'

'Not if there is any way it can be avoided. Any way at all, consistent with honour. But to arrest them must only inflame things beyond any hope of peace. Though we hope that danger is passed.' He stayed a little longer after that, though he appeared to have nothing much left to say and Susannah, who had work to do, began to grow impatient. She was about to drop a large hint that he should leave, when suddenly he moved towards the door, murmuring his farewells.

Halfway there, he came to a halt. 'Perhaps you heard, mistress – the King has raised his standard at Nottingham.' He smiled suddenly. 'It blew down.'

CHAPTER TEN

The October night was bitterly cold and they had hardly eaten for two days. Yesterday the last of the drink had run out too.

'Good stuff, that perry we used to get,' said Simon Milburn dreamily. The words floated only too clearly into the dark above the steady, rhythmic thud and creak and jangle of cavalry on the move. 'Remember that stop at Tenbury, the night after Powick Bridge? By, the beef was something too! I reckon I've never tasted the like, before or . . . since.' He ended lamely, his voice drowned in a united howl of outrage from his companions.

'Any more of that, Corporal Milburn, and I'll be wasting one of my bullets on you,' said the Captain, with more good humour than he felt. They had been ordered to march an hour ago, woken from sleep in the barns and outbuildings where they had been quartered, though it had been so penetratingly cold that few of them had slept much. Ludovick, who had declined the more comfortable accommodation available to officers so that he could stay with his men, had only just rolled himself in his cloak when the message came from Prince Rupert. As a consequence he had slept less than any of them and was in no mood to tolerate irritations.

'Not much of a threat that, with the weapons we've got,' muttered Lieutenant Haynes, younger son of a prosperous Worcestershire gentleman and only two weeks with the troop. He was gratified by the definite if faint sounds of amusement that greeted his remark, but the Captain simply gave them a brisk reminder that they were supposed to be advancing in silence.

The skirmish at Powick Bridge had taken place a month before, in the fertile countryside near Worcester, where they had been part of a small reconnoitring party under Prince Rupert, now the King's Lieutenant-General of Horse. Pausing to rest in a field near the bridge, relaxed in the afternoon sun, they had suddenly realised that a whole company of Roundheads was marching steadily into the lane beyond a distant hedge. In a moment, Rupert had flung himself into the saddle and shouted his orders, and then they were on the enemy almost before they knew it, scattering them into abject flight. Only two of Ludovick's company had been wounded, and those not seriously. The few fatalities had all been on the Roundhead side. After that brief but exhilarating episode, they had begun to believe they could do anything and Rupert had become the hero of the entire royal army.

Ludovick was glad that his men, new and untried as almost all of them were, had been given that encouraging introduction to combat, so that now, as they made their way in the dark to the summit of Edgehill, they were not wholly unprepared for what must face them in the hours to come.

They had waited long enough for this day. At first the forces that marched with the King from Nottingham had been too few even to defend his person, should he be attacked by any reasonably numerous force. Ludovick had fully expected some such attack in those early days. It had seemed to him the obvious course for the Parliamentary army to take.

Yet for weeks now the enemy force under the Earl of Essex had plodded after the Royalists through the Midlands and the Welsh borders, moving steadily further away from their London base, yet always avoiding any risk of conflict, except when it was forced on them, as at Powick. The delay had at least given the King's commanding officers the opportunity to raise and equip and train a sizeable number of men.

It was then that Ludovick would have welcomed the rents that were due from Blackheugh, since the King's resources were few (Ludovick's contribution had long gone) and Prince Rupert's nonexistent and many of the royal officers were reduced, like himself, to equipping their men from their own pockets; but his steward had written rather stiffly to inform him that many of his tenants refused to pay and there was nothing he could do about it. Ludovick knew his were not the only tenants showing defiance of their landlords this year. It was as if rebellion was everywhere in the air, in small things as well as great. Perhaps it was that sense of things beginning to fall apart that had suddenly, in September, brought hundreds more recruits flocking to the King's army; that and news of the iconoclastic activities of the Parliamentary soldiers in Worcester and elsewhere, who had destroyed stained glass and statues and altar rails and organs in every church they passed.

At least, ill equipped and hungry as it was, Ludovick had a troop under his command. He had at first been offered a wholly different set of men, all Protestant, who had immediately refused to serve under him. Some of them had even been so insulted at the very idea that they had deserted to Parliament. After that, Ludovick had recruited his own men, largely from the Catholic gentry of the west Midlands. It had taken some time to bring the troop up to strength, but now there were nearly seventy, as well trained as Ludovick could make them in a few short weeks and already bound together by the sense of comradeship and shared discomfort that he remembered from his days in Flanders. Though in Flanders they had always eaten well, slept in decent quarters and been regularly paid. And he did not remember that it had ever been as cold as this.

Edgehill was a long low ridge facing roughly north over the Warwickshire plain towards the village of Kineton, not far from the Oxfordshire border. More important, it effectively blocked the Earl of Essex's path back to London, which meant he would have to fight at last or risk being wholly cut off. Once that was done, the King's army would be free to march on London. A week or two, perhaps, and all would be over. At the least, they would have left Warwickshire behind them. They none of them liked Warwickshire. The population was almost unvaryingly hostile and staunchly refused to supply them with provisions, even when payment could be offered, which mostly it could not. It was natural enough, in the circumstances, that the soldiers should look back nostalgically on the harvest-time plenty of Worcestershire.

'Fight bravely tomorrow and we'll have plunder enough to fill our bellies,' Ludovick had promised his men as they set out wearily to occupy the ridge.

As dawn broke on that Sunday morning, the features of the plain below – clumps of furze, a single hedge, a distant view of the village of Kineton – took slow shape in the morning sun. By the time Ludovick's men were more or less in position, some latecomers among the cavalry were still making their way up on to the ridge. The King's army had been widely scattered last night, quartered in villages miles apart from one another, for it had been too cold to sleep out of doors. As a result it was taking a long time for everyone to reach the rendezvous.

It was mid-morning before they saw the foot move into their places on the centre ground, slowly straggling into long uncertain lines, while their officers, with much shouting of commands and beating of drums, tried to bring some order to their ranks. In Flanders infantry ranks bristled with the horizontals of pikes, the menacing verticals of muskets, emerging through the smoke of matches lit ready for firing. Here there were great gaps in the ranks, for many of the foot soldiers were armed with nothing better than clubs.

'They've been told to get hold of arms from the men they kill,' Ludovick said to Rob, in an undertone. 'Let's hope they stand their ground long enough to do it.' Conscious that the infantry were not alone in being nervous and untried, he rode again along the lines of his own men, looking out for those he saw to be most uneasy, pausing for a joke or an encouraging word as seemed most appropriate. He was grateful for the Blackheugh men, who (however unjustifiably) already had something of the manner of veterans, making themselves responsible for the mere novices. When he came back to where Rob was still watching the infantry, he saw that there seemed to have been a sudden outburst of new orders, and renewed movement in the lines. 'What's going on?'

'New formation,' said Rob. 'My Lord Lindsey's changed his mind.'

They watched in silence for a time, then Ludovick said, 'Swedish fashion now – look, they're forming up into squares, muskets and pikes together. That won't be Lindsey's doing. In his day they'd not have heard of such a thing.' The elderly Earl of Lindsey, General-in-Chief of the Royal army, had in his youth seen military service against Spain, but that was a very long time ago now.

The infantry lines shuffled and shifted uncertainly back and forth, while in front of them a group of officers on horseback appeared to be arguing. Among them the tall, scarlet-clad figure of Prince Rupert was clearly visible. 'I'd guess my Lord Lindsey and His Highness can't agree,' said Ludovick. The King had given Rupert an independent command, a fact that had already led to friction.

'I know it's not my place to say so, my lord, but His Highness doesn't command the infantry.'

'Do you suppose that'd make any difference if he thought he was in the right? Which I don't doubt he is. Lindsey's a fool.' He said that softly, since it would not do to encourage disrespect, though Rob heard it and grinned.

Later, a messenger passed near them, carrying despatches from Rupert to his younger brother Maurice, who led the adjoining regiment. 'The Prince and the Earl of Lindsey have fallen out,' said the man. 'My Lord Lindsey's resigned his command. Sir Jacob Astley commands the infantry now.'

Ludovick glanced at Rob, but said nothing. He hoped that inexperience protected his men from knowing how inauspicious a time it was for such a quarrel.

At last, in the bright clear light of the autumn morning, they could make out the lines of the Parliamentary forces emerging from Kineton and forming up about a mile away, where the land rose a little. For the Royalist horsemen watching the movement across the plain with nothing to do but wait, it was hard not to be painfully aware of their cold and hunger and weariness, and of that other increasing condition that turned their bellies to water and set many of them shivering more than the cold warranted. Even Ludovick, more used to battle than nearly all of them, felt his stomach twist into a knot and his mouth dry. He hated this time of waiting, always had done and probably always would. To distract his men, he led them in singing, anything he could think of, mostly bawdy songs, since that made them laugh and best took their minds off what was going on across the plain.

By midday even the infantry seemed to be in some kind of order. It was then that there came an odd period of near stillness, perhaps a human version of nature's warning of an imminent storm, though Ludovick could remember nothing like it in his experience. It was almost as if neither side wanted to fire the first shot, as if even now at this final moment they could not quite believe it must come to battle. He sat holding his restless horse in check, tense, alert, seeing how everything seemed picked out with unusual clarity, the many colours of the soldiers' coats and cloaks and sashes, the horses tossing their heads, gunners in position beside their cannons and culverins and fawcons between the ranks of infantry, bristling with pikes and winged by musketeers. At the head of each regiment the commanding officer sat his horse, Rupert magnificent in scarlet below the rippling silk of his standard, its movement echoed by the smaller banners of each troop. Ludovick's, in the Prince's colours, was carried by Cornet Will Dodd.

The King, a small upright figure in black velvet and ermine, escorted by the Prince of Wales and the Duke of York and a train of courtiers, made his way to the highest point and began to observe the enemy with a telescope. From somewhere behind the lines, they heard the barking of a dog – Rupert's dog Boy, perhaps, tied up for safety with the baggage train. Still the waiting went on. 'If this is it, why don't we all go home and get some sleep?' muttered Rob, with a carefully manufactured yawn.

A few moments later, orders came that the entire royal army was to move down the slope, to where the land fell less steeply. 'They'll not charge us, so we'll charge them,' commented Rob, with some satisfaction.

'Pray they let us get into position first,' said Ludovick. He was conscious for every minute of that lumbering descent how vulnerable they were to attack. But by some miracle – or slow-wittedness – Essex made no move at all for the whole two hours that the royal army was taking up its new positions.

Once they were in place, Rupert did the rounds of his regiments, calling out his orders with his usual briskness, softened by words of encouragement. Shortly afterwards, Ludovick's chaplain, Father Young, dressed like the rest of them in buff coat and scarlet sash, gave the troop a discreet blessing. Those who had them, put on their steel helmets, checked again that their swords ran free in their scabbards, made their carbines ready. Ludovick repeated Rupert's instructions and reminded his men that Essex's soldiers could be recognised by their orange-tawny sashes.

After that, the King rode along the lines of his troops, exhorting those who could hear to fight with courage and the conviction that right was on their side. The men cheered, even those who had heard nothing, relieving tension with noise.

At that moment a spurt of smoke and flame rose in the distance. A boom, and a moment after a cannon-ball flew across the plain, landing just below the King and rolling harmlessly away down the slope. King Charles dismounted quickly, took a match from the nearest gunner, and sent an answering shot towards the enemy lines.

Everything began to move at once. Through the continuing noise of gunfire, orders were called, drums beat, trumpets blared. Ludovick shouted a last reminder to his troop, 'Remember, lads, when you hear the command, straight at them, keep close, no firing till you've closed with them.'

The trumpets sounded the advance. Ludovick made the sign of the cross – *Sancta Maria, ora pro nobis!* – rose in his stirrups, turned to glance at his men. Would they remember the trumpet calls?

Down the slope at a steady trot, on across the plain, and then the call to charge. Ludovick released all the long tension in a great yell, spurred his horse into a gallop and rode furiously towards the solid ranks of the enemy with his troop at his heels, the thunder of hooves and the shouting of men drowning all other sounds.

They hardly fired or used their swords, for the enemy lines dissolved as they reached them, turning at once to a terrified rabble, riding for their lives. The force of the charge swept all before it, up the slope, over hedges and ditches, on to Kineton, where the Roundhead baggage wagons barred their path. Jubilant at the sight of meat and cheese and bread and beer, many of them forgot the fleeing enemy and fell to plundering, Ludovick's men among them, pushing food and drink into their mouths, stuffing pockets and saddle bags with anything that lay to hand. A trumpet called suddenly, then Rupert's angry voice bawled an order. Ludovick, furious, swearing, hit out at his men with the flat of his sword. 'Back on your horses, damn you! Remember your orders! Back to the field!'

It took some time and the help of Rob and Lieutenant Haynes (Corporal Simon Milburn, like the other Blackheugh men, was somewhere in the middle of the struggling mass round the baggage wagons), but at last he got enough of them mounted again, drunk as they already were, to ride back with Rupert and a few hundred others towards the din of the battlefield.

On the plain below Edgehill, the approaching dusk was deepened by dense smoke, acrid with the stench of gunpowder. Dim heaving shapes veered towards them and then vanished again, grunts and groans and shrieks mingled in the choking air; a snatch of psalm, an agonised prayer, the long curses of a dying man. Horsemen galloped past them and then were lost again in the smoke.

Closer to the heart of the battle, they came on the struggling infantry, desperately hard-pressed. Rupert shouted commands, Ludovick and the other officers bullied the men into some sort of order, ready for the attack. Already, the Roundhead foot were showing signs of wavering. A burst of fire from their own dragoons, and the Roundheads began to run – not far, just until the haze swallowed them up, but the worst was past. One charge more, thought Ludovick, and the field will be ours.

They did not charge. 'Too dark,' said Rupert. His face under the plumed helmet was grimy with sweat and smoke, but there was a note of regret in the hoarse voice. 'We can't tell friend from foe.'

More to the point, thought Ludovick, they had no fight left in them. Even he was weary beyond words. The excitement of the charge seemed long over, scarcely a memory. Now they knew only how much they had done, how tired they were, how worn their horses. 'Up the hill!' he shouted to his troop. 'Get fires lit. A night's rest, then we'll finish them off.'

They forced their horses away from the smoke and the fading sounds of combat, to the top of the hill where it had all begun long hours before. There, most of them simply dropped from their saddles and lay where they fell. Ludovick, trying to force himself to think what there was still to be done, even to make some move to do it, felt Rob tug at his sleeve. 'We've got some wood, for a fire – over here.'

They got the fire lit somehow, a feeble protection against the encroaching frost. All over the hill, and on the plain below, other points of flame sprang into the darkness. It was the only comfort they had, for there was neither food nor drink, for horses or men. Through what was left of the night they lay huddled about that little flickering glow, hearing the long humming moan of the wounded fall into silence as the hours passed and the deadly cold closed about them.

CHAPTER ELEVEN

Early in the morning of the ninth of November the drums began to beat all over the city of London, calling every able-bodied man to the muster at Finsbury Field. Walter Barras's heart seemed to beat in time with their rhythm as he dressed and swallowed a hasty breakfast – bread and cheese and ale served to him by Esther, whose green eyes met his every time he looked up, with shy, sweet admiration. She said nothing, of course, because they were not alone, but he was certain that she favoured him at last. Today, he thought, he would show himself worthy of her. Only let them choose him! He even sent up a prayer about it, for he knew he would not be able to bear it if he were turned away. At the same time, he could not quite believe that something so terrible might happen to him. Was he not called to be God's instrument against the ungodly?

What he did know was that he had never in all his life been as happy as he had during the past days, in this time of courage and hope and determination. Last week the men and women of the city (all Master Reynolds's apprentices among them) had flocked to St Pancras' Fields and Gray's Inn Lane and Piccadilly and all the other places where an advancing army might break through, to dig and to build, throwing up trenches and earthworks and always singing psalms as they laboured, united by a common purpose. Best of all, Esther had been there at Walter's side, her skirts tucked up and her shapely arms wielding a spade almost as effectively as he did, and sometimes (though he blushed to think of it) she would pause to look with what he hoped was approval at the working muscles of his chest and shoulders and arms, stripped of coat and shirt. They had talked too, more than he could remember they had ever done before. One day she had halted her digging to straighten her back and say, 'You know my Lord of Essex went out to bar the King's path to London?'

'And to bring him back here – yes.' He had thought he had known what was coming, for it was something that had been puzzling him too. While he waited for her to go on, he had tried hard to think of a reply that would justify the confidence she evidently had in his opinion.

'Well, he won a great victory at Edgehill fight.'

'Yes.' All the bells of London had rung in triumph at the news, and thanksgivings had been offered in every church. They had thought then that the war was as good as over, the King about to abandon his evil counsellors and return to the bosom of his loving Parliament.

'Then why is the King so close to London with a great army at his back?'

Walter had not after all found an adequate answer, so rather than admit his ignorance, he had said lamely, 'I don't doubt the tales we hear are mere idle rumours.' But he knew she had not believed it any more than he did. Why otherwise should they have been working so feverishly on the city's defences?

On Monday – the day before yesterday – they had stood together on the street corner to watch the Earl of Essex march into London, as they had watched him march out in September, full of pride and hope. But in September the army had stepped out briskly to the beat of fife and drum and the cheers of the people; regiment after regiment, cavalry, dragoons, infantry, artillery, all well armed and well drilled, fit for anything. John Lilburne had been with them, Captain Lilburne now, an infantry officer in the purple coat of Lord Brooke's regiment, and they had cheered themselves hoarse for him. He had distinguished himself at Edgehill, they had heard, holding his ground with courage against the enemy. He had come with victorious messages to London ahead of the rest, so he had not been part of the bedraggled remnant of an army that had trudged back into the city – more like, some whispered as they passed, a defeated army than a victorious one. They had been feasted and cheered, but the rejoicing had lost its edge. Among the whispers there were tales of the terrible Rupert and his fearsome cavalry charges that swept all before them; and Rupert was advancing on London with the

King at this very moment, already as close as Kingston-on-Thames, a day's march away if no one stopped him.

But they would stop him, with God's help they would halt his march and save their city from the fate that threatened if once that drunken, licentious army with its savage continental ways and its Popish officers was loosed upon their streets. Essex had brought too few men with him to do more than man the outer defences, certainly not enough to hold the city. But the people had not despaired. If the army could not do it, then the citizens would.

Parliament had declared that all apprentices were to be indemnified for any breach of their articles, if they offered their services for London's defence. Until now Walter's master had refused to allow him to join the trained band. 'A school for drunkenness, that's what it is,' he had said, though Walter had thought him rather out of date. It might have been true in the old days, but the trained band was now a disciplined and godly force. Not that he had dared to say so. 'You've less than a year to go till the end of your time,' Master Reynolds had added. 'Don't waste it.' But now, seeing what danger pressed, he had told Walter he could go with his blessing. 'If London falls you'll not get to the end of your time.'

Walter had been right to put his trust in the Lord. He was not rejected. On that day at Finsbury Field he stood with the hopeful thousands that waited to be inspected by a dazzling company of the best men from Lords and Commons, and it was the Earl of Essex himself, no less, who walked along the line in which Walter stood, and halted before him and nodded his approval.

They began training at once, under Major-General Philip Skippon, a hearty much-loved veteran with long experience in the Dutch service. Walter was issued with an eighteen-foot pike, which, for all its length and weight, he quickly learned to shoulder and manoeuvre with what he thought was commendable finesse. He wished Esther had been there to see him.

She was there the next day, for a time, watching the training, and the day after that. She was particularly attentive when he came home, plying him with the best food – 'after all your hard work,' she said.

It was the following day, just as Walter returned home from the training ground, that they heard the news they had all been dreading. Prince Rupert had attacked Brentford, driving out Denzil Holles's redcoats, savagely mauling Hampden's and Brooke's regiments, which had come to their aid. Now, at nightfall, Rupert's

men were running wild in the town, looting and pillaging like true
caballeros, the brutal Spanish horsemen for whom they were nick-
named. Many guns were in enemy hands, and banners too, and
worst of all John Lilburne himself was among the prisoners.

A breathless watchman ran shouting the news through the
streets, calling all the new volunteers to assemble at once at the
appointed places to march to the defence of London. Walter, excited
and frightened all at once – though no one must ever know how
great was his fear – pulled on his new buff coat, carried his pike out
to the street and there shouldered it. Esther came running and suddenly, startlingly, dropped a kiss on his cheek. Over her head he
glimpsed her father's face, shocked and disapproving, and for a
moment he felt dismayed. He could not hope to win Esther if her
father did not approve. What was more, he might well be in trouble
when he returned home.

But of course he might not return, and there were other things
even more important than Esther's kiss. Singing a psalm to keep his
spirits up, he marched away in the gathering dusk to join his new
comrades for his first taste of war.

The mist of the November morning was like Walter's fear, cold and
pervasive, at once a stench in his nostrils, a shiver down his spine,
a sour taste in his mouth. It hung heavily over their advancing army,
hiding the slopes running down to the river on their left and, half a
mile away, the little town of Brentford whose smoke thickened it –
not the usual coal-fire smoke (with Newcastle in the hands of the
Royalists, there was little coal to be had), but the different, distinc-
tive smoke of burning thatch, acrid and aromatic at once.

They had heard the noise from the town too, strangely close yet
somehow disembodied in the way of sounds in a fog: drunken
singing, laughter, shouts, all the din of a carousing army, taunting
them through the long cold hours of the night as they took up
their positions on Turnham Green common. Yet they could see
nothing of the enemy, even when the mist paled with the dawn.
Around them, fringeing the common, were gardens and orchards
and little fields, all dank and dripping and criss-crossed with narrow muddy lanes running between high hedges, punctuated here
and there with a building of some kind, a barn, a cottage. And in
every lane, along every hedge, there were crammed dragoons and
musketeers and pikemen, ready for the day.

Walter's company was lined-up on the common itself, with a row of Essex's seasoned soldiers between each of their lines, to stiffen their courage. It was only when day had broken as fully as it ever would that they had their first sight of the enemy, dim menacing shapes of men and horses moving out of the mist some distance away, forming into dense featureless blocks. Some were still singing drunkenly, but most of them were quiet enough, with an ominously purposeful look, Prince Rupert's dreaded cavalry among them, Walter supposed. His heart began to thud and he felt sick, and at first he was glad when, near him, someone quaveringly began to sing a psalm. Yet when it came to the point his mouth was too dry for singing and he could only croak uncertainly along. It did nothing to banish his terror.

He had never known time pass so slowly as it did that morning. He tried to talk to those around him, but it was hard to think of anything to say, and their remarks to him scarcely registered in his brain, though he heard one of the veterans say comfortingly, 'There are more of us, I'd say. And we've God on our side.' It should have encouraged him, but the cold seemed to have drawn all valour from him, and even his trust in God. He would have given anything to move. To wait and watch and be able to do nothing was intolerable. He itched to level his pike and step forward to meet them, longed for something to happen. Yet, what if he should fail when the time came? What if he should turn and flee? What if – as began to seem only too likely – he should shit himself where he stood?

The enemy lines took shape and then stilled. He knew that across that short distance they too were being watched, that those men too were waiting, wanting action to chase fear away. He wondered what kind of men they were, what they were thinking. Of drink, of rape and pillage, of killing? Was Lord Milburn among them, and if so what was in his black heart as he waited out there in the mist? 'Lord,' Walter found himself praying, fear abruptly pushed back, 'let me be the instrument of Thy vengeance this day!'

Then Major-General Skippon was among them, moving from company to company, as if seeking out every one of his soldiers for encouragement, down to the very youngest and most afraid. 'Come, my boys, my brave boys, let us pray heartily and fight heartily. Remember the cause is for God!' They cheered him with all their hearts and then they sang in earnest, finding their voices, dispelling quavering and hoarseness in a grand rousing psalm:

Let God arise, and then his foes
will turn themselves to flight . . .

Walter knew then, with joy in his heart, that if his own feeble
human nature was no match for his fear, then God's strength would
supply all that was needed. When the time came, he would not be
allowed to fail.

If the mist had been like his fear, the smell of spilled ale was sour
with his disappointment. It was the smell that reached them that
afternoon as they entered Brentford, going warily, for they could
still not be sure they would not find someone waiting for them in
the narrow streets. The smell was everywhere, catching in throat
and nostrils, too strong, too out of place to be remotely enticing. It
came, they found, from the overflowing cellars of the town's alehouses, where the Cavaliers, to spite their enemy, had smashed
every barrel they had not had time to drink dry.

Walter was surprised how badly let down he felt, and it had
nothing to do with finding neither food nor drink at the end of that
long hungry day. He knew he should not have felt like this, for the
town showed fewer signs of its recent sufferings than they had
expected. The buildings were still standing, with only a partially
charred roof here and there. No corpses littered the streets, and the
townsfolk – robbed, certainly, of everything of value, but otherwise unharmed – came running out to welcome them with cheers
and embraces, as friends and liberators. And before long women
and children (though he saw no sign of Esther) arrived from
London with wagon loads of food and drink, for townsfolk and soldiers alike, and all ate and drank in an atmosphere of festivity and
relief. London was safe, Brentford freed, the enemy gone.

Yet still Walter felt cheated. All that courage, all that waiting, and
nothing at the end of it but the enemy melting away in the mist,
gone beyond reach of a just vengeance. For these few days he had
thought himself a soldier. Tomorrow, with not the briefest fight to
his credit, he would be back in the workshop, a mere apprentice
again.

1643

Chapter Twelve

It had been at the end of January, on the day of the worst snow of the winter, that Richard had suddenly come to the house. Susannah had not even known he was back in Thornside. No one had told her he was expected, not even his sister.

She had not seen him since the previous summer, when he had gone to the support of the Fairfaxes. There had been a short-lived attempt at a neutrality agreement with the Yorkshire Royalists, but it had wilted under the disapproval of Parliament and the reluctance of many outside the immediate circle of the negotiators to abide by it. By the time the news of Edgehill reached them, even Yorkshiremen had resigned themselves to war. As expected, the Earl of Essex had appointed Sir Thomas's father, Lord Fairfax, as General for Parliament in the north.

For a time Richard had been said to be recruiting in the North Riding (Susannah had seen nothing of him), but then in December the Royalist Earl of Newcastle had marched south through Durham with a considerable army and established himself at York, putting new heart into all the Royalist forces in the county. After that, the Yorkshire Roundheads had been driven back to the West Riding, where their support was strongest, Richard with them. At Christmas-time, Matthew Fawcett had received a letter from his sister Judith in York, saying she had lately had a visit from Sir Ralph Liddell, quartered there with the Royalists, but no news of Richard had reached Thornside for a long time.

And yet there, suddenly, was Richard in person, struggling through the blizzard towards the house as Susannah opened the door. 'It wasn't doing this when I set out,' he had said with grim humour, raising his head just enough to look at her.

'Where have you come from, sir?'

'Leeds. Which we took a week ago. I've been four days on my way here. I began to think I wouldn't make it.' He peered through the stinging swirls of snow, and realised then that she was well wrapped in cloak and hood, with a basket over her arm. 'You're not going out in this, Mistress Fawcett?'

'You're out in it, sir.' She smiled, but her smile had a slight edge, which had an odd effect on him, as if the blizzard had somehow lodged itself inside him. He was about to argue further with her, and then realised she was still holding the door open and that already a small drift was forming on the flags inside. He stepped into the house and stamped the snow from his boots, while she shut the door, allowing quiet and warmth to settle about them.

'It's Doctor Fawcett I've come to see. Is he at home?'

'He's in the study. You know the way, I think, sir – please go through. I can't delay any longer.' And then she was gone, disappearing into the heart of a brief, fierce inrush of wind and snow.

For a moment he stood where he was, staring at the closed door, like one who has just seen a vision and now doubts the evidence of his eyes. And indeed so she had seemed to him, taking shape through the snow like some creature of legend or myth – a goddess too beautiful for the everyday. Conscious that his thoughts were verging on the idolatrous, and would have offended Susannah had she been aware of them, he blushed heavily and went in search of Matthew Fawcett.

Richard had left by the time Susannah came home from her shopping, but she discovered at once why he had called. Her father came to meet her in the hall, helping her out of her cloak while he talked. 'Master Metcalfe came to ask that I would go to the army, as one of the physicians to Sir Thomas Fairfax.'

'You won't get far in this.' But she thought at the same time that it was the logical thing for Richard to do. Like all good physicians, her father was qualified to minister to the needs of any soldier struck down by sickness, but unlike most physicians he was also skilled in surgery, and not ashamed to use his skill when the need arose.

'I shall leave when he goes, which will be as soon as the roads are open again.'

'Then you've given him your answer?'

'Yes.' He sighed. 'Susannah, you know I'm almost as much troubled by this war as poor Ralph. If a little less, then only because the rights and wrongs of it seem clearer to me. But I regret nevertheless that it has to come to this. In the end, I think we shall all be the losers for it. But there it is. I am a healer, so I must go where there will be most need of healing.'

'Then we must think what is needed,' said Susannah. She took her purchases to the stillroom, her father following. 'Where is Grandfather Fawcett's chest? Did it go into the attic?'

Matthew's father had been a surgeon and apothecary, born and raised in the very shop in the main street of the town where Susannah had just made her purchases. Matthew Fawcett had learned a great deal from his father, a man of much practical common sense who had urged him to train as thoroughly as he could with the aim of becoming a physician, and thus sure of a wealth and respect no mere surgeon could command. He had lived just long enough to see that ambition realised.

They found the chest, sorted the few things it contained, began to consider what ought to be packed in it. Later, in the hour before evening prayers, which, as often as possible, they set aside for reading, Susannah sought out a book her father had acquired in his student days, a manual on the treatment of wounds by a French surgeon who had served in the sixteenth-century wars. Matthew Fawcett turned the book in his hands, smiling reminiscently. 'Hmm. Ambroise Paré. I first heard of him from a pupil of his I met when I was studying in Paris. One Louise Bourgeois.'

'A woman!' Susannah, diverted, forgot all about the war.

'A gentlewoman. Midwife to the Queen of France. Or so she was when I met her. Greatly respected, and with reason. But that's beside the point. Let's see what Paré can teach us shall we?'

Susannah took the book and began to read selected passages from it to her father, sometimes in the original French, sometimes in translation, discussing various points. 'I can see I shall be better prepared than any surgeon with the army,' he said, when they parted to go to bed.

They spent the next day surrounded by lists that grew at one end as quickly as they were diminished at the other, by phials of medicines full or awaiting filling with the preparations made up by Susannah or her father in the stillroom, by piles of clean linen for bandages, and trays of implements, which Susannah checked against the lists and cleaned and then packed with the other things in the chest and the saddle bags.

On the second day the storm subsided and the sun shone and Richard sent word that he intended to set out the next morning, if things got no worse. He would send a packhorse to carry the luggage, though he hoped the doctor would be able to provide his own riding horse. They were rather short of horses at the Hall since the visit from Harry Middleton. 'We'll take Longlegs,' said Susannah. 'He'll carry two of us.' She hated riding pillion, preferring to be in full control of her mount herself, but this was no time to be ruled by petty dislikes.

Her father stared at her uncomprehendingly. 'Two?' He sounded genuinely puzzled.

'Me and you. Who else?'

'But – you're not coming with me!'

'I always come with you.'

'I'm not going to the bedside of a sick gentlewoman. I'm going to war.'

'I know. But every surgeon needs his mate. I've always been your mate – your apprentice anyway. Where would you find another so well prepared?' She sounded cheerfully unconcerned, as if she did not take his protest very seriously.

'Susannah, you can't possibly come with me! You are a young unmarried woman, gently reared—'

She felt as she thought she might have done if he had ever struck her. Never in all her life could she remember her father even hinting that anything should be forbidden to her because of her sex. She had always, in everything, been his friend and companion, his apprentice and latterly his colleague, at least as far as he was concerned. *A young unmarried woman, gently reared* – how could he use such words of her, speak of her so dismissively, as if she were like those other silly girls who giggled and gossiped on street corners, or like Anne Greatorex, who had screamed when the soldiers came? 'I'm not gently reared. I'm your daughter. Reared by you.'

He heard her, and a terrible weight of unease settled inside him. She was everything to him, the one precious thing his dear wife had left him. For her, he had given up a prosperous career in London. Had he stayed there he might by now have been a wealthy and fashionable physician, like Sir Theodore Mayerne, whom he knew slightly, who was physician to the royal family and immensely rich; or William Harvey, another royal physician, whose eminent position had enabled him to make the most of his studies. Matthew had been doing quite well for himself as it was, building up a considerable reputation. But he had wanted Susannah to grow up away from the unhealthy vapours of the London air, so he had brought her back to his home town, where he had bought a substantial piece of land, the rents from which were enough to keep them even without his medical practice; and he had not once regretted his decision. He had never given any very clear thought to her upbringing. He had simply brought her up much as he had been brought up himself, teaching her the same things; taking her with him wherever he went, so long as there was no actual danger of infection, simply because he could not bear to leave her behind. She had never given him cause to question the wisdom of what he did, because she absorbed everything so completely, asked such perceptive questions, learned so quickly, and very early became his friend as well as his daughter. He had never thought of her as a woman. She was simply Susannah, whom he loved.

But when Richard had asked him to go to the army, he had known without question that he must be parted from her. He had never been parted from her before and the prospect had pained him terribly, so much so that he had tried not to think of it at all while he made ready to go. Yet it had never once occurred to him that she might expect to go with him. This was war and she was a woman. If he had never known it before he knew it now. After all, it had never mattered before.

'I'm coming with you, father. There's no question about it.' He knew that expression, the sweet mouth set in an obstinate line, the clear eyes bright and unflinching.

'No, Susannah. In this I cannot be gainsaid. War is not for women. What's more it's the middle of winter.'

'I'm not afraid of bad weather. You know that.'

'There's the smallpox,' he went on, suddenly inspired. 'If anyone else should go down with it . . .' There had been a particularly virulent outbreak of the disease during the autumn, and the two of them, who had each survived childhood attacks of smallpox, had been kept very busy caring for the most difficult cases.

'We would know by now, if they were going to.'

He tried a different approach. 'What if Mistress Greatorex should be taken sick again? She depends on you.'

'Mistress Greatorex is perfectly well at the moment and has her mother to look after her should she need it. What's more, as far as I know none of your usual patients is sick or about to give birth or in need of you in any way; or me either.'

'Hmm. That's not the point,' he said, but he knew Susannah was as far as ever from accepting what he said.

In the end, confronted with an obstinacy he understood only too well – after all, he had it too – Matthew called Richard in to support him. He was afraid that if Susannah could not be convinced that her place was at home then she would simply saddle up their other horse and ride with them and nobody would be able to do anything to prevent her. He was deeply troubled by the whole business, for he knew that Susannah was (through God's grace) without fault, yet in this she seemed somehow to have wandered into error.

Richard was even more horrified than Matthew. 'Mistress Fawcett, your sense of duty does you honour, but it is misplaced. You are needed here.' She dealt with that argument, so he went on, 'You have no knowledge of war.'

'Nor had you until lately,' she said, with perfect truth. 'I shall learn.'

Her cool assurance, which had always seemed an admirable thing, began to irritate him a little. 'But a woman cannot understand these things. As befits one of your sex and birth, you have been sheltered from that kind of knowledge, as no man ever is. The women who go to war are either decent married women wishful to be near their husbands, who must be kept safe well behind the lines when hostilities start. Or they are – well, women of doubtful virtue, whose services before and after battle are necessary but whose company no man would wish for any virtuous woman. More than that,' he went on, sensing that she was about to make yet another objection, 'terrible things happen in war. Men lose control, behave like animals.'

'I know. I saw them at the Hall last summer.'

'That was nothing – nothing, Mistress Fawcett, believe me! What is more, there are sights in war that no gentlewoman should have to endure.' He had seen them himself already, and sometimes he would lie awake haunted by some horror he had witnessed. He knew things he could never tell her about, terrors in himself, and a capacity for cruelty in the heat of battle that horrified him. He respected Susannah greatly, but he was quite sure that she was wrong in this. Anywhere near a battlefield was no place for a gentle and lovely woman. 'The carnage of the battlefield has a peculiar horror. Wounds, too dreadful—'

'I'm not unprepared.' She explained what she had been reading lately, in a way that made him blench. Then she said quietly, with a note of utter conviction, 'God gave me a mind and body skilled in healing. It is His will that I use those skills in His service, in this war. I know it to be so. No man shall stop me.'

He could find no answer to that and knew he had failed. He wondered whether to enlist Anne's help, but decided that would not work. He consulted his mother, who had no real help to offer either. 'You should marry her, with all speed, if you've still a mind to,' was her advice. 'She has many fine qualities, but she'll get out of hand if she isn't checked soon. Her father has no authority over her at all. A strong husband is just what she needs.' He did consider taking the advice and proposing to Susannah again at once, but he was afraid she would refuse him, which would only make things more awkward.

In the end, she got her way, if only because Richard had no more time to spare for argument. He impressed upon her that she would be expected to stay safe in the nearest peaceful town while any fighting was in progress, in suitable company. Only when all danger was past would she be permitted to go to her father's assistance. She agreed meekly, to save time, and the next morning they set off, Susannah provided with one of Richard's steadiest horses, since he thought riding pillion unsafe on the snowy roads.

That had been the beginning of the adventure. They had struggled through drifts, which protected them from the fear of enemy attack, but made their journey very hazardous in places, and much slower than Richard would have liked. They had to spend several nights on the way, but Richard took care where they stopped, avoiding any towns where they might meet with Royalist troops, which slowed them still further. There had been a number of small but heated engagements during the winter months and, in spite of successes like Sir Thomas's attack on Leeds, the Royalists had, on the whole, consolidated their position. 'It's clear Newcastle has plans to settle the north for the King and then move on towards London,' Richard had explained to Matthew as they rode. 'We hold Scarborough still, and Hull, but we can expect no help from them while the enemy is so strong outside their walls. The concern when I left was to raise more troops. We are desperately short of men – and the money to pay them too. The West Riding has suffered grievously since the fighting began.'

'How many serve under you?' Susannah asked. She knew he was now a cavalry captain.

'Not enough,' he said. 'With things so uncertain it's not easy to find good horsemen willing to serve the Parliament. If they are not for the King, then they're for staying at home and minding their own affairs. Most of my troopers are farmers, or even clothiers and weavers and the like, honest men of their kind, but not of the quality of my Lord Newcastle's cavalry.'

'Who are all good men like Captain Harry Middleton, I suppose,' put in Susannah drily.

'I don't doubt he's proved a brave soldier,' said Richard. 'And there are better than he, of course, even on the King's side.'

Susannah, thinking of Ralph, glanced at her father and saw that his thoughts too were with his friend. He had told her before they left Thornside that his greatest fear was that he might one day find himself looking across a battlefield in the knowledge that somewhere on the other side Sir Ralph was facing death – his own, or that of men as honourable, killed by his hand.

Then they had come to Bradford. Won for Parliament a few weeks before Sir Thomas took Leeds, the fervour and godliness of its people had struck Susannah with impressive force. It was a quality she had since found almost everywhere in these deep Pennine dales, above all in the men who served in Lord Fairfax's army. She had wondered then, as she did even more now, that Richard should be so disparaging of the ordinary soldiers. There were those, of course, who were like most men she had ever come across, with minds full of horses and women and drink and little else, men who served simply for money or plunder. But from the little clothing towns high in the hills, other men had flocked to the army, men who sang psalms as they marched and fought with God's cause before their eyes. They might be poor – often without other employment, trade being so bad – but it was obvious to her, seeing them, which side in this war was blessed by God and must triumph at the last.

That had all been five months ago, when it had still been winter.

Now, as June turned to July, victory seemed a very long way off; especially since Friday's disaster. That there were not more men in the temporary hospital here in Bradford was due not to a lack of casualties, but to the fact that so few had been got to safety. Five hundred men had died on the battlefield, and more than a thousand had been taken prisoner. It seemed like the end of all their hopes.

Through the spring months the Fairfaxes' fortunes had swung this way and then that, from defeat to victory and back again. There had been the bitter day on Seacroft Moor, when the cavalry of the drunken and erratic Colonel George Goring had swept down on Sir Thomas's little army and savaged it; a defeat revenged at Wakefield, when against overwhelming odds not only had the town been taken but Colonel Goring too, now a prisoner of Parliament. But the Queen had returned that spring from the Continent, with arms and men and money begged and borrowed from Holland and Flanders for the King's cause; and on her way back to her husband she had charmed the governor of Scarborough into changing sides and declaring for the King. Worst of all, in the last few days news had come that the governor of Hull, Sir John Hotham, had followed his example.

That news, though devastating, had not surprised Richard, who had told Susannah that both the Hothams, father and son, had been restive for some time. 'Jealous that they were not given command of the army, I think,' he said. 'But I recall, too, something Captain Hotham said to me once. It stuck in my mind, because I had sometimes had the same thought. You know how it is, when you have something on your mind, and you think you are the only one who has ever thought such a thing, and then someone else gives voice to the self-same fear.'

She had nodded, waiting for him to go on. He spoke as if he were quoting the younger Hotham, but she sensed that the words were in fact his own.

'Hotham said: "I have an anxiety about arming men such as we have under us for this war. Once, no man of that kind would have dreamed of raising a hand to his betters, whatever he might say on the quiet. Now we pay them to do so, arm them, tell them it is the Lord's work. What happens when the war ends? Will each man then return quietly to his former state and forget he ever lived otherwise? I fear it may not be as easy as that – and if I am proved right, then our liberties will have been dearly bought." I would not do what the Hothams have done. I have given my allegiance to Parliament, and I shall stay true to that, as honour requires. But oh, I find myself wishing that it had all been ended last year, one way or another, before we find ourselves on a road whose end we cannot see!'

But whatever the reason for it, the loss of Hull meant that, in all of Yorkshire, only the West Riding was still in Parliamentary hands.

It was the obvious thing for the Earl of Newcastle to do after that, to march against the Fairfaxes and defeat them. Only when he had completed his hold on the north could he risk moving to deal with the forces of the Eastern Association, which now barred his route to London. For the Fairfaxes, driven back to Bradford without provisions to withstand a siege, the only possible response was to ride out and meet him with all the men they could muster, fighting him on their terms and not his. That was the theory, and to make it feasible they had begged for urgent reinforcements from Lord Mandeville (Earl of Manchester since his father's death), who commanded the Eastern Association, south of the Humber. But no help had come, and Lord Fairfax had marched out with a bare four thousand men to meet Newcastle's ten thousand and more on the bleak heights of Adwalton Moor, a few miles south-east of Bradford.

'If only Tom had been in command that day,' Richard had said, privately, to Susannah, just yesterday. But he had not, and though he and his men had fought with all their usual ferocity, the battle had been disastrously lost. Afterwards, Lord Fairfax had ridden with most of what was left of the army towards Leeds, leaving Tom to hold Bradford.

So here they were now, two days later, with the Royalist guns keeping up a constant bombardment from the hills above them, even though it was a Sunday and late in the day, and the fringes of the town had already fallen to the enemy. At this very moment Sir Thomas was in council with his officers, presumably discussing when precisely to surrender, since that would seem to be the only course left to them, apart from the pointless and bloody sacrifice of fighting to the end.

And what then? Susannah thought, as she replaced the dressing on the stump that was all that was left of a soldier's arm.

'If it was anyone else but Black Tom I'd say we was done for.'

She wondered for a moment if she had spoken her thoughts aloud, so neatly did the words seem to answer them. 'Black Tom' was the name most of the men gave to Tom Fairfax, because of his dark complexion, though he was 'Fiery Tom' too, which had surprised her at first, applied to so gentle, reticent and modest a man. 'What makes you say that, Robert Sykes?'

But she knew of course, for she had heard it all so many times before from the wounded men under her care. She heard it again now, as the man in the next bed woke and joined in their talk, and before long the two soldiers were comparing reminiscences of Wakefield, in which fierce fight they had both been wounded. 'And there was Black Tom alone with the Papists all about him, and does he lose his head? No, he does not. Puts his heels to his horse and springs forward, right over the earthwork to where we was with the gun. The next thing, the town's ours. All thanks to a good horse, he says afterwards.'

'Aye, that's Black Tom all over. I've never known him take the credit hisself, not for owt he's done.'

Susannah knew what would come before long, and sure enough there it was: 'Oh, I wish to God I'd been on Adwalton Moor! Maybe things would have been different, with just a few more of us there.'

Susannah thought it was more likely that there would simply have been a greater number of casualties, but she said nothing, merely secured the dressing and began to tidy her things away.

'Have a care, Robert Sykes, blaspheming like that,' said the other man. 'Good thing Black Tom can't hear you.'

'That's not blasphemy—' He fell abruptly silent. Susannah looked round and saw that Maud Laycocke was coming their way.

'Mistress Susannah, Corporal Skelton looks proper poorly to me. I think you should come.'

Susannah collected her things and accompanied the other woman the length of the hall. Like most of the women who helped with the wounded, Maud Laycocke had followed her man to the army. When he was killed at Adwalton Moor, Susannah had fully expected the widow to go back home, or at least to shut herself away in her grief. Instead, she had turned up as usual at the hospital, more silent, perhaps, but no less competent. Susannah, who until then had thought her light-minded (if useful), had been impressed.

Maud was right, too: the corporal had taken a turn for the worse. Susannah examined him and then gave Maud instructions as to what medicines to administer and how often. Behind her,

several of the other women, with little to do now there were so few
wounded, worked at a long table, cutting bandages from linen
brought in by the townsfolk – in case, Susannah supposed, Sir
Thomas decided to fight on, though then winding sheets might
prove more useful than bandages. They gossiped and laughed as
they worked, in a way that reminded her of women at the shearing
feast at Thornside, at which sometimes, a little disdainfully, she
had helped. As Richard had warned, few of the women – whether
sweethearts, wives or outright whores – were of good repute. Most
were dirty, foul-mouthed and loud. But they worked hard, cheerfully and without complaint, in the most difficult conditions. She
had come to feel a reluctant respect for them, and even some gratitude. They, she had soon realised, were more than a little in awe
of her.

'Hey, lasses, look who's here!' That was undoubtedly fat Joan
Rowbotham, one of the women at the table. Without looking
round, Susannah knew how she would be nudging her neighbour,
how they would all be exchanging knowing looks. She knew too
who must at this moment have come through the door at the far
end of the hall. Early on, one of the women had asked Susannah (a
little warily) if she had a sweetheart with the army, but her denial
had not put an end to speculation, especially as Richard sought her
out in all his moments of leisure. At least the women seemed to
think it was to her credit that someone so personable should be
paying court to her.

But when she did look round, Susannah saw that it was not
Richard who was making his way towards her through the chorus
of whistles and brazen comments. Captain John Lambert, another
of Sir Thomas's distant relations, was less liable than Richard to
crumple into pink embarrassment, perhaps because he was already
a married man and a father. Improbably elegant and self-assured, he
walked steadily up the hall, and even retorted with good-humour to
one particularly appreciative remark. He was only twenty-three,
but had already done good service for the Parliamentary cause, so
Richard had once said, a little enviously.

He removed his hat as he reached her, bowing slightly. 'Is your
father here, mistress?'

Susannah gestured towards the small side room, where her father
lay on a straw mattress on the floor. 'He's asleep, sir. I've taken the
night watch.'

'Then I fear you must wake him. Sir Thomas asks if you would both be so good as to come to his quarters, without delay.'

So a decision must have been made, Susannah thought, as she woke her father and together, escorted by Captain Lambert, they walked through the dusty, deserted, shuddering streets. But if it had, Captain Lambert was discreet and gave nothing away.

Richard was among those present at the meeting in Fairfax's lodgings, as was Lady Fairfax, a soldier's daughter of strong character and high principles, who had taken refuge in the town a few days before, when the Royalists overran her home at Nun Appleton. The town's surgeon, like Matthew Fawcett dragged from his bed, was there too, and two of the army chaplains, as well as an unknown man in travel-muddied clothes and two days' growth of beard. Susannah saw that Sir Thomas had a sparkle in his eyes, as if this whole desperate business was an adventure. She had seen that look before, but only when things were at their most hopeless.

'We have had two things in our minds this evening,' said Sir Thomas. As always when concerned with military matters he seemed to throw off his stammer, along with every other vestige of the private man. 'The one is, that we have only a single barrel of powder left. Our supplies of food are almost as low. The other, that by God's mercy Hull has after all not been lost to us.'

Lady Fairfax gave a muffled exclamation of pleasure; the officers of course already knew.

'So Sir John Hotham changed his mind?' asked Matthew.

'No, Doctor Fawcett. It was changed for him, by the good people of Hull. He is under arrest. As is his son.' He gestured to the stranger standing beside him. 'This gentleman found his way here today, with a promise that the gates of Hull will be opened to us, if once we make our way there.' Susannah watched his face, with its glowing dark eyes and a faint smile lighting it; he looked almost happy.

'We shall not surrender Bradford. I believe there are no terms that we could honourably accept. Instead, we shall meet with my father at Leeds, from where we shall make our way to Hull. Once there, we have a hope, in time and with God's help, of repairing our fortunes. In short, we intend this very night to break out of Bradford, all of us, that is, taking with us those civilians who choose.' Which was, Susannah thought, her heart thudding, why they had been summoned. 'I want no man or woman with me who is not whole-hearted for the attempt. It will be hazardous in the extreme. Those who remain in the town will of course be taking a different chance, though I have no doubt they will be accorded all the consideration that an honourable enemy can give them. The same cannot be said for we who break out tonight. What is more, any civilian who rides with me must know that, should he or she be wounded or fall into enemy hands, then he must shift for himself. The rest of us will not wait to see how he fares – or she.' He glanced at his wife, who smiled grimly back at him. Then, after a little pause to allow what he had said to sink in, he looked questioningly from one to another of the company. The town's surgeon announced his intention of staying in Bradford, as did one of the chaplains; both left the room. 'Doctor Fawcett?'

Matthew glanced at Susannah and then back at Sir Thomas. 'Hmm. I shall ride with you, sir. The wounded who remain here are for the most part recovered. I will go where I can be of most use. As for my daughter, that is for her to say.'

'I too shall come with you, sir,' Susannah said, conscious that Richard was looking at her with an expression of fierce anxiety. Sometimes his solicitude irritated her. In spite of all the evidence to the contrary he insisted on treating her as if she were as fragile as a thrush's egg.

'Then your attention, please!' said Sir Thomas. 'The foot have their instructions already, and will break out separately.' Susannah, aware from the corner of her eye that the door had opened, turned to see a small white-clad figure standing there, looking in some bewilderment for a familiar face. 'All mounted troops are to—'

'Sir, I had a bad dream.'

Sir Thomas looked in alarm at the little girl in the doorway, and then suddenly smiled and bent down, holding out his arms. The child ran to him and he lifted her up. 'Well, Moll my chick, you have woken just in time. We go on a journey tonight, and you must be ready.' Susannah half expected a horrified exclamation from Lady Fairfax, but none came. Then she thought: which would be worse, to risk the life of a child in the sort of adventure that faced them tonight, or to leave her here to the mercies of an invading army? It was probably an impossible question to answer.

By now the child's nurse was at the door. 'Oh, sir, I'm sorry!'

Sir Thomas carried Mary across the room and talked in a low voice to the nurse, presumably giving her instructions for tonight.

Susannah was moved by the contrast between the tall, dark soldier in his stained buff coat and the little girl with her bare feet showing beneath her frilled night-shift, whom he held so tenderly, kissing her before he handed her back to her nurse.

After the meeting, which was closed with prayers, the officers dispersed to give orders to their men and Richard walked some of the way to the hospital with Susannah, where she was to collect a few personal medical items that her father wanted to take with them. He had himself gone back to their lodgings to make a start on packing the saddle-bags, which were all they would be able to carry.

Richard was in a mood she had come to know quite well, at once tense and reflective, which came over him whenever he was about to face action of some kind. Unlike his cousin, he was not a natural soldier. She knew, though he had never told her so, that he was often afraid, that he hated fighting, that only his strong sense of duty kept him where he was. For that she deeply respected him. It was easier, much easier, for Black Tom, possessed by an ardour beyond his control.

'I could wish you were to remain safely in Bradford,' he said now.

'If little Mary Fairfax can go with you, then I think you have no reason to fear for my safety.'

'I have to say that I wonder at Tom, allowing it. She is but four, a mere baby. But then her mother was raised in the camp. And I suppose she might be used as a hostage, were she to fall into unscrupulous hands.' He sighed. 'I am thankful I have no such hard choice to make. Indeed, for myself this venture must be a blessing. Better than to wait for what tomorrow brings, able to do nothing.' He paused, then went on, 'I pray that you may not take any harm, that none of us may, of course. But if it should happen that I fall and you are left, perhaps to return to Thornside and see my mother again, and my sister, then I should like them to know that now, at this moment, I am filled only with a sense of God's great mercy towards me. He has wrought so many miracles in my life. I look back on the time when I first knew the workings of His grace in me, while I was at Gray's Inn. That I shall never forget as long as I live. I was wholly given up to darkness when in His goodness He sought me out. I give thanks for it daily. And you, Mistress Fawcett, do you remember such a day? You must, I am sure.'

'Yes, sir,' she said. 'Very clearly. I was twelve and my father was away. I can't remember why now. I think someone was sick at Richmond. But he was gone some days. The very first evening Margaret cut her hand, quite badly. It was bleeding fast and she was in pain, and frightened. I know I felt no fear, indeed no doubt. I thought only of all I had learned from my father, and I comforted her and bound her wound. It stopped bleeding and it healed well. To this day I remember that sense – how can I put it? – that I was doing what I was meant to do, that some power stronger than myself was working through me; that it was right, all of it.' She knew that she had not quite found the words to express the sense of intense concentration of mind and body and spirit that had come over her then, for the first time. She had come to accept it now, as part of the way she worked. Like Sir Thomas's fierceness on the battlefield, it was the force that drove her. But she would never forget the moment when she had first felt it.

Richard had heard her with great attention, but now he looked a little puzzled. It was hardly the usual conversion experience. In fact, to him it did not sound much like a conversion experience at all, but he did not like to say so. After all, Susannah was not like other women. He had always known that.

During the brief summer darkness, they gathered quietly by the church, the civilians on horseback among Sir Thomas's little company of soldiers, not more than fifty in all, Susannah riding pillion with her father, Lady Fairfax mounted behind one of the officers, Moll sleepy yet excited on the saddle in front of her nurse.

A short time after, they heard distant sounds of firing from the narrow lanes at one side of the town, and knew the foot were already engaged with the enemy. Immediately three men broke away from their own group and rode off, under cover of the commotion, along the road in the direction which the rest of them were soon to take. Those left behind sat straining ears and eyes, intent for anything that might warn them of trouble ahead. Not that there was any question that there would be trouble, only of what kind, and how great.

The men came back at last, and conferred briefly with Sir Thomas, who then gave the signal to advance. The company rode out of the town at a brisk trot, no one speaking, eyes peering watchfully into the lessening darkness. They covered the first mile unhindered, following the eastward road they had got to know so well during the past months, keeping to the shadow of the valley, where they could less easily be seen. Susannah, having nothing to do but sit there, holding on to her father for support, began to feel drowsy.

It was as dawn was breaking that she felt her father suddenly rein in the horse; for a moment only, but it was enough to jolt her fully awake. She looked up then and saw, drawn up on a ridge that crossed their path, a long dense line of horsemen, dark against the paling sky. 'There must be hundreds!' she murmured. That they were Royalist soldiers she had no doubt at all.

She realised then that Sir Thomas must have known about them all along. Not for an instant did he falter. With a shout he was racing up the slope towards the enemy, his tiny troop galloping behind him, and in a moment Matthew had urged his horse on after them, since any other course seemed out of the question.

On, up, and they were into the heart of it. Shots burst around them, shatteringly loud, bullets flew past their heads. Horsemen came at them from every side. Ahead, there was a confusion of noise and shouting, the whinnying of horses, the thunder of hooves, a child wailing. On still more, and the shots were all behind them. They saw a way through ahead, glimpsed Sir Thomas and the others riding clear in the distance. 'Get on with you!' she heard her father shout to their sluggardly beast.

Another shot. Matthew gave a cry, lurched in the saddle. 'I'm hit! Take the reins!' She reached round him to take them from him, supporting him, feeling, anguished, how he sank against her.

Quite what happened then she was not sure, except that the horse stumbled and the next moment she was falling, in a tangle of reins and swinging stirrups with her father's weight upon her. She felt the reins tugged from her hands, heard the thud of the horse's hooves, threw herself sideways so that they should not catch her head, and at the same instant her father tumbled clear of her with a terrible cry. Shaken, dazed, she glanced round and saw, closing in on them, horsemen without number. And through it all her father was moaning in agony.

She stumbled, half crawling, to where he was, angry that they had lost the saddle-bags with all the medical supplies. She felt someone grab her arm and try to drag her to her feet. Furious, she looked up into the dirty bearded face of a soldier, dismounted, one of a whole circle of men standing leering about her.

'Help me!' she cried. 'He's hurt. He's a doctor, not a soldier.' She

bent over him again, making a swift examination. His thigh had
been hit and was bleeding profusely from a wound which, even in
the grey light and with the torn blackened remnants of his breeches
concealing it, looked ugly enough. She pulled at her neckerchief
and tried to staunch the blood with it, only hearing him moan the
more. She needed good light, water and the right implements,
urgently. 'Is there a surgeon with you?'

They did not reply, but an officer came over and commanded
them to take the wounded man 'over there with the others'. She was
relieved that they brought a makeshift stretcher and lifted him carefully on to it, though he moaned again and she was frightened – she
who was never frightened – by the grey colour of his face. As she
walked along the ridge beside him, holding his hand all the while
and trying to reassure him, she realised there were other prisoners
somewhere in the throng behind her. She glanced round once and
glimpsed Lady Fairfax, who smiled, fleetingly, though she looked
tired and drawn. At the top of the hill they were taken in different
directions.

She and her father were brought to a cottage where a surgeon
examined Matthew, competently enough, Susannah thought. 'His
thigh bone's smashed,' he told Susannah, confirming what she had
already suspected. She wished she did not know only too well how
serious that was.

CHAPTER THIRTEEN

The Royalists under Prince Rupert stormed and entered Bristol on Ludovick's twenty-fourth birthday, the twenty-sixth of July 1643. It had been a fierce and bloody day and the losses had been terrible, but at the end of it Ludovick had ridden into the city at the head of his troop filled with a sense of happiness that he knew was out of all proportion even to so great a victory.

Certainly, the second greatest port in the Kingdom, after London, was theirs at last. Their own losses might have been severe, but the blow to Parliament was incalculable. Looking back, it was hard now to remember the tiny, ill-equipped, untrained army that had served the King in the days before Edgehill. From out of nothing, it seemed, supplies and arms had been organised, soldiers raised and trained, and it was Parliament now that was on the defensive. Apart from a handful of outposts in Lancashire, the north was all in Royalist hands, the Fairfaxes shut up in Hull. In the south-west, Prince Maurice was now in command of the Royalist forces and, in spite of the valiant efforts of the Roundhead Sir William Waller, only a few towns – Poole, Lyme, Exeter, Weymouth, Dorchester, Plymouth – still held out for Parliament. Many of them fell in the days following Bristol. Meanwhile, the Earl of Essex seemed to have lost all heart for war, especially since Rupert's raid on his forces at Chalgrove Field near Reading a month ago, where John Hampden, friend of Pym and most respected of Parliamentary leaders, had been killed. From Oxford, the Royalist newspaper *Mercurius Aulicus* crowed that Londoners were clamouring for peace.

But all that was a reason for satisfaction, even triumph, rather than the shining happiness that, at mass on the Sunday after the taking of Bristol, had filled Ludovick to overflowing. He had known then that the happiness had to do with his brother, and the conviction had come to him in the quietness of that thanksgiving mass that Charles had at last been ordained priest, reaching the crowning moment he had looked to ever since, as a small boy, he had known what he was called to do. It was an end, yet it was also a beginning, for he still had years of strenuous study and prayer before he reached his ultimate goal of admission to the Society of Jesus; but his feet were at last set firmly on his chosen path. Ludovick felt all that in the joy he shared with his brother. It had stayed with him long after they rode out of Bristol again, through the long slow weeks while the royal army laid siege to Gloucester, and it was with him still as intensely as ever on this late August evening as he made his usual evening rounds of his men.

Gloucester was Parliament's only outpost in that part of England, lying astride the supply routes from Wales to Oxford, where the King had his headquarters, and it had been a constant harassment to the Royalist training grounds on the Welsh borders. Once Bristol was secure, the King had assembled the largest army ever brought into the field and settled down to the business of starving Gloucester into submission.

It was, on the whole, work for engineers and artillery rather than cavalry, and Ludovick's men were restless for want of something to do. 'I'm sick of this sitting around,' Trooper Barty Robson (some kind of distant cousin of Rob's) had said the other day. 'Why can't we storm them? We took Bristol in a day. I can't see Gloucester's better defended.'

'Far from it, I'd guess,' said Ludovick. He had heard the same view expressed with equal force by Prince Rupert, who had tried to convince the King of its wisdom. 'But His Majesty doesn't want more losses like we had at Bristol.'

'Aye well, I can see his point,' said Tot Charlton. They still mourned Corporal Simon Milburn, the first of the Blackheugh men to die in this war; and there had been fifteen other men in their troop killed too. 'Mind, hanging about like this could mean more lost in the end.'

Ludovick thought that only too likely, if only from the sporadic outbreaks of sickness that always came at such times, especially in this hot summer weather. He knew that Rupert favoured a swift assault and then an equally swift march on London, taking advantage of the present demoralisation of Parliament. But, accepting his uncle's decision, the Prince had instead thrown himself into the slower business of digging trenches and devising ways of mining the walls.

It was a warm evening and the Blackheugh men had allowed their camp-fire to die down almost to nothing, once supper was over. They made a half-hearted move to scramble to their feet as Ludovick reached them, pulling off their hats. 'As you were, lads,' he said, and sat down among them. He had taken to joining them like this every night at the end of his round, rather than seeking out the quarrelsome, prickly company of his fellow officers, few of whom he much liked – or they him, come to that. He looked forward to these times when he became again simply a soldier among soldiers, sharing their talk and their songs, many composed by himself as a way of passing time on the march.

Rob poured ale into a tankard and handed it to him. Pipesmoke mingled aromatically with the lingering smoke from the fire, overlaying the less pleasing daytime odours of the camp. The faint glow from the ashes fell on weather-beaten faces and stained coats, softening all their harshness. Not far away someone was playing a fife and for miles around the air hummed with the murmur of voices. From close behind them came more earthy sounds of rustling and heavy breathing, where presumably one of the men had crept with a camp follower. Glancing round, Ludovick saw that Toby Milburn was absent and drew his own conclusions. Toby had a wife and children in Tynedale, but in Oxford, where they had been based during the winter, a large cheerful woman called Doll had attached herself to him and had been with him ever since.

There was a comfortable little silence, while the men drank or puffed on their pipes. Then Will Dodd commented, 'Rob says there's a Covenanting Scot rode in to the King yesterday.'

'Aye. The Earl of Montrose. He led them at Newburn.' That morning Ludovick had met him briefly in Rupert's company, a proud, deeply serious young man whose reception by the King had apparently not been what he had hoped, so far at least. Ludovick thought it unlikely he was the kind who gave up easily.

'What does he want then, my lord?'

Ludovick did not immediately reply. He could have said, truthfully, that Montrose had brought news of negotiations between

Parliament and the Scots, which he believed were about to be concluded with some kind of treaty of mutual support. There were, apparently, clear signs of a considerable army being made ready. The information had not impressed the King, who did not believe his Scottish subjects would be so disloyal as to break all the agreements he had made with them and ally themselves with his rebellious Parliament.

But to have said even a part of that would have reminded the Blackheugh men that they were very far from home and had left their families and friends at the mercy of an invading Scottish army. Ludovick might not have much sense of belonging himself, but he knew very well, as did all the Royalist officers, how strong were the ties that bound men to their homes. Encouraging soldiers to fight far from their own districts had been a persistent problem, only now being broken down. Very often, men would desert rather than travel into another county. He had no reason to think the Blackheugh men would do such a thing after so long with the army, but he did not want to take any risks on the strength of a rumour; which at present was all it was. 'You'd have to ask him,' he said at last non-committally.

'He's not just a Scot, man, that Earl of Montrose,' Tot Charlton said. 'He's a Graham.'

'Is that bad?' asked Ludovick.

'Aye, my lord, is it just! Rob'll tell you. You recall the tale of the scabbed sheep, Rob? Was it not your great grandfather had a part in that?'

'Aye, so I heard. Mind, that was the Liddesdale Grahams. He's not one of them, as I ever heard. Still, to my tale . . . You see, there was a day, oh, years ago now, the last century it would be, in the old Queen's time, maybe even before. A group of us Robsons had a mind to lift a few sheep, supplies being low. So off we rode into Liddesdale and took our pick from the Graham flocks and drove them back with us to Tynedale, the way it always used to be done.'

'Still is, now and then,' put in Tot Charlton, though he was quickly silenced.

'Now, it was night when it happened, as you would suppose, so we didn't get a good look at those sheep until morning. Out we go in daylight, then, to cast an eye over our new stock, and what should we find but that every single last one of them was dirty with the scab. You'll surmise how we felt. Cheated was the least of it, after all our efforts. So, there was nought for it then but to ride back to Liddesdale the next night and pay those Grahams a sharp lesson. Seven of them we hanged, and left a note for the rest. *Be sure next time your sheep aren't scabbed.*'

There was a burst of laughter, through which Tot Charlton said triumphantly, 'You see, my lord; never trust a Graham.'

They were still laughing when a man appeared on the fringe of the company and said something to one of the soldiers, who called out. 'My lord! There's a fellow here wants a word. Private, he says.'

Ludovick felt an odd sensation, as if everything had suddenly drawn away from him, leaving him isolated, held suspended in time and space. Not quite knowing what he did, he rose and made his way to where the man was standing, just beyond the reach of the light. He saw only a shadowy figure about middling height. 'I've a message for you, my lord. I've to tell you there was a ship landed in Norfolk a week ago, from Flanders. The man that was on it is at South Haddon now, will be for two weeks.'

Charles, Ludovick thought, his heart leaping: he's in England! Yet – he had not expected . . . 'Where's South Haddon?' he heard himself say.

'Northampton, sir, about five miles north-west of Northampton. A manor house, family name of Ashby. You ask for Master Miles Wood.'

'I'll find it,' he said softly.

He was dimly aware of making sure the man was given food, then of going to find Rupert to arrange leave of absence. It took him some time, for Rupert was not relaxing at his headquarters (that was no surprise), but in the trenches close to the walls of Gloucester, supervising the laying of mines. In the end, it was the large white shape of the Prince's dog, just visible in the darkness, that showed him where to find his commander. 'Be back within three days,' said Rupert, as he scribbled a safe conduct, valid at least through Royalist-held territory. Being devoted to his own brother, he had heard Ludovick's request with sympathy, but almost before Ludovick had time to thank him, he was already kneeling again over some device hidden in the darkness, Boy at his heels.

After that, Ludovick told a startled Lieutenant Haynes that he was temporarily in command, had a quiet word with Rob, packed a few necessities, and before midnight was on the road.

It was only then that what had happened began to reach him at all. The happiness was still there, more than ever in a way, for soon they would meet again, after years of separation. But it was tainted now by anxiety and unanswered questions. Why risk landing in Roundhead Norfolk, rather than at one of the ports safely held for the King? Why go to Northampton and not to one of the strongly Catholic regions, Northumberland or Lancashire perhaps? Or was he simply resting at a suitable safe house on his way to one of those areas? And why, oh why was Charles in England at all, at this time when Parliament was so rabidly anti-Catholic that priests went regularly to the gallows?

The first question he had answered himself before he had gone very far. With most of the fleet in Parliamentary hands the approaches were closely patrolled, particularly near the Royalist ports. Safer by far to land on some quiet shore where no Royalist shipping was expected. As for the other questions, they must wait for an answer because brotherly intuition alone was not enough.

He remembered little about the journey, except that he managed to evade inconvenient encounters with the enemy or with over-curious villagers; that he avoided towns and main roads, though sometimes forced to ask the way and, twice, to change horses; that, by hard riding, he came at dusk the next day to the edge of Northampton, skirting it carefully for fear of alerting its Roundhead garrison, and took a narrow north-westerly road that brought him, unerringly it seemed, to South Haddon and a modest old house tucked away in trees out of sight of its neighbours.

There seemed to be no one about. He dismounted at the front of the house and was stepping forward to knock at the door when he changed his mind and, leaving the horse tied to a convenient ring in the wall, walked round to the back.

There was a high hedge, with a gate, which he opened. Inside, a garden, roses edged with low clipped box, grass drenched with dew, a worn statue; and at the far end a man, alone, walking his way.

He was bareheaded, the bright hair shining out in the grey evening. Why did he not cover it? Ludovick thought with exasperated anxiety. He was so easily recognisable. Who could forget that hair; who, having seen him once, could fail to know him again? Why had he not stayed in Flanders, where he was safe?

But he was here, in the garden, and had nearly reached him. Ludovick broke into a run. They met. For a moment they stood there, face to face, blue eyes looking into blue eyes, smiling. Then they embraced. He forgot that he was exhausted from two days without sleep, and hungry, and afraid for his brother.

They began to walk along the grassy paths between the little box hedges, saying nothing at all to one another, content simply to be together, for in these first moments of meeting they had no need of words. The first to speak was Charles. 'Do you want to eat?'

'Not yet.' Ludovick knew he was incapable of eating anything at present. They walked on a little more, then he said, 'Why England?'

Charles smiled gently. 'Because I'm needed here.'

'But you were to be a Jesuit.'

'That can be done in England.'

'You're not staying at this house.'

'Not for long.' A little pause because, so Ludovick realised afterwards, he knew what effect his words would have on his brother. 'I'm bound for London next week.'

Fear clutched suffocatingly at Ludovick's heart. He came to a complete halt, simply because he could no longer put one foot in front of another. *Because I'm needed*, Charles had said; needed because so many priests had been betrayed, in that city where every man he spoke to might be a pursuivant seeking out priests for money, where one false step must mean certain death.

Charles halted too. 'Don't think of it, except that I have work to do. Men are killed in battle too, with more peril to their souls. I'd say the chances are at least even.'

Ludovick gazed at his brother's grave face and realised that the fear was shared, if not quite in the same measure. And what Charles said was true, when he thought about it: the risk was as great for him, at least until they had taken Gloucester and moved on London and brought the war to an end. And when it was ended then the danger would be over, for both of them. The King would hardly reward his loyal Catholic subjects with a strict application of the penal laws. He grinned, suddenly feeling very hungry, and then Charles took him into the house, where supper was soon brought. There were other people about, to some of whom he was introduced, though he hardly saw them. They were left alone over their meal and exchanged memories of their schooldays, washed free of fear by adolescent laughter.

They had that one evening together, and the night that followed, and the early hours of the next day. It was like sunlight on an autumn spider's web, a time of fragile yet perfect happiness. Not to waste the time, they hardly slept at all, but talked of friends and fears and hopes.

Next morning early, in a tiny chapel hidden under the roof, Charles celebrated mass for the household, and Ludovick for the first time received the sacrament at his brother's hands. Afterwards, there was only the briefest of moments alone, when the others had gone. Ludovick clung to his twin, the fear returning, worse than ever.

'I'll take care,' Charles said, gently extricating himself from the fierceness of his brother's embrace, so that he could look at him. 'After all, I shall be more use to my flock alive than dead.'

From somewhere a phrase came into Ludovick's head, *The blood of the martyrs is the seed of the Church*. He knew Charles was thinking it too.

Then he knelt for a blessing and felt his twin's hand warm and strong on his head, and the words Charles spoke were not in Latin, as he had expected, or even in English, but in the language of their infancy.

CHAPTER FOURTEEN

Walter Barras finished the saddle he was making and took it to his master for inspection. Abel Reynolds examined it with more care than usual. 'You've done well. I shall be losing a good apprentice – journeyman, as you'd soon have been.'

Walter, alarmed, stared at him. He knew times were hard. The excise lately put on leather, to help pay for Parliament's armies, had not been welcome to his master, though in these times saddles and harness were much in demand. Taxes had gone on beer too, and sugar and linen, all of which had made Mistress Cecily Reynolds, Abel's wife, complain volubly. Worse still had been the forced loan imposed on most London citizens just two days before. That day Abel Reynolds had offered up prayers for patience and endurance in God's cause. Now Walter wondered uneasily if he had been harder hit than any of them had thought.

Abel Reynolds smiled, only faintly, but then he was not a man much given to smiling. 'I promised a horse and arms for the Parliament. But it seems to me with Gloucester in such danger I should throw in a trooper too, for good measure. A dragoon, I fancy.' He paused and Walter began to see – or thought he saw, his heart beating fast, scarcely daring to hope – what he was about to say. 'They've musketeers and pikemen in plenty. It's horsemen they need. I know you've two months of your indentures left, but we'll overlook that – I'll sign the papers before you go.'

Walter felt as if a brilliant sun had suddenly driven back the clouds, as if the world with all its riches lay suddenly at his feet, his for the asking. It had been so dark a time, until lately, the London streets full of growing numbers of beggars made workless and homeless by war and lack of trade, troubled often with rioters clamouring for peace at any price. Then had come the news of Gloucester's valiant stand against the assembled might of the King's army, and overnight everything had changed. In Parliament, John Pym had forced through votes for money and supplies and recruitment for the army, against the growing peace-party led by his former ally Denzil Holles. It had been like Turnham Green all over again, a time when everyone stood together for a common purpose. Except that Walter had watched the preparations to send help to the besieged city with growing frustration, that he should have no part to play, except as one of the remnant of the trained bands left behind to defend London – which would have to be done if Gloucester fell and the King then defeated Essex, but was not an immediate danger.

And now this was in his hands. He tried to find the words, stammered, 'Oh, thank you, master,' felt Abel Reynolds' hand on his shoulder.

'Thank God that he has chosen you out, Walter. Serve Him with all your heart.'

'That I shall, master,' said Walter, his eyes shining.

Soon afterwards they went to supper, and Walter thought that Esther, far off at the other end of the table, was deliberately trying to catch his eye, as she had not done for a long time. He even thought she ventured a smile, just for him, though the candlelight was not bright enough for him to be quite sure. He wondered if she had been told what her father planned for him. Since Turnham Green they had scarcely ever been alone together, for Abel Reynolds had forbidden her to have anything more to do with him, except what was unavoidable for two people living under the same roof and eating at the same table. Abel Reynolds might favour Walter above his other apprentices, as being more godly and serious-minded, and always conscious of the debt he owed his master. He might even have been happy for Walter to have a brotherly affection for Esther. But as soon as he had realised that Walter had quite other ideas – and, worse, that Esther seemed to share them – he had put an end to all the old freedom between them. Whatever his feelings towards Walter, he had no wish to see him wed to his daughter. After that, Walter's only hope (a very faint one) had been that he might one day be able to set up in business on his own account and that then his master might look more kindly on him as a prospective son-in-law.

He had been right about Esther, for as they went to prayers after supper, she lay in wait for him in the darkness just outside the parlour door and caught his arm. 'You're going to be a dragoon, Walter.' There was an unmistakable note of admiration in her voice.

He felt his heart beat faster. He could only dimly see where she was in the darkness, but he could feel her warmth and the smell of her, very near. 'Aye,' he said breathlessly. 'Your father's very generous.'

She moved her hand up and down his arm, caressing it. If he had not known that someone might come by at any moment, he would have kissed her. 'You're the same age as Colonel Massey,' she said.

He was two years older than the heroic governor of Gloucester – and his deadly foe Prince Rupert, come to that – something that filled him with envy, but he accepted the comparison without correction. Nor did he remind her that Massey was a gentleman, something Walter Barras was never likely to be. Not that he minded that. All he asked for now was to be God's soldier. He did, though, admit to one regret. 'I should like to have served under John Lilburne.'

'He's free again now. Perhaps you will.'

'He's with the Eastern Association, in Colonel Cromwell's regiment. They're not going to Gloucester, and Gloucester's where I must go.'

It was Esther who kissed him then, but before he could take it any further Mistress Cecily Reynolds came round the corner and they had to go meekly on their way to prayers.

After that, his days became all military, his nights filled with thoughts of the excitements to come, when he was not fast asleep from sheer exhaustion. For the training was hard. Dragoons were part-way between foot soldiers and cavalry and much of their drill was carried out on foot. He had to learn to handle the snaphaunce musket, smaller and lighter than the matchlock used by the musketeers, and able (if absolutely necessary) to be fired from the saddle, an awkward manoeuvre which they practised at great length. After his first day's training he was too stiff to sit down, and it was several days before he felt quite at ease on horseback. In his early years he had almost lived in the saddle, working alongside his father in the stables at Blackheugh. But that had ended when he was ten and since then he had scarcely ridden at all, except when his master had some errand for him well beyond the bounds of the city. There was, however, a distinct prestige in being a mounted soldier and, even more, in the sword he had to carry – like any gentleman, he told Esther proudly when he returned one day from training. To his joy she continued to seek him out, though he felt a little guilty about it, since his master had been so kind.

'Best of both worlds, that's us,' one of his new comrades had said at the end of the second day. He was a former brewer's apprentice called Amias Stephens.

'Or the worst,' said Roger Tyler, a cloth merchant's son who always saw the gloomy side of things. 'When there's any work to be done, it's us have the doing of it.'

That meant, Walter realised with a sense of pride, that the safety of the entire army must sometimes depend on the dragoons, who while on the march were generally sent ahead to reconnoitre or to guard the dangerous ways, and in battle were depended upon to pick off the enemy cavalry. 'We are God's soldiers,' he said proudly, 'fighting for His cause.'

Roger was not encouraged. 'What I'd like to know is, how can it be God's cause, when it's going so badly? Seems to me God's showing what side He's on, and it's bloody well not ours.'

It was an argument that made Walter feel uncomfortable, but he knew he could not allow it to go unchallenged. '"Whom the Lord loveth . . ."'he began.

'". . . He chasteneth,"' added a voice behind him. He looked round to see that one of their corporals was standing there. Samuel Revol was an intensely serious young man with dark curly hair and glowing dark eyes and a phrase from the Bible for every situation, and they were already in awe of him. '"Ye have not yet resisted unto blood, striving against sin." That means keeping your tongue free of filthiness, Trooper Tyler.' Then, suddenly, he smiled at Walter, as if acknowledging a friend.

When the day came to leave, Abel Reynolds did something Walter could not remember he had ever done before, to anyone: he embraced him, rather abruptly and soon releasing him, but it was an embrace all the same. 'You go to do the Lord's work, Walter,' he said, in a voice rough with emotion. 'Keep that always in your heart.' Then he gave him a small book, *The Souldier's Pocket Bible*, for which Walter thanked him warmly.

Mistress Cecily Reynolds too kissed Walter with unusual warmth and the other apprentices clasped his hand and slapped him on the shoulder. Only Esther, inexplicably, would not even meet his eyes, and soon afterwards went upstairs. She was not standing there with the others in the doorway to see him ride away. He glanced up hoping to see her face at the window, but only blank glass shone back at him.

He pushed back the hurt, telling himself that it was only right that she should be obedient to her father. He had himself done wrong in accepting the encouragement she had lately offered him. Now, with his thoughts set on higher things, he must put her behind him.

They rode through cheering crowds to the beat of drums and the high piping of fifes, out of the city and into the wet summer countryside, where the air was sweet and fragrant and the city lads exclaimed in wonder at cows grazing in the wide green fields. Walter and his new comrades were posted in the van of the army, watchful for any threat, though they knew they need expect none so near the capital. This at least was friendly territory, and in every hamlet and village women and children and old men came running to wave and cheer, and cry, 'God bless you, lads!'

After a time, he found himself riding beside Corporal Revol, who had already begun to single him out. He knew that Samuel Revol was the grandson of a French Calvinist silk weaver who, in the last century, had moved his business from Lyon to the more congenial atmosphere of Elizabethan London, where he had prospered. Samuel had more education than Walter, and his family was wealthy, but they were of the same age and had already found that they thought alike on many subjects. 'Do you think it's true the King means to make a truce with the Irish rebels?' Walter asked him.

'Why else would my Lord Ormonde turn out every friend of Parliament from the council in Dublin?' The Protestant Marquis of Ormonde, of an ancient Norman–Irish family some of whom were themselves among the rebels, had been appointed Lieutenant-General in Ireland by the King. 'You see – there'll be a truce, then they'll start sending Papist Irish soldiers to fight for the King.'

And the King was already everywhere victorious, or almost everywhere. Walter tried not to think what it might mean for them all if this was how it ended. They had to trust that the Lord would prevail. He clutched at one recent piece of good news. 'By then maybe we'll have the Scots fighting with us.'

'Aye – but I'm uneasy that they'd have us take the Covenant first.'

To Master Reynolds, the Scots insistence that – in return for their help – every Englishman should take the Covenant, had been perhaps the most attractive aspect of the agreement. 'Why should you mind that?'

'Because it would bind us to their Presbyterian way. It would allow no room for Independency.' That, at least, confirmed Walter's suspicion that the corporal belonged to one of the sects which believed that every congregation should be free (within due limits, of course) to worship as it chose, without outside direction. 'I don't care for shackles on my conscience,' Samuel added.

'Sir Henry Vane's of the same mind, and Parliament sent him to make terms with the Scots.'

'Aye. That gives me hope that there'll be some form of words found to suit both sides.'

'Then you don't think it a danger to leave men's consciences free?'

After that, they became absorbed in a passionate discussion of their beliefs, at the end of which Walter found that, whatever he thought at the outset, he agreed with everything the corporal said. It was as if, through the other young man, he himself had found a voice. It was his own thoughts, his own hopes and fears, he heard from Samuel's mouth, more eloquently expressed, with more passion. He had known friendship before, others he could laugh with, drink with, wrestle with, even riot with, who were his own kind. But never before had he felt this sense of a mind reaching out to his, in harmony with his own. By the end of the day's march the two of them were talking together as if they had known one another all their lives.

They halted that first night on Hounslow Heath, the quartermaster finding lodgings for them in the little villages round about. Walter was just seeing to his horse, looking forward with a sense of excitement to the forthcoming gathering about the camp-fire at which he would further his new friendship, when he heard a woman's voice behind him. 'Walter!'

He thought, in a bemused way, that the voice sounded amazingly like Esther's, which of course it could not be. He looked round.

It could not be, yet it was: Esther, standing there in the doorway, with a tender, mischievous smile on her face. Walter stared at her in disbelief. She said, 'Aren't you pleased to see me, Walter?'

'What are you doing here? How did you get here?'

'I rode with the baggage. How else?' She came and linked her arm through his, coaxing him to smile. 'I couldn't stay at home without you.'

He felt his heart thud. Just yesterday all his dreams and hopes would have been held in those words. Now he did not know what he felt, except that he was bewildered. This morning he had left her behind and even put her entirely from his thoughts, knowing it was right to do so. Seeing her here now was all wrong, out of place. 'You can't – your father—'

'He'll come round, when we're married.'

'Married!'

'There's a minister somewhere isn't there? What's to stop us marrying?'

'Your father,' he said again.

'He's not here. Walter, you want to marry me don't you?'

'Of course!' His voice sounded strange; but then everything was strange, even unreal. 'But . . .' But what? He had no idea.

She slid her arms about his neck. He felt his body respond to her, but not as it would have done this morning, if she had kissed him goodbye. He felt a sense of panic. Perhaps this was all a dream. 'Trooper Barras—'

He looked round; and, pink with dismay and embarrassment, saw Corporal Revol coming towards them. Walter pulled off his hat and pushed Esther away. 'Sir!' Then he stammered out some kind of explanation, all the time conscious, with growing misery, of the chilly disapproval on Samuel's face. He understood it, for he too felt how much at odds all this was with the eager talk they had shared on their ride here today. He heard himself end, 'We want to be wed, you see.' Then he faltered into silence.

In a kind of dream he found himself brought before their Captain, a coarse, hard-drinking man who was clearly irritated by the interruption, but went so far as to ask them a few bored questions. Then, somehow, after a disturbingly short time, they were being married, in the very same church where many of the soldiers were quartered that night. Afterwards, there was a good deal of noisy drinking (to Walter's painful disappointment Corporal Revol was nowhere to be seen while that was going on) and then the quartermaster, with a lascivious eagerness, found them a room in the church tower where they could spend their wedding night.

Walter's new comrades saw them noisily bedded and then left them alone.

As far as bodily satisfaction went, it was all Walter could have asked for. Esther was his heart's desire. He had never wanted anyone but her. Yet, much later, lying awake in the small hours of the morning beside the warm sleeping body of his new wife, he found himself wishing it had not happened quite like this. He wished they could somehow have had her father's approval, and been married at some more suitable time, while his thoughts were not all on the coming campaign. It was unfair, perhaps, but he felt almost as if he had been pushed into marriage, not quite against his will, but before he was fully ready or had taken time to consider the consequences. Worst of all, it was a poor way to repay William Reynolds for all his years of kindness. Walter could only hope that they would be forgiven for it. He resolved that he would write to his master first thing tomorrow, in the most penitent and humble terms, so that everything would quickly be put right.

Asked a month ago what he most desired in life he would have said: to go and fight for Parliament, and to marry Esther. Now he had both those things and yet he felt something very much less than unalloyed happiness. It was strange, he reflected sadly, that the fulfilment of dreams should be so disappointing a thing.

CHAPTER FIFTEEN

'She's a born soldier's wife,' Trooper Stephens had said last night. They had been sitting in the drenching rain huddled over a sputtering camp-fire while Esther Barras served them all a meal whose savouriness was astonishing considering the scarcity of any but the most basic ingredients.

Walter had to acknowledge that Amias was right, in a way. Esther cared for him devotedly, washing and mending his clothes, cooking for him, seeking out the best food when they halted for the night. Her practical attentions lessened the discomforts of the long march in almost every way. What was more, she never complained, was unfailingly cheerful and was always ready to share a joke with everyone, sometimes of a kind that startled Walter, who was fast learning that Esther was not quite the simple and godly girl he had thought her to be. In fact, she soon made it plain that prayers and readings from the Bible and long sermons bored her intensely. 'I thought I'd got away from all that,' she said, when Walter remonstrated with her for lying in bed late one Sunday morning, missing a particularly fine sermon. She no longer seemed interested when he tried, as he still did now and then, to talk to her about the things that mattered most to him. An uneasy suspicion began to awaken in his mind that she had run after him not because she loved him, but as an escape from the tedium of life in her father's house.

Yet he had no reason to doubt her love. She was passionate in bed, tender whenever they were together, in fact seemed to hate being apart from him. As soon as the army halted for the night, she would be there at his side, cheerful and busy and full of concern for his needs. When, in the evenings, he sat among his comrades, she was there too, snuggled against him. Amias and Roger and the others welcomed her warmly, obviously appreciating her company, but her presence changed everything. There were things never talked of now, because Esther was one of the party, and also because the soldiers who sought refuge at his camp-fire were those who liked Esther rather than Walter; or Esther and Walter together, rather than the Walter he had begun to know a little on the first hours of the journey from London.

He noticed painfully that Samuel Revol no longer sought him out. He knew that he had disappointed his new friend, before ever their friendship had been allowed to develop, by showing that at this time when his heart should be set on God's work alone, he had given himself over to carnal things. Esther had not helped matters by openly refusing to take part in the gatherings for prayer and Bible reading that Samuel, troubled by the scarcity of chaplains, organised at some point each day. Since several of the other camp followers came, her refusal looked the more pointed. Walter did consider confiding in Samuel, telling him what precisely were his feelings for Esther, how it had come about that he had suddenly found himself married to her. But when he thought about it, that seemed disloyal to Esther, who was – for good or ill – his wife, and in any case he was not sure what his feelings really were, or how to put them into words; and he feared that Samuel would only despise him the more for them anyway.

The day after the wedding he had written to Master Reynolds, telling him that they were married, expressing all the gratitude he ought to feel towards his master – did feel, most strongly – and his penitence for the hurt they had caused him. He did not yield to the temptation to claim that it had all been Esther's doing. He had accepted what she offered and must take the consequences. He simply said that he was deeply sorry for his betrayal of his master's trust in him, that he loved Esther and that he would care for her as her father would wish her to be cared for.

They were a day's march from Gloucester when the answer reached him. It was harsh even beyond Walter's anxious expectations. *Walter Barras, your offence is beyond forgiveness. I thought you next to a son. Now I have neither son nor daughter. God will judge you both for what you have done.*

Trembling, Walter had read it to Esther. He thought it was as if God Himself had penned it, marking him out, only too clearly, for damnation. Esther simply took the letter, read it again herself, and then shrugged. 'He'll get over it,' she said carelessly. 'I'll write to him some time.' Walter wished he could look on the whole matter so calmly.

So it was that the glory of their coming to Gloucester, with the King's forces melting away like dew in the sunlight, was overcast for him by all kinds of unease. Not that there was any sunlight anyway, except in a metaphorical sense. It was raining as much as ever, so that the wide Severn valley looked grey and featureless, the roofs of Gloucester, the tower of its great cathedral, mere darker shapes in a gloom deepened by smoke hanging close to the city walls. They feared the worst, but as they moved nearer saw that the muddy wasteland near the walls was deserted, the only living things on it the fires burning in the heaps of refuse, their flames brave points of saffron and orange in the wet September morning.

They were welcomed in Gloucester as heroes and saviours, but even for those without Walter's troubles the sense of triumph was not as great as it might have been. They had done, magnificently, what they had set out to do. Gloucester was safe, reinforced with men and supplies. But they were all of them exhausted by the long march in appalling weather, and the relieved city had little in the way of material comforts to offer them, after so long under siege. 'Home, that's what I want,' said Amias Stephens that evening, as they sat in a smoky, crowded inn parlour, drinking sour ale. 'We've saved Gloucester. Now let's go back to London.'

There was a general growl of agreement from those around him, in which Walter did not join. He had no wish at all to go back to London, for there was no home for him there any more. He took another great mouthful of ale, trying somehow to quench the sudden sense of desolation. Esther had not said anything either, but she simply looked sleepily contented. He suspected that her thoughts were already on bed.

'*If* we can get back to London,' said Roger Tyler, whose natural pessimism was always made worse by drink. 'If the Cavaliers let us.'

'They've gone,' Amias reminded him. 'Scared off.'

'Scared off? Prince Rupert? If you believe that, you'll believe anything. Hasn't it crossed your mind it's just tactics? All they've got to do now is swing round and cut us off. Then we'll never get home.'

There was a moment of silence at that, before Amias dismissed it with a rather forced confidence. 'They tried that at Edgehill. It didn't work.'

Walter remembered the fear in London as the enemy had marched towards the city, the hours of waiting at Turnham Green. He wondered if anyone else was remembering how near they had come then to disaster. They might not be so fortunate another time. 'God's on our side, or we wouldn't be here now,' he said, but only because it seemed the right thing to say. After reading Abel Reynolds's letter, he was no longer very sure about God, at least in relation to himself.

Two days later they set out on the return journey to London, first marching north to Tewkesbury. Walter was more than ever conscious of the importance of the part he and his comrades played, always patrolling ahead of the army, or where it was most vulnerable, watchful for enemy movements; or, when they halted, foraging for food. They knew that the King's army was straddled across the roads by which they had come to Gloucester – whether or no they had been scared off by the Roundheads, the Royalists were certainly, now, making every effort to cut them off from London. After Tewkesbury, it was north again to Upton. But there, orders suddenly came to turn round and march back south, towards Cheltenham. 'You see, old Robin's got more sense than you gave him credit for,' Amias said to Roger, who the previous evening had cast doubts on the tactical skills of the Earl of Essex. 'We're keeping them guessing. There's one thing, their scouts aren't as good as ours.'

'Course not,' said Walter. 'They haven't got us.'

From Cheltenham, they marched on to Cirencester, where they took welcome food and ammunition, stored there by the Royalists.

'They're saying Exeter's fallen,' Roger Tyler said gloomily the following Monday morning, as he rode beside Walter in a south-easterly direction over the windswept, rain-washed uplands of Aldbourne Chase. From time to time, looking across the plain to their right, they could see the long slow lines of their army, cavalry some way off in the van, behind them the gloomy, mud-bespattered ranks of the infantry, burdened with pike and musket and knapsack, and then the lumbering artillery, which had constantly to be pulled and dragged and pushed out of the mud in which it had become embedded. Behind the guns straggled cattle and sheep, driven along to provide sustenance for the army in what had been relentlessly hostile countryside (though tomorrow that would change) and behind them again the baggage wagons, in one of which Esther was riding. Another detachment of cavalry, sometimes just visible, brought up the rear. Walter was very thankful to be on horseback, mobile and clear of the mud, as the men in the slow marching ranks were not.

Corporal Revol was a little way ahead of them and Amias applied to him for confirmation of the bad news. 'It's true, and Barnstaple and Bideford too,' said the Corporal. 'But remember the psalm, Trooper Tyler: "I have seen the wicked in great power and spreading himself like a green bay tree. But the Lord shall help his people and deliver them, because they trust in him."' His eyes shone as he spoke and Walter felt his spirits rise.

'They're saying too that the King's made peace with the Irish,' Roger said, unconsoled.

'If he has, it will avail him nothing,' said Samuel with confidence. 'The wicked is snared in the work of his own hands and he shall come to a bloody end.' He began to lead them in the singing of a psalm, which they followed rather half-heartedly.

> With glory and with honour now
> Let all his saints rejoice:
> Aloud upon their beds also . . .

'Wish I was upon my bed,' muttered Roger, and Walter hoped the Corporal did not see his answering grin, of which he was a little ashamed. He wanted rather to associate himself with Samuel than with Trooper Tyler.

'Never fear, Roger,' said the Corporal, more tolerantly than they expected. 'We'll be safe in Newbury tonight. Once there, we're as good as home.'

But later that day Prince Rupert's cavalry made a swift glancing attack on their own lumbering forces. It did little damage, but forced them off course, so that by nightfall they had only reached Hungerford, nine miles from Newbury.

The next night the Parliamentary quartermasters at last rode into Newbury to chalk up quarters for their men; and found that the Royalists had got there before them. The way to London was barred. That meant, they all knew, that there would be a battle tomorrow. It also meant that they had to camp in the cold and wet of the open fields, with little to eat or drink. For once Walter was glad of Esther's warm body in his arms, and the forgetfulness that their lovemaking brought.

Next morning, in the shivering dawn light, they saw the slope of the down stretching away from them towards Newbury, and knew that just out of sight the enemy waited. 'Not cavalry country this,' Corporal Revol observed. 'Look at all those little fields, and the hedges – even Prince Rupert can't charge through them. This is like Turnham Green.'

Except, Walter thought, that at Turnham Green they had been at the top of the slope, holding the ground. 'Do you think they won't fight then?'

'Oh, they'll fight, now they're there. But the Lord will destroy them, just wait and see.' Samuel sounded exultant.

There was no breakfast, for they had no food left. They were ordered to pull sprigs of greenery from the hedgerows to put in their hatbands, so they might recognise their own side in the fight. Samuel offered a lengthy prayer, for courage and victory, and then, more practically, brought out a leather flask of brandy which he passed round those nearest to him. That was the last thing Walter remembered clearly about the day of his first battle.

He had often imagined what it would be like, expecting it to be all fierce charges and courage and heroism. In the end, it was not like that at all. It was a day of confused impressions: rain, mud, terror, the screaming of men and horses, the roar of guns, a hard scramble up a slippery, muddy hillside; of long hours crouched behind a hedge firing and firing into the rain and the smoke, and the savage joy of seeing an enemy horse rear at his musket shot and throw its rider into his path, where a sword thrust finished him; of seeing men twist and writhe in their saddles, as his shots went home; of seeing rider after rider felled by a deadly fire from either side of a deep lane, along whose hedges dragoons and musketeers were ranged, until the bodies of the dead lay so thick they raised the level of the lane. He saw limbs torn off, blood and guts spilled on the ground, horses trampling the wounded and dying under their great hooves, a musketeer using his weapon as a club to beat off a half-maddened Cavalier with a face sheathed in blood; things that he thought would be seared in his memory for ever. Once, he was certain he saw Lord Milburn, without hat or helmet, just a foot or two away from him, and he levelled his musket and fired. The next moment, smoke hid his enemy and he did not know if he had hit him or not.

By dusk there was no joy, no satisfaction that they had held their own and even moved forward. There was only exhaustion, a jaw aching from teeth clenched too tight, arms and shoulders aching from constant loading and firing, everything aching from the damp and the cold. Amias, who had spent most of the day behind their lines, holding their horses, said, 'Have you noticed, their guns aren't answering one shot in three? Haven't done for an hour or more now, I'd say.'

'Out of powder maybe,' said Walter.

It was soon afterwards, as darkness fell, that all fighting stopped. They lay that night where they had fought, and the next morning woke to find that the King's army had slipped away while they slept. 'Was that a victory?' Walter asked Samuel, who had come to stand beside him, looking over the ugly debris of the battlefield. There were many bodies, most stripped by now of any personal belongings, but nearly all lay where the Cavaliers had fought most hotly, and Walter could see few green sprigs to match those that were already withering in their own hatbands.

'It was not a defeat,' said Samuel, 'and the way's clear to London. Praise ye the Lord!'

Chapter Sixteen

'I met Sir Ralph Liddell this afternoon,' Ludovick told Rob as they sat at supper in their attic lodging in Oxford.

'Oh, aye. What's he doing here?'

'Come for the Council, sent by my Lord Newcastle.'

'You didn't ask him to sup with you then?'

'He declined,' said Ludovick curtly.

He had been walking along the High, his mind on a song he had been setting to music, so that he had almost collided with Sir Ralph before he saw who it was. Both men had then come to a complete halt, immobilised by a thorough confusion of emotion. For a moment Ludovick had thought he saw, reflected in the other face, his own immense sense of pleasure at this sudden meeting. Then the beginning of a smile had been abruptly ended and the kindly mouth had set into the stern lines that were so uncharacteristic of it. Ludovick recognised that he had himself, just for that moment, thought that everything could suddenly be as it once was. The realisation of his mistake had hurt terribly. He had been about to say something, but then could not remember what it was and stood in silence, helpless.

Sir Ralph's hand had gone to his hat, as if to remove it, and had then stopped at the brim and fallen again. Presumably he had decided that deference was not after all due to a condemned traitor. 'My lord,' he had said stiffly. 'I did not think to see you here.'

'Nor I you, sir,' Ludovick had replied, trying to force some lightness into his voice, which had failed to function properly. 'May I ask what brings you here?'

'I come to represent my Lord of Newcastle at the Council of

War.' Sir Ralph had spoken brusquely, as if to make it clear that in answering the enquiry he was not in any sense admitting Ludovick to any part of their former intimacy. To underline the point he had added in reproachful tones, 'Your presence here does His Majesty's cause no good at all.'

'Perhaps that's for His Majesty to judge.'

There had been another awkward silence, growing by the minute. Ludovick had heard himself break into it, without quite knowing what he was saying. 'I'm lodged in St Aldate's, above the baker's just across from Christ Church. If you've a mind for music, sir, come and sup with me tonight.' He had wished the words unsaid almost at once, for he knew he had laid himself open to an inevitable rebuff. Things were quite bad enough without that.

Sir Ralph had made the faintest of bows. 'I must beg leave to decline, my lord. You know the reason well enough.' Then he had gone on his way. Ludovick had watched until he was out of sight and had then tried to remember where he himself had been going and why. By now the song had abandoned him completely and, since he could think of nothing better to do, he had gone back to his lodgings, where he still was.

'What do you think the Council will do?' Rob asked next, evidently deciding that the subject of Sir Ralph was best left alone.

'Listen to the Prince this time, I should hope,' said Ludovick. 'If they'd done that before we'd have taken Gloucester before Essex left London.'

'And we'd not have fought at Newbury. That's what they said anyway, that the Prince wanted to wait for the ammunition to come up.' There was a little silence. Newbury, if not precisely a defeat, had exacted a terrible price from the Cavaliers, who had lost many of their best officers and men, including Lord Falkland, whose quiet, moderating presence in the King's councils had been replaced by that of the ebullient and charming Lord Digby, one of Rupert's most lethal enemies. Ludovick's fellow lodger throughout the winter, an officer in Sir John Byron's regiment, had also died there, though Ludovick had not liked him much and had no regrets at being left sole occupant of their hard narrow bed. He had himself received a slight flesh wound in the calf, not yet quite healed, but he knew he had been lucky (though a good pair of boots had been ruined in the process). Of his own troop, fourteen men had died, among them young Lieutenant Haynes and Jack

Robson, one of the Blackheugh men. 'What does he want this time then?' Rob asked.

'Our new Lord Byron to command in the north-west, that at least.' Sir John Byron had recently been created a baron, in recognition of his courage at Newbury and elsewhere; and the loyalty of his entire family, since his five younger brothers were also fighting for the King. 'Also, that proper preparations should be made to receive the soldiers from Ireland, when they land.'

'Will there be any of your kin with them?'

'The Confederates haven't agreed to send any men yet,' Ludovick pointed out.

'That's not what they're saying.'

'I know. But they're wrong. The troops coming over – here already, for all I know – are from the regiments who've been fighting the Confederates. Good veteran soldiers,' he concluded, with heavy irony; though it was true enough, in its way.

'Ah, then you'll not be looking to them to make up your numbers.'

'I don't suppose they'll be looking to serve under me either.' Ludovick emptied his glass, then said, 'There's another piece of news I heard today: Sir Thomas Fairfax has got out of Hull. He's across the Humber, with a small cavalry force.'

'He can't do much damage with that.'

'Put him with what the Eastern Association already has, and there could be trouble. He may not be much talked of here, but he's a fine soldier. Still, with luck that'll mean we won't have to sit around in Oxford for long.' Ludovick pushed his scarcely touched plate from him and refilled his glass from the second of the three bottles of good claret Rob had unearthed from somewhere, with his usual unerring instinct for such things. 'Did you say you were off out with Toby Milburn tonight?'

'Aye. Unless you want me to stay.'

He knew that Rob had sensed his mood and was concerned about him. Indeed, he would dearly have liked the other man to stay, for he was afraid of his own company. When he had time on his hands he was only too easily tipped over into depression, and the meeting with Ralph today had already pushed him very near the edge. He knew that, once Rob was among his friends, he would very probably stay out until dawn, and Ludovick dreaded the long night hours most of all.

But he said none of this and Rob left shortly afterwards, supplied with a pass to allow him out after curfew. Ludovick could have gone to seek company of a kind at Merton College, where the Queen had her little court. He had begun an affair with one of her ladies last winter, picking up the threads again whenever he was in Oxford. But he was in no mood for the backbiting and affectation of the court, nor for sexual dalliance, come to that.

The only other way he knew of keeping the ghosts at bay was to get drunk, so he set out to do so, methodically. He had not in fact been drinking for very long when he heard someone coming up the stairs and thought, until the knock came, that it must be Rob, returning early.

It was Sir Ralph, standing rather awkwardly in the doorway. The light of Ludovick's single candle showed that he no longer looked stern, simply embarrassed and unsure of himself. 'Nothing much to do,' he muttered. 'Thought I'd take up your offer after all.'

Ludovick felt as if a great wave of relief and joy had broken over him. He held the door wide, ushered Ralph in, rushed round lighting candles, found music and a viol and a lute, and an extra glass, though he was unfortunately well on his way through the third bottle of wine by now. Ralph stood just inside the door, watching him. 'I should not like you to misunderstand, my lord. As far as my family is concerned, nothing has changed. But you and I – well, we find ourselves in this together. Let's put the past behind us while it lasts.'

After that, having made his position clear, he relaxed and came to look at the music Ludovick had put on the table.

When Rob came back in the early hours of the morning he found the two men engaged in an exuberant performance of William Lawes' song, *The Cats*, as harmoniously as if there had never been any rift between them.

CHAPTER SEVENTEEN

Autumn gave way to winter, a bitter cold winter with heavy snowfalls that turned in the London streets to deep mud-coloured slush, alternately freezing and melting again, each time creating more havoc. Food and fuel in this time of war were both short, and the most careful housewives set out while it was still fully dark to take their pick of the meagre supplies the city's markets offered. Cecily Reynolds, wife of Abel Reynolds, saddler, was an especially careful housewife, and even on this cheerless early December morning she was making her way home with a full basket well before most people were out of bed.

The talk in the markets today had all been of the death of John Pym. Even to Cecily, who had no great interest in political matters, the loss of so great a name meant something, though she was not sure what. His had been the guiding hand in Parliament since well before there was any thought of war. It was he who had kept all the different factions together through the past difficult months, and revived the courage of his quarrelsome colleagues whenever their spirits flagged. If anyone could be said to direct the war, it was not the Generals – the Earls of Essex and Manchester, Lord Fairfax, Sir William Waller – but John Pym. Without him, Cecily suspected, there might have been no war at all. Without him, once war had begun, things would certainly have gone even more badly for Parliament than they already had. Now he had died, they could only get worse. Perhaps, thought Cecily, suddenly hopeful, the war would be over soon.

She hated the war. If it wasn't for the war, everything would still be as it once had been: food on the table, good fires to sit by, the apprentices meekly at work, Walter now a journeyman, perhaps, using his skills to help his master's business; and she, Cecily Reynolds, would still have a daughter.

'We are childless, wife,' Abel had told her, as soon as he had read the fatal note from Walter, announcing his marriage to Esther. 'Let her name never be spoken in this house again.' And that was that. Cecily knew quite well that once his mind was made up, Abel was immovable, a man of unbending principle. Esther had defied his authority as no daughter should, so Esther had ceased to exist. Cecily knew he would never forgive her, nor Walter either, who had so gravely led her astray.

All the years of motherhood had been wiped out in the space of a few words. Her beloved Esther, the one surviving child of the seven she had brought so painfully into the world, was as dead as all the rest of them. But if Abel found it easy to accept, Cecily did not. Not once did she complain of his decision – it was just, she supposed, and besides a good wife did not question her husband's authority. But in her heart she questioned it all the time. She harboured thoughts that would have shocked Abel. She blamed the war, and those who had led them into it, not the Royalists, but the men who had so fatefully raised their hands against their King – after all, she thought, if you can defy the King, then are you not entitled to defy any authority? Not that she said so to Abel, of course. She blamed Walter too, naturally. And she blamed the Papists. She remembered, as her husband apparently did not, that Walter had been raised a Papist. The godliness they had seen in him had clearly been just a veneer, now stripped away. Papists sought to undermine order and authority, and how more surely to do it than by turning children against their fathers, by destroying an entire family?

So she was thinking no kindly thoughts – of John Pym or anyone else – as she turned the corner into their street. It was then that she glimpsed, some way ahead, a gleam of apricot-gold hair, bright in the grey early light. She quickened her step. Only Miles Wood had hair that colour. The young man had moved into an attic room in the house next door some time in the summer, and soon after his arrival she had found herself walking beside him in the street and they had somehow got into conversation. She had warmed to him at once. Of course, he was a fine-looking young man, not tall, but well made and graceful, with the most wonderful blue eyes. She might be old enough to be his mother, but she could still feel the attraction. More than that, though, he was an excellent and sympathetic listener, who somehow made her feel that anything she said would be safe with him, and that he would understand, without condemning. They had met and talked, out there in the street, several times since that first encounter, and by now he knew all about Esther and Walter and even about her unwifely feelings in the matter. On the other hand, Cecily knew nothing at all about him.

One of her neighbours had told her he was a charitable young man, much given to succouring the poor and needy, but no one seemed to know what trade he followed, if any. He was, apparently, single, and he had not mentioned a sweetheart, though since he almost never spoke of himself that meant little. Cecily had only his surface appearance to judge him by. He dressed simply, in plain dark clothes without lace or other adornment, and his hair reached only to the nape of his long graceful neck. He wore no jewellery, no ring on his finger, and his hat was plain, with a modest brim, as sober as the cloak he wore today against the cold. She supposed, from the way he dressed, that he had similar religious principles to their own, though she had never seen him in church on Sunday. Perhaps he belonged to one of the gathered churches that met – contrary to the law, but tolerated in these times – in certain parishes where the minister was sympathetic to them or even in private houses. But when she tried to ask him, he carefully evaded the question and turned the conversation back to her. She had never known anyone able to give such a sense of warmth and approachability while yet being so secret about himself.

She had almost reached him when he suddenly looked round and saw her – and then, to her surprise, quickened his pace, away from her. She saw then that there was a small boy hurrying along beside him, a grubby urchin. She moved faster herself, eager to reach him, and once more he gathered speed, this time apparently urging the boy to hurry too. Cecily felt both hurt and intrigued. She was suddenly eaten up with curiosity to know where he was going and why, to find out something definite about him at last. She continued to follow him, past her own house and on up the street, conscious that now and then he glanced round to see if she was still there. She had begun to think she was gaining on him at last when he suddenly grabbed the boy's hand and dived into an alley and was lost to sight. She ran to the alley, but though she walked its whole length and peered out into the street beyond, Miles Wood was nowhere to be seen.

Cecily turned round and retraced her steps; and as she stepped back into her own familiar street, suddenly spotted him, far ahead, slipping quickly into the door of a house on the other side, the boy at his heels. They must have looped round somehow, coming back into the street some way ahead and approaching the house from the opposite direction. Common sense told her to give up and go home. The whole exercise was more than a little pointless. But that last move of his, going to such great lengths to escape from her, intrigued her more than ever. It was almost as if he was afraid of her, yet what possible reason could he have for that? Quite clearly Miles Wood had something to hide. A woman, perhaps?

Telling herself that people with something to hide were up to no good and should be watched, she went towards the house. It was half-timbered and gabled and in a state of dangerous disrepair, not at all the sort of building for a tender rendezvous. With a sense of excitement, tempered by nervousness, Cecily pushed open the door. Inside was a narrow stinking stair, so she went up it, very softly, listening every step of the way. She thought, after a time, that she could hear voices from somewhere above, falling away to a gentle murmur. She came to a door, which was firmly closed. But it was made of poor wood, which had warped badly, and she found that at one side she could, by putting her eye to the gap, gain a clear view of the room beyond.

She was not quite sure what she had expected, but it was certainly not what she saw. There was a low bed, covered with badly soiled linen, on which lay an old woman, who was clearly very sick. Beside her, bending over her, was Miles Wood. She thought at first from the authoritative yet gentle way in which he moved that he must be a physician, though why that should be such a secret she could not imagine. Then she looked again. She saw him take something from a small container hung on a thong about his neck and then with his thumb make the sign of the cross on the eyelids of the sick woman, and afterwards on her ears and nose and lips. All the while he murmured soft words, which Cecily could not make out.

Then she knew why she could not make them out. It was not because she was some distance away or the other side of a closed door. It was because they were in Latin. Everything suddenly fell into place. Miles Wood was a Papist priest, performing his superstitious mumbo jumbo over a poor dying woman.

Shocked, Cecily leant back against the wall behind her, trying to gather her thoughts. Oddly, unreasonably, she felt terribly hurt, as if the young man had somehow betrayed her, as surely as Walter and Esther had done. She had thought him so attractive, so kind. So much, she thought, for trusting him with her fears and hopes and allowing him to offer sympathy for her despair! If he was attentive and sympathetic, that was because he sought deliberately, with forethought, to get her into his power and win her over to his corrupt faith.

She made her way softly back down the stairs and told herself that she should have known better than to confide in him. After all, if you could not trust those you loved the most, who in all the world could you trust?

1644

CHAPTER EIGHTEEN

Walking away from the market with a full basket on her arm, Susannah had felt full of hope, invigorated by a sense that the dark tedium of the winter might at last be almost over. The wind was strong, but it blew from the west and had a softness in it that she had not felt for a very long time.

Then she came to the house and pushed open the door and felt the weight settle again over her spirits. For what real difference could a change in the weather make to the condition of her life? Today, suddenly, the air was full of the sounds of water, of rushing burns swelled by melting snow and little streams freshly sprung to run down the ruts in the roads, and a steady drip, drip from trees and eaves of houses and byres. But that altered nothing, except to make her think of spring and new life, as everyone did at this time of year, taken by surprise by the realisation that winter – even one so hard as this – did not after all go on for ever.

But her father was still infirm and would never ride again to tend his patients. The long months of illness had left him, at fifty-five, an old man. He who had always been indefatigable was now content to sit at the fireside and read for hours on end, or talk over what he had read with his daughter. What activity he still enjoyed was all in his mind.

Susannah knew well enough what he had gone through. She had tended him with all the skill at her command, helped when necessary by the best surgeons she could call upon, and he had made a much better recovery than she had feared at one time. At first, it had been a miracle that he had lived at all, through days of agonising jolting over rough roads after the Royalists released them;

then, once home, that he had survived the amputation of his leg and the long weeks of fever that had followed; then, that he had gradually regained his strength, if with many setbacks, and learned at last, with the aid of a stick and a wooden leg, to hobble painfully about the place again.

It was only then, when she knew he would live and even be able to lead something approaching a normal life, that Susannah had begun to feel the sense of impatience and frustration that had chafed her through the winter months. She remembered how this time last year they had ridden through snow to minister to the army, giving all their energies to the supremely important work to which God had called them. This winter, Susannah had learned, reluctantly, to face the truth that she would never again ride anywhere with her father, because his doctoring days were over. He was, of course, still capable of making a diagnosis, should a patient call on him, but he no longer seemed to wish to do so. The theory of medicine interested him as much as ever, but not the practice to which he had given so great a part of his life. All this had brought home to her, as nothing else could, how much her ability to do what she was called to do had depended upon him.

Now, when people were sick or brought to bed with a child they turned to other surgeons or physicians, or to Margery Nelson, the midwife. No one thought of Susannah, partly perhaps because they assumed that she was still fully occupied with the care of her father. But she suspected, too, that they had seen her simply as her father's daughter, an efficient assistant but nothing more. They did not seem to know, as she did, that her knowledge and her skills were now, after years of his tuition, as great as his, or almost as great. Even Richard's sister could see no better role for her than as a kind of Dame Alice, charitably ministering to her husband's tenants, when her other duties allowed.

As if to rub it in there was the letter from Aunt Judith that Seth Atkinson the carrier had given to her at market today. Doubtless it would contain yet more strictures as to how Susannah ought to be married by now, how at nearly twenty-three she was almost past marriageable age. She was even beginning to wonder herself if marriage to a man like Richard might not be the answer after all. The example of Dame Alice came to mind again. She was running Richard's property for him, single-handedly, in his absence, and doing so with vigour and efficiency. She had learned to load and fire a gun and had trained every member of her household to do the same. During the past months they had repelled a number of unwelcome visits from marauding Royalists, riding out from garrisons at Castle Bolton or Middleham or Skipton to lay their hands on the considerable resources of Thornside Hall. What was more, rents and other dues were paid on time, for the most part, and then sent on to her son for his use. No steward could have done more.

Yet purposeful though Dame Alice's life might be, it was not the kind of life to which Susannah had been so sure that she was called. The trouble was that she had believed she was called to follow in her father's footsteps, as he had followed in his father's; but he was a physician, and that was something no woman could ever be, at least in a fully legal sense. Now she began to ask herself if her conviction about her calling might have been wrong all along. If Richard had been at home at the moment she might have been tempted to seek him out and test her feelings for him. She liked and respected him. But did that mean she could bear to subject herself to him and give birth to his children in return for the opportunity to continue in a small way to do what she had been so sure must be the pivot of her life? She did not know, and in any case she could not put it to the test, for Richard was in Cheshire now, as the news reaching them today had emphasised, and it was unlikely he would have time to come home for the foreseeable future. There had been no respite in the war this winter.

She stepped into the house, changed her clothes and went to where she knew she would find her father, by the parlour fire, reading, though with some difficulty because the light was bad, the clear cold light of the snowy days having given way overnight to cloud.

'News of a great victory in Cheshire, father,' said Susannah cheerfully. 'They're all talking of it.'

'Hmm?' said her father, with the vagueness that seemed to have come on him since his illness. 'Cheshire? I thought our men were in the east somewhere –Lincolnshire. Fighting with the Eastern Association.'

'So they were, last autumn. But you remember Sir Thomas was sent to the relief of Nantwich.'

'Yes, I remember now. There was that dreadful business on Christmas Day.' Master Johnson had preached in a high fury against Lord Byron's army, which, in the course of its triumphant progress through the north-west, had stopped to smoke innocent villagers out of their church and then murder them in cold blood, having first promised them safety. Matthew shook his head. 'It is what we most feared, Irish savagery brought to England. God keep us from greater ills!'

'He has done it, father: Nantwich is still ours, for Sir Thomas got there in time. And not only that – he routed Lord Byron's army, the Irish with it. God has revenged the blood of his people.' She began to describe the details of the battle as she had heard them recounted in the market-place, and then she realised her father was not really listening. He liked to have news of the war, though too often it saddened him, but the intricacies of battle did not interest him, so long as those he knew were safe afterwards. Susannah gave up and resigned herself to enduring Aunt Judith's advice. 'There's a letter for you.'

He took it and unfolded it and read for a little time. Then he gave an exclamation. 'She's sick, Susannah!' He read on quickly, then said, 'I don't like the sound of it. You'd better see.'

It was nothing like Aunt Judith's usual bracing tone. True, she had some astringent observations on the competence of York physicians – and their high fees, in these times when every citizen was already forced to contribute hugely to the Royalist garrison. But it was obvious that she was depressed and frightened and in pain, though her account of her symptoms was confused in the extreme. One thing was clear, however: she wanted her brother to come to her aid, being convinced that he would be able to work a cure where others had apparently failed.

Susannah put down the letter and looked at her father, the thin, tired old man at the fireside, with his wooden leg and the stump that gave him pain even when he walked just a short distance. 'You can't go,' she said. 'Even if the weather was better you couldn't go.'

'Hmm. No, I don't think I can,' he agreed. The tone of quiet resignation was a measure of how much he had changed. He took the letter from her and read it again. 'What do you think – is she terrifying herself over a trifle, or is it, well . . .?'

'It might be some simple disorder of the digestion, but it's not like Aunt Judith to be so troubled. However, without seeing her, there's no telling. Father, do you think she would accept me in your place?'

For a moment his face brightened, and then he looked at her and shook his head. 'Do you think I'd let you ride to York alone in these times?'

'I won't go alone. John can go with me, if you can do without him for a few days. Or there may be someone travelling that way, if we ask around. Also, it's safer than it's been for a long time. The Scots are keeping my Lord of Newcastle busy in Northumberland. Our own friends are harassing the Royalists to the south. With all that on their minds no one's going to trouble his head about a lone woman riding to visit her sick aunt. So long as I get all the right passes before I go, there should be no difficulty. If I find there's nothing much wrong with her, I can simply return at once, with John.'

'And if there is?'

'Then I'll do what I can. If I need another opinion, you can tell me who to call in, so that she has the best care.'

'Hmm. There's Doctor Baty. I believe he's still there. But I can give you a list, and letters of introduction.' He looked at her thoughtfully. 'Yes, I think perhaps you're right. I shall miss my dear friend and daughter, but that is selfishness. I can afford to lend you to my sister for a little while. Whatever you find, the best thing would be to bring her back here, for a little country quiet.'

CHAPTER NINETEEN

'Right, gentlemen,' said Ludovick to the junior officers of his troop, whom he had summoned to meet him in a corner of Christ Church meadow. 'I have just this minute come from a meeting with His Highness. His orders are that we leave for Shrewsbury tomorrow.' There was a murmur of relief and pleasure. 'I want every one of you here with a full complement of men tomorrow morning, one hour before dawn – that's five o'clock, for those of you who've not seen much of the dawn these past weeks. Mass will be said before we leave. Anyone arriving late or in a state of unreadiness will lose a day's pay.'

He himself was glad that at last they were to leave Oxford, where they had been stationed since the autumn as part of the city's defences. It had been particularly frustrating to be confined here in March while Rupert carried out the dazzling feat of relieving Newark with virtually untrained troops. Knowing that he was useful to the Prince, as almost the only one of his supporters who was favoured in the Queen's circle, was of little consolation to Ludovick. He detested the intrigues and petty jealousies of which he had been obliged to become a part.

'My lord, one thing—?' That was Tot Charlton, one of the Blackheugh men.

'Well, Lieutenant?'

'Is it true York's under siege?'

There was a sudden silence, into which Ludovick said, 'We've no certain news. But since Selby fell, it's been expected, of course.'

Joined in Lancashire by the defeated remnants of Newark's besiegers, Sir Thomas Fairfax had marched swiftly into Yorkshire and stormed Selby, taking prisoner a large part of York's garrison, which had been stationed there.

'That's bad, my lord,' said Cornet Arthur Hoskins, an opinionated young Shropshire gentleman. 'Maybe His Highness should have stayed up north, once he'd saved Newark.'

Ludovick could see that Lieutenant Charlton, for whom the north began at the Tees, and Newark was almost as much the far south as Oxford, was about to say so, and put in quickly, 'His Highness had no troops adequate to the occasion. It was a miracle he did what he did. And that, gentlemen, is why we're bound for Shrewsbury: to raise and train new soldiers for His Majesty in the shortest possible time.'

He dismissed them then, though he lingered for a while afterwards to deal with a number of individual difficulties. By the time he left for his lodgings, Rob at his side, it was growing dark. 'You go ahead,' he said. 'Start making things ready. I'm away to take leave of my cousin.'

'You'd be better getting a good night's sleep, if we're to be up so early. You were awake again last night.' Ludovick said nothing, so Rob went on, 'What's on your mind, my lord?'

'Maybe I've had enough of Oxford,' said Ludovick with a shrug. 'With the Queen gone . . .' He left Rob to draw his own conclusions from that. Two weeks ago, just before Easter, the Queen, heavily pregnant, had been sent for safety to Exeter. Her ladies had gone with her, among them Ludovick's current mistress. He did not, in fact, miss her very much, but he was happy for Rob to think otherwise. He could not have begun to find words to describe what was really on his mind. A simple, everyday fear, such as, for instance, he might feel before battle – that he could have explained; but not the spasms of gut-wrenching horror that jolted him awake in the darkest hours of the night and shadowed all his days. They had lasted off and on for about two months now, though there had been intervals of calm, the last ending three days ago. The worst part of it was that he knew quite well where they came from, but could do nothing about it, except pray with a kind of desperation for Charles, whose terror it was, that its cause might be removed from him, the danger overcome.

Now he said, lightly, 'Once we're away from here I'll sleep soundly again, you'll see.' He made for a narrow alley, instinctively putting his hand to his sword hilt as he did so: Oxford was a dangerous place these days. 'I'll cut through here. Expect me back within the hour.'

'I'll believe that when I see it,' said Rob, being familiar with Shane O'Neill's loquacity.

Ludovick's cousin had arrived suddenly in Oxford a month ago, with a deputation from the Confederate Irish, who were seeking concessions from King Charles in return for military help. The conditions they laid down had been reasonable enough, at least in Shane's eyes: full toleration for the Catholic religion, the return of all lands filched from Irish landowners within the last ten years, a pardon for all acts committed during the rebellion. 'We hold most of Ireland,' Shane had pointed out, when Ludovick had expressed doubts about the demands. 'It's the least we could ask for.'

'Maybe, but the King's hands are tied. You don't know the hatred there is for the Irish here in England; I do. Last month a Roundhead leader hanged thirteen prisoners, on the simple grounds they were Irish – which they weren't, as it happened. But suspicion is enough.'

'That kind of thing's been happening in Ireland for years now.'

'At the hands of soldiers. But here the people back the soldiers, that's the worst of it. If the King gave you even a part of what you ask, a good many of those who are fighting for him now would leave his service, believe me.'

Tonight, as they parted, he urged his cousin: 'Make terms quickly. We need your help, and you need the King on your side. The concessions will come afterwards, if you're patient. I know what I'm talking about.'

He slept worse than ever that night, and passed the next day in a daze of exhaustion, which made it hard to concentrate on all that had to be done. Leaving Oxford behind seemed to make no difference at all to how he felt. At the end of the first day's march, during which it rained incessantly, they reached Kiddington, where he busied himself with the practical details of seeing his men to their quarters. And it was there, while he was closely occupied with the most mundane of matters, that Ludovick suddenly knew that his twin was no longer afraid. He himself was as tired as ever, but he felt calm, even serene, though for him serenity was a rare sensation.

His own quarters were cramped and damp and shared with another of Rupert's officers who had a thunderous snore, but when at last Ludovick went to bed he slept like a child, soundly, deeply, without stirring. Next morning, in the darkness before dawn, it took Rob some time to shake him into wakefulness, but the sense of peace that had been with him through the night lingered as the day's march began. He felt profoundly relieved. Whatever evil had hung over his brother for so long had somehow been removed from him.

They made a halt some time around nine o'clock in the morning, to rest the horses and deal with a baggage wagon that had shed a wheel. All was put to rights and they were on the point of moving off again, when a squabble flared up between Toby Milburn and another man, a confused matter in which several of the women were involved too. Rob, called in to help but unable to resolve things, went in search of Ludovick. He found him mounted and ready to leave, sitting absolutely still in the middle of the road. He had an odd expression, as if he were far removed from the bustle that was going on around him. His face was parchment-white. 'My lord?' said Rob, anxious.

Ludovick gave no sign that he had heard, but turned his horse aside and dismounted. Rob thought he said, 'I can't breathe.' He stood by the horse with his hands clutching the saddle, his head bent, shivering. There had been sickness among the soldiers in Oxford throughout the spring, a sudden griping pain in the guts, vomiting and the flux. It was rarely fatal and generally short-lived, but violent while it lasted, and it always attacked without warning. Until now, Ludovick had escaped. Rob went and laid a hand on his arm; and at that moment he gave a moan and slid unconscious to the ground.

He came round to find several anxious faces bent over him. Someone had undone his neckband and loosened the lacing of his buff coat. Rob supported his head and put a cup of something to his lips. He drank, and then sat up, slowly. 'I'll send word that you're sick, my lord,' said Lieutenant Charlton.

Ludovick put a hand on Rob's shoulder and pulled himself to his feet. 'I'm not sick,' he said. 'It's over.'

So it was. The terror of the past weeks, this morning's sense of suffocation and the unimaginable pain, all had gone, and he knew they would not come back again, ever. That brought him no sense of relief. In their place was not peace or tranquillity, but a howling void. He walked to his horse – which was grazing beside the road – and mounted and looked down at the troubled faces of his men. 'What are you waiting for? Don't you hear the trumpet? Get moving!' And then, alone as he had never been alone before, he urged his horse to the head of the column.

Cecily Reynolds was among the crowd that gathered at Tyburn to watch Father Charles Milburn suffer the long-drawn-out agonies of the punishment for treason. Her husband Abel, proud of the part his wife had played in bringing the man to justice, was there too, having left his saddlery business to the care of his apprentices for the morning.

Cecily was not very tall and Abel suggested they push a way through to the front. 'You've a right to a good view,' he had said, but his wife said they would do well enough where they were and she knew what was happening without seeing it all. Which she did, for though she was not – like so many here today – a frequenter of executions, she had been in court when sentence was passed, four days ago, and had heard the judges's ominous words: *You must go to the place from whence you came, there to remain until you shall be drawn through the open city of London upon a hurdle to the place of execution, and there be hanged and let down alive, and your privy parts cut off, and your entrails taken out and burnt in your sight, then your head to be cut off and your body divided into four parts . . .*

'Justice is done,' her husband had said as they left the court, his hand approvingly on her shoulder. She had thought so too, glad that the ordeal of appearing as a witness was over. Because of her action – in giving information against the so-called Miles Wood, and then in witnessing to his priestly ministry and his efforts to make conversions – there would soon be one Papist priest the less in the world.

Near where they stood, a small group had collected, mostly women, many of whom were weeping. Some were running rosary beads through their fingers and murmuring prayers, quite openly, as if in their grief they had lost all fear for their own safety. Cecily was terrified that they would look her way and recognise her as the woman responsible for the young priest's arrest.

'Let's move into the sun,' she said to Abel, who agreed readily enough. Fortunately, Father Milburn had few sympathisers in the crowd, having been in London too short a time to have much of a following. Most of the people had come to cheer. Though, once surrounded by these like-minded men and women, Cecily felt very little more comfortable.

Yet she had no regrets about the information she had laid against him (she had refused the payment that was offered), or the way she had watched and followed him for weeks before that, until she had all the evidence she needed to ensure his arrest. Once that was done, the verdict of the court had been a foregone conclusion, and so had the sentence. There was the less likelihood of mercy, in view of the fact – well known among the crowd though not openly spoken of in court – that the young priest was so closely related to Lord Milburn.

A murmur of excitement, a spreading roar, and Cecily knew the condemned man was within sight of the scaffold. She stood on tiptoe, caught a glimpse of his shining hair, and at once sank down again, suddenly not wanting to see any more. She heard, though. The noise fell away, and into the quiet came the young man's voice, rising clearly over the crowd. She had liked his voice, with its odd unplaceable accent, always calm and careful, as if no word was ever chosen lightly. Now, he prayed for England to return to her true allegiance (there was a growl of anger at that), and thanked God for allowing him to seal his faith with his blood, as he was about to do. Then, he made a soft-voiced confession of his sins: impatience, an occasional rebelliousness, too great a love of the things of this world. After which he said, *In manus tuas, Domine, commendo spiritum meum*. Then the execution began.

Though she could see little, every stage of what came after unrolled in Cecily's head. It was enacted for her through the groans and shouts of the crowd, which rose and fell with each act of the drama, and were broken into more and more by the cries of the victim. She heard the words torn from him in his agony: 'Father forgive!' and then that terrible plea, 'Father, receive my spirit!', again and again. Cecily began to wish she had a good view of the proceedings after all. Perhaps if she had it would have shut out the picture in her head of the young man's blue eyes, looking at her, as he had once in court, not with hatred, but with understanding. Was that 'Father, forgive!' for her?

It was over at last, a job well done. As Cecily made her way home, letting Abel talk without hearing a word he said, she found herself thinking that it made no difference, after all. Not even the death of a Papist priest could bring Esther back to her.

Chapter Twenty

All Good Friday afternoon the streets of York had been filled with the clamour of marching feet and clattering hooves, shouted orders and the steady beat of drums, and beneath it the excited chatter of citizens gathered to watch the new arrivals.

The noise washed against the walls of Aunt Judith's tall narrow house in Micklegate, but scarcely intruded on the third-floor room where Susannah fed and washed and dressed her aunt, and administered the medicines prescribed by her doctor; or read to her from the Bible or talked soothingly, or simply sat and watched, as she had day after day since she came here two months ago.

She had seen at once that there was no question of taking Aunt Judith back to Thornside. It was obvious to her that the old woman was dying from an extensive cancerous growth and there was nothing to be done except ease her pain as far as possible. Susannah, who had only forthrightness in common with her aunt, told her the truth, which she had guessed already, while being too frightened to admit it. Once she knew the worst, Judith Moorhouse became calmer, took the advice of her very competent doctor, received visits from her lawyer and her parish priest and seemed comforted by Susannah's stated intention of staying with her until the end. She was a cantankerous woman at the best of times and in the pain of this last illness she was more difficult than ever, but at the end of Susannah's first week in York she had said grudgingly, 'I always thought your father was a fool to bring you up as he did, but I'll say this for you – you've a soothing way for a sick-bed. There's no one I'd rather have by me than you.'

The weeks had passed and Susannah had scarcely known what

was happening outside the house, what the weather did, how the seasons changed, what battles were won or lost. All her life shrank into this little space, confined by it and by the demands of her aunt's illness. This was what she had to do and so she did it, without wasting energy on anything else.

On that cold Good Friday, the military sounds reached her from outside, but she gave them little thought; until suddenly they seemed to gather and crash against the front door and then burst into the house with an explosion of angry voices rising up the stairs. It was enough even to trouble Aunt Judith, who muttered irritably about unruly servants. Susannah went to investigate.

She found most of the household standing in the hall, the cook, the two men, and young Molly, her aunt's personal maid. They were engaged in angry altercation with a soldier, who stood in the open doorway with a paper in his hand, a group of other soldiers just visible in the street behind him. 'What's going on?'

Molly looked round, 'Mistress Fawcett, this man says we are to have soldiers quartered here!'

'That's out of the question,' said Susannah. 'This house belongs to Mistress Moorhouse and she is gravely ill. Besides, she's paid to keep her house free of soldiers.'

'No one's exempt now, mistress, orders of my Lord Newcastle. My compliments to your aunt, but she'll have to bear with it. Captain Percy, sir, these are your quarters. And you too Ned Bell and Thomas Dobson.'

Before Susannah could say another word he had stepped back into the street, leaving the hall occupied instead by three men. The two privates wore coats of undyed wool, much stained, the sleeves embroidered with a cross in blue and red, though Captain Percy, a fair man with lively moustaches, wore bright blue and a good deal of silver lacing. He took off his hat and bowed. 'Your very humble servant, mistress. May I say how honoured we are to be granted the hospitality of so fair a lady.'

Susannah, who did not like the way he looked at her, gave him a cold stare and then instructed Molly to make two rooms on the first floor ready for the men. She hoped they would be far enough from Aunt Judith not to disturb her. Then she returned to the sickroom, angry that such a thing should be forced on them at such a time.

The next Tuesday, about dinner-time, Molly told Susannah that a gentleman had called at the house. 'I told him my mistress weren't seeing no one, so he said he'd speak to you instead. He's a soldier, like Captain Percy.'

'I'm not seeing anyone either,' said Susannah. 'You may tell him so.'

'He said you'd know him, mistress. Sir Ralph Liddell, he says.'

Susannah had not felt such unalloyed pleasure for a long time. She left Molly to sit by her aunt and ran downstairs to where Sir Ralph waited in the hall. He kissed her warmly. 'My dear Susannah, this is a surprise! Just a courtesy call, I thought, and here I find you. I'm grieved to hear of your aunt's condition, of course. But do I understand you're here alone – your father isn't with you?'

'No, he's at home,' she said, leaving the details for later. She led him into the parlour and brought wine and cakes.

'I cannot stay long,' he said. 'You will understand that our duties press in these times.'

Susannah realised then that she had very little idea what precisely was happening 'in these times'. Last week Lord Newcastle – now a Marquis – had arrived in York with a large number of soldiers, but that was as much as she knew. 'Did you come here with my Lord Newcastle?'

'Yes.' Then he said, with some urgency, 'Tell me, how sick is your aunt? Can she travel? Or is there someone else you can call upon to care for her? You ought not to stay here. You know we expect to be under siege at any moment? The Fairfaxes are already at Tadcaster, and we hear that my Lord Leven with the entire Scots army has met with them there. If you leave at once there is still time to escape before they close in on us.'

'My aunt is in no condition to be moved. I have promised to stay with her until the end. I'm a woman of my word.' She smiled gently. 'Remember, sir, that army you fear has no fears for me.'

'That makes your position the more hazardous,' he said, his expression grim. Then: 'Oh, this wretched war, that sours every friendship!'

Trying to divert him, she said, 'What news have you of your family? Lady Elizabeth and Mistress Dorothy – are they well?' Then she recalled that the Scots were presumably once more in possession of his home county.

'I was at home a few weeks ago. They were all well then. But the war has made life very difficult. Even our own soldiers made heavy demands on us. Now – I don't know. I can only pray.' He sighed, then made a visible effort to throw off his low spirits. 'I trust your father is well?'

It did not, of course, make things better when she told him about her father's wound. 'He must be desperately anxious about you,' he commented. 'At the very least you'll have great discomforts to face in the days to come. There will be nothing brought in to market. My Lord Newcastle has already ordered rationing of food. Can I really not persuade you to leave?'

'No, sir. On that I'm immovable.' She looked at his anxious face. He looked older, she thought, and tired. 'I never thought to see you dressed as a soldier.'

'I'm captain of a troop of foot, brave fellows, all of them.' He sounded, suddenly, almost proud. 'Newcastle's Whitecoats, they call us. Tell me, who have they quartered on you? I hope they behave themselves courteously.'

She gave a non-committal answer – after all, she saw little of the soldiers, but drunken singing, tobacco smoke in every corner, gobbets of spit on the stairs and a good deal of stifled female giggling were hardly evidence of wild behaviour. 'I wish it could have been you instead.'

'So do I. A pity I didn't think of it in time. Though, to tell you the truth, not knowing you were here, I was not seeking to be on closer terms with your aunt.' He looked embarrassed. 'Forgive me, in the circumstances . . .'

Susannah smiled. 'I would have felt the same.'

For the next few weeks nothing much seemed to happen. Sir Ralph called twice more, but only briefly. He told Susannah that the combined forces of the Fairfaxes and Lord Leven had begun to surround the city, but so far were not strong enough to seal it off entirely. 'Let's hope relief gets through before they bring up reinforcements,' he said.

'Do you expect to be relieved?'

'We hear Prince Rupert's on his way. He's in Lancashire, and lately took Stockport and Bolton.'

Susannah felt as if her stomach were turning right over. Then she reminded herself that it was only the armies outside the city that had reason to fear the terrible Prince. But then the men in one of those armies were her friends. It was uncomfortable and confusing.

Early in June, a frightened Molly told her that the Earl of Manchester and Lieutenant-General Cromwell had marched up with the army of the Eastern Association to complete the ring about York. The next day the citizens heard the first cannon fire.

After that it became a daily noise, booming through the summer heat and the constant sound of rain, sometimes lessening, sometimes intensifying, sometimes giving way to the noise of some greater explosion, but always there, night and day. It irritated Susannah's nerves – though she grew used to it, in a dull kind of way – making her anxious only when, as happened now and then, something landed nearby, setting the house shaking to its foundations. These days, whenever she opened the window, the air that flowed in was heavy with smoke and dust.

On Trinity Sunday (Susannah knew it was that day, because Molly, who had gone regularly to church since the siege began, told her so) she allowed the servants to go together to the minster, where there was to be a great service of intercession for the safety of the city. The soldiers had been out since early morning, at their various duties, so that the house was empty of all but herself and Aunt Judith. By now the old woman was kept in a constant stupor with increasingly heavy doses of opiates and, though Susannah still read or talked to her, she doubted if she was heard. Now, shut in that room with only the sound of laboured breathing and the far off rumble of guns, Susannah felt a great relief, to be at last, almost, alone. Never since she came to York had she had space or time to herself. She passed each day in this room, slept in this room on a truckle bed at her aunt's feet. She had not been outside the house for weeks now, and for the past month it had been filled with people.

She had a sudden longing to wander about the empty house, to take temporary possession of its space, to be truly alone, to let the quietness – in here if not outside – seep into her brain.

Her aunt was not stirring, so she left the door ajar, just in case, and made her way down the stairs, feeling as if with each step a burden was slipping from her shoulders. On the first floor, she saw that the door of Captain Percy's room was not quite closed and on impulse pushed it wide. The room smelt of sweat and tobacco and unwashed feet, and the musky perfume the Captain wore, but was otherwise tidy, except for something dropped on the floor near the door, which she picked up. She thought at first it was a necklace;

then she saw that the polished wooden beads were arranged in an ordered repetitive pattern, ten at a time, then a space, then a single bead, another space, another ten; and that there was a silver crucifix hanging from it. She realised that it must be a rosary, and remembered what Fairfax's men used to say about Newcastle's Papist army. They were right then, for here was proof.

A sudden enormous reverberating explosion shattered the morning. Between shock and guilt Susannah dropped the rosary and ran up the stairs to her aunt's room. The old woman had not stirred, but still lay exactly as she had before; the room was unchanged, neat, over-warm, oppressive with approaching death. But from across the city, from the direction of the minster, came the lingering noise of the explosion, cries, shouts, a scattering of musket fire. She went to the window and pushed it open, but though the air was thick with the smell of gunpowder and burning buildings she could see nothing, except two women anxiously conferring before running off in the direction of the noise. A little later, a group of soldiers followed, running too.

It was tormenting to be shut in this place, with no means of knowing what was happening. Long after the service should surely have ended, there was no sign of the servants, no noise of passers-by in the street. Eventually the distant sounds subsided once more to the usual cannon fire, but still no one came.

It was well into the afternoon when at last she heard their voices outside, the door opening, feet on the stair. She ran out to meet them, and saw Molly, bright-eyed with excitement, looking up at her. 'They mined the wall, just by the minster. We had to stay there, all this time. There was fighting and people were hurt, but they didn't get through.'

Someone moved into Susannah's line of vision, gently pushing Molly out of the way. She saw that it was Captain Percy. 'Mistress, if you please—' She saw that he was quite without his customary roguish expression. It made her feel uneasy, though she was not quite sure why; she did not much care for the Captain's usual manner. He came a little way up the stairs, removing his hat as he did so. 'Mistress, I believe Captain Sir Ralph Liddell is a friend. I regret—'

She felt her breath catch in her throat. He must have seen what she thought he was going to say, for he raised a hand and said quickly, 'No, mistress, not what you fear. But he's hurt. I saw him carried away. He's in the surgeon's hands now.' He stood beside her on the small landing. She smelt the faint perfume, the masculine sweat, and saw kindness and compassion on his face. 'I will let you know how he does.'

There was nothing to do but thank him and return to her aunt, with the guns' dull rumbling going on and on and on. That night beacon fires burned on the minster tower, signalling the city's plight to its distant friends.

CHAPTER TWENTY-ONE

A week after Trinity Sunday, Aunt Judith died at last, as peace-fully as was possible in the circumstances. With a great sense of relief, Susannah made the arrangements for the funeral, which was necessarily a quiet affair. After that, there were all kinds of tiresome details to be sorted out, with the lawyer and the doctor and the servants: bills to be paid, legacies to be settled – to the poor of the parish, to the servants, who were to be kept on for the time being, and, surprisingly, to herself, for Aunt Judith in gratitude to Susannah had left her the bulk of her property. A house in York was not much use in time of war, but Susannah thought that when peace came she would let it; the rent would be useful – always sup-posing that it was still standing when peace came, for many of the city's houses had already been destroyed. As for peace, it seemed further away than ever.

When Susannah had last been free to walk in the streets of York, they had been filthy and treacherous with trodden snow. She knew time had passed, that it was now summer, but it was a shock all the same to emerge into the stinking oppressiveness of late June; and the sudden near reality of a siege that had until now been distanced for her. Out in the streets the noise was terrible, endless. Smoke often shut out the sun. There were soldiers everywhere, grey-faced men as weary of the siege as most of the citizens, but grimly deter-mined not to give in. Beacon fires blazed nightly from the minster tower, but no help came and the siege was as close as ever. Nearly thirty thousand men enclosed York in an iron band. Nothing got through, whether in or out, not messengers nor food nor arms nor news, not least because the city's many gates had been barricaded for fear of an assault, the suburbs demolished or burnt to reduce cover for the enemy. The citizens only had rumours and the ration proscribed by the city's governor – beans and bread and beer – enough for one meal per person per day, though other things could sometimes be had, if you were rich. The rain, incessant for so long, had ceased about the middle of June and the stench in the crowded streets mingled powerfully with the smells of gunpowder and burning. The dust was worse than ever.

It was only when the funeral was over that Susannah realised how completely exhausted she was, though it was an exhaustion of the mind as much as the body. She found herself longing for the clear air of Thornside, for quiet, for her father, for all the things that now seemed impossibly far away, like a dimly remembered dream.

The day after the funeral, she went to see Sir Ralph. Captain Percy had told her he had at first been too ill to see anyone, but was now somewhat better. Even so, knowing a little of what explosions could do to the human body, Susannah had feared the worst. She was relieved to find that he had not in fact been injured by the explosion at all, simply shot in the thigh during the fighting afterwards. The musket ball had been awkwardly though not dangerously lodged and the surgeon had taken some time to remove it, after which Sir Ralph had been very ill with fever, but was now quite clearly mending, if still very weak. He answered her many questions about his injury, amused at her interest. 'I can see that for you my importance has grown in direct proportion to my wounds. I must regret I wasn't able to contrive something rather more severe for you to investigate.'

She had the grace to blush a little, but she laughed too. 'I can't help wanting to know about such things.'

After that they had a lengthy discussion about medical matters, and she was reassured to find that Sir Ralph had not lost his engaging curiosity. In fact, he seemed much more himself, as if there was some relief for him in being temporarily removed from the war.

Two days later, early in the morning, Susannah was jolted sharply awake by some change in the air. She lay still, listening, and then realised that what had woken her was not, as she had thought, a new sound, but an absence of sound. She was hearing nothing – or nothing, at least, but the singing of birds wakening to the dawn in Aunt Judith's little garden, a city stirring to everyday life. The guns had ceased.

It was not until Captain Percy returned from night duty that they learned precisely what had happened. 'They've gone, every one of them,' he said triumphantly. 'Fairfax, Manchester, the Scots. Not a one of them left. I will say this for them though, they were good enough to leave us their boots. Four thousand or so, brand-new.' He gestured towards his own fast-disintegrating footwear. 'I've a hope for a pair myself.'

'But where have they gone, sir?' Susannah asked.

'That's the beauty of it, mistress. They thought he'd come from the west – well, you would, wouldn't you, when he was last heard of at Knaresborough? So they've marched themselves up that big hill beyond Long Marston, halfway to Tadcaster. And what do you suppose? There he is now, fast coming this way from the north. Marched right round them without them even getting a whisper of him.' His eyes were shining.

'Him?' But she knew, even before the Captain replied.

'Why, Prince Rupert, of course.'

Susannah felt odd, at once relieved and apprehensive. She heard Molly say, 'Will there be a battle, Captain?'

'Sure to be, sweetheart,' he said. 'And I wouldn't be in the enemy's shoes when it comes – barring the ones they've left behind them that is.'

Susannah wondered if Sir Thomas Fairfax had ever before faced Prince Rupert. She thought not, and feared for him, and those with him, her friends.

Soon afterwards, having breakfasted, Captain Percy went out again. He was singing as he left the house, a cheerfully satirical Royalist ballad whose words hung in the air when he had gone.

> *Tis to preserve his Majesty*
> *That we against him fight . . .*

York was full of jubilation that day. Citizens poured through suddenly reappearing gaps in the walls to scavenge what they could from the enemy camp, though the soldiers had already scoured it pretty thoroughly. Later that morning, Susannah, a little ashamed at giving in to idle curiosity, went with Molly to watch the terrible Prince himself ride into York, with a handful of officers in his train. Behind his horse ran a large white poodle, Boy, the Prince's reputed familiar, his link with the Devil. To Susannah he looked like any ordinary dog, trotting obediently beside his master, with an occasional pause to sniff some interesting roadside smell. As for the Prince, he was very tall, splendidly dressed and undeniably handsome.

They heard that he rode out of York again early the next morning. They watched from their own windows a little later as the Marquis of Newcastle passed in his coach through Micklegate Bar, with a perfectly groomed military escort, who did not, Susannah thought, look much like soldiers going to battle.

It was well into the afternoon when the rest of the garrison marched out, with a great noise of beating drums and whistling fifes and tramping feet. A good many of them appeared to have been celebrating the ending of the siege and were none too steady on their feet. Molly waved and shouted to Captain Percy and the two familiar figures in the ranks behind him, pikes over their shoulders. Captain Percy at least waved back, as jaunty as ever.

After that a strange silence settled over the city. It was a heavy grey day, oppressively hot. Susannah wished she had some useful work to do, to occupy her mind and stop her from thinking of what her friends might even now be enduring out there in the July heat. She wished she could have been near them, on the fringe of the battlefield, ready to tend their wounded and share in the bitterness of their defeat, if that was what it must be. She did not want to be here in York among the victors when news of it came.

Then she thought how hard it must be for Sir Ralph, alone on his sick-bed while his troop marched out to fight, and she went to see him. He was clearly delighted to see her, though he scolded her for coming unaccompanied. She diverted him by changing the subject and they began to talk of family matters, but it was obvious that his attention was elsewhere. After a while he suddenly burst out, 'Why can we hear nothing?'

'Perhaps the wind's in the wrong direction. Or they're too far away.'

Ralph shook his head. 'No. We would hear something.'

'It's not so long since the garrison marched out.'

'Long enough. Though God knows they should have been gone hours since.' He sat up. 'I can't bear lying here. Forgive my impatience, Susannah, but would you help me to a chair?' She did so, but he seemed no less restless afterwards. 'I heard there was trouble this morning – mutiny, some called it, though I doubt that. Besides,

you can't call it mutiny when the men at the top are the instigators.'
Susannah thought, with fascination, that he must mean Lord
Newcastle, who was notoriously temperamental, and his right-hand
man, Lord Eythin, who was rumoured to be an old adversary of
Prince Rupert. 'It's true we've had a hard few months of it. The
pay's in arrears as usual, and you could say the men deserve a
breathing space. Still, I know those lads and they'd have marched
out at once, given the least encouragement. But there, they've gone
now.' Then, in another tone, 'Pity you don't sing. Music is a good
way to forget your troubles.'

'If you heard me sing you'd want your troubles back,' said
Susannah, at which he laughed.

'Now, it's not that you can't sing, just that you have your heart
too set on other things.'

Time passed and it began to grow dark. Still there was no sound
of battle. 'It's time you went home,' said Sir Ralph. 'There'll be no
fighting tonight.'

Susannah helped him back to bed and was about to leave when
the storm that had threatened all day suddenly broke, with lightning and thunder and a deafening torrent of hail that clattered on
the roof and the window. 'I'll wait till this is over,' she said.

But when the brief storm ended it gave way not to silence, but to
a new sound, the one they had been expecting all afternoon. Far
away, familiar and yet different in its intensity from the sporadic
daily cannon-fire of the siege, it came to them through the heavy
air: the sinister rumble of guns, like continuous thunder from the
west. For a few seconds they sat quite still, listening. Sir Ralph
closed his eyes. 'God have mercy on us all!'

Susannah reached out her hand and laid it over his, saying nothing. There was no more talk of her going.

After a time, Sir Ralph said, 'There's wine on the table there. My
Lord Newcastle sent it when I was hurt. Obliging of him, but I've
not been inclined to broach it before now. This would seem to be
the moment.'

Susannah found glasses and poured wine into them and they
drank, trying to talk lightly, of unimportant things, but always
falling silent again to listen to the guns. Once, Ralph said, 'They
began so late. Why wait till it's almost night?'

'I expect there's some good military reason, sir,' said Susannah.

'My dear, one thing war has taught me is that military reasons have little—' He broke off, listening.

There was a new sound, coming nearer, a confused noise of stumbling, running feet, horses' hooves clattering on the cobbles, voices shouting in alarm. Further off (roughly, Susannah thought, from the direction of Micklegate Bar) came more shouting, fiercer and angrier. Ralph put down his glass. 'God help us, what's that?'

'Shall I go and see?' If only the house looked over the street! The shadowed garden was still and quiet and told them nothing.

Ralph sank back again. 'No, most certainly not. Whatever's going on, I'm sure the streets are no place for you. It's early yet. It may be that things have gone badly in just one part of the field. It wouldn't be the first time.'

Susannah lit the candles, for it was fully dark by now, and they sat in silence again, ears strained to catch every sound. Sometimes there would be a brief lull, followed again by that noise of hurrying feet and shouting. Steadily it increased in volume, until there could be no doubt that out in the dark streets of the city were men crying and shouting in pain or terror, frightened horses, the clatter and rattle of carts and wagons. There could no longer be any doubt, as time passed, that what they heard was an army in rout.

Close on midnight, Susannah could stand it no longer. She took a candle and went downstairs to see if the landlady or any of her household had news. She found them gathered in the kitchen, clearly terrified, an old woman and an older man. 'Don't go out there, mistress!' they warned her. 'They're at the gates! They'll tear you to pieces!'

Susannah could not imagine who would be likely to tear her to pieces, and she went to the door and opened it. She was startled to find herself face to face with a man, who said hastily, 'Sir Ralph Liddell – is he here?'

She just had time to say, 'Yes, up there,' before he pushed past her and ran up the stairs. She followed quickly, full of anxiety.

The man had reached the foot of the bed. She saw Ralph struggling to sit up, astonished and dismayed at once. 'My lord . . .! But where is—? Susannah!'

The man turned, looking where Ralph looked, and then stood still. Susannah stood still too, just inside the door with the candle held before her . . . A face, blue eyes shadowed by black brows; and something that ran through her from head to toe, to her fingertips, her scalp, her spine, something that was like fear but was not, though she shivered . . . She quite forgot everything she had been thinking a moment before.

From a long way off she heard Ralph say, 'For the love of God, what news?'

The man looked as if he, like her, were waking out of a dream. 'I beg your pardon, sir.' He sounded dazed. He turned slowly. 'I thought to find you alone.' He spoke with an odd lilting intonation, as if he were not quite at home with English. Susannah found herself staring at the back of his head, dark hair just visible beneath the wide hat brim, and Ralph's face beyond, anguished with impatience. 'York is lost,' the man said abruptly, and then fell silent. He went to the table and poured himself some wine, drinking it in one swift movement and then instantly refilling the glass.

Ralph watched him with a little frown. 'Stop pacing the room and sit down,' he said. It was clear that he was trying very hard to be patient. 'I want to know what happened.'

Not quite sure what she was doing or why, Susannah came nearer, putting her candle down on the edge of the table. The flame shivered, for her hand was trembling. The man turned to look at her again.

'My lord,' said Ralph with weary resignation, 'may I make known my kinswoman, Mistress Susannah Fawcett of Thornside, daughter of a dear friend – parted, alas, by war. You may remember that Dorothy stayed with them, once. Susannah, my one-time ward, my Lord Milburn.'

Now it was a different kind of shock that made her stare at the man. How could Sir Ralph speak so casually, as if to meet this man in his room, on apparently friendly terms, was the most natural thing in the world?

He took off his hat. She saw then how dirty and dishevelled he was, and how very tired. She also thought she glimpsed just a little of her own revulsion mirrored in his face, though why that should be she could not imagine. 'Your servant, mistress,' he said, as curtly as good manners allowed.

'Now, I beg of you, tell me what happened out there!'

He seemed to put Susannah completely from his thoughts, sitting down on the edge of the bed and giving all his attention to Ralph. 'God knows what happened. I've never known His Highness in such a mood, unsure of himself. Maybe he was tired. Maybe it was the other generals – there was some unpleasantness. Whatever it was, he lost the initiative. To do that, when we were so heavily outnumbered . . .! We thought that was it for the day, and then they attacked, suddenly. So here we are.' He drained the glass again and then sat twisting it in his hand, his head bent. 'I never thought to see such butchery, not in England.'

'And my regiment, the Whitecoats?'

There was a little silence. Then: 'I'm sorry, sir. Cut to pieces, every one. They stood to the last man.'

'All of them?'

'All of them, God rest their souls.'

Ralph put a hand over his face. Susannah slipped round the far side of the bed and knelt beside it, one hand on his arm. She knew the other man was watching her, but she did not look at him. 'God give you comfort, sir,' she said softly. Ralph closed the fingers of his free hand about hers.

After an interval, Lord Milburn said, 'What of you, sir? They told me before the fight that you'd been hurt and your life feared for.'

Ralph rubbed his eyes, making a visible effort to be calm. 'I'm almost recovered. The worst part was to lie here while . . . To know I couldn't be with you today.'

'Thank God you weren't,' said the young man fervently, 'or I'd not be talking to you now.' He stood up. 'I must go. I've to meet with the Prince.'

'What then?'

He shrugged. 'Leave enough men here to hold the city for a few days more, I suppose. Then take what's left of the cavalry and ride west again. Men are still getting through from Ireland, and we need every one.'

Sir Ralph glanced at Susannah. 'And tonight, my lord? What are the chances of getting safely away from York, for a woman, that is?'

The other man looked at Susannah too. 'Tonight, no, it would be too dangerous. But tomorrow – there'll be the usual truce to bury the dead, I suppose. Under cover of that, with a strong escort per-haps. But even then—'

'Mistress Fawcett has friends with Sir Thomas Fairfax. If safe pas-sage could be arranged to his quarters, that would suffice.'

Susannah was about to protest at the high-handedness of making such arrangements without reference to her, and then she realised that there was nothing she wanted more than to go home, as soon as possible. Lord Milburn was silent for a long time. She thought he was about to refuse or say something rude, but in the end he simply said, 'I'll see to it.'

'And if I may ask one last small favour, my lord – would you be so good as to spare a moment now to see her safely back to her house in Micklegate, so she may make ready to leave?'

Again that momentary pause, and the abrupt reply. 'That too.' Then he bent and clasped Ralph's hands and said in quite a different tone, husky with emotion, 'I pray we shall meet again, dear sir, before too long. And in happier circumstances.' Then, a cold glance: 'Mistress?'

Susannah kissed Sir Ralph, said, 'Let us have news of you,' and then followed her reluctant escort in silence down the stairs. They had no light with them and all the while she felt as if strange impulses ran back and forth through the darkness between them, setting her nerves tingling. Hatred, she thought: I abhor him and all he stands for. Yet she had hated before, felt anger and disgust. It had been nothing like this.

They reached the door, she heard him fumble for the latch, then it opened, letting in a faint light. She stepped forward, conscious that her shoulder brushed his. She felt it like a shock through her body. Then she looked into the street and her mind was swept clear of everything that had fogged and cluttered it; everything but a burning sense of outrage at the indescribable chaos that lay before her. She had been familiar all her life with sickness and pain and death, she had seen, she had thought, the worst that war could do to men. She had seen nothing like this.

There were a few rushlights set in sconces along the street, and over all a livid and fitful moon, hidden from time to time by shredded rags of cloud like the torn banners of a defeated army. By their dim light she saw men passing along the street, stumbling, supported by comrades, desperately seeking a resting place, their faces haggard with pain and fatigue and fear. They could hardly make any progress for the dreadful litter of the wounded and dying who choked the street. Here and there a wagon had been abandoned, right in the middle of everything, tipped sideways so that its groaning mass of casualties was thrown into an agonised, struggling heap. Voices cried or screamed for water, for help, in an extremity of pain. Other men were silent, shaking and staring into space. An overpowering stench of blood and filth hung on the oppressive air and caught in her throat.

Susannah turned to the man at her side as if he had been any unknown officer, passing in the night. 'This is shameful! Where are the surgeons? Who's caring for these men?'

She thought, with disgust, that he smiled, though bitterly enough. 'Where do you find surgeons sufficient for these numbers, mistress? Among your Roundhead friends?'

'Something must be done. They can't just be left like this.'

'They'll be moved under cover, when it's possible. The hospitals are full, believe me. This is war, Mistress Fawcett.'

She subjected him to a glance of withering scorn. 'I know that. It's no excuse.' She ran down the steps, and he followed her.

'Mistress, where are you going? You must not walk unescorted.'

'I'm going home.' Relieved, he went with her. She asked, 'Where are the hospitals, do you know?' She wished now that she had not been too wrapped up in her aunt's illness to find out such things.

'What's that to you?'

'I shall find them more quickly if I know where I'm going,' she said, exasperated by the triviality of his questions.

'You said you were going home.'

'To get my things, that's all.'

He stood still, grasping her arm. 'Mistress Fawcett, Sir Ralph would never forgive me if I permitted that. This isn't like treating a servant with the toothache. Leave it to the camp followers. They know what they're doing. You should be safe within doors, at least until I've made arrangements for your journey.'

'Sir, I was a camp follower myself until last summer. I have no intention of standing idle now just because these men are not of my party.' She began to walk on and he had to move quickly to keep up with her. When they came to the house she said, 'I bid you good-night, sir,' and went indoors.

He stood staring at the closed door for a moment, then he shrugged and went on his way.

As Susannah stepped through the door she was met by the sound of hysterical weeping. In the kitchen she found Molly in tears, cook flustered, the men drunk and still drinking. Molly raised her head to wail, 'Oh mistress, Captain Percy's dead! They were all cut down, all of them.'

'I know,' said Susannah. 'Now you must dry your eyes and do what you can for the living.' She set them tearing sheets for bandages while she gathered her medical supplies into a bag, which she slung over her shoulder. Then she kilted up her skirts and set out into the streets with a nervous and still tearful Molly at her side.

She saw that by now there were other women working among the wounded, binding superficial wounds, bringing drinks or food. She set to work herself where she saw the most urgent need, removing musket balls, staunching bleeding. Molly began by shuddering and even screaming at what she saw, until Susannah told her sharply to show more self-control, after which she proved helpful enough; though often she had to look away and once, having stood by as Susannah dealt with a particularly horrible facial wound, she turned aside to be sick.

By the time dawn broke some attempt was being made to reduce the chaos in the streets. Volunteers began to carry the wounded to the emergency hospitals or into private houses, though the streets were still so clogged with men that it was not easy to get through. A number of clergymen had emerged to offer what consolation they could, among them two who were quite obviously Papist priests, though no one but Susannah seemed to think anything of it. For many of the men there was no other kind of help to be given. One such, Susannah found in a corner near All Saints' church, where someone had left him, presumably thinking it out of the way of trampling feet. He was not dead yet, but from the way his guts spilled out of the wound in his belly Susannah knew he had not long to live. She wondered that anyone had bothered to carry him into the city, with what was obviously a mortal wound. She covered it as best she could, wished she had not exhausted all her stock of opiates and bent to moisten his lips with a sponge soaked in water. Then she realised with a little shock that the face was familiar; at least, she thought it was. Pain and the approach of death changed a man's features and those she looked at now seemed to have little to do with the blustering boy who had confronted her at Thornside Hall; but she was almost sure. She said softly, 'Harry Middleton', and saw his eyes briefly open, though there was no recognition in them.

She went to where one of the Papist priests was muttering his superstitious prayers and directed him to the boy. She had no idea what made her do it. She had no reason to think kindly of Harry Middleton, and her father would have been scandalised. She had only some vague idea that since he faced certain torment beyond the grave, then he might at the least be allowed some consolation, however illusory, in the last moments of his earthly existence. It would make no difference at all in the end.

The sun rose and soon it grew oppressively hot. The sickening stench of congealed blood and festering wounds and excrement would have been unendurable by anyone who had not been working in it from the beginning. There were flies everywhere, and rats in the quieter corners. The numbers of wounded in the streets were beginning slowly to diminish and other traffic was moving against the flow: frightened citizens anxious to get out of York before the siege resumed, their laden carts adding irritability to the bloody congestion. Meanwhile, through the gates came more and more soldiers carrying in the dead from the battlefield – or those of the dead whose rank entitled them to ceremonious burial. Often Susannah and the others tending the wounded found themselves caught up in some heated altercation with those trying to push a way through.

By mid-morning Molly was near to dropping with exhaustion, so Susannah sent her home. She had no intention of resting herself, while there was still so much to do. She was tired and hungry and hot, her clothes were drenched with sweat and dirt and her face and hands sticky with blood, her hair straggling from her once-white coif. But she did not let such minor inconveniences upset the single-minded concentration of which, once, she had spoken to Richard, and which kept her working quietly, calmly, efficiently, when others might have given up.

Around midday she did pause at last, long enough to take food and drink brought out to her by a woman from a nearby house. She longed to sit down, but she knew that if she did it would be the harder to get up again. She was about to return to work when a hand touched her arm. 'Mistress Fawcett?'

She glanced round, and then had to put out her hand to support herself on the wall. She had forgotten how disturbed she had been, last night, when they had come face to face by candlelight. Now, in daylight, it all came back in a rush, only worse. He had taken off his hat and his face was cruelly lit by the sunlight, unshaven and dirty, the eyes shadowed. But she only saw the eyes, not the shadows. She was not tall, but he was not very much taller than she was . . . Deep blue eyes almost on a level with her own. Looking at them, she could not think clearly, could not, in fact, think at all.

He said nothing for a moment, and when he did speak his voice sounded shaky. 'The arrangements – as I promised Sir Ralph. A cornet will ride with you, with a white flag. In half an hour, I think. He will come to your house.'

She had completely forgotten Sir Ralph's request and it was some time before she understood what the young man was telling her. When she did at last she said, a little dazedly, 'But that's impossible.'

'Why?'

She gestured around her. 'You can see for yourself how much there is still to be done.'

'Then let others do it. If you don't go now you'll be shut up in the city again and God knows how long it'll be before you can leave, or what dangers you may face. Besides, I promised Sir Ralph.'

'You did. I did not.' She tried to bring herself under control. Whatever might lie behind the odd sensations that still distracted her, they were of no importance. 'Now, excuse me, sir. I have work to do.' She walked steadily away from him, resisting a strong temptation to look back.

He came after her and tried to argue with her, but she set to work on a shattered leg and he could not in decency continue the argument over the wounded man. 'Damn you then for an obstinate Roundhead!' he exclaimed. 'I wash my hands of you.' Then he left her. She was thankful that her patient was too ill to hear what had been said.

Rain came at nightfall, making it imperative that the last of the wounded should be brought under cover. Susannah saw three men carried into the tall house in Micklegate and gave instructions to the servants as to how they should be cared for, returning from time to time to make sure that her orders were being carried out. Soon after dawn, she stayed long enough at the house to snatch something to eat, and it was then that a messenger came from Doctor Baty, inviting her to come and assist him at St Anthony's Hall, one of the old city guild halls now converted to a hospital. As she made her way there she glimpsed a file of riders clattering towards Monk Bar and recognised the tall figure of Prince Rupert, with a detachment of cavalry behind him. He looked nothing like the triumphant figure of three days before. 'I can't see his dog,' a woman said.

'I heard it was found on the battlefield, dead,' her companion replied. 'They were surprised. He must have forgotten to tie it up.'

CHAPTER TWENTY-TWO

'I really must urge you to go and take some rest, Mistress Fawcett,' said Doctor Baty, who had been conferring with Susannah over the bed of a feverish patient, while his apprentice noted down what medicines he prescribed. Like most physicians – and unlike Matthew Fawcett – he never actually laid hands on his patients, leaving that to the surgeons and the women. But for all that, Susannah respected him, for he had ably attended Judith Moorhouse in her last illness.

She knew he was right. She had been at St Anthony's Hall since dawn and it was now well into the night again. She had not slept since before the battle and she was exhausted. She knew she risked making some serious mistake.

On her way out of the hall, she passed a trooper whose bandage was badly stained with fresh blood, and stopped beside him. 'Let me take a look – that shouldn't still be bleeding.' His shoulder wound was not particularly severe, but the bandage had almost worked loose. She began to unwind it. 'You've been fidgeting about.'

He grinned. 'I'm glad you got to me first. That one over there was on her way.' He nodded towards a large and dignified citizen's wife who had come, with marked condescension, to give her assistance to the doctors. 'She put this on, and none too gentle she was about it either.'

That, Susannah thought, probably explained the bleeding. She began quickly and neatly to place a pad over the wound and bind it firmly in place.

'Now if they all had your pretty eyes,' the soldier went on, 'we'd every one of us be feigning sick, when there was naught wrong with us at all.'

'Well, that would soon end the war,' said Susannah. From wounded men she would accept remarks that she would coldly have repulsed from anyone else. To keep cheerful through what some of these men had to endure was an admirable thing, and if that led to lightness of talk, then that was only to be expected from Royalists.

She was conscious of someone coming up to the bed behind her. A voice said anxiously, 'Rob, what's wrong?'

'Just a dressing worked loose,' said Susannah, turning her head in the expectation of seeing a stranger; and instead finding herself looking up into the face she had last seen furiously confronting her in the street yesterday afternoon. He did not look angry now, only startled and confused, as she was. She had no resources left to try and control her emotion. She felt herself blushing, and was annoyed that she could do nothing to stop it happening. She mumbled something, she was not sure what, and stood up and walked away, towards the door and the stairs that led down to the garden and the street beyond.

She was halfway there when she heard steps behind her and knew he was following her. She was angry with him for it, because she hated the way he seemed able, just by his presence, to sweep away all reason and control, so that she was no longer in command of herself. She had experienced nothing like it before and it distressed and enraged her, the more because the man who had so overturned everything that she knew of herself was someone she could only despise.

She said nothing as he reached her, and they descended the last of the stairs in silence. In the street he continued to keep up with her, though she tried to think of the right words to send him away. If she had been less tired she might have succeeded, but, as it was, what with exhaustion and the effect of his nearness, she could not assemble anything coherent.

She stumbled suddenly on some piece of debris and her companion's arm slipped about her waist, steadying her. She felt as if she were drowning, gasping for air. She knew she was dangerously close to allowing herself to relax against him; no, not relax, for the shivering pleasure she felt at his touch was not in the least restful. 'No . . .' she said faintly.

The arm was withdrawn. 'I beg your pardon, mistress,' he said. 'It was only to stop you falling.' He sounded breathless too. On a little further. Then, 'I want to know – why did you refuse to leave? You could have been among your friends by now.'

'I told you why. Because there were wounded men to be seen to.'

'Your enemies.'

'You know surgeons treat all equally.'

'But there were others to do it. Now you have to stay till the siege ends.'

'I shan't be idle. Tell me, my lord, if you were a surgeon, would you not have done the same – with wounded men from among my "friends", as you call them?'

'No!' he said vehemently. 'Never!'

She studied his face, as far as she could read its expression in the moonlight. There was no softness in it, only repugnance and, she thought, something that might have been pain. 'Why not? "Blessed are the merciful" – or do Papists not have that teaching?'

'I don't need lectures in mercy from a Roundhead,' he said harshly. They had reached the Ouse bridge, crossing the river towards Micklegate. There, once past the buildings that encroached upon it, he propped his back against the parapet, facing her. 'In Queen Elizabeth's time, a housewife was pressed to death on this very bridge. They placed rocks on her body, more and more until she died. You would have stood by and cheered – she was a Catholic, you see. Her crime, to be true to her faith.'

She felt buffeted by the bitterness of his tone, and angered too. 'You've no right to ascribe feelings to me. You scarcely know me. I'm not personally responsible for what men did years before I was born.'

'No,' he said after a pause. 'I think I rather wish you were.'

She could think of no possible reply to a remark of such obscurity. 'I'm tired,' she said. 'I'm going home.' She began to walk on and felt him fall into step beside her.

'Forgive me, mistress,' he said, in quite a different tone. 'I've never before met a Roundhead I could remotely say I liked. Now, to see your generosity and compassion, to have to admit that is what they are . . .' He stopped again, shaking his head. 'It's all wrong: some malign conjunction of the stars perhaps. And my brother not long dead at the hands of your kind, God forgive me!'

So that was it. Killed in battle, she supposed. She wanted to ask, but could not quite bring herself to intrude into a private grief. If he did not know her, neither did she know him. 'War's like that, my lord,' she said gently. 'But I have killed no one, ever.'

'I'm not talking about war.' Suddenly he took hold of her shoulders, almost shaking her. 'Swear then that you have never wanted the death of any priest, that you've never rejoiced to hear of it!'

It was something she had scarcely ever thought about. Papist priests were, by their very nature, subject to the death penalty if caught. She supposed that she believed, regretfully, that the law was just. But what that had to do with either of them tonight she could not imagine. She began to wonder uneasily if Lord Milburn was a little mad. 'I've never rejoiced in any death,' she said, 'even if sometimes I might see the necessity for it.'

'Then if you found a priest – say, doing what you were doing, caring for the wounded – you would betray him to the authorities, so he could be arrested?'

'I've met them, my lord, in the streets and in the hospital. I've spoken with some of them. I may not like what they are, but they seem quiet and devoted and I see no cause to interfere.' Then she went on, 'My lord, this is not fair. I'm too tired to think clearly. I don't understand what you seek to accuse me of. But I know I've done nothing at all to make you think so badly of me.'

'No,' he said. 'No, you haven't.' He began to stride away from her up the slope of the cobbled street and she had to hurry to catch him up, though why she should want to catch him up she could not imagine. He did not look at her and they walked on in silence, very fast, until they came to the door of the house. There Susannah had a vague thought that she ought to say something – thank him for escorting her, perhaps, though she had not asked for an escort, nor, for that matter, had he offered one, and his company had hardly been reassuring. She turned to face him, and he stood gazing back at her, saying nothing, though he was frowning slightly.

Then, suddenly, he grasped her hand and turned it palm uppermost and pressed his mouth to it. The shock of the gesture and the fierceness of it made her catch her breath. She stood looking at his bent head, while his lips seemed to sear her hand, burning her to the bone. Her fingers closed about his cheek, feeling the stubble on it, the line of the jaw. For that moment she was no longer separate, a woman standing in the street with a man she scarcely knew, but part of a single being, fused into one by a rush of feeling beyond words or understanding.

As suddenly, as shockingly, he let her hand fall, as if he, not she, were the one who had been burned. He said, in a tone that was so abrupt as to be scarcely courteous, 'Good-night, mistress,' and then he turned and walked away. It was some time before Susannah had stopped shaking enough to step towards the house and open the door.

Sir Ralph was woken early next morning by the sound of guns, from somewhere roughly north-west, he thought. He lay with his eyes closed, listening, and then became aware from some small sound that there was someone in the room with him. He assumed it was his landlady, bringing breakfast. 'Back where we began,' he said wearily.

'Aye,' said a voice that was certainly not that of his landlady.

He sat up, wide awake. Ludovick was sitting on the chair at the foot of the bed, gazing into the empty hearth. 'What are you doing here, my lord? I thought you'd ridden out with the Prince.'

'As you see, I did not.'

'I heard all the cavalry had gone.'

'I asked to serve with the garrison.'

'Good Lord, why? There was surely no need to put your head deliberately into the lion's mouth. What if the terms go against you?'

Ludovick shrugged but said nothing. Ralph tried to read his face, but it was half-turned away from him and there was not enough light. Then he remembered the crudely triumphant news-sheet he had happened upon one day in the spring. 'I heard about your brother,' he said quietly. 'I'm sorry.' There was no sign that he had even been heard. He wanted to ask more – 'Is that why you stayed, because you hope to meet his fate?' – but he could not bring himself to do so.

Ludovick had heard him, and he had also seen what was scarcely even implied, because he had wondered it himself. Yet he could not really say what had made him stay in York. His feelings were by now so confused, so painfully impenetrable even to himself, that to understand them was beyond him.

When he first knew Charles had gone, he had wanted only to die too. 'Do that,' Rob had said with the harsh logic that was the only thing that could have stayed his hand, 'and you cut yourself off from him for ever.' Ludovick had not even been sure about that. He had to believe that Charles was, somewhere, still living and in bliss, but he had not felt any sense of it, not since that terrible day. There was only the void. But he knew that if there was any truth in what his twin had died for, as there must be, then for him to take his own life would only deliver him to still more unbearable torment, made worse by the knowledge that the separation was eternal. His life was not his to dispose of. That did not mean that he need take any especial care to preserve it, and in wartime death lay daily in wait. He had, for a while, become extravagantly reckless in everything he did, until one of his soldiers had died because of it, and he knew it was not just his own life he was risking. After that, grimly, he had known he had to leave it to God. Yet it was possible that some hope of an end had been in his mind when he asked to stay in York. Unless it was the other thing.

He only knew that he hurt so much that he could not bear the mere thought of being touched, whether physically or by any call on his emotions. Yet into this universe of pain had come Susannah, unasked, and he found that he was filled with a hunger he had never felt before, for the thing he dared not allow himself to feel.

But he could say none of this, and did not even attempt to. He simply sat in silence with his head in his hands. Seeking at last to break through the brooding atmosphere that had settled over the room, Ralph said, 'How do things stand now?'

'What things?'

'I gather my Lord Newcastle has gone overseas, Eythin with him. I heard too that Sir Thomas Glemham has been raised to command in the north. But I don't suppose the siege will last long.'

'I shouldn't think so.' Another strained silence.

'My lord, I'm wondering as I lie here,' said Ralph with exaggerated pensiveness, 'whether you came to my lodgings this morning to disclose to me your innermost heart, or to delight me with your wit. I've still not made up my mind.'

In spite of himself, Ludovick laughed. He shifted to the edge of the bed. 'Forgive me, sir. How are you? Have they let you get up yet?'

'I've sat there by the window two days now, and yesterday took a couple of halting steps. Alarming how weak one becomes! On the other hand, I reckon to have made great strides since the battle. My surgeon's been too busy elsewhere to order me back to bed.'

Ludovick said nothing. The black frown had returned. Ralph sighed, and then remembered, with compunction, what should have been uppermost in his mind. 'I was forgetting: Susannah, Mistress Fawcett . . . You were able to arrange a safe conduct for her, before all this started again?'

There was a sudden rush of movement as Ludovick got up and went to the window, and stood there with his back to the room and his head, shielded by his arm, resting against the glass. Ralph could see that he was breathing hard. 'What's wrong, my lord? Has she taken some harm?'

'No, no she's quite safe.' The words were almost inaudible. Then he burst out, 'What in hell's name possessed the girl's father to send her to York at this time of all times?'

'He wasn't to know what would happen,' said Ralph, calmly enough, though he could not shake off his anxiety. It was clear that something was wrong, though he could not imagine what.

'This is no place for Roundheads at any time.'

'Then she's in some kind of trouble. What's amiss?'

'Nothing. Except that she's still in York. She wouldn't leave. It seems she fancies herself as some kind of female surgeon.'

'You mean she's been caring for the wounded?' Ludovick nodded and Ralph gave a rueful sigh, which had relief in it too. 'I suppose I should have guessed. A strong-minded young woman, Susannah. Please God she takes no harm in the end.'

'You have no business to number rebels among your friends.'

'Oh, come now, my lord, that is the bitterness of civil war, that it tears friends apart.'

'I have no ties with any fighting for the Parliament, nor ever have had.'

'Then you're the exception, and should give thanks for it.'

'I shall only ever give thanks,' said Ludovick harshly, 'when we've put to the sword every man and woman and child who ever stood with Parliament.' He left soon afterwards, and Ralph wondered uneasily what Susannah had said or done to make him so bitterly angry.

Increasingly, as the days went by, the stench of gangrene filled St Anthony's Hall, driving away all but the most strong-stomached surgeons and nurses. Susannah was kept busy scraping putrid flesh from infected limbs, and trying to ease the fever that went with them. It was harrowing work, and depressing, for once gangrene set in, only amputation could save a man, and often not then. It was no place for the less sick patients, and she thought it only right when Ludovick came to take Rob away to his own quarters.

The previous day he had talked to her briefly, asking her how Rob was doing, and she had wished he had not, for he had over-thrown all her concentration for the rest of the afternoon. When he came for Rob, she was at the other end of the hall, and this time he made no attempt to speak to her, not even glancing her way when he passed her. She was relieved, but she was hurt too, and angry – with herself as much as with him.

Two days later, about dinner-time, he suddenly sought her out. 'I've food with me, if you care to eat. We can go by the river.'

Put like that, so abruptly, it was hardly an irresistible invitation, but she was weary of disease and death, and due for a break, so she went with him to a quiet place where a flight of steps ran down to the water's edge, full in the sun. They sat there, and without a word he took bread from his pocket and broke it in half, and two wrinkled apples. She began to eat, wondering if any of this was real, or if it was all a dream. It was so very different from their previous meetings in the dark, with so much suffering about them. Here, the sky was blue and the water shone and some-where across the river a blackbird was singing. The guns seemed very far away.

Ludovick was sitting one step below her, gazing out over the water, and he did not seem to know that she was watching him. She saw that he had washed and shaved, but he did not look as if he had slept very much. The breeze lifted his hair from his neck, revealing the long oblique line from ear to jaw. His hair was not particularly long, only just reaching his shoulders, a soldier's hair, not the arti-ficial beribboned lovelocks of a courtier, though it evidently curled naturally, loose dark curls clustered about a long neck.

She finished her share of the bread and picked up the apple, and he turned his head then to look at her and she sat without moving, absorbing him. He had a long oval face, the chin dimpled, blue eyes under the heavy curve of his brows, a straight nose lightly dusted with freckles, a supple mouth. For no good reason that she could think of, words read long ago in one of her Latin lessons with her father came into her head. Except that there was every reason . . . There had been apples too in the little scene in the poem . . . *Ut vidi, ut perii, ut me malus abstulit error! How I saw, how I fell, how . . .*

She realised that she had whispered the words aloud, for she saw recognition on his face. His eyes held hers. She heard him murmur what came afterwards, '"Nunc scio quid sit . . ."', falling into silence before the final momentous word. She seemed to hear it shouted into the silence – *amor. Now I know what kind of thing is love . . .*

She did not know how, for she made no conscious choice, but she bent towards him. She felt her lips reach his and then she slid down to the step where he sat and he put his arms about her and her body was pressed against the unyielding bulk of his buff coat, and she knew there was no kind of barrier between them any more.

When the kiss came to an end, as finally it did, he held her face in his hands and looked into it. '"Nunc scio quid sit amor,"' he said softly, finishing the sentence this time. Then, after another slow kiss, 'Where did you learn to quote Virgil?'

She told him, while his hands touched face and hair, stroked her neck, as if shyly exploring. He watched her intently as she spoke, sometimes asking a question. 'That's a lot of learning for a woman,' he said at last. What was it Dorothy had written? *Mistress Fawcett is very virtuous, though I think has too much learning to please a husband.*

'Why are you smiling?' The smile gave him a boyish look, full of mischief, which made her feel as if her heart was turning right over.

'Just something I remembered. Tell me, are you very virtuous, Mistress Susannah?'

'I hope so, my lord.'

'Then why do you allow so notorious a malignant to kiss you?' There was no answer to that, nor could she have given one if there had been, for he kissed her again. She only knew that all the usual everyday rules had somehow been overthrown, all that had guided her life until now. She was intoxicated, bewitched, possessed. She wanted only to seize what she found so suddenly within her reach, hold it to her for the short time that was all they could have. She had no thought for past and future, only for the present.

After that, there followed a lifetime telescoped into a moment's breath, a week holding in it all the experience of years. He came to seek her out whenever he had a break from his duties, though often they would have only a few minutes together. Unless she had some urgent task to do she would go with him and they would walk or sit by the river, or if it was raining in a quiet corner of a church. She never knew quite what to expect. Sometimes he brought to their meetings the bitter mood of the first days, at other times he carried her along on a tempestuous voyage of discovery, tossed this way and that by laughter and surprise and sudden devouring passion. Whatever she did, she had thoughts only for him, a craving of body and mind that could not be satisfied. When she heard the guns and he was not with her she prayed for his safety, knowing in the little that was left of her good Calvinist soul that to pray for him was pointless, for he of all people must be beyond God's mercy. Once, as she laughed at some silly remark of Molly's, and saw the girl look at her strangely, she realised that she was behaving exactly like all the foolish girls she had so despised, and she did not care. This was different, because it was happening to her. She was not herself, yet somehow she felt she was more fully, truly, herself than she had ever been. *Now I know what kind of thing is love . . .*

Early on Saturday morning they walked near the minster, since he had little time before he had to return to his post on the walls near Monk Bar. 'My lord, I've meant to ask you,' she was saying, 'Sir Ralph said you'd been his ward. How did that—?'

A group of riders passed them, with an escort of soldiers. She glanced up without more than a passing interest, and then she saw the face of the first rider, a tall, elegant young man with brown hair. She knew the face so well, but it was like seeing again something dimly remembered from early childhood, something that did not fit here, into the life she led now. She completely forgot what she had been saying. Instead, she suddenly recalled the young officer walking towards her in the hospital at Bradford, through the crude approval of the women. 'That's Captain Lambert!'

Her companion looked at the rider, well past them by now. 'Colonel Lambert, I think you'll find. You know him then?'

'Yes. He was with Sir Thomas Fairfax, last year.' She knew Ludovick had withdrawn from her, suddenly reminded as he had not been for the past days of the things that so implacably divided them.

'He and Sir William Constable are sent to meet with Sir Thomas Glemham. We've asked to discuss terms. You should soon be able to go home.' His face was without expression.

'Yes,' she said. She felt sick, weighed down with sudden misery. 'What will you do?'

'That depends on the terms.'

She looked at his sombre face and a terrible possibility occurred to her. 'My lord, what of the sentence against you? Will they—?' She could not bear to put the thought into words.

'Demand my blood for the safety of the city? I doubt it. If we'd held out for an unreasonable time . . .' He shrugged. 'But we haven't, and they've won York against all their expectations – and ours.'

Two days more, and the terms were agreed. That day Ludovick did not come to St Anthony's Hall. Anguished, Susannah waited until Doctor Baty sent her home for the night and then went to Ludovick's quarters, but he was not there, had not been there all day. She went home to tell the servants what she was doing and then called on Sir Ralph, whom she had not seen since the night of the battle. She found him slowly packing his belongings.

'You're leaving too, sir?' She was dismayed beyond all reason, as if the whole little world of York, of these past strange months set apart in time, was dissolving about her.

'The surgeon has declared me well enough to travel.'

'Then you'll go home?'

'Not at once. We're bound for Skipton first, under the terms of the surrender. After that we shall see. Now more than ever the King needs all the men who are fit to serve him.' He straightened and then sat down, facing her. 'You'll be among friends again soon, my dear.'

'Yes.' She felt tears rush to her eyes, she who never wept, and had to bend her head so he should not see.

'You must carry my warmest good wishes to your father. One day, please God, we shall meet again as friends in a land at peace.'

'Yes.' But she did not want peace. She wanted this time of war, this time that was so swiftly nearing its end.

'Susannah, what's wrong?'

'Nothing,' she said, forcing a smile. 'Nothing at all.' She went to kiss him. 'Goodbye, dear sir. God keep you safe.'

Then she turned towards the door, which at that moment was thrust open. Ludovick stood there, with eyes only for her. 'They said I'd find you here. I've looked for you everywhere. We march out at eleven tomorrow. Susannah, I've no more time.'

Ralph looked from one to another in astonishment and disbelief; and then with a slow, dismayed realisation of what it was he was witnessing. They stood facing one another, saying nothing, but he knew they had completely forgotten that he was there. He was convinced that if he were to try to cross the floor between them he would find he could not, for the strength of the force that linked them.

Troubled beyond words, he mumbled something about settling a little matter with his landlady and left the room. He knew that as he did so the two young people had met and were in one another's arms.

After a time, Ludovick said, 'There are no words to say what I feel.'

'No,' said Susannah. 'Nor for me.' She clung to him again.

'One day,' he murmured, his lips on her neck, 'I shall come to you again and it will not be like this.' His mouth moved to her face, over it, seeking her mouth. Then, through kisses, 'May God and his angels keep thee safe, dear heart, till then.'

Till then . . . But she knew that there could be no *then* for them, ever.

Late next morning the defeated garrison passed beneath Susannah's window towards Micklegate Bar. Under the generous terms of the surrender, they marched with arms shouldered, colours flying, the musketeers with bullets between their teeth and match lit at both ends. But no one watching them could have been fooled into thinking that they were anything but defeated. Many were drunk. Nearly all, soldiers and camp followers alike, were dirty and ragged, and most of them stumbled and slouched rather than marched.

She saw Sir Ralph, awkwardly mounted on a slow steady-looking gelding, and then Ludovick, his face shuttered against all emotion. She prayed that he would glance up as he passed the house, but he did not.

When he had gone she lingered at the window for a long time, seeing nothing. The sound of the drums throbbed in her head and tugged at her nerves and she felt as if steadily, inexorably, with every relentless beat, her heart was being torn from her body.

CHAPTER TWENTY-THREE

'Jesu!' said Ludovick wearily, as he rode back to join Sir Ralph at the head of the column. 'If we all get out of here alive, it'll be a miracle.'

'You'd have more chance if the Roundheads didn't seem to want the opposite,' said Sir Ralph. He had tried protesting to their escort about the treatment of Ludovick's troop, but without success.

The matter of Toby Milburn and the watch had been just the latest incident in a humiliating and uncomfortable journey. Yesterday, as they passed between the files of Parliamentary soldiers beyond Micklegate Bar, they had been systematically plundered. Their Roundhead escort was meant to protect them, but they were selective about it, and clearly thought Papists were fair game.

When, at the end of the afternoon's march, they had halted for the night at Hessay, Ludovick's troop had found itself with the worst quarters, which had consisted of a dilapidated barn offering little protection from the persistent, drenching rain. Early this morning, they had crossed Marston Moor, passing the mass graves in which two of the Blackheugh men now lay, Rob's cousin Barty and Will Dodd. The three who were left had taken off their hats and crossed themselves as they passed, at which their escort had jeered at them.

After that, their way had led through the fringes of the Earl of Manchester's camp, and the Roundhead troopers had fallen jubilantly on their baggage wagons. Far from protecting them, the soldiers in the escort had joined in. One of them had taken a watch from Toby Milburn's woman, Doll, which he had then dangled in front of an enraged Toby. 'Got it at Bolton did you, damned pillaging Papist dog?'

As a matter of fact he had, but Ludovick laid a hand on his arm, warning him to say nothing. Toby had shrugged him off and thrown himself on the Roundhead, his hands at the man's throat. In the end, rather than see Toby shot, Ludovick had hit him over the head with his pistol butt and dragged him clear.

Toby, dazedly rubbing his head, had been furious. 'Bloody interference! What's it come to when a man can't protect his own property?'

'We've no rights till we're away from here,' Ludovick had said. 'Shut up and get back in line. And keep a hold on your temper.'

Toby had muttered something inaudible and probably mutinous, but had obeyed. Ludovick was grateful to Doll, who said cheerfully, 'The watch doesn't work anyway,' which gave them an excuse for a laugh at the Roundhead's expense.

In a way Ludovick was glad of the necessity to be constantly on his guard to prevent trouble. It gave him something to occupy his mind. He could not remember ever having felt as he did now, disorientated, without moorings. It was more than just the black melancholy that had dogged him since childhood, more even than grief and sleeplessness, though he had slept little since Charles's death and not at all since the night before Marston Moor. Now, though, to everything else was added a restless longing for what he had left behind in York, combined with revulsion that he should feel like this.

It was as if he were haunted by her, as if she were some malign but beautiful spirit sent to lure him to his destruction. He seemed to hear her voice in his head in every quiet interval: clear, resonant, musical, pitched exactly where it was most certain to find a way into his blood and his nerves, setting him on fire. Her eyes too seemed there in the darkness of his present mood, and the feel of her in his arms: her smooth skin, the curves of her body, the breasts he had once caressed. He knew that when they had been together the rest of the world had somehow ceased to exist. He had never felt like that with any woman in his life before, least of all with one who stood for everything he most detested.

He told himself that physical need lay behind it. It was a very long time since he had lain with a woman and he needed one badly. If he could have bedded Susannah, none of this would have happened. That would have got her out of his system and he could then have left her behind without a second thought. He resolved that as soon as they reached Skipton he would find himself a woman – any passable woman – and exorcise that particular ghost.

'How about a song, to take their minds off things?' said Sir Ralph, breaking into his thoughts.

Ludovick saw that they were close to the furthest outpost of Manchester's army, where a knot of dragoons, some on foot, some on horseback, were more intent on their approach than on watching for any external threat. 'When we're clear of this lot. I don't doubt they'd take exception to anything we'd a mind to sing.'

Sir Ralph followed his gaze. 'Aye, you've a point there. In fact, I'm not sure that isn't John Lilburne, there on the right. I wouldn't want to get on the wrong side of him.'

In the end, the trouble came from behind them, from somewhere in the region of the pillaged wagons. They heard a shot first, then furious voices. Ludovick swung his horse round and spurred her towards the disturbance. He knew he risked being fired at by an over-zealous guard, but that did not trouble him in the least.

He saw very quickly, with relief, that it was nothing to do with Toby or any of the others. Well beyond the wagons, he came on a group of Roundheads surrounding a pinioned prisoner, whom they had evidently taken as he tried to break through their lines. He was a young lad, about sixteen or so, well dressed, though his clothes were much splashed with mud. He had an old sword buckled to his side. 'No pass, no papers of any kind,' one of the Roundheads was saying, accusingly.

Just as Ludovick was beginning to think there was something familiar about him, the boy looked round and gave a delighted exclamation. 'My Lord Milburn! Oh, I'm glad to see you! You'll vouch for me, won't you? They say I'm a spy, but I'm not, I tell them. You know I'm not. I only want to find my father.'

Ludovick dismounted and pushed his way forward, though he sensed the hostility that closed about him and knew that the slightest wrong move would only make matters worse. 'This is Master Mark Liddell, son of Sir Ralph Liddell.' He spoke calmly enough, but he felt bewildered.

They took some time to be convinced, and even then it was clear they did not entirely trust him. 'Right then, we'll go and ask Sir Ralph to confirm it.' One of them grasped Ludovick's arm. Ludovick sensed his pleasure in being able so discourteously to

handle one of his betters. 'You come along too, my lord. If you're
lying, you'll be strung up along with this one.'

'That wouldn't be in accordance with the terms.'

'Nor is spying.'

They made their way, leading the horses, to where Sir Ralph had
last been seen. As they went, Ludovick asked Mark, 'What on earth
are you doing here? Is something wrong at home?'

'No, my lord – there are Scots all over the place, but otherwise
everyone's just the same. That's just it. I'm sick of doing nothing. I
want to serve the King, like my father does. There's no honour in
sitting quietly at home, but Cuthbert can't see it. Oh, my lord, can
I serve in your troop?'

He was like an eager puppy, anxious to please, sure of his welcome. Ludovick cursed him for it, though he only said, 'Let's see
what your father has to say.'

Sir Ralph's reaction was precisely what Ludovick would have
expected. He was angry and dismayed and above all anguished that
his young son should walk with such blithe innocence into the
bitter complexities of the war. 'As soon as we halt again,' he said
sternly, brushing aside all Mark's pleading, 'I shall arrange a safe
conduct for you back to Widehope and there you will stay until I
come home again. You should be at school.'

'I'm sick of school. If it wasn't for the war I'd have left by now.' He
turned eagerly to Ludovick. 'You will let me serve in your troop,
won't you?'

'I don't recruit schoolboys. You're much too young.'

Mark gave him a sly sideways look. 'How old were you when you
first went as a soldier, my lord?'

Ludovick cursed that he had ever been tempted to tell soldiering
tales to the Liddell boys in those long-ago days of peace. 'That's not
the point.'

'You were only sixteen, you said so. I'm seventeen, a whole year
older.'

Since it became clear very quickly that, safe conduct or not,
Mark had no intention of riding meekly back to Widehope, Ralph
decided that he should come with them to Skipton, and from there
his father would himself escort him home again. For some reason,
Mark seemed to take that as the preliminary to an agreement that
he should remain with the army, and was jubilant, ignoring all Sir
Ralph's warnings and reproofs. His enthusiasm was infectious and

the rest of the day's march was immeasurably lightened by it. He insisted on being taught soldiers' songs and begged for tales of battles, though the answers he was given were selective in the extreme. Ludovick's troopers treated him with a rough protectiveness.

'Tiresome boy,' said Sir Ralph in an undertone to Ludovick. 'To be fair, there are lads as young as he is fighting in this war. One or two. But —'

'They're not your sons.'

Ralph gave a rueful half smile. 'No. Yet if he should refuse to go home – what then? What's to stop him running off again, until he finds some troop that'll take him on, as he surely will?'

'Best to keep him under your eye then,' advised Ludovick.

At Skipton, among friends again, they had the first firm news of the war, and it proved to be cheering beyond all their expectations.

The Queen, they were told, had gone safely on her way to France, leaving her baby daughter at Exeter. Freed of anxiety for his wife, the King had led his army into Devonshire against the Earl of Essex, who was retreating steadily before him, Sir William Waller having made no attempt at all to stop the royal advance. In the west of Scotland a force of rebel Irish had landed to join with their Highland kin, so causing the Scots to look anxiously over their shoulders. Meanwhile, Rupert was in Lancashire, making his way back to the training grounds on the Welsh marches, there to employ his formidable energies in building up a new army.

The north might be lost, for the time being at least, but the situation was very far from hopeless.

CHAPTER TWENTY-FOUR

By six o'clock in the evening of Tuesday the sixteenth of July the defeated Royalists had all left York. Almost at once the victors of Marston Moor marched in to take over: Susannah watched them from the window too. Sir Thomas Fairfax rode with the group of officers at their head, his face marked by a scarcely healed wound, his expression almost as sombre as if he were one of the defeated – but then she remembered how he had always been more light-hearted in defeat than in victory. Colonel John Lambert was there too, and Lord Fairfax, looking a good deal more tired and old than when she had last seen him.

The victors went first to the minster to give thanks where it was due. 'You see – they'll smash up the place before they're done singing psalms,' said cook, but Susannah pointed out that the terms of the surrender forbade any damage of that kind. She had heard people say that Lord Fairfax was behind that clause, and she could believe it. After all, he was a Yorkshireman, with a Yorkshireman's pride in his county's capital.

She felt in a strange state of suspension, as if life had momentarily drawn away from her, leaving her adrift between two quite different worlds, to neither of which she quite belonged any more. For the moment, nothing seemed quite real. She felt as if she were waking slowly from a dream to reality, or perhaps the other way about, she was no longer sure.

That afternoon, four soldiers were quartered on them, and later, after supper, Molly came to say there was an officer at the door. Remembering the day Sir Ralph had come – was that really only three months ago? – she went down, and there in the hall found a tall, broad young man with soft fair hair and an anxious expression.

'Master Metcalfe!' She stood staring at him, quite unable to think of anything further to say. He might have been a stranger. In fact he almost was a stranger, so long was it since she had seen him, such a lifetime had passed since then.

He kissed her, and she noticed that the kiss was rather longer and more lingering than the simple greeting warranted. 'I thank God you are well!' he said fervently, stepping back to look at her.

'And you too, sir,' she said, feeling dazed, not quite knowing what she did or said.

They talked, or rather he questioned her and she answered, giving him the news he had not heard, of her aunt, of herself and how it had felt to be among enemies in a city under siege for so long; all the trivial things that had slipped to the back of her mind and could only with difficulty be dragged up again. Then he promised he would arrange her return home as soon as possible, preferably under his own escort, since he had matters to attend to in Thornside. For that at least she was thankful. She was weary of York, weary of everything, and wanted only to be home; though she would hardly have been surprised if she were to be told that Thornside was after all simply a figment of her imagination.

She went to St Anthony's Hall only once more before leaving York. All but the most severely wounded men had ridden out with the garrison, and the few left behind were quickly handed over to the care of the Parliamentary surgeons. There was little left for Susannah to do. Giving her mind to entirely practical matters, she went to see her aunt's lawyer to arrange for him to manage her newly inherited property, though there would be little enough profit in it as long as the war lasted. Then she paid the servants what was due to them and packed her bags.

The journey home passed in a kind of daze, though she remembered being struck by the greenness of the countryside, the freshness of the air, once away from the city – its suburbs now a mass of blackened rubble – and the ruined fields about the battlefield. Richard talked a good deal, sometimes in answer to her questions, when she thought to put any to him. He was very ready to tell her all he had been doing since they last met and she had little need to interrupt him; she had never known him so voluble. For the most part his talk drifted over her, only half heard, but once or twice something he said caught her full attention. For instance:

'. . . It is a great mercy. God made them pay for the blood of Bolton.'

'What happened at Bolton?'

'You did not hear, then? How the Prince took Bolton on his way to York, and put it to the sack? I wonder they didn't boast of it.'

She had heard; at least, she had heard of it as a victory, one of many on that journey. Now Richard recounted the full horror of it, not just the plundering and the burning, but the merciless slaughter of the population of that godly town. She thought, feeling sick: Was he there? She knew at once that he had been, for she remembered he had once mentioned Bolton. They had rarely talked of the war, but in one of those dark, bitter moods that sometimes came on him with inexplicable suddenness he had said something about Bolton, something about an Irish prisoner hanged over the walls while they laid siege to the town. Then: *So we gave the men their heads afterwards.*

'Stop, stop!' She broke into Richard's horrible narrative, because the picture in her head, of Ludovick doing those things, was beyond bearing.

'Console yourself, Mistress Susannah, that God's ultimate judgement on these men, when it comes, will be terrible, more terrible by far than their late defeat.'

She said nothing, for it seemed as if there was no consolation whichever way she turned, however she looked at it. After a little while she said, 'Tell me, sir, would you ever, in any circumstances, for any provocation, do such things as were done at Bolton?'

'How can you ask!' he exclaimed indignantly. Then he said, 'Though if it were an Irish town, and I knew myself to be the instrument of God's vengeance, perhaps, yes. But I pray that I may never find myself in such a position. Even at its most noble, war is still an evil, civil war worst of all. And even I, sometimes, have done things I would not wish to dwell on afterwards.'

After a pause, he began to tell her, as he had once before, about his anxieties as to the outcome of the war, though those anxieties seemed now to be more than a vague unease. In particular, his meeting with some of the soldiers of the Eastern Association seemed to have alarmed him. 'I knew Lieutenant-General Cromwell when I was first in Parliament, and greatly admired him. But I have to say that having now seen what manner of men he has serving under him, I begin to have serious doubts about his judgement.

'It is not just that so many of his officers are not quite gentlemen.

There is a Captain Harrison, for instance – a butcher's son, of all things, and inclined to an unseemly showiness of dress, as if he were of better birth than he is. But that would not matter so much, were it not for the religion of these men. Anabaptists, antinomians, all kinds of sectaries, allowed to speak and worship and even preach just as they please. If I tell you that John Lilburne seems a meek, modest man in such company, you will see the scale of it. General Cromwell would claim that his first concern is that they make godly soldiers, but then I begin to have doubts of his religion too. I'm told he did not subscribe to the Covenant until the very last moment, and such tardiness must be suspicious. I am surprised that one who is a gentleman himself should be so blind to the consequences of allowing such licence to his men. It is in danger of contaminating the more orderly troops. Things are being said that once would never have been dreamed of. Some men hold forth against tithes, crying that they should not have to pay for ministers they do not like, as if they had the right to pick and choose as the fancy takes them. I hear there's even a book lately brought out in London that argues for liberty for all religions – not just the wildest sects, but Papists even, and Turks and Jews. I trust it will be burned before it gets into the wrong hands. But that anyone should have thought to put such a thing into words . . . The times are troubled, Mistress Susannah. As I always feared, this war looks set to unravel all that holds England together.'

All the old certainties, everything she had believed to be true . . . Yes, even within herself the war had unravelled things and then tangled them up again beyond re-ordering. All her pure, clear sense of right and wrong had grown clouded. She had learned that Ralph, that dear friend, with his kindness and his sense of honour, was not after all unique among Royalists. She had shared weeks of hardship with men and women whose loyalties and hopes were wholly different from her own, yet who were simply men and women like herself. She had seen her enemies brought low by wounds and sickness and the imminence of death, and learned that they too could face the very worst with courage and patience and even trust in God. She had mingled with Papists, and found them to be not greatly different from herself, misguided perhaps, but to be pitied rather than condemned. And where still she could condemn, where she could have no doubt that evil lay, there, inexplicably, she loved.

*

She reached home, and everything was strange and familiar at once. Even her own voice, to her ears, sounded odd, with a timbre and intonation that belonged to an earlier time, long gone. She felt ill at ease, unsure of herself.

Yet she was welcomed with thankfulness and love. Her father hobbled about her in a state of smiling beatitude that told her as no words could how much he had missed her, how deeply feared for her. In church the next Sunday, Master Johnson gave thanks for the safe return of their dear sister Susannah Fawcett. Richard's sister wept over her and then begged her to admire the way young Philip had grown and thrived, even in her absence – though certainly thanks to all the skill she had previously lavished upon him. Dame Alice greeted her more austerely, but with obvious affection, whose motive became only too clear the next day, when Richard came to the house and proposed to her.

She heard him in a silence that lasted for a long time after he had finished speaking. In fact, so anxious did it make him that he was the first one to break it. 'I know the times are uncertain. Perhaps you think they are not right for marriage. Yet if God wills it, as I believe He does, then it is not for us to hesitate. You know, I think, that my constancy in this thing has been tested in the fire, tried above the ordinary. My respect for you can never have been in doubt.'

'No, never,' she agreed. What should she say? What every instinct urged her to say, 'No, I cannot marry you?'

Once, it had seemed clear to her that marriage was not for her, that God had quite another purpose for her. But since then so many things had whittled away at that certainty, leaving her now without a clear and unequivocal answer. Indeed, she found herself wondering, 'What if it had been *he* who asked me this?' The very thought of such a thing was ridiculous, unimaginable, and shot through with pain. Yet might not even the most foolish thought be sent to point her in the way she should go? She knew that she must keep her eyes open for any sign of God's will for her. On the other hand, she knew that she must not lightly, out of hand, dismiss the possibility that God might have sent Richard to her in her present uncertain state, to win her at last. 'I must have time to consider what you ask,' she said eventually.

'You have known my heart for four years now, mistress. Surely in that time you have reached a conclusion?'

'If you press me to give you an answer now, sir, then I shall refuse you,' she warned him; so, visibly shaken, promising to return in the morning, he left her.

It was cold and raining, but she pulled a cloak about her and went up onto the fell and there, buffeted by the wind, walked with bent head, seeing nothing, struggling through her confusion and her pain to understand the mind of God in this thing He had placed before her.

What Richard offered was what he had always offered, marriage, children, the management of his household: the ordinary lot of the majority of womankind, the one most of them eagerly sought. Yet she saw now, what she had never realised before, that her past rejection of marriage, to Richard or anyone, had been more complicated than the simple acceptance of God's will that she had thought it. She saw, with astonishment, that she had even been afraid of marriage: not simply because it would put fetters on her freedom, but also because of what she had seen as the brutal subjugation of the act of coition, the agony and terror of childbirth, the exhaustion of its endless repetition, the lifelong burden that each child must place upon its mother.

The strange, wonderful, intoxicating yet inexpressibly painful thing that had happened to her in York had changed all that. She understood now why a man and a woman might wish to put aside all their fears and seek in marriage the union of body and soul that chastity denied them outside it.

Except that marriage was quite a different thing from love, at least from the consuming fire that was like a sickness of the blood from which, in time, with God's grace, she might be cured. Love of that kind was no good ground for marriage, which was only to be entered on *reverently, discreetly, advisedly, soberly*, as the idolatrous Book of Common Prayer for once wisely put it. It should be based not on unthinking passion, but on respect and affection, a sure foundation from which a steady and enduring love might grow. That, certainly, she would find with Richard (though she was not too sure how sober his feelings were), who was precisely the kind of godly man she ought to marry, if she were to marry at all. Yet how could she marry one man while she was still burning with fever for another? The very thought of doing so both depressed and repelled her.

And there, she saw suddenly, was her answer. She loved, but her feelings were so immoderate, the object of her love so hopelessly, ludicrously ineligible, that there was not the remotest possibility of any happy conclusion. And since she knew that, loving one man, she could not now bring herself to marry another, it was the surest sign she could have been given that God did not mean her to marry. He had another purpose for her, and that most certainly the one she had always believed it to be. The fact that she now looked forward to the rest of her life with less hope and enthusiasm, felt less of the single-mindedness that had been her driving force, made no difference, for God did not arrange for everything always to be easy. That it was His will must be enough.

Of course, that did not tell her what precisely His will was for her. She had no intention – it was certainly not God's intention for her – of becoming merely some sort of wise-woman, an eccentric crone dispensing love potions and remedies for sickness with equal confidence. She did not want to give anyone cause even to look on her in that way. She would have preferred simply to set herself up in practice as a physician like her father, which as a woman, of course, she could not do. While the war lasted, there was a need even for unrecognised medical skills, but she could not leave her father again, at least not yet – she could see how scarred he had been by her long absence. However she did it, she supposed it would be a slow and difficult business. But a way would be shown to her, in God's good time. Until then, she must be patient.

Her most immediate difficulty would be to convince Richard that what he saw as God's will was not in fact such at all. She wished now that she had followed her instinct and refused him at once. She feared he would take it hard.

Going back down the lane towards the town she passed three women gossiping in the shelter of a tree, their hands busy with their knitting. Their talk reached her in gusts on the wind, something about an acquaintance just delivered of a dead child, after a long labour. 'Dead, the bairn was. Just as well, the state it was in. Such a time Mistress Nelson had getting it out of poor Bess. All night, and all her private parts torn afterwards. You should have heard her yell.'

'I heard she'll not last the week.'

'Not the day, I'd say, the way she looked when I was there this morning.'

Susannah flinched at the picture the talk brought to her mind, and felt anger too. There was so much barbarity in life, so many evils that men and women brought on one another. She had seen so much of agonising and degrading death, its stench and its horrors. Was birth too meant to be as harsh, to lead so often to a horrible end? She thought of her mother's lingering death, her father's helpless anger in the face of it, his long determination to understand what had gone wrong and to learn, somehow, to prevent it happening. That determination had dwindled now to an occasional rumination, leading nowhere, and not expected to do so. But he was old; his daughter was young and called to something apart from the common lot of women. What more fitting than that she should take up where he had left off, and somehow try to bring an end to a small part of all that needless suffering?

Suddenly, with the force of a storm breaking, she knew what she was meant to do next, where her decision of this morning was taking her. Elated, excited, eager to begin, she ran the last part of the way home.

At the door she halted, considered, and then turned round and made her way instead to the Hall, where she asked to see Richard and told him, as gently as possible, that she could not marry him. Then, that hard thing over – and feeling a good deal more sober – she went home to tell her father everything, beginning with her refusal of Richard's proposal. Rather to her surprise, he was not pleased. 'I don't understand you, Susannah. Why refuse him? He's a godly young man, well born, well endowed with this world's goods, which, though I know it is not of the first importance, is nevertheless not to be lightly disregarded. Where else will you find such a man, at your age too?'

'Nowhere, I suppose, but then I do not want such a man. Nor any man.' But one, echoed her heart, though she pushed the rebellious thought firmly aside. 'And since when have you wished me married and away from you?'

'Hmm! Marriage is the natural state of humankind, Susannah. A barrier against sin and a consolation, as I know myself. If I'd never married, I should not have had you. One day you will want children, and then it may be too late.'

Susannah resisted the temptation to point out that, lacking all natural motherly instincts, she had no wish to bear children. She suspected that he would either disbelieve her, or be dismayed. 'If in my selfishness I've not wanted to lose you too soon,' he went on, 'then I have still known it must come one day – and who better to give you to than a gentleman I know and like so well, and who is such a near neighbour? I shall not live for ever, you know – and what when I die? I don't want to leave you a withering old maid, turned in upon herself, perhaps driven mad by melancholy and loneliness.'

Susannah laughed. 'Dear father, you know I'm not made of such feeble stuff as that! Besides, if it's what God wants of me, then he will not allow me to be the worse for it.' Before he could protest again, she put in, 'I shall attach myself as a pupil to Mistress Nelson. Then I shall apply to be licensed as a midwife.'

That brought on her head a storm of quite another kind. Matthew Fawcett was appalled that she should lower her sights from a good marriage to the pursuit of a demeaning craft. 'For a woman of your quality, to ally yourself with such as her! Besides, you are unwed, you have never borne children.'

'I didn't notice that you used that as an argument against men midwives.'

'That's different.'

'If it is, then the difference is in my favour, for I have a woman's body.' She knelt down beside him and put her arms about him. 'Father, have you ever known me to be wrong in these things?' He shook his head. 'Well then, trust me now. I know what it is I must do.'

'But what can you learn from Margery Nelson?'

'I don't know. I shall discover. Perhaps only what not to do. But there will be something.'

That night when she went to bed she was filled with such a sense of peace as she had not felt for a long time, and fell asleep quickly; and then dreamed that she lay stark naked in the sun by the river in York and Ludovick lay beside her and was kissing her and his hands were doing things they had never done to her in life, slowly, sweetly; and then she woke suddenly before it was all ended and felt her body throb agonisingly with unsatisfied desire, and she wanted to weep. Instead, she put her hand to her mouth and pressed her teeth into it until it hurt, because it was the only way to drive out the other pain. Then she stood beside the bed and prayed earnestly that this torment might be taken from her.

As soon as it was light she went to Mistress Nelson's neat cottage and put her request to the woman in as pleasant and meek a manner as she was able.

The midwife, hands on hips, looked her up and down with a hostile light in her eyes. 'You want to be apprenticed to me! Well now, there's a thing. Going to set yourself up in opposition to me, is that the idea?'

'You were once an apprentice yourself.'

'To my mother, who taught me all she knew, so that I'd one day step into her shoes. You're not my daughter, and far too old to be too. Why should I train a rival?'

'I should only become your rival if I were one day to surpass you in skill and knowledge,' Susannah retorted. She strongly suspected that she had already reached that point, but she could not yet be certain, and in any case she had no intention of saying so. She knew Mistress Nelson would contemptuously have rejected the idea. She might, too, have guessed that Susannah was as much concerned with establishing her position in the eyes of the community as in actually extending her knowledge.

'But once you've plundered me for all I know, and got your licence . . . You know, I suppose, there's no one to go to for licences now, what with the Bishops gone?' Then she paused. Susannah realised that she had suddenly seen what might be read into her words; that in the present unsettled state of things, any unscrupulous woman could set herself up as a midwife, without a licence, without any training even. Perhaps she thought too that it would be easier for Susannah to do so than for many women, and wished to forestall her. She went on, 'Still, if that's what you want, who am I to stand in your way?' She smiled, maliciously. 'Mistress Fawcett my apprentice—!'

'I said pupil, not apprentice.'

'What's the difference—? Ah, I see. You don't want it all legal and tied up. No, Mistress Susannah, if I'm going to take the risk of training a rival, I'll have it all in writing, everything properly drawn up.'

Susannah had no intention of binding herself for years to come, with no prospect of setting up on her own until the apprenticeship was over. Yet, in spite of her dislike of Mistress Nelson, she did genuinely want to learn anything that the woman could teach her. In the end, by the simple expedient of offering her a payment far in excess of the usual bond for an apprentice, she managed to persuade the midwife to take her on simply as a pupil, with a month's notice on either side to end the agreement. That much at least she put in writing. She knew quite well that Margery Nelson would crow over how Doctor Fawcett's proud daughter had bound herself as a pupil to the woman he and Susannah had, until now, so openly despised, but that too was a price she must pay for what she wanted.

She began her tuition next day, when Mistress Nelson sent word to meet her at the house of Joan Lupton, wife of the wheelwright, who had just gone into labour with her fifth.

The midwife was at the door of the house when she reached it, about to go in, but she turned and stood gazing at Susannah, looking her up and down with mock amazement. 'Well, well, we're very fine this morning! We're not going to church, Mistress Fawcett.' She spoke the name with contemptuous emphasis. 'Those things won't be spotless very long, I can tell you.'

'These are my working clothes,' said Susannah; she had dressed, as usual, in her sober grey-green gown, the skirts kilted up over her russet petticoat, with clean apron and neckerchief and cap.

'Oh, I'm sorry I spoke! I forget you're a gentlewoman and I'm just a humble midwife. Just so long as you don't come crying to me when your fine linen's red with blood.'

'My father always used to say that only the very best is good enough for the welcoming of a new life into the world,' said Susannah quietly. Even now it was a thought that moved her.

'Aye well, much good it did when your mother was in labour,' said the midwife.

Susannah caught her breath. 'What killed her was the afterbirth not coming away,' she said, when she had herself under control again.

'Aye, and he didn't get it away did he?'

'Have you ever done that, and the mother lived afterwards?'

'If she's died it's been for other causes. Milk fever or such. Anyway, what's that got to do with the clothes I have on my back?'

Susannah did not say, as she might have done, that the stinking garments the midwife wore, stained with the blood of many births, were enough to turn the stomach of any more squeamish patient; though when they came into the crowded bedroom she had to admit that neither Joan Lupton nor her neighbours seemed to notice what either of them was wearing, still less to mind. Perhaps, in the gruelling toil of childbirth, such things were unimportant after all.

Susannah forced herself to behave in every way as the meek pupil, obeying each order she was given, standing quietly by when nothing was required of her, watching and holding her tongue, except when she wanted to know the reason for something the midwife did. Margery Nelson was evidently an advocate of the birthing stool, a specially designed seat which Susannah had never seen in use before, since her father, like most physicians, regarded it as a primitive relic of the past and insisted that the women he attended in labour should remain lying in bed.

'All right for fine ladies, that,' the midwife said, 'but my mothers like to be up and doing. It's quicker that way, in the end.'

Susannah, watching Joan Lupton crouched on the stool, thought she did indeed suffer less than many women she had seen in labour; but then this was the swift and uncomplicated birth of a fifth child. On the other hand, most of her father's patients had been gentle-women, and she had heard it said, often, that low-born women always gave birth more easily than their betters, being less sensitive by nature. It was a theory she would have liked to put to the test.

Within two hours the bloody miracle of childbirth was over, the infant washed and swaddled, put to the breast and then placed in the cradle, while his mother, grateful and happy, rested. Susannah took off her stained apron and washed her hands at the well out-side, drawing further scorn from the midwife for her finickiness. Then they were both entertained by the father with cakes and wine before going on their way, with a generous gratuity added to the midwife's fee. 'Not always like that, of course,' said Mistress Nelson. Then, a grudging concession, 'Well, you did all right, I'll say that for you.'

Susannah was not in the mood for mutual congratulations. She said, trying to choose her words with care, 'Tell me, mistress – it seemed to me that this was one case where nature could have been left to run her course. I think in your place I should not have done anything, beyond giving what encouragement was needed. Yet it seems you thought differently.' She had in truth been appalled by the degree to which the midwife had intervened at every stage of labour, with what seemed to her quite unnecessary manipulation of an infant who was showing every sign of doing quite well on his own account. Ignorant interference in the birth process was one of the things that most enraged her father, who had too often been called to deal with the results of such clumsy handling.

'Is this how it's going to be – one case, and you're carping at what I do?' retorted the midwife. 'You're my pupil, remember.'

'Of course. But I can't learn if I don't understand why you do what you do. After all, when your practice differs from my father's, it may be that you're right and he's wrong. I only know that in this he wouldn't have done as you did. He always says that whenever possible it is best to let nature take her course.'

'He sounds just like my mother,' said Mistress Nelson contemptuously. Her mother had been the town midwife before her. 'That's the old way. I can tell you, I've seen more living infants into the world than my mother did in all her lifetime. Or, I don't doubt, than your father ever has. What does a man know about it, when all's said and done?'

Susannah thought it wiser, after that, to say no more. When she reached home she wrote a careful account of the birth and its treatment in one of the large leather-bound volumes in which she and her father kept their medical records, and then she sat down to talk everything over with him. At the end, he said suddenly, 'You remember I spoke to you of Madame Bourgeois?'

'The one who was pupil to Ambroise Paré?'

'And midwife to the Queen of France, yes. I always had in mind to get hold of one or other of the books she wrote, but never got round to it. I don't know if it's still possible, but my bookseller has contacts in Paris. Shall I write to him?'

Susannah knew then that her father had accepted the decision she had made.

Dame Alice Metcalfe, who had secretly been anguished by her son's obvious misery at his rejection, and had tried in vain to make Susannah change her mind and accept his proposal after all, was outraged when news eventually reached her of the young woman's latest whim.

'I thought better of her, I have to admit,' she said to Richard, more calmly than she felt. 'But there we are: I was wrong. Console yourself, my son. She would never have done for you. She should have been checked long before this, if she was ever to make a biddable wife.'

Richard smiled ruefully. 'Like you, madam?'

His mother had not seen him smile for some days now and was less offended by this uncharacteristic impertinence than she might otherwise have been. She said with dignity, 'I was a very biddable wife to your father. However, we are not talking of me. We must look now to finding a wife for you. As you know, I always favoured Barbara Chaytor.'

Barbara Chaytor was a pale, shy young woman, on the fringes of their own social circle, whose name had occasionally been connected with Richard's before he began his doomed courtship of Susannah. Even in those days the thought of marriage to her had depressed him. 'Is she still unwed, then?'

'To my knowledge, yes. She was most eligible, of good birth, assured of a substantial dowry. Unfortunately, her family have sided with the King. I'm not sure her father hasn't died now, but I do know for certain that she had a brother killed at Marston Moor. They are a godly enough family – or were – but I think it unlikely they will look kindly on marriage to one of your allegiance at this time. We must either wait a little, to see what happens, or think of someone else. There is the matter of an heir to consider, of course. You're nearly thirty.'

'I can afford to wait a little, I think,' said Richard with a sense of relief. 'Once the issue of this war is known, then it will be clearer what I have to offer, or she to give in return.'

'Richard,' his mother said after a moment, 'the war is something that has lately troubled me very much. After Marston Moor it looked clearer, but now the news is not good.'

'No.' They had heard only the previous day that the Earl of Essex, penned into the Fowey peninsula by the royal army, had fled by sea, leaving his infantry, artillery and large stores of ammunition at the King's disposal. 'It's being said that the Irish have won a great victory in Scotland too. You know the Earl of Montrose has put himself at their head?'

'I thought he was a Covenanter. What's he doing leading Papist Irish?'

'God alone knows,' said Richard wearily. 'What I do know is that he has the Scots watching their backs, instead of giving wholehearted succour to our cause.' He had been uneasy enough about the course of the war when it was going well and he still had hopes of Susannah – could that really only be a month ago? Now it felt as if everything had turned sour and stale and without hope.

'Yet in the end right must prevail.'

'"If we beat the King ninety and nine times he is the King still,"' Richard murmured. 'So, I'm told, my lord of Manchester said once.'

'There's nothing new in that. Nor would you wish it otherwise, surely? The war was entered on to induce the King to listen to good counsel. When victory comes – so long as it comes – then he must do so.'

'But what if he will not? What then do we do? There are things being spoken of . . .' He broke off and then, after a pause, went on, 'If the Scots abandon us, then the Independents have the larger voice, with their talk of every man being free to follow his own conscience. Where then is order and authority?'

'What does Tom Fairfax say in all this?'

'Oh, you know Tom. He's a soldier. He seeks to win the war by whatever means, and looks no further ahead than that. His complaints are all of divided commands and arrears of pay. I suppose he would say, if asked, that he will do what he has to do and the rest is in the Lord's hands.'

'Then perhaps you should follow his example,' suggested his mother.

A week later Richard left Thornside to rejoin his troop, which by now was besieging Scarborough. Susannah, absorbed in her new work, scarcely noticed his going.

1645

CHAPTER TWENTY-FIVE

There were four men of various ages sharing the small room and one bed above the baker's shop in Oxford, and tonight they were all there at once, along with five of their friends, and even – God help us! thought Ludovick – the mother of one of them.

At least Goodwife Pugh sat knitting peacefully by the apology for a fire, which would have been wholly inadequate on this bitter January day had there not been so many crammed into the room. Fuel was very hard to come by in Oxford at present unless you were extremely rich, as few Royalists now were, since their pay was catastrophically in arrears. Now and then the widow would bend down to prod the last few charred splinters of wood together with her foot, in the hope of making the fire last longer. Otherwise, fingers busy, she simply sat watching her son Davy with her usual mixture of pride and anxiety. A gaunt, dark woman, she put Ludovick in mind of one of those Spartan mothers he had read about at school, who commanded their sons to come home from battle either bearing their shields as victors, or carried on them, having died valiantly. She was fiercely protective of her son's honour, wanting him always to be first in the fight, while in quarters she fussed over him like any other mother of an only son. But she made herself useful too, organising the cooking of meals, keeping order among the other Welsh camp followers with military discipline.

Davy – Cornet David Pugh, to give him his full title – was one of the group engaged in a very noisy game of cards at the table that took up most of the space left by the bed. With him was the other Welsh lad who normally occupied the room, his cousin Gilbert, and two of their compatriots who were quartered elsewhere, their sing-song English competing with Mark Liddell's Durham lilt, the flat Cheshire vowels of Corporal William Gartside and the Northumbrian burr of Tot Charlton, who had called to see Rob but could never resist a game of cards. They had been growing noisier and more hilarious as the afternoon passed. Mark Liddell, who shared his father's lodging but had become a firm friend of Davy Pugh, almost exactly his own age, had reached the stage of uncontrollable giggles, more from excessive high spirits, Ludovick thought, than the effects of what little alcohol they had consumed.

Rob, who sat on the bed beside Ludovick mending a stocking, said something, but the words were lost in the din. When he repeated it, all Ludovick heard was, '. . . Browne got his hands on a hundred casks of wine today.'

In May last year, as a result of an inexplicable decision by Rupert's enemies on the King's council, Abingdon had been abandoned to the Roundheads and was now under the command of Major-General Browne, who had proved a constant harassment to the convoys bringing supplies to Oxford. There had been several attempts to retake the town but all had failed. 'Maybe it's the only way he knows to keep a hold on his men,' Ludovick suggested. 'I've heard they're near mutiny. But then that's true of half Parliament's army.' A sudden louder burst of laughter swamped Rob's reply.

'I think,' said Ludovick, the next time there was a lull, 'I must be getting old. I can't stand much more of this noise.' He had been trying to tune his lute, but had long since given up. He got to his feet. 'I'm away to see Sir Ralph.'

'You should bring his landlady back with you,' suggested Rob. 'Set her singing, and she'd sharp clear the room.'

'She'd never make herself heard.' He took his lute with him, protected under his cloak from the bitter rain. Oxford had become a stinking dungheap, its streets disgusting with excrement and rubbish, haunted by rats and other vermin, and by soldiers who had nowhere else to go, lying drunk in corners. The stench hung over everything, augmented now by the smell of charred wood, since the disastrous fire last October that had burned down a large part of the poorer quarter of the city. Ludovick had long ago come to hate the place. He was sick of war, too. It had struck him the other day that he had now been a soldier for a good third of his life. Yet he could not imagine that things would ever be any different.

For the most part he was too busy for such gloomy reflections. After an autumn of vigorous recruiting, his troop was now at something approaching full strength. Through the winter, a constant series of raids on nearby Roundhead strongholds had helped to sharpen their military skills. Prince Rupert, now overall commander (next to the King) of the royal armies, was as restlessly active as ever, though as much at war with the growing number of his enemies at court as with the Parliamentarians.

Then there was Mark, who was a perpetual anxiety to Ludovick. Nominally a part of Ludovick's troop, he was given relatively safe duties to do whenever there was any possibility of danger, something he increasingly resented, especially as his friend Davy had no such protection. Sir Ralph would have kept him under his own eye, but he now had command of a troop in Colonel George Lisle's regiment of foot, and felt Mark was safer with the cavalry, which was, in any case, what the boy wanted.

As Ludovick neared Ralph's lodgings the sound of enthusiastic female singing greeted him from somewhere at the back of the house. He mounted the stairs, wincing as the singer managed somehow to slide into three different keys in the space of four bars, if what she sang could be dignified with such technical terms.

'She's in lamentably good voice today,' he commented to Ralph, when the older man had welcomed him and pulled up a chair for him. 'Rob thinks I should borrow her, as a sure means of clearing my quarters of noisy youth.'

Ralph grinned. 'Why yes, at twenty-five I can see you'd feel yourself a bit past the pleasures of youth.'

'Half an hour of Mark and Davy and I feel ninety.'

'Mark has long had that effect on me,' Ralph conceded. Then, more gravely, 'Two visits from you in one week. I'm honoured. What's gone wrong?' He had never actually said so, but Ludovick knew that Ralph had disapproved of the succession of feverish if brief affairs with which the younger man had filled his spare moments throughout the winter; until last week, at least, when the husband of his latest bedfellow had challenged him to a duel. It had ended without serious bloodshed, but it had brought him up short, forcing him to look at what he was doing. He had not much liked what he saw. It was not working anyway, for no other woman seemed able to drive out his burning obsession with Susannah.

'I've decided there's more solace in music than women,' he said.

At the end of a pleasant afternoon, he left for his own lodgings in good time before the curfew, and was met at the bottom of the stairs by a messenger, summoning him to Magdalen College, where Prince Rupert lodged. 'Another attempt at Abingdon,' he thought, as he walked into the Prince's room and saw the familiar faces there: Rupert and Maurice, of course, and Dan O'Neill; and Sir Henry Gage, governor of Oxford since November, a well-respected Catholic soldier with long experience in the Spanish service in Flanders, where Ludovick had known him slightly. There were also a number of 'Irish' officers, among them a man who had once refused to serve under Ludovick, though they were now at least on speaking terms.

An hour later, he had returned to his lodgings, sent Mark home, emptied the room of all but his officers, who were then sworn to secrecy and given their instructions. By early evening, they were part of a considerable force riding out of Oxford, on the now familiar southward road.

They had been on their way for perhaps half an hour, when one of Ludovick's men began to whistle softly between his teeth. Turning to silence him, Ludovick caught sight of the face of the man next to him, lit briefly by the glow from a farmhouse window.

He swung his horse round and rode back to the man, who now had his head bent, so that his hat brim hid his face. Ludovick grasped his bridle, praying that he was mistaken, that it was one of the other men. But it was Mark Liddell's young face that looked up at him, briefly angry, then dismayed. Ludovick dragged furiously at the bridle, pulling Mark to the side of the road. 'What in hell's name are you doing here?'

'You let Davy come, my lord. That's not fair!'

'Davy told you?' Ludovick snapped, further enraged.

'No. I knew there was something up, so I followed him. Are we bound for Abingdon?' His eyes were shining with excitement.

Ludovick cursed himself for not having made absolutely sure Mark had gone home to his father. 'You're not bound for anywhere but Oxford,' he said. 'With all speed, or I'll have you sent home the first chance I get, if I have to take you myself. Don't you dare disobey my orders again!'

'You gave me no orders, my lord,' Mark said irrepressibly, and then quailed a little at the waft of anger that reached him. 'Very well, my lord,' he said, all meekness.

Ludovick reminded him of the password, so he could pass the Oxford sentries safely, and then watched until he had disappeared into the darkness. Then he hurried to catch up with the others, feeling unsettled and uneasy.

They reached Culham village, south of Abingdon, some time after midnight, and fell on it, surprising its Roundhead outpost. In less than an hour of fierce fighting they had secured the village and the bridge and were able to move forward across the long causeway running over flooded fields to Abingdon bridge itself, though not very fast, for the causeway was narrow and the flood-waters stretched level and dark on either side of it. Ahead of them, the sound of firing told them the advance party was through, but had met with some kind of resistance.

The next moment Ludovick thought he saw something move in the water; and then suddenly there was a mass of seething black shapes coming towards them. Shots burst into the night. There was a cry from somewhere in the ranks ahead, then shouting, and men scrambled out of the water, some mounted, some on foot, slashing and thrusting with pike and sword at horses and men.

The Royalists fought back fiercely, but the waters hampered them, and the enemy's greater knowledge of the treacherous ground; and the darkness that made it cruelly hard to tell friend from foe. Slowly, surely, they were forced back to Culham bridge, slithering in the mud, men and horses falling around them, some swept away by the swift currents of the river.

Beyond the bridge was a narrow, high-hedged lane, and there the fighting grew desperate, for the few Roundheads left in Culham came to the aid of their comrades, so that the Cavaliers were pressed on both sides. By the time dawn came, those who were left had forced a passage back to the village, but they knew it was over.

Somewhere, a trumpet sounded the retreat. Ludovick made his way through the crush, shouting to his own men, trying to put some order into their withdrawing. The firing was more scattered now. He saw Davy Pugh riding towards him. He was shouting something, though it was a moment or two before he could make it out. 'My lord, come quick – it's Mark.'

He had not thought he could feel so cold. He heard himself say, 'He went back to Oxford.'

'No, sir. He's here. He's hurt.'

The questions would have to wait. He followed Davy to where he had left Mark, in the shelter of a doorway. The boy was unconscious, the blood seeping in a widening stain through the front of his buff coat. Ludovick did not need to examine him to know it was bad. In any case, there was no time.

He staunched the wound as best he could, then took Mark on to his saddle, anguished by the boy's moaning. It ceased not long after they left Culham. By the time they reached Oxford he was dead.

They had carried him, with the other wounded, to Magdalen and the attention of the Prince's surgeon. Rupert himself was there, watching over Sir Henry Gage, wounded too, and dying. The Prince said suddenly to Ludovick, 'There were five in the advance party from Ireland, I think.'

'I believe so, sir,' said Ludovick. It seemed a trivial point, until the implications suddenly reached him: the advance party had got into the town, but presumably were still there, prisoners of the Roundheads. 'Jesu!'

Rupert strode to the door, calling for a messenger to ride to Abingdon at once: no exchange of prisoners anywhere until the safety of the Irish soldiers was assured. Through the clamour, Ludovick heard the surgeon pronounce what he already knew – that Mark was dead. He left Davy to watch him and made his way to Sir Ralph's lodgings.

The older man was already out of bed, writing a letter in the quiet of the morning. He looked up as Ludovick came in. 'Is Mark at your quarters? He hasn't been back all night.' He did not sound particularly concerned; but then he trusted Ludovick to watch over his son's safety.

He saw the look on Ludovick's face, and put down his pen and stood up, as if bracing himself for what he suddenly saw was about to come. 'That's why you're here, isn't it?'

'Yes,' said Ludovick, and then told him, as simply as he could, as if reciting a tale that had little to do with either of them.

A silence. He waited for Ralph to turn on him in fury, to shout, *Why did you not see him safe home? I trusted you and this is how you reward me! You have wronged me more than ever your father did. At least he only took my land. For this I can never forgive you; I wish to God we had never met!*

Nothing happened, though in the silence Ludovick wished desperately that it would. In the end Ralph only came round the table towards him, pressed a hand on his shoulder, said, 'Take me to him,' and then walked towards the door at his side.

On the way to Magdalen they said little, though now and then Ralph asked a question, which Ludovick answered as best he could. He found it very difficult to speak at all. Then they came to the room where the boy lay and Ralph went in and knelt beside the body of his son and took it in his arms, crushing it to him as if he hoped somehow to press into it some of his own life. Then he began to weep, the harsh dry sobs of a man not easily broken, who had never had much cause to weep.

Ludovick could bear it no more and left him alone with his grief. I have done this, he thought.

Just beyond the door he met Rupert, who was in one of his thunderous rages. 'We were too late. Browne hanged the men from Ireland before the messenger got there. Damn him to hell for it!'

CHAPTER TWENTY-SIX

Richard Metcalfe had spent the winter in London, attending to his Parliamentary duties. The capital was not a cheerful place, though in a way it fitted only too well with his present mood. Fuel was short, prices high, the people sullenly murmuring, to be diverted only by a series of executions: the usual Catholic priest, one Henry Morse, following on a more notorious victim, the former Archbishop of Canterbury, William Laud, now an old, sick man. And there were two others, whose fate disturbed Richard very much more, because they had once been his friends: Sir John Hotham and his son, letters from whom had been found in the Marquis of Newcastle's baggage after Marston Moor, proving their treachery beyond denial. That had made their deaths inevitable, yet Richard had found himself thinking: There but for the grace of God . . . Had they been guilty of anything much more than the same kind of confused unhappiness that he felt so much of the time, about the whole sorry business of this war?

So many men had fallen to wondering where it was all leading them. Men who had once stood together with John Pym against the King's evil counsellors were now fighting amongst themselves, the Earl of Manchester and Denzil Holles against Oliver Cromwell and Sir Arthur Hazelrigg and Sir Henry Vane. In many ways Richard found himself in sympathy with Manchester's party, at one with the Scots in their strong Presbyterianism, opposed to the least toleration, urging the making of terms with the King. He was glad to be associated with the moves to establish a Presbyterian system in England. He voted for the outlawing of the Book of Common Prayer and its replacement by a new Directory of Worship.

Yet he saw the other point of view too, for all his reservations about it, the more so when he saw how dismally the recent negotiations with the King at Uxbridge were failing. Whatever the hopes of Manchester and his friends, it was clear that the King had no intention of agreeing to any terms they could accept. And if that was the case, then the war must go on, and if the war must go on, then it must be fought with vigour and trust in God, not in the half-hearted way Manchester and Essex had been conducting it lately – not least because defeat would bring disaster on them all. He preferred not think what victory might bring.

What was clear to him, though, was that his whole life was about to change, in two ways. The first was unequivocally welcome. The second caused him a good deal of apprehension, when he allowed himself to dwell on it. It was that change which necessitated a brief return to Thornside early in March.

On that first Sunday in March, the Reverend Nathaniel Johnson had news for his congregation, in the form of a letter from his brother, who was now an army chaplain. He read it from the pulpit before the sermon. *Let glory be given to God, that Shrewsbury has fallen to us,* Jeremiah Johnson had written. In taking the Royalist stronghold, heart of the King's recruiting grounds, Colonel Mytton's troops had captured the magazine, stores, cannon and innumerable prisoners, including many Irish, left behind by the terms of the surrender when their comrades marched out. *Thirteen of these men paid with their lives next day for the innocent blood they had shed*, the minister read.

It was a little while before Susannah, listening to him, realised precisely what Jeremiah Johnson was saying: that by the terms of the town's surrender some of the garrison had been left behind as prisoners, and had then been hanged. She remembered something Ludovick had said once, about many of the so-called Irish fighting for the King: that they were as Protestant as she was, and sworn enemies of the Irish rebels. She wondered now if it was true. At that moment a man in the front pew looked round, and she saw that it was Richard. Catching her eye, he blushed so deeply that he had to look quickly away and bend his head to hide his confusion.

After the service she paused to speak to him, expressing her surprise at seeing him there, when she had understood there was so much to be done in London. He blushed again, painfully, but then brought himself under some kind of control, beginning his reply a little falteringly but gradually regaining his composure. 'I have business to attend to,' he said. 'I have set my feet on a new path. My soldiering days are over, I am glad to say.'

'Why, sir? What's happened?'

'The self-denying ordinance, as they call it.'

'I thought the Lords threw that out.'

'It is to be brought back again, in some form.' Susannah knew what her father would say to that – much the same as he had said on first hearing the proposal that no member of either House was to be able to serve as an officer: 'What are they thinking of? All their experienced generals wiped out at a stroke.' But not quite all, as she had pointed out to him then. Essex and Manchester might no longer be eligible for army service, but there was at least one fine soldier who had never been a member either of Lords or Commons. 'But I saw the Lord's hand in it,' Richard added now. 'I have resigned already.'

'I thought you'd want to stay, with your cousin appointed General of this new army they're making.'

'Ah, but it's John Lambert who's been appointed Commissary-General in the north, for the time being. It's him I'd serve under. Unless Tom asked for my services, which I doubt. Even Lambert's likely to go south soon. He's been given command of one of the New Model regiments. Tom can have his pick, you know. Only the best.'

'Unless they're in Parliament.'

'I think the new self-denying ordinance will be worded so that men like Cromwell can be retained. Tom wants him for his General of the Horse. As for me, as I say, I am glad to turn my back on soldiering.'

'Perhaps I understand that, when I hear such things as this morning's news,' said Susannah. She saw that he did not see what she meant. 'The hanging of those prisoners. Once that would not have been done.' She remembered the scrupulous courtesy of the dealings between Newcastle and the Fairfaxes in those early years of the war, where prisoners were concerned.

'Once there were no Irish brought to fight in our English wars. There is more too: I have later news than our good minister – news that shows how little Prince Rupert understands the clear difference

there is between Irish and English. In revenge for those hanged at
Shrewsbury, he has lately put thirteen of our prisoners to death, and
swears he will do the same for every Irishman hanged – as if Irish
and English were somehow equal!'

'Then that will stop it, I suppose.'

'Oh, no. It's done according to the law. Since last October, when
the ordinance was brought in.' It was his turn now to realise he was
not understood. 'Now all Irish, or any Papist Englishmen born in
Ireland, are condemned to die if found in arms against Parliament.'

She thought with a shudder of one Papist born in Ireland, and
was thankful the ordinance had not been in force last summer.
Then she remembered that since he was under sentence of death
anyway it would make no difference to him.

She realised suddenly that Richard had spoken again, and just in
time caught what he was saying, for it was news of such importance
that to have ignored it would have hurt him very much. '. . . I am to
be married very soon.'

'Oh!' she said brightly. 'I'm so glad for you, sir.' She felt an odd
combination of regret, very faint and wholly illogical but distinct all
the same, and relief that Richard had so clearly come to terms with
her rejection of him.

Her father had accepted her decision the more quickly because
he took so much vicarious pleasure in her new work, which she
always talked over with him afterwards, sharing her anxieties, her
triumphs, any new ideas she had, valuing his opinion. Others, evidently, had not been so sure that she was right. Once, soon after she
had begun work with Margery Nelson, the Minister had taken her
on one side after one of the Wednesday prayer meetings. 'I'm troubled, Susannah, lest you fall into the error of mistaking your own
inclinations for the will of God,' he had said very gravely. 'You must
earnestly seek His mind in this, and allow yourself to be guided by
those who are better able to discern where the right lies. You are but
a young girl remember, and a maiden. Ask yourself if it is seemly for
such as you to do this work.'

'If I were Mistress Nelson's daughter you wouldn't say that,
whether I was single or not.'

He considered that for a moment, but she noticed that he
avoided making a direct answer to it. 'What troubles me as much is
your determination, told me by your father, never to marry. Mistress
Nelson is married, remember. In fact, I can call to mind no spinster

midwife. Certainly that calling is a bar to the kind of marriage that might otherwise have been yours – to such a man as Master Metcalfe, for example. On the other hand, once your sights are lowered, there are still many good men who would provide you with a fitting husband. Think of it, Susannah.'

She had not made an impatient retort, for after all he was the Minister and she knew she ought to take what he said seriously. It was just that she did not seem able to make him understand what she knew to be God's will for her.

When, soon afterwards, Richard brought his bride home to Thornside Hall, Susannah discovered what kind of woman he and his mother now considered suitable to be his wife. Barbara Chaytor – now Metcalfe – was a pale brown-eyed young woman with a look of permanent anxiety, but then, as a Royalist marrying into a Parliamentarian family in wartime, perhaps she had reason. When Susannah was introduced to her she blushed awkwardly and stammered, and Susannah thought it likely that someone had been unkind enough to tell her that once Richard had wanted to marry this neighbour of his. She was quite obviously in awe of her new mother-in-law. Susannah hoped Richard would be patient with her, but he looked ominously grave for a bridegroom. He returned to London only a week later.

After the wedding, her father did not say, 'Well, that's your chance gone,' but she knew he thought it. Perhaps even she thought it, just for a moment, if only because, eight months after those heady days in York, the fever of blood and heart seemed to have subsided to an occasional disturbance. Ludovick, his face, his voice, his strange moods, his kisses, all had faded now beyond her recall. She could still have told what he looked like, what colour his eyes were, and his hair, but she could no longer hold them in her memory, to gaze upon. All she had now were the troubling feelings, the urges and needs she had not known were there until he had woken them. They disturbed her dreams, but awake she was too busy and occupied to consider them.

It was in her work that she found a real and absorbing happiness and satisfaction, greater than anything she had ever known before. If she had ever doubted the rightness of her choice – which she had not – she would by now have been sure of it.

Not that it was always easy. In particular, her alliance with Mistress Nelson became progressively more prickly. On the whole, the midwife had come to respect her for her obvious abilities and her quickness to learn, when she thought something worth learning. But there was no more liking between them than there had been at the outset. Mistress Nelson had ceased to mock what she called Susannah's finickiness, but that was because it now irritated her almost beyond endurance and she was more likely to explode about it, though never, as yet, in front of a patient.

As for Susannah, though she acknowledged that in some things Mistress Nelson was skilled, in her way, there were far more things she could not like. For instance, the midwife was fond of charms and spells, and would never begin work without tying magical herbs or branches to the bedpost. 'Makes them feel safe, so it does no harm,' she would say, a view Susannah could not share. But her most serious fault, in Susannah's opinion, was the one she had questioned on their very first meeting, her tendency to interfere during labour when no interference was necessary or even wise. More than once a baby had been brought from the womb dead or severely damaged, or a mother had suffered horrible injuries, as a direct result, Susannah believed, of the midwife's mishandling, though Mistress Nelson would always find some good reason why things would have been worse without her intervention. Faced with what she saw, Susannah no longer confined herself to polite questions, and the friction between them was growing as a consequence.

'Wait till you're called to a labour alone, and you'll not be so quick to find fault,' the midwife would say, though since she had no wish at all for Susannah to set up in competition with her, she always somehow managed to part from her with some remark designed to restore the peace between them, at least on the surface. She even went to the length of lending her the much-handled book on which she relied for her authority, *The Birth of Mankind* by Richard Jonas, which Susannah took home and read, aloud. 'Hmm,' her father said at the end. 'Sometimes I think it was better when midwives were unlettered and passed on their knowledge by word of mouth. Then at least they couldn't read pernicious rubbish like that.' He frowned. 'Still no word of Madame Bourgeois' book. I should have thought he'd have found a copy by now.'

Matters were brought to a head with Margery Nelson late on a Sunday night in April. Susannah was sitting up after everyone else had gone to bed, noting some conclusions she had reached about a recent case, when there came a wild knocking on the door. Margaret must already have settled to sleep for the night on her mattress by the kitchen fire, so Susannah, hearing her stirring, called, 'I'll answer it!' and took her candle and went to the door.

There she found a distraught woman, who clutched at her out of the night. 'Thank God it's you that's answered! Oh, Mistress Susannah, come quick, please! It's my lass. She's bleeding to death, and I don't know what to do.'

Susannah pulled on a cloak, while trying to bring to mind the woman's name (Mary Wetherald, she remembered at last), gathered what medicines and implements she might need and went with her to her cottage. The girl lay in the single upstairs room on a bed soaked with blood, and she was bleeding still. She was grey and exhausted, her skin clammy, her breathing already failing. Susannah examined her quickly, and was appalled by the signs of injury she found. She sent the mother from the room and questioned the girl as to what had been done, and by whom. Then she hurried home for more medicines, and returned to stay for most of the next two days and nights at the bedside, until the bleeding at last slowed to a normal trickle.

'You know Jane's miscarried of a child?' she said to the mother, when at last she could be reasonably sure that the girl would survive.

'Aye,' said Mary Wetherald miserably. 'You won't say nowt about it, mistress, will you?'

Susannah considered the matter. 'The minister ought to be told,' she said at last, 'for fear it happens again.'

The mother clung to her, begging her to say nothing. 'She'll be made to do penance, then they'll all know what she did. It wasn't her fault: he promised to wed her. Oh please, mistress, say nothing!'

Susannah was moved, but she steeled herself to do her duty. If the girl was not brought to see the implications of what she had done, then she might even be tempted to risk another pregnancy, and (moral considerations apart) next time she might not escape so lightly. It was only right, too, that the man responsible should be brought to a proper sense of his sin. But first she had to confront the woman she saw as the worst sinner of all.

She went straight from the sick girl's bedside to confront Mistress Nelson, though by now it was late in the evening. The midwife admitted her, but barred her path just inside the door, hands on hips, eyes bright and belligerent. She had clearly gauged Susannah's mood.

In as few words as possible – she was too angry for any preliminaries – Susannah explained what she had found at the cottage and what she had been told. Mistress Nelson looked unperturbed at the implied accusation. 'Her courses had stopped,' she said, 'so I gave her an infusion of rue. You'd have done the same.'

'Her courses had stopped because she was pregnant. You know that quite well. You procured an abortion for her, from which she has almost died. What's more, it didn't end with your infusion. Instruments were used.'

'Not by me. If she interfered with herself, that's not my fault. If she'd done what I told her she'd have been none the worse. What's more, no one would have been any the wiser. That's the trouble, they get so desperate they try anything they can think of and that's when the damage is done.'

'How can you say such things! If you gave her anything to aid her then you committed a crime.'

'Don't get all virtuous with me. When a girl's desperate, who am I to turn her away?'

'You took an oath that you would never deliberately cause a woman to miscarry.'

'Aye, so I did. And I keep it, as best I can. But face it, mistress, what's right and wrong isn't always that clear. If a girl's been stupid, and I can stop her having to pay for it for the rest of her life, then even you should see I have no choice.'

'If a girl has done wrong then she ought to face the consequences.'

'The world would be overrun with bastards if you had your way, I can tell you. Not just bastards either. There are lawfully wedded women who can't face another bairn, another mouth to feed. Act quickly, and no one knows, not even their husbands half the time. I know how many are prevented, and you'd be surprised. That's apart from those babes that don't live long after the birth – not that I've ever connived at that, except where the babe was deformed, of course.'

'It would serve you right if I reported you.'

'It's only the girl's word against mine, and you can be sure I'd deny it. And think of this – if you carry tales to the authorities, what will become of that lass? She's guilty too, more than me. Do you really think she deserves hanging?'

Susannah realised that there were limits to her indignation, though she did not know precisely what penalties the girl might have faced. But she did know that she could no longer, under any circumstances, work with Mistress Nelson. She told her so, adding that if the midwife tried to prevent her from attending such births as she was called to, then Susannah would reconsider her decision to remain silent about the crime. She was sure that, for all her defiance, the midwife knew she meant it and would not take the risk.

Susannah did, however, tell the minister about the incident, though she let him think it was simply a miscarriage. When she called at the vicarage soon afterwards, Nathaniel Johnson told her that he had seen the girl and admonished her with considerable severity. 'However,' he added, 'her sin was never publicly known, so she cannot be said to have set a bad example to other maidens in the town. In which case, I do not feel the need for her to make a public penance.' For that, Susannah was profoundly thankful.

She went home, and found her father opening a parcel of books, among which, at long last, was a worn copy of *Observations Diverses* by L. Bourgeois. 'Hmm, I see what happened,' said Matthew Fawcett, reading the letter enclosed in the parcel. 'She died some eight or so years ago, but that wasn't the difficulty. Customs, that was it. They thought it some Popish work and wouldn't let it through.' He turned to the title page and then showed it to Susannah with a smile, so that she could see the elaborate decoration topped with a crowned, resplendent Madonna and child.

A little apprehensively, Susannah took the book and began to turn the pages, and as she did so all the unpleasantness of the past days seemed to fall away. Here, inside, in spite of the unquestionably Popish exterior, she found laid before her the work of a practical, intelligent woman, writing, not from superstition and dead tradition, but from her own direct experience and from years of careful observation. 'I think,' she said, looking up from the book, 'I'll learn more in one reading of this book than I've ever learned from Margery Nelson.'

CHAPTER TWENTY-SEVEN

Corporal Walter Barras could not remember a May as hot as this. There had been hot May days in London, when the holiday had come as a relief, when dogs had lolled in the shade too hot to move, when children had been hushed into immobility and young men's tempers had flared easily into anger. But nothing had been quite as bad as this. It was not even fully light, the Hampshire countryside around them was scarcely visible, yet already the air was like hot breath on their faces.

The drums were beating to wake them. Like the others stretched along the line of the hedge, Walter sat up and reached sleepily for his boots and coat, which he had folded together to make a pillow of sorts, since they were certainly not needed for warmth. The coat was new, a good bright red cloth, faced with the Fairfax blue. They were all supposed to have been issued with them, so that every soldier of the New Model Army could immediately be recognised by friend and foe alike, but as yet many of them still wore their own coats. It was the same with the regular pay promised to all those fortunate enough to be recruited for the new army; it came in fits and starts, more frequently than in the past, but not as often as they had hoped. As far as the coats went, though, Walter could be said to have been lucky. At the very moment that they had learned that their troop (or what was left of it after the many desertions of the autumn, which had included that of their captain) was picked for the new army, his old coat had fallen to pieces, and he had no one but the army to buy him another.

By the time he had seen to feeding his horse, the drum was beating again, for prayers this time. He went with the rest of the troop

to stand, head bared, before Captain Bartholemew Potter. Until this
year, Captain Potter had served in the Eastern Association under
Lieutenant-Colonel John Lilburne. That incorrigible rebel had left
the army, after refusing to take the Covenant, not simply on the
grounds that he disliked its Presbyterian connotations, but also
because he had come to believe that all oath-taking was against
scripture. The men who had served under him now formed a large
portion of the New Model Army's dragoon regiment.

Captain Potter led them in the singing of a psalm and then asked
Lieutenant Samuel Revol to read to them from the Bible, which he
did, in his clear, expressive voice. Many of the soldiers, like Walter,
would be listening with especial care, noting passages that they
might wish, later, to discuss among themselves. Walter loved this
time of prayer and reading and reflection at the start of each day
and at its end too, when all the details of their work, great and
small, seemed drawn together and hallowed. In the Earl of Essex's
army, Samuel had been almost alone in the example he set. But in
this New Model Army even the senior officers seemed to encourage
their men in such exercises. Colonel John Okey, who commanded
the dragoons, was no exception.

Samuel came to an end and closed the Bible. 'Lord, lay Thy
words to our hearts.'

There was a little moment of quiet; and into it, jarring, disruptive
of the mood of devotion, broke the distant laughter of women,
Esther's infectious gurgle loudest of all. Once Walter had loved that
sound. Now he only wondered painfully what unsuitable thing she
was laughing at this time.

She had not come to prayers, though several of the wives were
there, more every day. After prayers Walter would have to steel himself to rebuke her for disturbing their worship. If he did not then, to
his shame, someone else would, most probably Samuel. Once – a
long time ago now – he had even rebuked Walter himself, for not
keeping his wife in better order. That had prompted Walter to try
and tell Samuel something of the difficulties there were between
himself and Esther, and his friend had listened sympathetically and
encouraged him to speak of all the unhappiness of the past years.
'You should send her back to her father's house,' he had suggested.
'Just until the war's over.' Then, that had seemed a good suggestion
and even one capable, with tact, of being put into effect.

Even with the changes in the army, Esther was resolutely

impervious to good influences, though she did, generally, take part in some kind of worship on Sundays. Once, she had unwisely grumbled to Walter that the army was now worse than her home, for prayers and psalms and other pious exercises. 'God won't give us the victory if we don't serve him,' Walter had told her. Certainly the sins of the past had brought them no success, in spite of Marston Moor, in spite of the difficulties of the Royalist armies.

'God won't give us the victory if we're not saved,' Esther had retorted. 'And if we are saved then it doesn't matter whether we go to prayers or not, for it's been fixed from eternity and we can do nothing to change it. So I shall do as I please.' The pert, triumphant note in her voice had enraged him, the more because Samuel had been standing nearby, well within earshot.

'That's downright antinomianism,' Samuel had said, accusingly, and Esther had only laughed, though not quite as confidently as she might have done, for she was a little in awe of Samuel. There was something rather daunting about his grave intensity, and he was one of the few men who seemed impervious to her charm. 'Remember, sister – sin is a sure sign that you are not saved.' At which Esther had shrugged and turned pointedly to talk to someone else, in the insolent way Walter had come to hate.

Hate was a strong word, but whatever he felt for her now it was very far from the love he supposed he had once felt. Esther was thinner, browned by the sun, with a sparkle she had not had before. He desired her as much as ever, but he no longer even tried to tell himself he loved her. He was most certainly ashamed of her.

It was the child that had finally destroyed all the tenderness he had for her, the child that never was. When, not long after that first battle at Newbury, she had told him she was pregnant, he had been delighted, so delighted that he had not then realised that she did not share his happiness. He had done all he could to care for her, ignoring her exasperation at his solicitude. Winter drew near, a bitter winter. Not wanting her to live from hand to mouth in the discomfort and disease of army quarters, he had gone, meek as could be, to London to plead for her father's forgiveness; only to have the door shut in his face. After that, Samuel, unexpectedly, had come to his aid, finding comfortable lodgings with a neighbour of his own family, where Esther could stay when campaigning began again in earnest in the spring. But she had refused to stay behind. Rattling along in wagons, tramping the rough roads, tending the sick and wounded, she had inevitably lost the child, though with little inconvenience to herself. Her relief had only made Walter's bitterness the greater.

Last autumn she had miscarried again, just about the time of the disastrous, shameful episode of Lostwithiel, when the Earl of Essex had fled by sea, abandoning his army and all its equipment to the King. Walter's troop, with most of the cavalry, had managed to make their escape from Fowey before the King's forces finally closed in. Even so, it had been humiliating, and not at all the way a soldier fighting for God's cause wished to be led. Walter had begun to think, one way and another, that God was still set on punishing him for the sin of marrying Esther – as if the daily hell of their marriage was not punishment enough.

This morning, as the sun rose and it grew ever hotter, they went from prayers to breakfast. Passing close to Esther as he lined up for his ration of biscuit and small beer, Walter murmured, 'Your laughter disturbed our prayers this morning. I wish you would not stay away.' It was not much of a rebuke, but it was enough to make her scowl and turn from him. Later, as they sat on the grass to eat, men and women together, she sat with her back to him and chattered away to the others as if nothing had happened.

'Poll Betterton says her Will's regiment's ordered to march in the rear today,' he heard her say. 'But they say they will not.'

Poll Betterton had been a friend of Esther's for a long time. Her husband too had served under Essex, as a pikeman, and was now a sergeant in Fairfax's foot regiment. 'They can't do that!' Walter broke in, and then wished he had not, so scornful was the look Esther turned on him.

'Why not? They're the General's own regiment. They've a right to march in the van. They always had that right under my Lord of Essex.'

'I heard,' said Roger Tyler, 'that there was a complaint made to the General that all should take their turn at the rear.' It was the least popular position for the foot soldiers, especially in this hot weather when they had to march through the great clouds of dust thrown up by the army ahead of them, which coated their clothes with dirt and filled mouths and noses until they were near to choking.

'Well, that's as maybe,' said Esther. 'But they won't have it.'

Walter realised that Samuel, who was sitting beside him, had suddenly pulled off his hat and was scrambling to his feet. He looked round and saw Captain Potter coming towards them, presumably to give his orders for the day. They all followed Samuel's example, listening attentively to the instructions. 'We're still bound for Newbury then, sir?' Amias said at the end. His voice had a slightly satirical note.

'That's right.' The Captain gave Amias a sharp look, warning against further comment.

Amias had reason to be wary, for their first days in the field with the New Model Army had been filled with vigorous but inconclusive marches. First, they had heard they were ordered to relieve Taunton from Goring's siege, so off they had marched to the west. They had been at Blandford, no more than two or three days' march from Taunton, when word had come that they were to send only a small force on to Taunton, while the bulk of the army was to turn round and march back to lay siege to Oxford, which the King had just left. Captain Potter, who had been standing near the General when the message came from the Committee of Both Kingdoms, which directed operations from London, had said that Sir Thomas Fairfax had looked tight-lipped with rage, but had said nothing, except to convey the orders, briskly, to his senior officers.

'Black Tom hates sieges,' Captain Potter had told them. He had first come across the General at Marston Moor last year, and liked to give the impression of being something of an authority on the man. 'You can be sure of one thing – the King won't have left Oxford unsupplied. And it must be the best fortified city in the kingdom. We could be tied up there for months. They should have ordered us north. From what we hear, Sir Marmaduke Langdale's giving the Scots a hard time. They were wavering already, what with the news of what Montrose is up to back home. We should get up there quick, before the King joins forces with Langdale.'

When the Captain had gone, Roger Tyler said, 'I don't know what they were thinking of in London, giving the command to a man like Sir Thomas. Old Robin was bad enough. I was the first to say he was too old for war. But this one – for all he's young enough, I'd say he's well past it already.'

'He has to obey orders, like the rest of us,' Samuel said.

'Oh, Roger thinks we shouldn't have northerners put over us,' said Amias.

'That's not what I meant. But he's too sickly to lead an army. It's been one thing after another ever since he took over.'

Sir Thomas Fairfax had come to Windsor, where the New Model Army had assembled in early April, with his arm still in a sling from a wound suffered last autumn. The sling had gone by the time they left Windsor a month later, but by then he had been shivering from an attack of the ague – something he regularly suffered, they gathered – and had spent much of the time sick in his quarters. It had been an inauspicious beginning, and by all accounts he suffered from the stone too, and rheumatism, as well as various weaknesses from countless old wounds.

'He's served Parliament well in the past. He has a name for valour,' said Samuel, striving to be fair.

'That was in the north,' Roger pointed out. 'That's not the same. Anyway, you know how northerners boast up their exploits.' He cast a sly sideways glance at Walter, who aimed a mock blow at him. When he had dodged the blow and righted himself again, Roger added, 'Anyway, whatever he did once, I'd say he's past it now. You see, we'll end up like we did with Old Robin – devil take the hindmost, and the Generals snug and safe.'

They were ready in good time that morning to provide support and protection for the foremost infantry regiment. As they rode to take up their positions, Walter saw that the men in the van were in total disarray. Here were no orderly columns of footsoldiers, pikes neat as a well-planted spinney, muskets smartly shouldered, but a disorderly rabble, jostling for position, pikes and muskets all mixed up together. 'One thing,' Walter thought, 'the General's regiment would never have behaved so ill.' The regiment ordered to the van today was Harley's, led by Lieutenant-Colonel Pride, whose men were largely recent conscripts – 'Gaol scourings,' Will Betterton had called them, with good reason. 'Scum.'

Riding nearer, Walter saw here and there a face he knew, and then he remembered what Esther had said this morning. He realised then that Fairfax's troop had not after all obeyed orders. What was more, they were disputing the place with Harley's regiment. Weapons and fists were raised, the shouting grew louder and more furious, while one of the drummer boys began to bang his drum with a brisk wrathful rhythm, as if deliberately stirring up the men's tempers. The two Lieutenant-Colonels, Thomas Pride and Thomas Jackson, were trying vainly to restore order, thrusting their horses into the rabble, swords drawn. Before long, Walter thought, with a certain shameful excitement, it would surely come to blows.

'I'd lay odds on Fairfax's lads,' Amias said, his eyes shining as much as if he had been at a cock fight.

'They're in the wrong, mind,' said Walter.

'Not the way—'

'His Excellency!' hissed Samuel. They looked round at the frail dark man on horseback, riding at a brisk trot towards the arguing men. A sudden little silence fell, spreading out from the watching dragoons to the fringe of the dispute, and then settling, momentarily at least, over the entire company.

'There'll be trouble now,' Roger murmured. One thing they had learned about their new general was that he would stand no nonsense where discipline was concerned. Very early in their march from Windsor he had called a halt for the court martial and hanging of two men, for mutiny and plunder. Since then others had been executed for similar offences.

Sir Thomas Fairfax drew rein beside Lieutenant-Colonel Jackson, who removed his hat and spoke in a low, troubled manner to his superior. Behind him, the men of his regiment began to protest loudly – recklessly, Walter thought. 'We've always had the van, your excellency,' one of them said, more clearly than the rest. 'It's our right!'

Fairfax looked the men over, his scarred face sombre, though he said nothing. There was another moment of tense stillness.

Then all of a sudden the General dismounted, awkwardly – it was obvious he was still far from well – said something to Jackson; and then, more clearly, with a commanding gesture of his arm, 'Follow me!'

He signalled to the drummers to beat out the order to march and strode to the head of his own regiment – or what, in the confusion, seemed to be more or less its head. The drums began to beat. After a moment of stupefied bewilderment, the men shuffled into place behind him and fell into step, their Lieutenant-Colonel alongside. Then the General, a thin, sombre, solitary figure, led them on a little way, before swinging suddenly to the right, until he faced back along the waiting ranks of the army. He did not even hesitate, or glance round, but simply continued to march.

'He's leading them to the rear himself,' said Samuel, amazement in his voice. They could none of them remember ever having seen any senior officer – still less a general – marching on foot with his men.

At the first halt of the day, after two hours of marching in burning heat, they learned that Fairfax had led his regiment to its allotted place at the rear of the army and had there continued to lead it, on foot, until the halt came. By then, Will Betterton told them, he was grey with exhaustion, but no man in his regiment was ever likely to murmur against his orders again.

'Well, Roger Tyler,' Samuel said, when Betterton had finished his story, 'what have you to say about General Fairfax now?'

CHAPTER TWENTY-EIGHT

'Friday the thirteenth today,' said Rob, as they rode north-east from Daventry in the dampness of the June morning. 'Maybe that's why the Prince won't fight. He's superstitious.'

It was not superstition that had made Ludovick more than usually edgy, but he said sensibly enough, 'His Highness knows we haven't a snowflake's chance in Hell without Goring. He should have been here long since. When he does come up, then we'll face the enemy.'

'If it wasn't treason to say so, I'd wonder why the King ever let my Lord Goring go off like that.'

'It is treason: His Majesty is the fount of infinite wisdom.' Ludovick spoke lightly, but he was thinking: We came this way the other day; we're near the place now.

'Not when my Lord Digby's advising him.'

'True. And Goring's an insubordinate drunkard, but that's probably near treason too. To be fair, he's able enough, when he's sober.'

Someone, behind him – Tot Charlton, he thought – said, 'What's this place?' and another man answered, 'West Haddon.'

And not far away was the manor of South Haddon, in whose dew-drenched garden he and Charles had met for the last time, nearly two years ago. During the past weeks they had ridden backwards and forwards through this remembered landscape, as if fate wanted to rub his face in the agony of it.

He realised Rob was speaking again and made himself pay attention. 'Mind, half Fairfax's men are raw recruits, never seen battle. You'd have thought we could at least put the wind up them, outnumbered or not.'

'I never thought I'd hear you speak like a courtier,' he said, rather more sharply than he meant to. 'Digby and the rest can laugh all they like at the "New Noddle". You should know they've got the old Eastern Association at the heart of them, and the pick of Essex's veterans. And Fairfax has a free hand at last. It's my belief he'll show what he can do. It's only the stupidity of the men in London has kept him off our backs so long.'

They reached Market Harborough in the late afternoon, sufficiently far ahead of the bulk of the army to be sure of finding lodgings in the town. Ludovick saw his men safely installed and then went, with that still inescapable sense of dread, to find Sir Ralph, who was quartered in a nearby village.

After his son's death Ralph had made the difficult and dangerous journey home, to offer some kind of consolation to his wife. On his return Ludovick had avoided him, until one day Ralph had sought him out and said bluntly, 'I need your friendship the more at this time, not less.' Ludovick had felt ashamed that a mixture of grief and remorse had blinded him so selfishly to Ralph's need. He had felt even worse when Ralph, understanding, had added gently, 'It was no more your fault than it was mine, though maybe we can neither of us believe it. If anyone was to blame, it was the lad himself. And this accursed war. Who knows – maybe he's got the best of it.' The despair in his voice had been so uncharacteristic of him that Ludovick could have wept, except that he seemed encased in a layer of ice, through which the painful feelings underneath could not escape.

Tonight he took a bottle of wine with him to Ralph's quarters – one of the spoils of the recent sack of Leicester, though he did not tell Ralph that; the older man had been shaken by the savagery of the storming of the town. 'The worst excesses of the continental wars brought home to England,' he had said sadly, though it had been tamer by far than anything Ludovick had seen of the continental wars. But then Ralph was growing increasingly troubled by the universal decline in discipline in the Royalist armies. Now, he took the glass Ludovick filled for him and drank and then said, 'I wonder sometimes what I'm doing here. Then I ask myself where else I could possibly be, and there's no answer. Perhaps tomorrow will bring an end, one way or another.'

'Not if the Prince has his way. Unless Goring arrives.'

'How many men has Fairfax got under him?'

'About fifteen thousand now, I think. There's a rumour that Lieutenant General Cromwell has joined him, with his men.'

'And what have we? Perhaps nine thousand at most, without Goring. So, it'll be north again tomorrow.' He smiled. 'Maybe we'll end up at Widehope. I'd be sorely tempted to stay there.'

The talk faltered into silence, while Ludovick struggled to think of something safe to say. Once, they would have passed the time with music, but for a long time now neither of them could find the heart for music. Ludovick was glad when he felt he could decently take his leave and return in the dusk to his lodgings and the easier company of Rob. He took the bottle, still three quarters full, with him. 'One thing I won't do, is drink when I'm low spirited,' Ralph had said. 'More than for thirst, that is.'

Ludovick had no such scruples and, having refused most of the supper Rob had prepared, stayed at the table to finish the bottle. Rob, who was sitting on a stool near the fire cleaning their boots, watched him for a time, then said, 'What's up, lad?'

'Nothing. Why should there be?'

'I've never known you like this out in the field. In Oxford, yes, or at Blackheugh, or in London. Then after Master Charles, well . . . But never otherwise.'

It was true, for Ludovick had almost always been able to push his own troubles aside when there was work to be done; but not this time. 'If you know me so well you should know there's nothing wrong,' he said curtly. The bottle was empty now, and he was still almost sober. 'Is there any more of this, or was it finished?'

'You should keep a clear head,' said Rob. 'What if we're surprised?'

'Jesu, can't you mind your own business? You're my servant, remember, not my bloody parent!'

For a moment the room was filled only with the sound of vigorous brushing. Then Rob said quietly, 'I'll keep that in mind, my lord.'

Ludovick hated himself for his ill temper, but he was past doing anything about it. Since there was nothing more to drink he went to bed and lay there with his back to Rob, while little scenes from the past scalded his closed lids – Rob teaching him to ride, with a patient kindliness no other adult at Blackheugh had ever shown him; Rob his companion on the grim journey to France; Rob giving up all hope of secure employment to aid his flight to the Spanish service; Rob always there, in good times or bad. Unable to bear it any longer, full of remorse, he turned round, an apology on his lips. But Rob was stretched out on the floor by the fire, sound asleep.

Ludovick fell asleep himself just a short while before there came a banging on the door. It was still dark, but the streets outside were echoing with horses' hooves and running feet and shouting voices and the blare of trumpets, and the distant throbbing of drums. He read the message that was handed to him. 'Fairfax is nearer than anyone thought,' he said to Rob, in a voice husky with sleep. He reached for buff coat and boots, pulling them on as he talked. 'We march out to meet them, at once.'

'Yes, my lord,' said Rob stiffly. It was only then that Ludovick remembered last night. Now, with a bustle of activity around him and other concerns on his mind, the whole thing seemed very trivial. He felt irritated with Rob for his apparent sulkiness. He must know him well enough by now to realise he had not meant it.

Tot Charlton arrived for his orders. 'Has my Lord Goring come, sir?'

'Not that I've heard,' said Ludovick. He thought: Rupert won't have changed his mind in this – he must have had it changed for him. After all, the King was still in overall command and could follow what advice he chose.

In the grey early light they took up their positions on a ridge two miles south of Market Harborough. There was still no sign of Goring and his three thousand horsemen, but across the gently undulating fields another higher ridge hid the little village of Naseby, and for a short time in the early light they glimpsed a distant moving line of red, before it slipped out of sight again. A little after, Ludovick, shading his eyes to see better, thought he saw them reappear.

'They're further off, I think,' he said. 'Can you tell?' He glanced round at Rob, who sat motionless on his horse, staring into the distance with a blank and chilly expression, as if he had heard nothing. Sulking still, thought Ludovick.

Rupert's scoutmaster seemed as obstinately impervious to sight and sound as Rob, for he returned from reconnoitring the enemy's movements to report no sign of them at all. Impatiently, the Prince took a handful of troops, Daniel O'Neill among them, and set out to reconnoitre for himself.

'Scoutmaster-General Ruce wouldn't spot a dungheap if he rode clear through it,' Rob said, not to Ludovick, but to Davy Pugh, who waited nervously beside him, with the banner (faded, but carefully mended by Goodwife Pugh) flapping in the wind over his head. 'The Prince now, he'll find them. It's my guess they're on the run.'

Knowing it was said only for Davy's benefit, Ludovick muttered in an ironic undertone, 'As likely it's Goring come at last.' Then he grinned at Rob, who immediately looked away, though he must have heard. Ludovick felt exasperated. He wished he knew whether Rob was truly hurt, or whether – more likely – he was deliberately acting the simple servant, knowing how much Ludovick would dislike it and wanting to teach him a lesson. In which case Ludovick had no intention of humouring him. Ignore him, and he would soon forget his grudge.

Ludovick was riding along the ranks of his men, repeating the usual instructions ('Keep together, knee to knee!' 'No firing till you see the whites of their eyes!' 'No plundering till the battle's over – and that's when I say it's over!') when a messenger rode up at full gallop, drawing rein just long enough to gasp out the Prince's orders to advance, in full battle order, in the direction that he and his party had already taken. The enemy had been sighted.

They rode at a brisk trot down the hill and over the intervening ridges to the gentle slope that Rupert had chosen for their position. Good for attack, bad for defence, Ludovick thought. They were given just time enough to draw breath before trumpets and drums sounded the advance.

Perhaps a hundred times Ludovick had been a part of the thunderous excitement of a charge, but it never failed to catch him up, taking him out of himself. He roared with the men around him, 'Queen Mary!', the King's choice of cry, giving a comfortable English sound to the name of his beloved wife. But any word would have done, so long as they could bawl it to the sullen sky.

They were scarcely aware of the obstacles they crossed, ditches and swampy ground, close-growing clumps of furze, then the upward tilt of the slope towards the nervously advancing cavalry of Commissary-General Ireton.

Musket fire from dragoons behind the hedge to their right, scarcely felt, a brief moment of combat and then the exhilaration of the chase, on and on with the enemy flying before them, all the way to Naseby village. Then, time to gather the men together, bully

them into turning round. A little way back, and they found the
Roundhead baggage train barring their path, an untidy, sprawling
town of wagons and superfluous guns and campfires, all ringed by
musketeers, who, summoned to surrender, fired at them. Rather
than waste what was left of their energy, Rupert led his weary men
away from the train, round and back to the battlefield by a longer,
unimpeded route.

The valley was veiled in smoke, a mass of confusion and noise.
Red coats were everywhere, falling in waves on the struggling
Royalist infantry.

Ludovick and his men rode after Rupert across the field, on and
up to where the King tried to rally what remained of his left wing.
Between them, shouting and threatening, they got the troops into
some kind of battle order, while just a carbine-shot away the New
Model re-formed for another attack. For a moment an uneasy
silence lay over the field, like the stillness before battle, though
Ludovick could not remember anything like this, in the very heart
of a fight. He saw how many there were facing them, rank on rank
of fresh troops, against their exhausted few.

The New Model dragoons were mounted now. Then they were
coming at them at a brisk, business-like trot, orderly, disciplined,
purposeful . . . A single volley from their muskets, and the wavering Royalist cavalry turned and fled. The King and Rupert and the
few men who still had heart – however desperate – for the fight,
held their horses against the force of the retreat and cajoled and
shouted and laid about them with their swords to try and turn the
tide. But it was useless. In the end, they could only join the rout.

Ludovick, bitter and angry, dragged at his reins. As she turned,
his mare caught her foot in a rabbit hole. She stumbled, and then,
hit by a musket shot, fell to the ground, throwing her rider clear.
Ludovick lay where he was, in the midst of thundering hooves, too
winded and dazed to move. As if in a dream, he saw a horseman
draw rein above him, sword in hand. 'This is it,' he thought, without emotion.

Then somehow Rob was in the way, urging his own horse
between them. The sword slashed down, but it was Rob who took
it in his breast and slid in silence to the ground.

With an anguished cry, Ludovick jumped up. He scarcely felt the
hand grasping his arm. A voice called, 'Leave him, my lord – take
the horse!' Then the onrush of riders parted him from the place

where Rob lay and he was dragged and pulled on to the riderless horse, swept along with them.

In some oddly detached part of his consciousness he knew of the pursuit and the flight, yet he saw and heard nothing but the thunder of hooves beating in his brain.

When at last the men about him drew rein and dropped exhausted to the ground, he halted too, but stayed in the saddle. He sensed rather than heard a voice, from a great distance, asking him a question, but the sound was drowned by the drumming in his head and the single urgent purpose that had taken shape there. He said only, 'I'm going for Rob,' and turned his weary mount back the way they had come. There was a press of men about his horse, and a hand grasped the rein, but he drove his spurs into the animal's heaving flanks and forced it into a canter. The man holding the rein was dragged a little way, then had to let go.

Ludovick was not conscious of any danger or of anything but the need to find Rob. Though he rode alone, the insistent thudding of hooves never left him, hammering ceaselessly on in the dark. If there were other sounds, if there was anything to see on the road, he did not know about it. Only Rob's name repeated itself over and over against the monotonous noise in his head.

Then a new sound slipped suddenly into his brain above the beating of hooves, a wailing and moaning like the cries of souls in torment. Soon after, the darkness was pierced by a searing vision: a kind of horrible, garishly coloured embodiment of the pain he had scarcely begun to feel. He saw wagons overturned on bruised and bloodied grass, emptied and broken, one wheel still turning slowly above the litter of bodies obscenely scattering the ground. They were women, all of them, lying there; or once, perhaps, they had been women. Now, the fortunate ones among them were dead. All, alive or dead, had been slashed about and cut and mutilated to a point where every little mark of human individuality had gone. Somewhere in the midst of it all a bloody twitching figure sat propped against the wagon under the turning wheel, whimpering through the ghastly disfigurement of a face that had once, he knew, with the logic of nightmare, been that of Goodwife Pugh. Over it all the sky was brilliantly, improbably blue.

For a few moments he could not go on. He sat still on his horse, shaking with nausea, pressing his hands to his face, as if by shutting out sight from his eyes he could somehow drive the image from his brain. He was glad when the darkness closed in again, though the face of Goodwife Pugh lingered on when the rest had gone. It was still there when he urged his horse on again.

He knew, single-mindedly, as the one remaining certainty, where he would find Rob, so he rode straight to the spot where the gorse blazed over the rabbit warren and the still figure lay face down on the reddened turf. Seeing him lying there, with the wind stirring the yellow flowers above his head, Ludovick almost expected him to move at any moment, to turn on his side and sit up, as if waking out of sleep.

. . . It was no false hope, after all, for there he was, raised on one elbow, grinning from a white face, the dark stain clear on the buff coat; grinning and grinning and saying nothing. 'I'm sorry, Rob,' Ludovick said. 'I'm sorry.' But the man only went on grinning . . .

The horse tossed its head and stamped, uneasy at the stillness, and the illusion broke. The man had not moved, for he was no longer a man, merely a corpse, small and pathetic, one of hundreds on the field. Ludovick's eyes took in the whole scene, the scattered weapons and dead horses, and the other bodies, lying in the awkward positions of the violently dead, the only living things the men and women who went from corpse to corpse, stripping and plundering . . . The squalid everyday hell of the aftermath of battle, too grey and ordinary to drive out the horrors from his brain.

He did not know quite what happened then, but he found himself soon afterwards riding back the way he had come with Rob's body across his saddle bow, while all the time the drums thudded on and the wheel turned above the mutilated women.

CHAPTER TWENTY-NINE

By dawn on that Sunday morning the little town of Ashby-de-la-Zouch was in chaos, its streets crammed with exhausted men, many of them already asleep in the first corner they could find, others seeking food or drink or some kind of lodging among the terrified townsfolk in the overcrowded houses. It had taken Sir Ralph Liddell some time to find Ludovick, in an attic room in an alehouse under the castle walls, and he was not best pleased when Toby Milburn, on duty outside the door, refused to admit him. 'My lord said he wasn't to be disturbed. Not on any account.' Then Toby added, 'He's got Rob in there with him. Dead, in the battle.'

Ralph hesitated, torn between respect for another man's desire for solitude, and his own wish to offer consolation.

Then came the shot, exploding into the dawn. He turned; Toby too. Something heavy must have been wedged against the door, for it would not budge, not for what seemed an age. When it did at last they fell together into the room.

The smoke was already clearing. Rob's body had been decently laid out on the bed. Beside it knelt Ludovick, stripped to his shirt, his back to them. Ralph ran.

He held his sword in both hands, inverted, its point against his chest. Ralph dragged him backwards, cried to Toby, 'Take the sword – wait outside!' Then, as Toby obeyed, 'You've seen nothing!'

The door closed. Ludovick tried to free himself from Ralph's grasp. 'Damn you to hell! Why can't you leave me alone?'

'Because I'm fool enough to care you don't destroy yourself,' said Ralph, holding him more firmly. He saw that there was blood on the shirt. 'Come now, my boy, let me see.'

Rather to his surprise, Ludovick sat still then, while he examined the wound. The sword had drawn blood, but it was nothing much. Ralph glanced at his face, and saw his eyes move to some point near the bed. He looked round, saw a stool, on which Rob's few possessions had been laid, a leather flask, a few coins, a knife. In that moment Ludovick launched himself towards them, his hand reaching for the knife.

Ralph seized his wrist, just seconds before his fingers closed on the weapon. 'No, lad, no!' By some awkward sideways manoeuvre he kicked the stool out of reach. Then he flung himself on Ludovick and pushed him to the floor, pinning him there.

He wished he was younger and not so tired, for Ludovick fought like a wild animal, kicking out with his feet, battering with his fists, twisting and turning to find the weak point in Ralph's hold, not caring in the least if he hurt him. Ralph gritted his teeth and held on against blows and bruises and a constant flow of obscenities. He would have called for help, but he did not want to shame Ludovick any more before his men. He prayed that exhaustion would win the fight for him.

At last the abuse tailed off, relapsing first into what he took to be Irish and then into silence, and the blows became feebler and less frequent and then ceased altogether. The body below him went suddenly limp, the breath wrenched out in sobbing gasps.

Even then, Ralph did not let go, but waited until he was quite sure that it was the stillness of exhaustion and not a ruse to lull him into lowering his guard. Then, still wary, he drew back far enough to be able to check the wound – the bleeding had stopped. Then, painfully conscious how much depended on his finding the right words, he said gently, 'I'm sorry about Rob. I know he was more to you than just a servant.'

Ludovick made an odd choking noise. Then: 'It should have been me. He got in the way.'

'So that's how you thank him for his gift,' said Ralph. 'By throwing it back in his face.'

He heard Ludovick's sharp intake of breath. Then the young man turned his head away, so that Ralph could no longer see his face. 'I never asked to be given it.'

'That's the thing about a gift,' Ralph went on, afraid with every word he spoke that he might suddenly undo everything he had done so far. 'Whether you want it or not, you must accept it with good grace and make the best of it.' Trite moralising, which he himself would have rejected – he was angry that he should have thought of nothing better. Ludovick's reply was inaudible. 'What did you say?'

'I said: "It's out of my hands."'

'What's that supposed to mean?'

'I can't make any choice at all for good or ill if I've no power over my own mind.'

Ralph frowned, trying to understand. He sensed that there was something more here than simple grief. 'There's no reason to suppose you lack that power.'

Ludovick closed his eyes. 'Once, I had, most of the time. Not any more.'

There was a silence, while Ralph considered the words, wishing he had the skill to read another man's thoughts. Ludovick had never been easy, always subject to sudden black moods. For the most part they seemed to have cause enough: the death of his brother, defeat in battle, a hopeless love, guilt at Mark's death; and now this new loss. But Ralph remembered that there had been other times, especially before the war, when the cause had seemed less clear. He said, very gently, 'Grief sends us all a little mad. That's part of our condition, and we must bear it as best we can.'

'You never went mad.'

'Not every man wears his heart like a banner. Some of us continue to eat and drink and walk about, like ordinary men, while in truth are not in the world at all, but shut in some deep pit from which there is no escape.' He saw the blue eyes look speculatively up at him and realised with relief that he had touched a sympathetic nerve. 'You see, I've felt it too.'

'If that was all!' Ludovick flung an arm across his face. 'It's in my blood. It's always been there. Some said my father was mad. His sister surely was, for she had to be shut up, and even then she hanged herself.'

Ralph reached out and touched his hand. 'That old story! Oh my boy, how long has that been on your mind? It's not true anyway. As to your father, that I don't know, though I'm certain that you're nothing like him. But your aunt – she was as sane as any other young woman, until she fell in love. True, that's a kind of madness, but there'd have been no harm in it, if your father hadn't opposed the match. The man died too. There was talk that your father –

well . . .! I do know your aunt was sane enough when he locked her up. Six months she was there, all alone in a place that was said to be haunted. What with grief and terror, it's no wonder she hanged herself.'

Ludovick moved his arm, and Ralph was astonished at the extent of the relief revealed on his face. 'Are you sure? Rob never said.'

'I don't suppose Rob knew. But I'm as sure as any man can be. I'd heard the old tales, so I took very good care to ask questions where it mattered, amongst those who knew your aunt. I didn't want my daughter married to a man with tainted blood. It wasn't easy. It had all been hushed up, and those lies spread. I'd guess even your father was wary of a charge of what must have been close enough to murder. '

'My father said—'

'Would you take his word against mine, my boy?'

Ludovick gazed at him for a moment and then shook his head. There was a moment of silence, at the end of which Ralph realised with a sinking heart that it was not settled after all. 'It wasn't just what you said,' Ludovick whispered. 'There were other things in my head – foul things . . . They're still there.'

'Do you want to tell me about them?' Ralph asked, as he used to do when the children had nightmares.

'No!'

Ralph stroked his tangled hair. 'You're tired. You haven't eaten since God knows when. It's just your mind playing tricks, that's all. Don't think of it.' He risked standing up. 'We'll be moving out of here soon. Don't you want to see Rob decently buried first?'

Ludovick sat up. He was shivering. Ralph helped him into his buff coat. It was then that he suddenly saw the pistol, in the corner against the wall, which was scorched with the marks of an explosion – as if, thought Ralph, someone had thrown the weapon in a rage across the room, where it had then gone off. He picked it up.

'It failed,' said Ludovick, bleakly. Then, 'We quarrelled, before the battle. Rob—' And then suddenly he began to weep.

Some time later they left the room together, to go in search of the chaplain, and someone to see to the burial. 'Father Young's in the back,' Toby told them. He looked as if he would have liked to ask questions, but did not dare. 'With Davy.'

'Is he hurt?' Ludovick realised with shame that he had taken no thought for any of his men, apart from Rob.

Toby shook his head. 'It's his Mam, sir,' he said, with no trace of the amusement that was usual when any of them spoke of Goodwife Pugh. 'The other women too. Though Doll got away, thank God.'

'What happened?'

It was clear on Toby's face, horror and revulsion and a reluctance to speak. 'The Roundheads cut them about. All the Welsh women-folk. Most are dead. Not Goodwife Pugh though, not yet.'

So it had not been simply a delusion of madness. After the first shameful sense of relief, Ludovick found himself wishing that it had.

1646

CHAPTER THIRTY

Almost a year had passed since Naseby, and in that time, through countless dangers and difficulties, the Lord had unequivocally shown his hand.

So many memories crowded his head that Walter could scarcely remember in what order they had all happened. Naseby was the first of the great victories, of course, and as clear in his mind as ever: the desperate struggle, hope and fear swinging this way and that; Black Tom everywhere on the field, wherever he was most needed to give heart to his men, his dark eyes alight, his head uncovered because he had lost his helmet somewhere, but did not care; Colonel Okey crying on them to trust in God, for He would not desert them. Twice he had commanded them to mount their horses and charge, and they had scattered the infantry and seen the enemy's proud cavalry melt before them.

After Naseby, they had marched ever further into the south-west, once the scene of their greatest disgrace, now, as garrison after garrison fell before them, to be won for God's glory.

It had not been easy, none of it had. They had pressed on so fast that they never had time to rest, through heat and rain and fog and snow and ice; through hunger and sickness. There had been new and terrifying dangers too, especially from the Clubmen, angry countryfolk, sick of marauding armies, who everywhere had armed themselves with clubs and staves, and had only been kept in check by the General's tact and patience – and force, when necessary.

So many battles fought and towns stormed: Langport, where they had fought every bloody inch of the way through the narrow, deadly lanes, to defeat the undisciplined, desperate rabble of

Goring's army; Bridgewater, burning around them as they marched into it; Torrington, where a great explosion had shaken the town, scattering them with debris, felling a horse just beside Sir Thomas, though never a man of theirs was killed; Tiverton, where by a miracle a cannon shot had snapped the chain of the drawbridge, which had come crashing down so that they could enter the town, with little loss of life; Bath, where Walter had been one of a party who had crawled over the bridge in the dark and suddenly seized the ends of the muskets of the Cavaliers at the far side of the gates, shouting for them to surrender, and so startled and terrified had the Royalists been, that they had done just that, and the city had fallen to Parliament.

Then there had been the greatest prize of all, Bristol, that great seaport, which Prince Rupert had held with an abundance of stores and too few men, and the plague raging within the walls. The General's Council of War had advised against a storm, fearful of the plague, but Fairfax had overruled them. The Lord would keep his servants safe, he had told them. He had ordered a day of solemn prayer and fasting, led by the eloquent chaplains Hugh Peters and William Dell. And then they had stormed the city, and indeed no Parliamentary soldier had caught the plague, though many lives had been lost in the fighting, and Walter himself wounded. He had staggered from his sick-bed to watch the proud Prince ride out with his defeated army. Like many of his friends, Walter had murmured at the generous terms of the surrender. The Prince had left the city at the head of his troops, magnificent in scarlet and silver lace, riding a superb black Barbary horse; and Sir Thomas Fairfax had escorted him, exchanging courtesies for all the world as if he were seeing off an honoured guest. Behind Rupert had ridden his officers, equally splendid, and among them Walter had glimpsed Lord Milburn. He had felt sick with rage – by the laws of England that man at least should not have been allowed to go free. The only consolation was that the hour of judgement could not long be delayed.

For so it had gone on. Earlier this year, the Prince of Wales, trapped in Cornwall, had fled to the Scilly Isles, and after that Exeter had fallen into their hands, along with the infant Princess Henrietta. In Scotland, Montrose had at last been bloodily defeated, at Philiphaugh. By then, Wales was all theirs, as the north had been long ago. Then came news of the surrender of the last army the

King had in the field, under Lord Astley at Stow-on-the-Wold. 'You have done your work, boys,' the old General had said to his captors, as he was taken prisoner. 'Now you may go play, unless you fall out among yourselves.'

In Oxford, the King still had a shadow of a court and commanded what was left of his army, taking account of those who had deserted or gone into exile or made their peace with Parliament. There had been a great many of those, not simply because the King's cause faced defeat, but because after Naseby the royal correspondence had been captured, with proof positive that the King had offered full freedom of religion to Papist Irish rebels, in return for their support in his fight against Parliament. The fact that he had not in the end concluded an agreement was neither here nor there. That he should have been working towards one on such terms was more than enough, even for many of his staunchest friends.

Best of all perhaps, Rupert was no longer in command, for the King had dismissed him the moment the news of the surrender of Bristol reached him. Later, some kind of reconciliation had been patched up, but Rupert was now, in these last days of April 1646, merely one of many Royalist officers penned in Oxford – or very soon to be penned in, for with the west thoroughly subdued, Fairfax was marching to close the siege about the King's headquarters.

Except that, astonishingly, the King no longer had his headquarters there, or anywhere, it seemed. 'He's gone,' Samuel had reported, soon after they reached Newbury. 'So they're saying anyway. Left Oxford yesterday, in disguise. Seemingly he's vanished from the face of the earth.'

They had still not heard what had become of him when they came within sight of Oxford, on the first day of May. Fairfax immediately began an examination of the city's fortifications, Colonel Okey with him, while part of Walter's troop was sent to patrol an area to the north of the city, close to the Banbury road. 'Black Tom looks deathly sick to me,' Samuel said to Walter as they rode.

'Aye. He'll be as glad as any of us when this is over.' None of them worried any longer that their General's poor health might prevent him from leading them effectively. Nothing, they now knew, would ever do that.

They came over the brow of a hill, began slowly to descend the long slope at the other side, their eyes scanning the landscape below: a wood, loud with cuckoos, bordering a gentle river, little more than a stream; cattle grazing in green meadows. A group of horsemen emerging suddenly from the trees.

Samuel called a halt. They watched the riders, moving along the track that crossed the meadows: no gleam of red, nothing at all, in fact, to mark who they were. There were many marauding former soldiers on the roads these days, robbing and terrorising peaceful countryfolk. On the other hand . . . 'The King – maybe it's the King!' said Roger excitedly.

'I doubt he's still so near Oxford,' said Samuel. 'But we'll take a closer look.'

They went cautiously, keeping as far as possible to what cover there was, making their way along a ridge roughly parallel with the track the men were following, just below its crest so that they should not be outlined against the sky. The riders were moving steadily, but not very fast. There were four of them, though one appeared to have a woman riding pillion behind him. As far as they could tell, all wore buff coats and carried weapons of some kind. 'That man there in front,' said Amias, when they paused for a more careful look. 'He's small of stature. Dark too. He could have shaved off his beard.'

Walter glanced at Samuel's face, but saw his friend smile. 'I told you – I guess the King's well clear of here by now. Still . . .' He pointed out that the track would soon take the riders through another small wood, before it emerged again into open country. 'On your horses, lads. We'll give them a warm welcome, other side of that wood.'

It was not the King, but Walter knew the first rider the moment he came out of the wood, the sun full on his face. With hate in his heart he levelled his musket and fired. It was the second rider who fell. The first was already past Walter, trying to rush the line of dragoons closing about them; just too late. No one cried for quarter. They fought fiercely, even the woman, and did some damage. But it was soon over.

The air was hazy with swirling dust. Bodies lay on the baked earth, congealing blood already thick with flies. The woman bent over her man, howling with anguish. Walter, dismounted, stooped to raise her to her feet – and got a punch in his face for his pains. He stood there, a little dazed, his eyes watering, dabbing a bleeding nose and washed by a wave of laughter from his companions; and only then saw that two of the cavaliers had after all forced a way out of the ambush and were riding off with four of the dragoons fast gaining on them. The pursuers reached them, closed with them: shots. One fell, the other beat them off with his sword and then broke into a breakneck gallop, and soon disappeared from sight, the dragoons at his heels. Walter was ready to ride after him too, but Samuel said, 'Not with your nose bleeding like that. Let's see who we've got here.'

They had secured the woman and searched all four bodies by the time the pursuers returned. 'We lost him,' said Amias Stephens, out of breath. 'Gave us the slip over the hill there. Not a sign of him.'

'Then I'm going after him,' said Walter. 'I know who he is, and I'll not give up till I have him safe.' He glanced at Samuel. 'With your leave, sir.'

It had been something they had agreed together before they rode out of Oxford: 'If we're attacked, it's every man for himself,' Ludovick had said. 'Unless the odds are in our favour.' Which, as there were only five of them – himself, Toby Milburn and Doll, Davy Pugh, Tot Charlton – they knew was unlikely. When the moment came, Ludovick had fought as fiercely as any of them, and had not himself fled until he was sure the others were beyond help. It was not his fault that, of them all, he had been the only one to escape; but for the first hour or so after the incident he tussled with an urge to turn his horse round and go back to share their fate.

He had left Oxford thinking it better to die fighting for his life in the open than shut up like a cornered animal, waiting for the end. He had not been the only man in the city on Parliament's list of those exempted from pardon, but he was the only one with a formal death sentence hanging over him from before the war ever began; Dan O'Neill had been in Ireland since last summer, negotiating with the Confederates, led now by his kinsman Owen Roe O'Neill. Rupert – also on Parliament's list – had urged Ludovick to go, but he had taken little persuading. He would have gone alone, except that Davy and the Tynedale men had wanted to take their chance with him. So had Ralph. Told of his plans, he had said wistfully, 'I'd ask to come with you, if I thought you'd have me.'

Ludovick had not allowed himself to be moved. 'I wouldn't. You'll be safer by far here in Oxford. I've cost your family too much already.'

Now he was profoundly thankful that he had not yielded to Ralph's plea, or his own reluctance to part from his friend. They might never meet again – most likely would not – but it was one death the less on his conscience. One day perhaps, if he lived, he would be able to think of Ralph living peacefully at Widehope, as in the old days; if anything could ever again be as it was. Perhaps his old friend would now do the sensible thing and make his peace with Parliament, as so many others had already done, paying the necessary fines to lift the penalties from his estates. 'The war's as good as over,' he had said to Ralph. 'You owe it to your family not to suffer any more for a lost cause.'

'That's rich, coming from you!' Ralph had said.

'I've no choice in the matter. And no family. You have.' He wondered if, by now, Ralph had taken his advice. And if he would ever know. One thing, though, Ralph had left with him to carry into the bleak future. As they parted he had handed him a letter. 'I want you to take no risks – but it's a long time since Elizabeth heard from me. If you could find a way to get it sent to her . . .' Then, when Ludovick had promised that he would, he had added, 'You're wrong, you know, when you say you have no family. Whatever I said once, you'll be welcome, if ever you come to Widehope again.'

But it was a dream, and now he was alone as he had never been in all the wandering years of his life. The last of the men who had ridden with him from Blackheugh were dead, and so was Davy Pugh, who had almost got away at the end. They had set out with no very clear idea where they were going, except that they would go wherever the Royalist cause still had a small flame burning – Scotland perhaps, or Ireland. Now Ludovick was free to make his own choice, without need to take account of anyone else. The thought gave him no pleasure, though the choice was easy: Ireland it should be. But first, he decided, he would take Ralph's letter to Widehope himself. It was well out of his way, but it was perhaps the least he could do in return for that staunch friendship. So he turned his horse not west, towards the Welsh coast and Ireland, but north.

By the following afternoon, in spite of the need for caution, he had made good progress and reached the painfully familiar countryside near Market Harborough. Then his horse cast a shoe, forcing him to go on foot, at least until he found a blacksmith or a change of horse. It was hot and he was tired, and it seemed hours before he reached a small village. The inn had no reliable horse for hire, but there was a blacksmith, on the further edge of the place. While he waited for his horse to be shod, he took himself to the inn, and sat down to ale and a pasty, not having eaten since yesterday morning.

The inn parlour was dim and cool, the door standing open to the road so that the innkeeper's three children could run backwards and forwards from sunlight to shadow with the ceaseless swooping movement of swallows to a barn. Their shrill laughter and the patter of their bare feet filled the quiet of the afternoon, along with the singing of a woman from the inn kitchen; soothing, unwarlike sounds. Ludovick began to feel drowsy and even considered asking for a bed for a few hours, to catch up on lost sleep – he had spent the previous night in the fields, and it had been bitterly cold.

Suddenly the children ran right past him, across the parlour to the kitchen door, their voices raised in high-pitched incomprehensible chatter to whoever was in there. Ludovick heard someone reply, and their answering chorus, and then suddenly realised what it was they had been saying, over and over. 'Soldiers, mother! Soldiers – come and see!'

He heard them then himself, hooves thudding to the rhythm of a brisk trot, the jingle of harness. He edged to the window and peered out. Dragoons again, as yesterday morning, only about a dozen or so he thought, but they were almost at the door. He did not wait to find out if they had any idea he was here. He ran through the kitchen, pushing past the children and their startled mother, and out by the back door.

The land around the village was open for the most part, with little cover except scattered furze bushes. A path ran behind the houses in the direction of the forge, so he took it, and then, cautious, watchful, turned into the alley along which the sound of the blacksmith's hammering reached him. He found to his dismay that the man was still only shaping the horseshoe. 'A few minutes yet, your honour,' the man said, with a cheerfulness that set Ludovick's teeth on edge.

Cursing under his breath, he glanced down the street. The soldiers had made a halt outside the inn, but they were already beginning to move on again down the street, coming his way. It would have to be the fields then, on foot. He turned and ran back along the alley, rounding the corner, to find that the troop had split up, for a group of them were riding along the lane from behind the inn. It was clear enough now that they had come expressly to find him. It was also clear that if he ran out on to open ground he would be seen at once, and he could not hope to outrun mounted dragoons.

Behind the forge was an assortment of sheds and barns, grouped round a yard. He ran into the nearest, in which he could just make out stalls empty of animals and a ladder, leading to a hayloft. He sprang up it, and then dragged it after him, out of sight. At the end of a bitter winter there was no hay left to conceal him, but by lying flat on the floor against the further wall he might be safe, if they did not think to look up here.

The sound of hammer on anvil ceased briefly, and then resumed. He imagined the troopers asking questions, the blacksmith answering. He laid his pistol on the floor beside him and watched the opening where the ladder had been, a small square of light in the darkness.

He heard the clatter of hooves in the yard, voices calling, the men fanning out, a few to each building.

He made out two voices below. He lay very still, listening, trying to interpret what he heard. They seemed to be making a thorough search, even thrusting their swords into straw and sacks and any possible place of concealment.

A moment of silence. Had they gone? No, voices again, someone saying, 'Up there.' Damn! he thought, closing his fingers about his pistol.

They must have found another ladder, for he saw its upper edge appear in the opening, come to rest on one side. Shortly after, a head appeared. The man's eyes looked straight at him.

As he called to his companion, Ludovick flung himself forward, pistol held club-like, by the barrel. One blow, and the man fell back with a muffled grunt. Ludovick moved to the ladder, but the other man jerked it away, shouting for his comrades.

The sound of running, then a shouted order. 'No firing: I want him alive.'

He smiled at that. If they had to take him alive it gave him the upper hand. The opening was too narrow for more than one man to pass through at a time, and he had enough ammunition to fire several times. Even without that he could have kept them at bay indefinitely with his sword; or until they – or he – grew tired. He wondered how much they wanted him, if they knew who he was.

He moved back to load his pistol, which was not easy in the dark, then crept to the edge of the opening. The men below seemed to be having some sort of conference as to what to do next. Stupid of them not to watch out. He levelled the pistol and fired. Nothing; just a click. He pulled the trigger a second time. Still nothing. He forced himself to patience, moving back out of sight (they had looked round now and seen him) to reload the pistol. He heard them putting the ladder back in place. Someone was coming up. He had the pistol ready by the time he appeared. It failed again. 'Jesu Maria!' He hurled it at the startled face of the man and then flung himself after it, sword in hand. The man lost his footing and fell back, cursing – Ludovick heard his officer rebuke him for that.

He wondered whether simply to try and fight his way past them. But he could not be sure that they would worry too much about not killing him, if the alternative was serious injury to themselves. Not that he minded the possibility of being killed. What he did not want in the least was to be taken prisoner.

He stayed where he was, watching for the next man to appear.

No one did. He heard them talking it over again, in low voices. Then someone ran outside for something, coming back soon afterwards. He could hear them in the corner of one of the stalls, moving things about. Then a moment of silence. A voice said, 'Right, now!' An odd little noise, sharp and sudden. What was it?

Flint on steel: they had lit a fire. He heard the crackle as it took hold. Almost at once smoke began to trickle up through the cracks in the boards.

He heard their voices recede, and the clatter of their feet, but he knew they would not have gone far. There was only one way out of the loft, and a single door to the barn.

He delayed only until he was sure the fire was spreading and then he grasped his sword and slid down the ladder. They had been waiting in the doorway, screened by smoke, but they closed on him at once. He backed against the wall, away from the fire, drawing on all his skill to fend them off while he edged round towards the door. His mind felt suddenly clear, logical. He had been taught to fence by the best teachers, and he even enjoyed that brief, doomed exercise, his blade swift and lethal against their clumsy over-cautious swordsmanship. He wounded several of them, one badly, before he reached the door.

He backed through it, still fighting, beginning to turn. In a moment he would make a run for it, fling himself on one of their horses.

He heard the shot almost at the same moment as he felt the sharp hot pain sear his upper arm; his right arm. His sword clattered to the floor. He bent to take it in his left hand and they were on him.

He was flung to the ground, kicking and struggling until his strength gave out. Even then, when at least five of them had him firmly held down, the rest went on kicking him, in a way that told him they knew quite well who he was.

They dragged him into the yard, where quite a little crowd had gathered to watch the afternoon's excitement. The blacksmith had his horse ready and they flung him face down across the saddle, wrists and ankles tied together under her belly. He heard orders called, the clatter of hooves, then his own horse moved with the rest, in an orderly trot out on to the road.

He could see very little, apart from the changing patterns of the road under the horse's hooves, and the dust thrown up to sting his eyes and coat his mouth. He could feel the blood sliding down from the wound in his arm, gathering stickily about his fingers, turning the rope that bound him to a dark rusty brown. Now and then a spot fell, spreading, into the dust. His head throbbed painfully, flies buzzing about it. He could hear cuckoos calling above the noise of the horses, sometimes the sounds of cows or sheep; once a scrawny dog came into view, barking at him, teeth unpleasantly close to his unprotected face and hands. He was relieved when one of the troopers hit out at it with his musket and it ran off.

Soon afterwards the soldiers began to sing a psalm, vigorous and triumphant and sharply rhythmical:

> Let God arise, and then his foes
> will turn themselves to flight,
> His enemies for fear shall run
> and scatter out of sight:
> And as wax melts before the fire,
> and wind blows smoke away,
> So in the presence of the Lord
> the wicked shall decay . . .'

To shut out the noise, he found himself murmuring other more familiar words, not aloud, but in his head, through its throbbing: *Sancta Maria, Mater Dei, ora pro nobis peccatoribus, nunc et in hora mortis nostra . . . Now and in the hour of our death*. It looked at the moment very much as if that hour was almost on him.

CHAPTER THIRTY-ONE

All through the heat of the afternoon they rode, never halting once. After a time Ludovick lost any sense of what was happening. Disjointed sounds clamoured in his head, along with alternating circular patterns of light and darkness, and then, increasingly, weird delusions over which he had less and less control. The road seemed to heave, the ruts turned to great waves like those of a stormy sea, until he closed his eyes, and even then the nausea did not go away. He was fiercely thirsty. Later, the calling of the cuckoos seemed in some confused way to form itself into the great black shape of a bird, which swooped down and fastened its talons into his upper arm, draining the blood from his body, taking all that was left of his strength with it. Then it was not a bird any longer, but something more horrible . . .

Suddenly the singing stopped, and it was cool, and when he opened his eyes he saw that they were in a wood and it was growing dark. His head began to clear a little. Brambles reached over the path they took, to catch in his hair and scratch his hands and, once, to tear painfully along his cheekbone. Then there were cobbles below him, rimmed with weeds, and the order came to halt.

It was an enormous relief to be free of the constant jarring of the journey, but he ached to slip off the horse, to lie quietly down somewhere. As if from a great distance he was aware of men dismounting, of a discussion of some kind taking place. Then a knife slashed the cords about his ankles, and hands dragged him to the ground.

At that moment his numbed and swollen feet failed him and he slid, humiliatingly, to his hands and knees under the half-heard jeers of the troopers. He fought an almost overwhelming urge to lower himself the last few inches to the cobbles and lie there waiting for unconsciousness. Instead he groped above him with his left hand until he found the stirrup and slowly, with a great effort, dragged himself upright, supporting himself against the horse. Through his dizziness, he saw that they were in the yard of a decaying farmhouse, shut in by a dense wood, but it was too dark to make out much detail. He yawned then, noting with detachment the chill trickle of perspiration on his skin, the raging thirst, all the signs that the still oozing wound in his arm had already cost him more blood than he could well spare.

'Right. Get him inside.' Two men took his arms and led him, stumbling like a drunkard, towards the farmhouse. Darkness; a lantern lit in a sparsely furnished room; a chair to which, very soon, they bound him. They were not gentle and the pain made him vomit. The officer said, 'Now, outside, all of you.' Ludovick looked up at the man's face, and realised he had seen it before.

'You were – yesterday – the ambush . . .' His voice sounded ridiculously faint and strained. The man said nothing, so he added, 'You were there, the Captain—'

'Corporal,' said the man, 'Corporal Walter Barras.' Silence. 'That name mean something to you then?'

'No,' said Ludovick. He closed his eyes, wishing he could be left alone.

'Jack Barras, then. You'll recall him.'

He did not bother replying. A hand struck his cheek. 'Answer me!'

With a great effort Ludovick opened his eyes. 'I recall no Jack Barras. Or Walter.' He began to wonder if the corporal was mad. Not that it mattered much if he was; it could make little difference to him in the end.

'Meant nothing to you, then? Just servants, to do your bidding, whatever the cost.'

'I've had no servant called—'

'Your father did. Jack Barras, head groom at Blackheugh.'

Not madness then, but a grudge. 'Not lately.'

'No, not lately, thanks to you.'

'I don't understand.' Then, need overcoming pride, 'Would you bring me some water, if you please?'

'Water? Oh no, my Lord Milburn. I want to see you suffer. That's what makes me angry; when they kill you it'll be clean and quick, not like your brother suffered, not what you deserve, all because you're a lord. Well, it's my job to get you to the block, but I'm going to see justice done first.'

'For what? I don't know you, or your father.'

'You don't recall the great barbary horse, dapple grey, only half broken, brought to Blackheugh by your father in 1627? About this time of year, it was.'

He remembered then, a clear picture of the horse taking sudden shape through the memory of what had come after. It was a very long time since he had brought it to mind. He remembered he had never seen anything so beautiful, the small perfect head, the power of those graceful limbs. Spirited and dangerous, the creature was, so that even Rob told him to keep away, though he said love and trust would win it, given a chance . . . But what could that possibly have to do with anything? 'I was eight,' he said. 'A child.'

'Aye. A spoilt pampered brat, all in your silks and velvets. A lute at your fingertips, dainty food on the table, soft bed to lie on, everything the heart could desire. And never a thought for the consequences of what you did.'

There was a certain wry amusement in hearing so strikingly misplaced a view of his childhood. Had it really looked so enviable? Perhaps it had, but Rob had always known better. In that cold spring Charles had been sent away to school in France, and he had been left to face his father alone. 'I shall have that wildness beaten out of you if it's the last thing I do,' his father had said, soon afterwards. Then he had made some remark about bad blood and its fatal admixture with the wild Irishness of his mother.

'You rode that horse, remember?'

Yes, he had ridden it, going before dawn to the stables. He did not really want to remember, but it was all coming back now, dragged reluctantly out of him by this stranger who was apparently not a stranger. Made desperate by misery, clutching at anything that might hurt his father, he had taken the thing his father most loved – no, not loved, but sought to subjugate, for he had to have everything broken to his will. And the horse was not subjugated, for it would not let its new master mount it at all. Ludovick had watched as his father had been thrown time and time again, afterwards lashing the horse with his whip in one of his cold furies. But it had let the child climb on its back. It had been a terrifying ride, for he had never been quite sure what the horse would do next, and he had little control over it. He thought there might have been some vague idea in his head that if he were thrown and injured, then his father would be sorry and send for Charles to come home. But he had not been thrown and the horse had at last carried him safely back to the stable yard. Where his father had been waiting for him.

'Just a toy for a spoilt brat,' said Walter. 'Not a thought for what you did to my father.'

'What did it have to do with your father?'

'Don't you even remember that? What happened when you rode back into the stables, without a care in the world?'

Oh yes, he remembered, would remember as long as he lived, but it had nothing to do with Jack Barras, whoever he was.

'I recall, though – they took you indoors. To make sure their precious boy didn't see anything unpleasant, I suppose. But I saw, all of it. Ten years old, not much older than you. I saw what was done to my own father there before my eyes.'

Ludovick watched the other man's face, knowing he would hear the rest even though he had said nothing to encourage it. He felt quite sure that Walter had never spoken of this before, to anyone, but that the time had come when he could no longer keep silent.

'Maybe you don't know what your father was like when he was crossed.' He stopped. 'Smile would you? Comical, isn't it? You're your father's son all right. But God will judge you, Ludovick Milburn, and then you'll not be smiling, believe me . . . What's that you say?'

'I wasn't,' he said wearily. 'I knew my father better than you think, that's all. But I'm not responsible for the wrongs he did.'

'No? When it was for your disobedience my father suffered? It should have been you there, not my Dad. But it wasn't. I saw my Lord Milburn shout at my father – no, not shout. He never shouted, just spoke in that cold way he had, like ice given a voice. You could feel it freeze your very marrow. Told him he'd betrayed his trust, to let you ride that horse. Then had him stripped, there in the yard in front of everyone, and beat him. I stood there and watched my own father beaten to death, and no one said a word, no one.' His voice was harsh now, tears running unchecked down his face. 'Only Rob Robson, he said something once, I didn't hear what, but your father pushed him out of the way and just went on and on. Then he gave my Dad a kick with his foot. Then he gave some order and walked away, and I ran out and they told me he was dead.' He was sobbing openly now. 'In any right-ordered country they'd have had him brought to court for murder, but he was a lord and my father just a groom, and a long way from any justice. So he had us turned out of our house, my Mam and all us bairns, driven out of Tynedale with not a penny to our names.' He rubbed his sleeve across his face, then studied Ludovick's expression. 'You didn't know, did you? They never told you? Too busy making sure you weren't hurt, making a fuss of you, I suppose. Had a special supper ready, did they?'

Ludovick said nothing. His silence seemed to enrage Walter the more, as if he blamed him that he offered no further small wrong to latch upon. 'Tell me – what did you do that day? What did they say?'

He said it again and again, until Ludovick, to shut him up, burst out, 'He beat me too.' Fresh from killing a man, he had come to beat his son.

A little pause, then: 'All fathers beat their bairns.'

'Not like that.' Not so often, at the least excuse or none at all; not taking pleasure in every whimper of pain. Though it was not the beating he remembered, since that was nothing new. Afterwards he had been shut in the tower, alone in the room where his mad aunt had hanged herself, the room where the redcap was said to lie in wait for unwary lodgers. Even in daylight he would see the red eyes watching him from the corner, waiting for night. As soon as it was dark, they would come right down to where he lay, even though he pulled the blanket over his head and did not move. Night after night he had felt the long talons fasten on his back where the whip had scoured it, drawing blood to dye the wraith's cap and feed his hunger. He had felt himself daily grow weaker, felt the marks of the talons burn on his body. Sometimes he had screamed and screamed, but no one had come. If ever he had truly been mad, it had been then. It had ended in delirium and long months of illness, after which at last, afraid that he would die, his father had been persuaded to send him to join Charles at school in France – not from love, but because, since Charles was even then promised to the priesthood, he had no other heir and, until he had, he could not afford to lose this one.

Ludovick realised Walter was standing over him, watching him. He wondered if anything of what he had been thinking had shown on his face. There was certainly some indefinable change in the other man's expression. 'Did you love your father?'

Ludovick gave a ghost of a laugh. 'Jesu, can you think anyone ever loved him?' Then, soberly, 'I cursed him once. I think if I'd been older, and stronger, I might have killed him. It's a wonder no one ever did.'

There was a stool at the far side of the room and Walter suddenly pulled it towards him and sat down. He looked almost as tired as Ludovick felt. 'By God's grace I was spared such a sin. He has been good to me.'

By God's grace . . . Walter had thought himself God's instrument in what he had done today, and in what he had been about to do; a man chosen to bring justice on the lesser sinner, since the greater had gone to a more perfect judgement. Now he wondered if, rather, he had allowed his own carnal feelings of anger and horror and hate to blind him to what was really required of him. There was reason enough for him to look on this weary, wounded young man as God's enemy, as he was Parliament's, and it was his simple duty to take him to meet his fate in London. But the hatred he had nurtured over the years now seemed a squalid and unworthy thing. Was it even possible that this man – that child – had been as much a victim of Lord Milburn as he and his father had been? It was not a question he cared to answer at present, but to have been brought to ask it was enough to drive away all desire to inflict more hurt. He felt suddenly empty, as if a great purpose had been taken from him.

He got up suddenly and went to Ludovick and began to untie him, while he called for someone to bring water and someone else to go in search of a surgeon. 'We'll be in London before long,' he said. 'Let God be your judge, not I.'

Much later, lying on a mattress in another room with his wound dressed, Ludovick woke from a brief sleep and looked across at the soldier seated at the table by the door, a candle alight beside him, empty plate and tankard nearby. If he was not quite asleep, he was certainly not very wakeful, but then the prisoner was obviously in a bad way (the surgeon had said so) and needed little watching. Ludovick did indeed feel terrible and would have been content just to lie there and wait for what was coming. But he did not want to face a public execution in London, if he could help it, and this was likely to be his only chance to escape that fate. He lay looking

about him, taking in everything he could see, willing himself to be
ready to move, when the moment came.

The instant the soldier looked away, he lurched to the table,
where he snatched the tankard and knocked the man unconscious
with it. The room was on the ground floor, so he went to the window. Opening it was almost beyond his strength, but he did it at
last, though he was not sure how he got through it. He found himself in the wood, stumbling along with no idea where he was going
and no other aim than to get as far as possible from the house
before he dropped.

Then he was lying in a dark hollow beneath the trees, too
exhausted to go any further, feeling the cold seep into him from the
undergrowth.

Some time afterwards, he opened his eyes, and the early sun was
shining and a dog was standing over him, barking excitedly. He
heard someone call, and then come running through the wood
towards it, and he knew he could only lie there and wait to be
found.

CHAPTER THIRTY-TWO

It was only just beginning to grow light when the Fawcett household was woken by a loud hammering on the door. Margaret, stumbling sleepily to answer it, came soon afterwards to Susannah to tell her that young Will Alderson was downstairs. His mother had gone into labour at last.

The Aldersons had a small farm on the northern slope of the dale about three miles east of Thornside. Susannah took the child up on the pony with her and they rode through the brightening dawn to the woman's bedside. Mistress Nelson continued to be called to the bedsides of the poor and those who liked the old ways and felt the safer for charms and incantations; Susannah was the favourite of the godly, which for the most part meant the more well-to-do. Since the safe delivery of Richard Metcalfe's daughter Grace four months ago she had also been much in demand among the few gentry in the neighbourhood.

Jane Alderson's labour was a long one, though without complications, and it was not until late in the evening that everything was done, the infant washed and swaddled and put to the breast, food and drink shared in celebration with friends and neighbours, and Susannah thanked with what was certainly unnecessary effusion for her part in the matter.

'I'll see you home, Mistress Susannah,' said John Alderson afterwards. Susannah protested that it was not necessary; she would be home before dark and in any case on these June evenings it hardly grew fully dark at all.

'You can't be too careful these days,' one of the neighbours said. 'Wat Thornton had his horse stolen from him last week, coming back from Richmond, in broad daylight too. If it's not beggarly Cavaliers, it's Parliament men with too much time on their hands.'

'Oh, but I've nothing worth stealing,' said Susannah cheerfully. 'Besides, I think I'm a match for any man.' John Alderson had some sympathy with that view, particularly today, but still he persisted, until she convinced him that he ought to stay with his wife and that she had no wish at all for an escort.

In truth she always enjoyed the solitary journey home after a delivery, whether mounted or on foot. In the quietness she could think over what had happened, give thanks or resign herself to God's will, according to how the birth had gone, or simply enjoy the tranquillity after hours of concentrated exertion. She rode now into the soft evening, with her head full of a picture of the tired, smiling mother suckling her infant, the other children clambering on the bed to see, the father holding his wife's hand with relief and thankfulness. It was odd, she thought, that however often she saw it she never failed to be moved, as she was rarely moved otherwise, by the safe delivery of a child.

There were a few people about on the road this evening: a group of lead miners returning home from their work; a family stacking peats, newly cut for fuel, the children yawning hugely as they hauled the last of the great turves to the pile. They called to Susannah as she passed, for they knew her well. Then she was alone on the road, riding into the setting sun, with a curlew still calling overhead. Sheep scattered at her coming, a lark sang high above the fell to her right. On her left, where the land sloped in gentle undulations to the river, the dale was already shadowed, the hills beyond deeply purple.

It was then that she saw him, black against the molten gold of the sunset: a single rider on a big horse, sitting very still smack in the middle of the road, barring her path.

She felt her heart thud painfully, her mouth dry. She remembered the warnings. She knew they were well founded, for more than once in the past year she had herself seen groups of marauding ex-soldiers riding through the dale, in search of whatever they could lay their hands on. A single man might be less of a threat, but she was unarmed and – for all her facile, boastful confidence – a woman alone. She drew rein, wondering if she would be wise to turn round and go home another way. The rider began to move, coming nearer.

The track curved a little and he no longer had his back full to the sun. Neither rider nor horse now looked as large and threatening as they had a moment before. She urged Longlegs on again, cautiously, her fear subsiding. She would probably find it was someone she knew. In fact, already something stirred in her memory.

Then she halted again, not from fear, though her heart was thudding more than ever. It could not be . . .! It was all over, that, long ago, something that had happened in a strange period of her life, taken out of time, set aside and shut away now for ever.

He came on, steadily, at a slow trot. She heard the soft thud of the hooves. The horse was an unpretentious animal, brown and solid, but the rider sat gracefully, in the way of a man trained to the saddle from his earliest years. His cloak was thrown back and she could see he wore a badly stained buff coat, and a sword hanging at his side. A wide-brimmed hat shaded his face, though she could see the hair curling under it, dark hair, and his face was fair.

He was there, directly in front of her, smiling not quite confidently. He took off his hat and bowed from the waist, though his words, spoken in the lilting voice she felt rather than heard, were not in the least ceremonious. 'I thought you'd never leave that house. What have you been doing there all this time?'

She stared at him, registering that he must have been watching her movements, from early this morning if not before, hanging about all day until she should return home. 'Waiting for a baby to be born,' she said dazedly. She had forgotten how he looked, the blue eyes under the strong brows, the effect they had on her. Her head seemed to swim, she could hardly breathe. She managed to say, 'What are you doing here?'

'Did I not promise I'd come to you again?' he said, but lightly, so that she was not sure whether to take him seriously or not. He swung himself from the saddle and then stood looking up at her. 'Come down, Mistress Fawcett, and talk with me!' With so much pleading in his voice and his eyes she would have done it even if she had not wanted to. She slid down beside him, felt his hand touch her arm as she did so, and then she was standing very close to him, looking into his face. Her heart seemed to be beating uncontrollably somewhere in her throat. She felt his hands close on her elbows. 'I had forgotten how lovely you are.' He sounded as if he too could not breathe very well. They stood there for what seemed an age, saying nothing, just gazing. At that moment she wanted more than anything else in all the world to kiss him, to be kissed by him. But they had only just met, after two years of separation, and they had scarcely known one another even before then.

She walked on a few steps, leading her pony. Her legs felt absurdly weak. 'Where have you come from?' The words tumbled out, not really meaning anything, but she had to break the silence, disperse the emotion that lay in it.

He fell into step beside her. 'Widehope, a few days ago.'

That jolted her out of her agitation. 'Oh! How are they all? Is Sir Ralph home again?'

He shook his head. 'He was still in Oxford when last I heard. I carried a letter for him.' Elizabeth Liddell had welcomed him kindly enough, once she knew why he had come, but he had refused her rather half-hearted invitation to stay. It was obvious they had troubles enough without taking him in. He had been relieved that he had seen no sign of Dorothy. 'They're well, I suppose, but the war has cost them more than ever I guessed.' He had in truth been appalled by what he had seen at Widehope. He had remembered it as a place of sunlit prosperity, a lovely and harmonious place, like something from Virgil, but it had been clear at once that those days had long gone. House and fields and family alike had a weary uncared-for look, as if there was too much to be done and too little time and money and energy for the doing of it, as if the heart had gone out of them all. Even when the north had been in the hands of their own party they had suffered from the depredations of the soldiers. Since the Scots had occupied the area for the second time after Marston Moor they had endured punitive taxes, again and again, had seen cattle, sheep and horses driven away to feed the armies, had the house pillaged twice of everything of value, while rents only trickled in (if they were paid at all) and the colliers, inclined to sympathy with the enemy, often refused outright to work. Their neighbours, once good friends, had proved little help, for many of them supported Parliament – John Lilburne himself owned lands bordering on Widehope. Elizabeth Liddell, burdened by yet another infant, fruit of Sir Ralph's last consoling visit, seemed to have aged far more than four years since Ludovick had seen her last. 'You know Mark Liddell was killed?'

'Yes. Sir Ralph wrote to my father . . .He was just a boy.'

'I know.'

All the passion that had hung in the air seemed to have dispersed. Ludovick's face had something of the dark withdrawn look Susannah remembered from York. They were two people who hardly knew one another, walking side by side, staring into the distance and talking of the war that marked the differences between them. 'You can't have come all this way just for a letter. Is it to do with the King?'

'The King?' He looked genuinely puzzled.

'He's at Newcastle.'

'So I heard.'

'They say he's a prisoner in all but name. I thought perhaps you might have some plan to get him away. It's not so far from here.'

'Do you think I'd tell you if I had such a thing in mind?' he returned lightly; then added, 'Though as I see it, he chose to go to the Scots. He must have guessed what would happen.'

It did not sound much like the view of a devoted Royalist. She studied his face. 'Don't you care that he's a prisoner?'

'I care for whatever best serves the cause nearest my heart.'

She did not ask him what that was, sensing that she would find the answer disquieting. She thought: Sir Ralph and my father were divided by little more than a scruple – even now, what unites them is greater than all their differences. But between me and this man there is an unbridgeable gulf. 'Why have you come?' she asked. She thought it sounded almost like a reproach, which perhaps it was. The pain of their parting at York had faded long since. She had accepted that they would never meet again and had come to terms with a life that was deeply satisfying, in which he could have no place. She had even learned to ignore the occasional restless stirrings of her body. And now here he was, stepping back into her life as if those few brief meetings in York had given him every right to do so.

He turned his head to answer her and with that one glance seemed to stride the gulf between them. 'Can you really not believe it was just to see you?'

'Because of a promise you made once? No, I don't believe that.' But with his eyes on her she could almost have believed anything.

She thought she saw in his face an acknowledgement that she was right, but what he said next surprised her. He spoke slowly, as if he were trying to understand his own motives. 'I came because I had to see if you were as I remembered – if I'd been wrong to think it was something different, not as with other women.'

'So there have been other women.' She felt an unreasoning tremor of jealousy and was reminded again how little she knew about him.

'A few,' he said, not quite truthfully.

'But you've never married?' She realised she could not even be sure of that.

'No. Nearly, once.'

'Who was she?'

He coloured slightly. 'Mistress Dorothy Liddell.'

She remembered that at York something had been said about his having once been Sir Ralph's ward. She had meant to ask him about it, but the moment had never seemed right. Now, questioned further, he told her the whole story, and she began to realise, with a certain unease, that she was walking beside Dorothy's mysterious lover, the cause of all that girlish unhappiness. She was surprised that Sir Ralph should ever have thought him eligible as a husband for his daughter, but then she had not heard his side of things.

There was a little silence at the end, and then she said abruptly, 'Have you come to any conclusion then?' He looked puzzled. 'Is it something different?'

He halted, looking at her. 'What do you think?'

'I think it's too soon to know,' she replied, though her heart was thudding again in that painful way. She was dismayed by the way her mood and her emotions kept swinging so violently from one extreme to the other. She had forgotten what it felt like not to have herself under perfect control, to feel that she was at the mercy of some power – some person – outside herself, to be melted by a soft-spoken word, to be tossed high like a bow on a kite's tail by a long look from a pair of blue eyes.

'For you, perhaps,' he said softly. 'Not for me.' Then they heard voices and looked round and saw the peat cutters coming their way in the now deepening dusk.

Ludovick glanced about him, as if seeking a hiding place, but there was no cover near. 'I can't stay,' he said.

She was suddenly fearful for him, beyond all reason, as if the approaching family were a troop of soldiers instead of innocent neighbours who could have no idea who it was Susannah Fawcett was talking to on her way home. 'You shouldn't have come. It's not safe. People talk. And there are soldiers at Castle Bolton. Sometimes they ride this way.'

He pressed his hand lightly to her mouth. 'Hush! I'll take care; I'll go now. But, listen, do you know a little valley, just as you go down into Swaledale, by the Muker road?' She nodded. 'There's a ruin in the trees there, near the stream. If you can, meet me there at midday tomorrow. If you don't come, if something stops you, then I'll watch for you, as I did today.' He did not wait for her answer but sprang into the saddle and rode quickly away, towards the road that led over the fell to Swaledale.

Susannah rode the last mile home in a daze, seeing nothing that was about her. She stabled Longlegs and went into the house and up to her room, and only later remembered that she had not entered an account of Jane Alderson's labour in her book. She was going downstairs to do it when she met her father, hobbling through the hall in search of her. 'John said you were back. I thought you'd gone to bed without saying goodnight.'

She kissed him, that and nothing more, but he must have sensed something different about her, for he said, 'What's wrong?'

'Nothing, father,' she said. 'Nothing at all.' She had never even hinted to him what had happened at York. By the time she returned home she had known it was behind her, for ever she thought; no point then in disturbing her father with any of it. As for what had happened today, that too was just an incident, a chance meeting, which very likely would end as suddenly as it had begun.

But later, in bed, she lay staring into the dark with such a fiery joy consuming her that she felt no need of sleep.

It was about three miles from Thornside to the gill Ludovick had spoken of, scoured from the southern slope of Swaledale by a rushing beck, impetuous with waterfalls. On its steep banks ash and willow and sycamore, oak and scots pine, alder and birch jostled for space, their many shades of green broken here and there by splashes of white blossom: hawthorn thick as cream and languorously perfumed, rowan delicate as lace. At the head of the gill Susannah dismounted and followed the line of the beck down from its source on the open moor, leading Longlegs. They slithered together through the trees, while she looked for a ruin of some kind. Around her the wood was loud with birdsong, underlaid by the splash of water and the soft rush of wind in the boughs. After a time it began to rain, but she knew of it only by a gentle spattering overhead and an occasional dash of moisture on hand or cheek.

She had begun to think she must somehow have missed the ruin, when she saw it suddenly, a grey-lichened shadow among the greenness, on the further side of the beck. Not that it really deserved so portentous a name, for it could scarcely have been much of a building, even when it was new, just a small shed briefly used for some agricultural purpose, or perhaps to provide casual shelter near the site of a now worked-out lead vein.

She saw the horse first, grazing quietly in the dappled sunlight just beyond the tumbled heap of stones – only half of one wall remained. Then she saw its rider, sitting in shadow lower down the bank, his arms linked about his knees, his eyes watching her. She halted, her breath caught in her throat, unable to move for a good few seconds. Then she smiled and found a way across the beck and up the other side. She tethered Longlegs near the other horse, and then turned to find Ludovick beside her, and his arms about her.

The world shrank to their embrace, to his body against hers, the smell of him suddenly coming back to her, fresh air and echoes of perfume, lingering odours of tobacco from inns passed through, sweat-stained old leather and the last component that was essentially him, indefinable, unmistakable. Then his face was on hers, a little rough at the jaw, his mouth soft, tender, and then urgent with the hunger of his need, which was her need too.

'You came,' he said, when at last they paused to draw breath. 'I feared you wouldn't.'

She was startled even to think there had been any question about it, or even any choice. She had herself never doubted that she would come. Now, for the first time, she wondered: 'What does he want of me?' and then thought how foolish she was to ask, for what did any man want of a woman he met secretly like this? Suddenly, she doubted him, doubted herself, though her need for him was consuming her. 'Let's walk, and talk,' she said unsteadily from somewhere within the tumult of her emotions. He took her hand in his and they walked through the wood, not seeing anything around them and saying nothing at all. She knew it was a device to stave off what might otherwise happen, to give her time to know what she was doing; if indeed she wanted to do it. Whole minutes passed and she could not gather her thoughts or find anything to say. From his silence he seemed to be in as bad a way. At last, she said, 'Did you stay here last night?' Before she saw it she had thought of the ruin as something much more substantial, imagined him taking refuge there.

'I'm staying near Muker – a Catholic family I know.'

She thought, the Middletons live near Muker. 'Will you stay long?'

'That depends.' But he did not say on what, and she did not ask. He halted, taking her arm. 'Susannah, look at me.' She did so, though all the little threads of calmness she had been gathering together blew away in a moment, beyond her reach. 'I love you.'

'I know,' she said.

'You don't say, "I love you too."'

'I can't think. I don't know what I feel.'

'Yet you came.'

'I don't know why I came.' But she did. Her body told her so, the wild joy that had kept her awake last night. The trouble was that she knew what she felt, but could not yet allow herself to see what the implications were, or to face them.

He tugged at her hands, whispered, 'Come closer and you'll know.'

'I think I should go.'

'You've only just come.'

'I shouldn't have done. I'm not sure . . .'

He gazed at her and she had to lower her eyes, not to be drawn to him against any last resisting instinct. She heard him say, 'I know I've nothing to offer, nothing but what you see. I don't know what lies round the corner, for either of us. I only know I had to see you, that this now is all that we have. That I love you. And that I want nothing from you that's not freely given, from the heart. If you have doubts at all, then you must go. Now.'

'I need time, I think,' she said.

'We have no time. You know that.'

She knew that whichever way she looked at it, deceive herself as she might, he was simply trying to seduce her. It was the thing every girl was taught to resist, the thing she had never doubted she was well fortified against, whatever the circumstances. Now she realised that the most impregnable defences are useless if the will to hold them is not there. Her will had dwindled to a tremulous, feeble glimmer and was close to extinction. She feared – no, she knew – that she herself wanted to extinguish it, but shrank from doing something so momentous, so contrary to what she had always been taught.

'Susannah!' His voice in the stillness was soft, imploring, breathless with desire. She raised her eyes and knew she had to stay for one more kiss before she left him.

'Let's sit down.' He spread his cloak on a level place on the grass, quickly, as if there was no time to waste. Then he took her hand and drew her down beside him and she sat there, looking at him. He reached out and took the coif from her head, so that her hair fell loose about her shoulders. Then she leaned towards him, mouth meeting mouth. After a moment he pressed her gently back. She felt his hand on her cheek, running down her throat, sliding on to her shoulder, then under the rim of her bodice, seeking her breast. She knew then that the last barrier had fallen, the last flicker of her will had gone out. She was all desire, naked unresisting desire. She put her arms up to draw him nearer, felt his hand push her skirts aside, move up to the place where all feeling was centred. 'Let me come, love!'

He came, and it was not paradise, for there was pain and bleeding and it was over too soon, but for a moment she had come near to some delight beyond imagining, which until now she had not even known was within her reach. It had left her, not disappointed, but hungry, wanting more.

He saw the blood and looked at her face and knew, even in his indolent contentment, that he had not carried her with him to the end. Once, he had asked Selina to show him how a virgin should be won, but today, in his hunger for Susannah, he had not considered her needs or her pleasure. He felt ashamed, for he had never before been so heedless, and he loved Susannah as he had never loved any other woman. Perhaps that was the trouble. 'I hurt you,' he said. 'Forgive me.' He wanted to say, 'Next time it will be different,' but he feared that after this there would be no next time, that she would not want it. Then she smiled at him, tenderly, and reached out to stroke his hair, and he felt relieved.

'This – it was of my choosing too, not yours only,' she said. 'There's nothing to forgive.' Then, suddenly sure, 'I love you.'

He kissed her, gently this time. 'And I you. As long as there is breath in my body, I shall love you.' He held her face in his hands. 'No dishonour will come to you from this, I swear it.'

'I'm not afraid.' Nor was she, for after all her doubts it had not felt wrong, and she knew God watched over her, as He did over all His Elect.

'You've no need to be. You see, I cannot get children.'

She was startled, even a little shocked by what that assurance implied. 'How can you possibly know that? Unless you've lain with very many women.'

'There've been enough.'

'And some had children from other men?'

'Yes, more than one. Or miscarried of them.'

She realised that implied rather more women than 'a few', but she let it pass. 'Do you mind?' She knew how important such a thing was to most men.

'Not now. Before the war, when I thought of getting an heir, then I did for a time.'

'Did Sir Ralph know?'

'He'd scarcely have wanted me wed to his daughter if he had.'

'I suppose it was something he'd not easily have thought of. He's never had any trouble of that kind.' She gazed up into the creamy blossoms of the hawthorn above them. She thought its perfume – sensuous, cloying – would stay with her until the day she died. 'Will you be here tomorrow?'

He ran a finger over her face, tracing her features as if he wanted to imprint them on his mind for ever. He was smiling slightly. 'Do you want me to be?'

'You know I do.'

'Then I shall be here, all day.'

He was there, waiting for her, without buff coat or sword, because the day was hot, a lithe graceful figure in a worn doublet of slate-coloured satin, its silver lacing frayed and tarnished. She no longer felt any doubt or hesitation. Her longing for him, the clamorous need of her body, overcame any other thought or principle. He met her with a kiss and then they found a sunny hollow in the wood and she sat down and he said, 'I should like to undress you. Will you let me?'

She was already melting from the look in his eyes and the touch of his hands, but she said, rather breathlessly, 'Only if I can do the same for you.'

He grinned. 'You drive a hard bargain, Mistress Fawcett.'

'Fair shares for all, my lord.'

'Then, firstly, you are Susannah, and I am not 'my lord', but Ludovick; and I shall begin.' Kneeling before her, he took off coif and neckerchief and began to undo the lacings of her bodice. She put up a hand then, staving off her own fierce desire.

'My turn now.' Her hands were trembling as she unbuttoned his doublet. When she had it off he pulled her to him. She could feel his body through the linen of his shirt, warm, very close. She did not know if it was his heart or hers that beat so fast. She felt his hands seek out the lacings of her bodice.

They went on undressing one another, slowly, by turns, with kisses and caresses between each garment, teasing out the pleasure for as long as they could bear. Her bodice, his boots, her skirt, his stockings, her petticoat. Dressed now only in her shift, she unlaced his shirt and pulled it over his head. About his neck she saw that he wore a rosary – for concealment, presumably – and, hung on a silver chain, a waxen disc set in silver and imprinted with a lamb and a cross. 'What's this?'

'An *Agnus Dei*,' he said. 'Blessed by the Pope.' He put it briefly to his lips, though his eyes never left her face. Then he kissed her too, little teasing kisses. It was only then that she saw the ugly red mark on his upper right arm. She gave a cry and touched it, her fingers light and gentle.

'You've been hurt!'

He tried to stop her mouth with another kiss but she made him tell her how he came by the wound, listening in dismay to his account of his capture, though he gave few details. He saw her relief when he told her how he had been taken in by a kindly Royalist family, hidden from the soldiers searching for him and nursed back to health. He saw her anxiety give way to a lively physician's curiosity, displacing all the passion of the lover. She wanted to know precisely what the surgeon had done to him; whether he had been feverish and for how long; what medicines he had been given, if any; how quickly the wound had healed; whether it still pained him. He soon gave up answering her questions and pressed his hand to her mouth to silence her, laughing. 'So that's why you wanted to undress me! I'm a mere medical curiosity. I suppose you'd sooner I was a corpse, then you could carry out a full dissection.'

'Of course,' she said, then added with an earnest primness belied by the brightness of her eyes, 'They don't let women dissect, you see. It's very discouraging. I have to make do as best I can with living flesh.'

She pushed him to the ground, slipping off the short linen drawers so that he was entirely naked. Then she sat back on her heels and gazed at his body. She had seen men stripped before, but always in the defencelessness and indignity of wounds and disease; never like this, laid before her in all the pride of passionate youth. He was small-boned and not very tall, but his shoulders were well muscled, his hips narrow, his legs long, all perfectly proportioned. It was not curiosity she felt now, nor even the satisfaction that came from looking on a young and healthy body, but delight and wonder and desire all mixed up together. 'You're beautiful,' she said after a moment, running her hands down the fair, taut skin. 'Did you know that?'

He smiled and pulled her towards him. 'Then we're well matched, dear heart.' His voice was ragged, shaking with desire. He tugged at her shift, took it off, laid her naked on the cloak. 'Now, love, no more. Lie there—' He bent his head to kiss her, her eyes and mouth, her throat, her breasts, and she lay under the touch of his hands and his lips, surrendered to him, her fingers threaded through his hair. He did things to her then that she had never dreamed of, sweet forbidden things that shocked her and yet set every part of her on fire and ravished her senses and made her sob with pleasure.

This time there was at the end no pain, no regret, no remnant of hunger, only an explosion of joy, like a great flower bursting into sudden exultant bloom, like all the beauties of light and colour the soul could imagine fused in one perfect moment. She laughed out loud and held him pressed to her as he cried, 'Love, love, love!' and then relaxed, the weight of his satisfied body suddenly heavy on hers.

Much later, after a time of quiet and tenderness, she felt a sudden chill recollection that there was a world outside this place, without its exquisite simplicities. She said, casually enough, 'How much longer can you stay?'

They had been lying side by side, their bodies touching with all the ease of their growing familiarity. Now he rolled over and looked earnestly into her face. 'For ever and ever, dear heart; until eternity. I shall come every day to this wood for as long as I live and you shall meet me here and we shall pass the days in love until we grow old and tired, and then we shall fall asleep in one another's arms, and the birds will cover us and we shall lie there until our bones fall to dust. And then for ever the earth will be so rich and fruitful where we have lain that a thousand flowers will spring up in this place, even in winter time.'

It was like some foolish old song, a fantasy sprung from all the ardour of young love, yet spoken in that soft lilting voice with his eyes, very blue, on her face it almost convinced her for a moment, as if it held some concrete promise for the future, certain of fulfilment.

It was an illusion that lasted through the summer days and nights, for they met almost every day and her life became centred on their meeting place, on her lover and all they shared together.

When she was with him he absorbed her completely. Away from him, she carried him with her, in her heart and her mind, her blood, her limbs, her organs, every part of her. He was there with her every moment of every day, all through the long wakeful hours of the night as she lay listening to the hooting of the owls and wishing she were out there with him, wherever he now was. What impinged upon her of her old life seemed somehow turned topsy-turvy, seen from where she now was. Worship on Sunday and midweek, once the mainstay of her life, had somehow grown arid and meaningless, something to be endured until it was over. Now it was outside that she felt most in harmony with what was around her, among the multiple greens of trees bursting into new leaf, the grass growing lush and emerald, cranesbill and dog roses and cow parsley crowding banks and the borders of woods with a tangled riot of colour, cattle suckling calves, sturdy lambs careering happily after one another in the dusk, everything alive and growing so fast you could almost see it grow; and the couples, driven by the same fruitful urge, who passed hot afternoons and warm evenings in woods or hay byres, in a way that once would have drawn from her disapproval or disgust. Now she knew what they were seeking, and she only smiled to herself because she, among all of them, had truly found it, for there had been no man like her lover, no woman so blessed, so happy as she was, no love like the one they shared.

Only when she attended a woman in labour did her old concentration and singleness of purpose return to her. Otherwise, she did everything in a dream, scarcely knowing what she was doing. Once, Anne Greatorex, speaking to her after church, got no reply and had to repeat herself three times before Susannah, vaguely, answered. Anne laughed. 'If you were anyone else, Susannah, I'd swear you were in love.' Susannah felt herself colouring and turned away quickly, for fear that Anne should read the truth in her eyes.

For it was true, of course. She had known at York the name of what she felt. Now it was a consuming fire against which her feelings then had been a mere candle glow. At York she had been distracted from Ludovick by the needs of the wounded. Now nothing distracted her for more than a moment. He had brought with him to her home all the strangeness of York, its apartness, but focused and intensified a hundredfold. He had searched out and woken in her things she had not known were there, delights, sensations, depths and joys.

She ate no more than was necessary for life, she slept little, so that her father grew concerned. 'But you've a good colour, it's true,' he said after dinner one day, having commented anxiously on how little she had just eaten. 'You don't look as if anything ails you.'

'Then don't worry about me,' she had retorted, kissing him. Then: 'I said I'd call on Mistress Robinson today.'

'I thought you said she was imagining the symptoms?'

'I don't want to be caught out. Don't worry if I'm gone a while. You know how she talks.' And she went to saddle Longlegs for the ride over to Swaledale where Mistress Robinson, her most remote patient, lived; though she did not, of course, see Mistress Robinson that day.

The May blossom browned and the petals fell and the leaves darkened. Susannah came to Ludovick through haymeadows and arrived with the hem of her skirts dusted with pollen from the buttercups. 'Oh, fie, Mistress Susannah!' he said. 'Adorned with gold dust like any vain court lady!' And then they laughed and danced about the wood, she who had never danced, for she was neither fine lady nor idle country lass and had always had better things to do with her time.

There were days of soft rain or showers when they heard the pattering far over their heads, and he made a tent with his cloak against the ruined wall, and they lay dry and warm and let the world do its worst while they loved.

There was a day so cold and wet that they huddled together, shivering, trying to reach completion without exposing the least corner of flesh to the air. They did it at last, a little fumblingly, and were consumed with laughter at how ridiculous they were, how absurd were human creatures in the act of love.

There was a hot day, baking hot, when they wandered out of the wood and up on the fell, away from the tormenting flies and the midges, in search of what little wind there was, and stopped by a tarn, and stripped, and she splashed on the edge, while he swam slowly, smoothly, through the dark still waters. Then they lay on the grass allowing the sun to dry them, and then they dressed and he sat there with her leaning against him, and after a time he began to sing. She had little knowledge or understanding of music and it had never meant much to her, but even so the beauty of his voice stirred her, its effortless sweetness floating over her head into the summer afternoon.

> Dear, leave thy home and come with me
> That scorn the world for love of thee;
> Here will we live . . .

When he came to an end she turned to look up at him. 'What was that song?'

'Something by one William Lawes. He was killed at Chester last year.' Then, as if he regretted that reminder of the war, he brushed her face with his hand and said, 'It seemed to speak to us.'

'Except that I've already come to thee.' A little later she said, 'Sing something else!'

This time it was an older song, one that even Susannah had heard before, long ago, though she suspected she had then thought it lascivious.

> Shall I come sweet love, to thee
> When the evening beams are set,
> Shall I not excluded be . . .?

She laughed and said, 'I hope that's not a question you want me to answer.'

'Ah, but now – would you not like me to climb in by your window tonight and come creeping into your bed?'

She shivered with pleasure at the thought, but said, just in case he was serious, 'It wouldn't be safe. My father—'

'I forget there are other people in your life.'

A chill seemed to come over them both. She shivered again, but this time she felt cold.

'What do you tell him?'

'Oh, that some woman is in labour and has sent for me.'

He laughed. 'Then I've brought an increase after all. So many infants in so short a time!'

'I don't always say the same. Sometimes women think they're in labour when they're not. Sometimes they call me for other things. Sometimes there really is someone.' She felt suddenly dejected at the thought of so much deceit, and it must have shown in her voice or her face, for he said, with a note of astonishment,

'You love your father.'

'He's my best friend and companion.' But I have lied to him, for the first time in my life . . . She did not want to think of it. 'Let's go back to the wood.' So they went and made love and drove the rest of the world back where it belonged, out of their lives again.

There were other days after that when he sang to her, because she begged him to. He sang in Spanish and French and (seductively) in Italian and even, once, a strange sad Irish lament that tore at her heart. Another time he sang some foolish improper song while he undressed her, his voice part of the lovemaking.

There were other days when they talked and talked. Soon after his arrival she brought him news of the fall of Oxford, though his hosts (they *were* the Middletons) had already told him of it. Fairfax had been generous in his terms. Parliament's excepted persons, the Princes Rupert and Maurice among them, had been given passes to leave the country. The King's second son, James Duke of York, had been sent to London, to join Prince Henry and Princess Elizabeth, who were already there, prisoners of Parliament. The rest of the garrison had been allowed simply to go home, there to pay the fines that would enable them to live in peace. 'I suppose Sir Ralph will be back at Widehope,' Susannah had said. Her father had expressed the wistful hope that they might now meet again, but she did not mention that to Ludovick, not wanting to bring her father between them again.

That was one of the few days when they talked of the war and the things that divided them. For the most part they avoided such hazardous matters, not wanting to bring any hurt into their time together. Sometimes they talked of their lives before York and since. Susannah had little to tell, for he was not much interested in medical matters and there had been few other excitements which he did not already know of. Ludovick told her a little about Rob's death, and Mark's, and talked of his brother, and, when she asked, something about his life before the war. His face shadowed as he told her, without detail, what she asked and no more. She saw that there were dark things he would never speak about, and she hoped her love would bring the healing that words could not.

Sometimes she brought food to their rendezvous, because she suspected he would not otherwise eat enough, and they shared bread or oatcakes or cheese or bacon, much as they had in York, and washed it down with clear cold water from the beck. Like every moment they spent together it was special, set apart.

There was a day when the air was full of the scent of fresh-mown hay and he did not sing, because the songs of the haymakers came to them from the meadows by the river beyond the gill. That day he was in a mood she had not met before, quiet and thoughtful and especially tender. When they had made love, he said, 'Today is my birthday.' Then, 'For the first time in three years I'm happy. I didn't think it was possible to be so happy in this life.' She had remembered then that it was three years since the brother who had shared this birthday had died. Without a word she had kissed him.

The next day was hot, oppressively hot, and she rode on to the fell through meadows full of men and women and children getting in the last of the hay before the threatened storm broke.

She was late, because for once she had indeed been called out to a woman in labour, though fortunately it had been a quick and easy birth and she thought she still had time to go to the wood before Ludovick left. He usually stayed there until well into the afternoon. Sometimes they had not parted until dusk. But it was already early evening.

He was still there, sitting in his usual place by the ruin, though he got swiftly to his feet as she came into sight. She knew at once that something was wrong. His face had lost all its relaxed happiness and he held her with a kind of desperation. She saw that he was wearing his sword and his buff coat and his cloak. Her heart seemed to stop. He was dressed for a journey.

'I must go, tonight. God knows, I've stayed too long already. They came to the house this morning, first thing, soldiers, looking for me. They had a report I'd been seen, more than once. I only hope to God they hadn't seen you too, but I don't know. I got away and came here. I don't think I was followed. But I've heard them passing on the road, the last time not more than an hour since.'

She clung to him. 'They know who you are then?'

'Yes, I don't know how.' He was holding her as if he could not bear ever to let her go again. 'I was afraid you wouldn't come, that I'd have to go without seeing you.'

'There must be somewhere else you can hide. There are caves. I know places—'

'So long as we go on meeting, you're in danger. And what point is there in staying if we can't meet?'

'I'm not afraid. I would face anything for you.'

'Do you think I could bear it if any harm came to you, because of me?'

'Don't go, please, love!'

'We have until dark, that's all.'

And already the shadows were deepening under the trees. Far off, ominous, they heard the first thunder roll round the hills. All the little familiar sounds of the wood, birds and animals, all were hushed, except for the sound of their breathing, the beat of their hearts. 'One last time!' she begged, and so they lay there by the ruin and made love with a desperate, anguished passion.

Afterwards they held one another for a long time. 'Come with me, Susannah. We can be married!'

Come with me . . . She thought of riding with him into the growing night, fleeing the pursuing soldiers, sharing every danger, every adventure. 'Where will we go?'

'Ireland.'

Where the men who had plundered Anne Greatorex and killed her husband and child were still holding their own; his kin. He had taught her to understand something of what lay behind that bitter rebellion, but to understand was not enough. The cause closest to his heart was one she could never serve, nor even wish well. How could she marry – perhaps by some superstitious Popish rite – a man whose life was given to something she hated? What would she do at his side, but live a passive silent witness to things she could not approve, things that must in time make them hate one another as passionately perhaps as they had loved? She saw it all with livid clarity, as if the lightning that suddenly lit the wood to the last thin blade of grass had shown her the truth about herself and the man beside her. The love that had been everything through this magical summer was suddenly not enough, and the realisation struck the warmth of it from her body. She shivered.

When the thunder ended, he said quietly, 'Forget I said that. I should never have asked it of you. It's not just the danger. I'm going to fight. I have no choice now.'

She knew that he too had known a moment of bitter illumination.

Lightning again, searingly bright, immediate thunder cracking overhead . . . She stood up, pulling him to his feet. 'It's not safe here under the trees.'

He held her so close that there was not a thread of air between them. 'Let it strike us both then, now, this minute, before we have to part!' But the next flash showed only that his face was wet with tears, as hers was. He held her more tightly than ever. 'Know one thing, Susannah – with all my heart and soul I'm bound to thee, to eternity. What we have done together, here – that has bound us as surely as any marriage vow. That I promise thee; and that as long as I live there will be no other woman to hold this place in my heart.' She felt him fumble with something, which he then pressed into her hand. 'My father's ring,' he said. 'It's no use to me now. But if ever times change and we can meet freely again, then I shall come to claim it, and you too, as my wife, if you will have me.'

She knew that was a delusion, for their love had only flowered because they had been able to shut out the world and all its hatreds and fears and suspicions, and their own divisions with it. She could not believe that the world would ever change enough for them to live openly together within it. Yet, defying that truth, she tried to shout, 'I shall love you too, for ever!' But the storm had broken, and its din drowned her words, reverberated through their clinging bodies. Rain fell with a sudden drenching force, penetrating the leaves in seconds. 'I must go,' he said against her ear.

'Not in this – you can't go in this!'

'What better cover than a storm?'

Always, always, one last embrace, one last kiss, but there could be no always and it had to end. Then he was mounting his horse, soothing its fears, reaching from the saddle to hold her just once more, almost sweeping her off her feet with the fierceness of his hold on her. Then he had turned his horse and set his spurs to it and was riding away through the torrent, leaving her standing alone in the wood in the dark with his ring biting into her hand, so tightly did she hold it.

CHAPTER THIRTY-THREE

Every year at the end of August Thornside had its feast to mark the festival of St Aidan, to whom the church was dedicated. In the old days the feast had taken place under the benign patronage of the church, but Nathaniel Johnson had little time for dead saints and still less for drunken village festivals, with all their accompanying temptations of dancing and races and wrestling and the selling of vain trinkets. Not that he could do anything to stop the proceedings, for it was the time of year when people who had moved away came home to see friends and relatives, when everyone forgot work and troubles for a whole week and enjoyed themselves to the full. It would have taken place if the church had fallen down and Master Johnson been swallowed up by the earth. So he had to content himself with a fiery sermon against wantonness and vanity, and hope that the more sober of his parishioners would set an example by refusing to associate themselves with the event.

Conscious that if he stayed in London he would not be seen to be setting an example, Richard had come home, and after church that morning he saw his wife and mother and sister into the coach and then hung back to walk some way with Susannah and her father. 'I had hoped to call and enquire after you both,' he said, 'but time is pressing. I understand we are more in your debt than ever.' Two weeks ago, Susannah had been summoned to Barbara Metcalfe, who had miscarried of a child almost before she knew she was pregnant. 'We have cause to give thanks to God that you are so near,' Richard added. He spoke almost as if he were alone with Susannah. Both she and her father had often been concerned by the intimacy of his manner towards her, which seemed to have increased since his marriage.

Now Matthew saw that Susannah was making none of her usual effort to bring him into the talk – in fact, she seemed only to half-hear anything that Richard was saying, as if her thoughts were far away, as they so often seemed to be these days. He said, 'I've heard it said, now the malignant party's defeated, Parliament has hopes to send the army to subdue Ireland.'

'That is certainly my hope, as soon as may be.'

'It must be the more pressing, after the late victories by the Irish rebels.'

'More than that: there are too many regiments standing idle, with nothing better to do than listen to the pernicious nonsense poured into their ears by Lilburne and his like.'

'I thought Lilburne was in the Tower.' He had been sent there on the orders of the House of Lords for a publication defaming the Earl of Manchester.

'When has that ever stopped him? Sometimes I think the Star Chamber treated that firebrand more lightly than he deserved. However, until the matter of the King is settled, our hands are tied.'

'Will the Scots hand him over, do you think?'

Richard glanced at Susannah, hoping for a reaction from her. In the past, she had been the one to ask the questions and show a lively interest in the course of the war. 'We hope to make terms of some kind with all parties. We shall see. As you say, Ireland gives cause for alarm.' He saw that he did after all have Susannah's attention, and enlarged, 'Though it looks as though the rebels are close to falling out among themselves. What better moment to move against O'Neill and his savages? But our hands are tied until this land of ours is settled in peace again.'

Susannah, realising that she was not to have news of Ludovick – why after all should she have hoped for such a thing? – lost interest in the conversation, and soon afterwards Richard left them.

'I wish I knew what ails you,' said her father, as they reached the house. It was something he had said very frequently, in one form or another, since the night of the thunderstorm, when Susannah had come home very late, soaked to the skin and so distraught that he could get no sense out of her. It was also a question she had never satisfactorily answered, and did not now. 'Nothing ails me, father.

You worry too much.' Then she made her way upstairs to take off her cloak and change her shoes.

She had tried, desperately, to pull herself together, to control her misery and throw off the weariness and nausea that seemed to have clung to her since Ludovick went away, as if in his going he had taken all the savour from her life. Her father, finding no other explanation, had apparently decided she was working too hard, and rebuked her gently for overtaxing her strength, urging her to work less and rest more. She did not tell him that work was the only means she had of shutting out her pain.

It was work that took her out into the streets of Thornside on the Tuesday of the feast. Tuesday was always market day, but this week, because of the feast, it was more like a fair, with stalls on every corner selling every imaginable item, the streets thronged, jugglers and fiddlers and ballad singers and wrestlers providing entertainment. There had, in previous years, been a stall set up especially for the occasion by a linen weaver from somewhere outside the dale, and Susannah had last year bought linen from him at a very good price. It had proved to be strong and hardwearing, exactly what she needed, not only for her own use, but to make sheets and swaddling bands for mothers too poor to afford such things for themselves.

She pushed her way through the throng, her only aim to do what she had to do and get home again as quickly as possible. She soon began to feel swamped by the clamour and the heat and the dust and the stench of too many bodies in too close proximity. She felt more sick than ever, and dizzy, and desperate for air. She found herself by a stall selling ribbons and trinkets, none of which she was remotely interested in, and stood there trying to remember what she had been doing and why, trying to gather her thoughts. A group of women were chatting over their knitting beside the stall, their voices coming and going around her, odd phrases drifting unheeded in and out of her mind. 'No, it was the night Annie's little lad was born,' one of them was saying. 'That's three months ago now. You'll mind that well enough, Mistress Susannah?'

Susannah looked up at the large woman beside her. 'Mind what?'

'The night of Annie Sutton's lying in – when she nearly lost the bairn after waiting all that time. I was saying . . .'

She remembered it well enough: a difficult labour, an oppressively hot day and night, and the knowledge that so much anxiety and hope depended upon the outcome of this delivery – and irritation that she had to cope with it all while the familiar monthly pain nagged at her. She suffered few inconveniences with her courses, but the first day always brought some pain. The week after that, Ludovick had come.

She felt as if someone had suddenly drenched her with cold water. Time had for so long ceased to have any meaning for her, every moment of each day being measured in the intensity of what she felt, its joy or its pain. She had not realised that so many weeks had gone by; months . . . The women had moved on to some other topic, but she broke sharply in, 'How long is it since Annie Sutton's lying in?'

'I said, mistress – three months. First week in June, it was.' The woman stared at her. 'Does owt ail you, mistress?' There was a concerned murmur from the others.

Susannah was thinking: And now it's almost September. Three months . . . *I cannot get children*, he had said. The nausea and the tiredness – how could she of all people have been so blind as not to know what it meant?

She stammered some kind of reply and then turned and pushed her way back through the crowd. She was not too hot now, for there were cold shivers running all over her body. Once home, she went straight to her room and stripped and stood before the polished metal that served as a mirror and examined her breasts, noting their fullness, the darkened nipples. When she dressed again she was shaking.

Her father was in the garden, but at the further end, lovingly removing scarcely visible weeds from his tulip bed, and he did not see her go to the sheltered and sunny corner where a shrubby plant grew, and pick a handful of its leaves: herb of grace, rue, an efficacious plant with many uses, but never before, in her hands, the use to which she was about to put it. She had parted with Mistress Nelson because of this very thing.

She took the leaves into the house and made an infusion of them and poured it into a glass – rather more than she needed, more than was safe, but she had to be sure. Then she raised the glass.

She had it at her lips, had almost swallowed the first mouthful, when she seemed to see Ludovick's face, looking at her so earnestly in the dappled light under the trees, his hands holding her so that he could gaze into her eyes. Her summer love, gone for ever . . . *I cannot get children*. She had believed him, and she thought he had believed it too. In any case, by the time he had said it, very possibly it had already been too late.

She knew she could not do it, at least not now, not yet, not while she thought of how this thing had come about. She emptied the glass out of the window and washed it and put it away. But what was left of the infusion she poured into a phial, which she stoppered and pushed to the back of the highest shelf, just in case.

She slept not at all that night, nor for many nights afterwards. Her father grew more anxious than ever, for she was scarcely eating either. Each day she would examine herself for signs that she had been mistaken, or if not mistaken, that she was about to miscarry. She prayed with a desperate hopelessness that she would begin to bleed. She took long vigorous rides, walked for miles like one possessed, even when there was nothing to do and nowhere to go.

One day she found herself at the edge of the wood where she and Ludovick had met so often. She thought that perhaps some purpose had brought her here, that in this place she might somehow find help. It was cold in the wood, and dark, and swept by a chilling wind and spatters of rain. There were even some leaves already blown from the trees. It seemed quite another place from that summer scene of love and happiness. She felt horribly alone, and full of terror. She sat on the grass near the ruin, where they had lain so often, and tried to recall something of the warmth and laughter of that time, some of her certainty in their love, in the rightness of what they did. But he had long gone and she was here alone, pregnant with his child and facing disgrace.

Other women, confronted with a like disaster, sought out the man and hoped for marriage. Ludovick had offered her marriage and she felt sure that he would not have refused her now, had he known. But how to seek out a man who might, perhaps, be somewhere in Ireland, a war-torn and savage land of which she knew nothing? She wondered if Sir Ralph, presumably back at Widehope by now, might know how he could be reached, but she thought it unlikely. And it would mean telling Sir Ralph why she wanted to find Ludovick, and she shrank from the very thought of such a thing. And then to undertake so hazardous a journey on so slender a chance that it would bring her any good. True, if she were to find him it might ensure that their child was not born a bastard – but was bastardy much more to be dreaded than to be the acknowledged child of a landless Papist under sentence of death for treason? It would not after all be something she would want to broadcast to the world. She knew that the arguments against their marriage were not made null by what had happened. Unless times changed beyond all imagining, there could be no future for them together.

She could still take the route that had already so greatly tempted her. It was by no means closed to her yet. But if not, if she chose instead to bear her bastard here in Thornside, among the people who knew her – what then? The very thought of telling her father what had happened filled her with a crawling horror. He who thought so highly of her, who trusted her so completely; no, she feared it would kill him to know that his daughter could have done such a thing. But if she were to bear this child, then he must know.

Unless – she suddenly remembered her aunt's house at York, hers now. It had been little use to her as yet, having been occupied by a succession of soldiers. But no one in York would know that she was not a widow or a woman deserted by her husband. There she would be able to bear and raise her child, free from prying eyes, in the city where she had first met its father. Except that she would need money. She could in time earn her living as a midwife, but during the months of pregnancy and lying-in, and while her child was an infant, she would need something put by, to be sure of a subsistence. This year's harvest had been bad, which would mean high prices for the most simple foods.

Besides, Thornside was her home. What was more, she would still have to tell her father something and she thought it might distress him almost as much to think she was leaving him for no very good reason. Then there was that last, inescapable possibility: if anything were to happen to her, if, like her mother, she were to die in childbirth, who in York would care for her child, as her father, even in his shame, would surely do?

But to stay . . .! There was not just her father to be told. That might be the hardest, but then as yet she had scarcely considered the rest of it, the disgrace that must come on her, the effect it would have on her work. She knew she had never been much loved, except by those grateful mothers whose children she had successfully delivered. Aside from her father, she had no close friends. But she was deeply respected. What would it be like to lose that respect? She could not begin to imagine and hardly dared to think, but she knew that if she were to stay and bear this child, then she would find out only too soon.

Cold, wet, as frightened and alone as she had been when she came, she stood up and began to walk home. Only one thing had been changed by this journey: she had somehow made her choice, if it could be called that, when every possible path made her shrink. She would stay in Thornside and bear her child, facing the consequences whatever they were.

The first thing would be to tell her father. But not yet, not yet . . .

In the end, she did not wait until she no longer had any choice. She found she could not endure the waiting, or the loneliness. She wanted to get the first terrible step over with, and soon.

Such a simple thing: it was a Sunday evening and they sat side by side by the parlour fire, and she spoke suddenly into the quietness. 'Father, I have something to tell you.'

'Hmm.' He scarcely looked up from his book.

'I'm with child.'

Silence. He stared at her. She saw disbelief, incomprehension. 'What did you say?'

She rose to her feet to answer him, bracing herself for his reaction.

What happened then took her entirely by surprise. He threw down his book and hobbled over to her and put his arms about her. She saw that there were tears in his eyes. 'My dear, so that's what's wrong! Oh, why did you not tell me before? To carry this burden with you for so long, alone . . . What you must have suffered! It was the night of the storm, wasn't it? I knew something had happened.' He held her, kissed her. Then, his voice suddenly harsh, 'Who did this to you? He shall pay for it, Susannah, I promise you.'

It was only then she realised that he had immediately assumed she had been raped. She was moved beyond words by his tenderness, his trust in her, his concern to comfort her. If only it had been true, then she would have had nothing to fear. She was, for just a moment, strongly tempted to let him go on believing it. She knew that the world outside would not look so tolerantly even on a woman made pregnant by rape, but with her father beside her, with his love and trust in her undamaged, she knew she could face anything.

But to let him go on thinking that she had been wronged was to cast a slur on her memory of Ludovick. She could not allow it to happen. Gently she disengaged herself from her father's misconceived embrace and said, her voice shaking, 'No one did this to me, father. It was as much my doing as his.'

Even then he was not easily convinced. She felt guilty, he assured her, as any woman would after a rape. She blamed herself when she ought to blame the man. He was so blindly, so persistently understanding that in the end she found herself crying out, 'I loved him, father – I loved him!'

There was a long and terrible silence. He stared at her, and he seemed to be looking at a stranger, and one very little to his taste. Susannah shivered and sat down again. 'You say you lay with a man, knowingly, of your own free will?' She nodded. 'Who is he?' His voice was hard and cold.

'You don't know him.'

'Then that had better be remedied, and soon. There has already been more deceit than enough. He must marry you.'

'That can't be.'

'Don't tell me he's married already!' She saw now the look of a man whose trust had been so blown to pieces that he would believe almost anything of her.

'No. He's gone away and I don't know where he is.'

'Then he must be found.' But she would tell him no more, though he stormed at her as he had never done in all her life before, beside himself with rage and grief. Once he cried, 'How could such a thing have happened, and I not know of it?'

How indeed? she thought bleakly. Through deceit; and for that she had no excuse, even to herself. Yet she could never have told him who she had met and loved, or how, or why, could not tell him now, under any circumstances. To tell him would bring no healing, only make everything worse than it already was. Her love for Ludovick had driven a wedge between herself and her father, and the damage was beyond mending. If she looked at it coolly – something she only did now and then – even she could not understand how she could have loved such a man. To try and make her father understand was beyond her powers.

At the end of a miserable week, during which her father went about in a silent state of shock that puzzled and distressed Margaret, who could not know what was behind it, Susannah was called out to a delivery that went wrong.

The labour itself was uneventful enough and the mother bore it well, but the moment the head began to emerge Susannah saw that something was not right. She knew that such things happened from time to time, but had come across nothing quite so bad as this. She looked down at the monstrously deformed thing that lay in her hands and felt herself go cold with horror. It was still alive, though – please God! – it would not live long. With a haunting sense that this was her doing, that somehow she had brought the contamination of her sin to this place, she wrapped it well and laid it out of the mother's sight in the cradle. She knew what Mistress Nelson would have done, for she had seen her do it once, with a baby that was quite obviously gravely malformed – she had pressed a pillow over the face of the infant, before calmly announcing that, mercifully for all concerned, it had been born dead. Susannah could not bring herself to do such a thing, and so she had to tell the mother the truth, or as much of it as she thought she could bear. Fortunately, it died soon afterwards.

She went home with the sense of horror hanging about her still, unable to throw off the conviction that it was all somehow her doing, that she had been found out, if anyone cared to look a little below the surface. Worse than that, she saw in it a clear warning. She thought: What if this is what I give birth to, when my time comes? It would be too late then. She would have endured all the shame, all the disgrace, brought all the pain on her father, for nothing, because there would not even be a whole and healthy child at the end of it.

But it was not yet too late. There was still time, now, today, for her to go at once to the stillroom and take the drug she had put aside. Then she would tell her father she had miscarried, and he would be greatly relieved. She could not now undo the hurt she had caused him, but perhaps time would bring healing, and there would be no further disgrace for either of them to endure. What was more, she would be able to continue with her life's work as if nothing had happened, for no one else would know.

She reached the house and put out her hand to open the front door, and at that moment felt the first faint fluttering movement of the child in her womb. She halted, put a hand to her abdomen. Movement was not health, and there was no certainty about anything, but nor was there any reason why a bastard should be less whole and strong than any other child, except that many bastards, after birth, were neglected and uncared for. But not her child, and

Ludovick's. She had not wanted children, most certainly did not want this one, but because she had loved its father then she would love it too, and cherish it, as far as lay in her power.

She had thought that telling her father would be the hardest thing she would have to do, but it was not. She knew that Nathaniel Johnson had to know, before it became obvious to everyone, and she told him herself, on a grey wet October day. His disbelief was almost as great as her father's, and his wrath too. But before Matthew Fawcett's anger she had felt shame and misery. Before Nathaniel Johnson she felt only rebelliousness. He called her things her father would not have dreamed of, even in the worst of his hurt and distress: 'Whore, unregenerate child of the devil! You that I believed to be of the company of the saints found wallowing in filthiness!'

Filthiness, that love in the wood, the joy and laughter and sweetness of it – no, she could not accept what he called it. She stood before him and said nothing, because she had no choice, but her spirit was on fire with indignation. He spoke to her as he would have spoken to Nan Bestwick or any woman of loose morals, as if there was no difference between them.

Like her father, he tried to get her to name the man, with a view to salvaging something by an enforced marriage. When that did not work, he turned to Matthew, who had been present all the time. 'Then she must be put away, out of sight, that her sin may not prove a stumbling block to the weak. I know of a godly household in Colchester—'

Susannah saw the anguish on her father's face and knew it was a measure of his love for her, however deeply she had hurt him. 'I cannot send her away, Nathaniel. She's all I have. If anything should go wrong . . . I lost her mother that way . . . I beg you, don't ask it of me!'

'Did I not warn you, time and time again, not to make an idol of her? You have loved the creature above the Creator, and now you too shall be chastised for her sin and brought low.'

Matthew began to weep, but when Susannah went to put her arms about him, he thrust her away. 'No, you have brought this upon us!' Yet still he begged the minister to change his mind.

'She may remain in this place on one condition only,' said Nathaniel Johnson at last. 'That she acknowledges her sin publicly before the town, so that none may think we condone such filthiness.'

Susannah thought again of York; her father could come there with her, now that he knew. She put it to him, but he was implacable. 'I do not want to go to York, nor do I think you should. You ought to do this thing. You have sinned and now you must declare your repentance.'

So she agreed, with a sense that somehow after that she might find herself restored to what she had been, in the eyes of those who mattered most.

Her father stayed away from church the next Sunday morning, pleading indisposition, and Susannah did not try to make him change his mind, not wanting him to witness her humiliation.

There had not been so many in church since Thornside feast. Margery Nelson was there, craning her head to see Susannah, with triumph in her eyes; and more terribly Richard, though she had not known he was at home again. Draped in the white sheet of repentance, she walked the seemingly endless distance from the west door to the chancel steps, hearing the whispers swell to a drone of excitement. She stood before them all, staring far over their heads, until Master Johnson had mounted the pulpit for the sermon. And then into the sudden silence she made her declaration, in a clear, expressionless monotone. 'I freely confess, before God and before you all, that I am a fornicator. I have sinned most grievously. I acknowledge my sin. I ask for God's mercy and your prayers.'

As she came to an end she found she had somehow met the eyes of a girl sitting near the back, watching her with sombre intentness; and realised it was Jane Wetherald, whom she had condemned for doing what she herself had so nearly done. She wanted to say, with real remorse this time, 'I'm sorry; I understand now,' but of course she could not. Instead she looked up again, back at the whitewashed wall above all their heads.

She continued to stand there while the Minister preached a furious sermon against the sins of the flesh, and then through the psalms and prayers that seemed to go on for ever. As soon as the service ended she walked as quickly as she could without openly hurrying to reach the door before anyone else, to make her escape.

She was not quick enough. In the churchyard a group of men and women – mostly young - were already waiting for her, jeering.

She tried to ignore them and walk on, but they followed her, shouting more loudly than ever: 'Whore! Slut! Dirty hypocrite!' She quickened her pace, but they went faster too. Out of the churchyard, into the market place. They were catching at her skirts now, making obscene suggestions. Some threw mud and even stones. She turned into the lane that led towards home, and there they closed about her, and she knew they were not going to stop at insults. 'Whore! Thought that was it, did thou?' They fell on her, pulling her hair, tearing at her clothes, kicking her, hitting her. She tried to fight back, to kick and scratch and bite in return, but there were too many of them. She flattened herself against the wall, putting up her hands to protect her head. Then someone aimed a kick at her belly and she screamed, terrified for the child in her womb. She sank to the ground, bent double, trying somehow to keep both herself and the child safe. She wondered, in a detached sort of way, if they would kill her.

Then something in the noise changed, the blows dwindled to an occasional furtive kick. She did not dare move, but she listened, trying to work out what was happening. She suddenly realised she was hearing Richard's voice – by some miracle – and he sounded angry. She heard one of the women say, 'Sir, Nan Bestwick was whipped at the cart's tail, for what she's done. Why should she get off so light? Isn't it a sin when gentry do it?' Around her there was noisy agreement, but the blows ceased altogether.

'It's a sin, no matter what,' said Richard. 'But the law is the law, and you are breaking it. Now, go home, all of you, before I'm compelled to take steps to make you.'

She heard the muttering, sullen and resentful. Then she felt them move away, heard their departing steps, and one or two last jeers thrown at her in their going. Then she dared to look up and saw Richard bending over her, his expression full of anxiety. 'Are you hurt?'

Slowly, with his hand at her elbow, she stood up. Her clothes were torn and muddy and in disarray. She knew she was covered with bruises, and there was a painful cut on her lip. Her legs were shaking so much she could scarcely stand. 'Nothing that will not mend,' she said unsteadily.

'Then I'll see you safe home.'

She glanced at his face and saw its tight angry look, and the coldness in his eyes when she said, 'I can't thank you enough.' He took her arm and they walked together along the lane, like two old friends. Except that they were not friends any more, and could not be.

'I was simply doing my duty as a magistrate. You know that whatever friendship there was between us, is ended.' He sighed. 'I did not think this of you, in all the years . . .' Then he broke off. 'You shall not call on any of my household again, of course, not in any capacity.'

'No,' she said. 'I did not think I should.' But her heart sank.

She reached the house and there he handed her over to her dismayed father.

She recovered quickly enough from the incident, but of course nothing could ever be as it once had been. The whole district knew the story now and talked of it for weeks afterwards, enjoying it the more because she had fallen so far. Nan Bestwick falling pregnant was scarcely news at all, the godly Susannah Fawcett in such a condition was the source of endless lip-smacking speculation. There were even lewd songs made about her and sung in the town's alehouses. Children shouted obscenities after her in the street and once a man cornered her in a quiet place, clearly thinking her fair game. He had her pushed against a wall with his hands up her skirts before she was able to break free. After that she made sure she never went out alone. Colourful rumours were passed round, growing more lurid by the day, though one such piece of gossip, brought home by Margaret one market day, was no rumour at all, as it happened. 'Ellen Hall said she saw you one day last summer, talking to a man on the fell. She didn't know him, but she said he had dark hair and the look of a soldier.'

Susannah remembered that first meeting and the peat cutters making their way home in the dusk. She felt a sudden bitter pang of loss. Later, her father asked, 'Susannah, was that the man?' No answer. 'Who was he?'

In the end she said, abruptly, 'He was a Royalist, now gone overseas. I met him first at York.' And then she went up to her room so that her father should not question her further.

During the last months of her pregnancy she left the house only to go to church, which she continued to do in the hope that she might somehow find acceptance again, not for her own sake, but for the sake of her child. No one ever spoke to her, and scarcely even to her father, but if nothing else it kept them in touch with the news, read or announced from the pulpit. Susannah listened only in the faint hope of hearing news of Ludovick, but none ever came. Otherwise, it all seemed very far away, the war and its consequences, the coming of peace – in England, at least – but not of an end to uncertainty. Four hundred thousand pounds paid to the Scots, to ensure their withdrawal; the King handed over to Parliament, escorted south to Holdenby House in Northamptonshire through the worst of the January snows; moves by Parliament to make terms with the King and to disband most of the army, leaving only a small force for the conquest of Ireland. All part of a world far removed from her.

At home, her father scarcely spoke to her, except, sometimes, to urge her to eat some particularly wholesome food, or to rest. She knew, though he did not say so, that he was deeply worried about her and terrified, in spite of everything, that he would lose her as he had lost her mother. In the end she spoke to him about it, because she knew she had to protect her unborn child against that possibility. 'Whatever happens, father, I beg you to care for this child. Bring it up as lovingly as you brought me up.'

'No,' he said bitterly, 'I would never make that mistake again.' Then, softening, 'I'd not let any grandchild of mine want for anything, however ill-gotten. I think you know that.'

The baby was born early in March, on a wild wet afternoon. The wind lashed the rain against the windows of her room, while inside by the fire the fierce pangs of her body did their work. Her father, now all loving concern, wanted her to lie in bed like his gently-born patients, but she had no wish simply to wait passively for the moment to come. She had him bring her the birthing stool that had been made to her order some time ago and crouched on it by the bed, arguing fiercely with her father while he hovered anxiously over her.

At dusk the wind died down and the rain ceased and into the candlelit quiet Susannah saw the child emerge, a tiny creature covered with the greasy coating of birth. She saw her father bend over to cut the cord, heard the first cry, growing in force.

'A boy – a healthy little boy!' It did not sound like her father's voice, but was somehow harsh and muffled at once. She heard herself laugh, foolishly. Margaret took the child somewhere out of her sight, but her father stood tensely over her until the placenta came away, completely, without trouble. Afterwards, as he helped her to bed, Susannah saw that there were tears in his eyes, though he would not look directly at her, but simply turned to take the child from Margaret and hand him to her. The baby was washed now, and closely swaddled in clean linen. He had a tiny red crumpled face, a black fuzz on his head; and an unerring instinct, when she put him to the breast, for the nourishment that would give him life. As she felt him suck, she found she was weeping; yet she laughed too.

Then her father suddenly leaned over and kissed her and she looked up and saw that he too was smiling through his tears. 'God knows I wouldn't have chosen it to be this way. But I thank Him all the same . . .What will you call him?'

'Daniel,' she said. 'He'll need all the courage I can give him.'

1647

CHAPTER THIRTY-FOUR

It was two days into June, and Walter and seven others, uneasy and restless, were making an unauthorised patrol of the lanes about Holdenby House.

'There's one thing I've thought these past days,' said Amias, when they had been riding in a watchful silence for about a quarter of an hour. Walter, in command of the troop during Samuel's absence, gave him a questioning look. 'Colonel Graves is very thick with the King, since he came back from London.'

Walter recalled the little scene, watched this morning from where they waited – ready to ride, yet suddenly redundant – at the front of the mansion in which the King was held. They had seen the prisoner ride away from the house, in the respectful company of his servants, the few courtiers allowed access to him, the Parliamentary commissioners, and Colonel Graves, who commanded the garrison at Holdenby. There had been a military escort too, but a small one, made up of men carefully selected from Colonel Graves's own regiment. Yes, thinking of it now, Walter recalled how the Colonel had ridden close to the King, his hat in his hand, head bowed, listening with great attention, yet occasionally speaking at some length.

'You're right, Amias. He's getting as fawning as Major-General Browne.' The former governor of Abingdon was one of the commissioners sent to Holdenby by Parliament, and it was obvious to them all that His Majesty had long ago won over that devoutly Presbyterian officer.

'They'll have given him his orders,' said Roger: 'Get well in with the King.'

'Then it's my belief we soldiers have to make terms with him before they can,' said Amias. 'Who has a better right to settle things, after all? We gave our blood for the nation's liberties.'

'Do you really think we'll ever get our liberties restored, with this King?' Walter put in. 'As soon as he's back in Whitehall, he'll overturn everything that's agreed and we'll be back where we began – or if not that, then it'll be men like Holles he'll turn to for counsel. And Holles says we're traitors, for daring to petition for our rights.' He drew a deep breath and then plunged on, fired with the ideas he and Samuel had talked over so often. 'It's my belief we have to have a settlement without the King. Without lords too. And our rights written down, for all that can to read and know what they are, so that no one will be able to overturn them ever again.'

'And votes for all men, and Parliaments every two years, and no more tithes – you've been reading John Lilburne.'

'To read and talk and think is no crime, so long as the Lord lights the way.' But Amias was right. Samuel had friends among John Lilburne's circle in London, who supplied him with everything they put into print, which he and Walter then eagerly read. As usual, the fact that Lilburne was in prison made no difference to his flow of words.

'But to do without the King . . .'

'We've done without him since the war began.'

Corporal Will Harper said with exasperation. 'What business is it of ours how the country's governed? We're soldiers, that's all.'

'Are you content with the way things are?'

'No, because I'm owed four months' pay at least, like everyone else. But just let me get what's due to me, and I'll be content. As I see it, that's all any soldier can ask for.' The Corporal, a large fair young man, good looking in a florid way, was new to their troop, but Walter already felt he did not much like him.

'Then we're mere mercenaries. That's not why I fought, not for money.'

'You don't want your back pay then?'

'Of course I do, for it's justly due to me. But without the rest – no, I shan't be content. Amias is right. We've given our blood for the liberty of England. For that, we deserve to have a voice.'

'That's all very well,' said Roger, 'but if Parliament makes terms with the King, then we shan't have any say in the settling of things, as you said yourself. And the way things are, we're like to be disbanded or sent to Ireland before the week's out.'

Walter knew they were all thinking, as he was, of the letter Samuel had sent five days ago, from Bury St Edmunds, where he had gone to meet with the other representatives elected by the soldiers – agitators, as they called them. Samuel, being the most eloquent of their company, had been their choice. The letter had told them that Parliament, now dominated by a Presbyterian faction under the leadership of Denzil Holles, had at last formally voted for the long-threatened disbandment of the army. Walter had read it to the men of his troop, and to a handful of men from Graves's regiment too, since their senior officers had prevented them from choosing agitators of their own. He had read slowly, translating the coded words that scattered it as he came to them. He and Samuel had worked out the code together before parting.

The disbandment is to begin on the first day of June and finish within the fortnight, Samuel had written. *All to go, except those that choose to serve in Ireland, and what cavalry is needed to keep the peace here. The General's foot is to be disbanded first, at Chelmsford, and Ingoldsby's after . . . We ask for a general rendezvous, so that they may not pick us off one by one. We must stand together in this – all, men and officers in unity. Parliament has voted two months' arrears, to pay us off. If they vote ten times as much, no man must take it, nor agree to go to Ireland. We stand for a full settlement or nothing, all of us as one, from the General to the least drummer boy. We must do it, for our safety and our liberty . . . Make sure all know of this and act upon it.*

By the time the letter came to an end, Roger had been chewing his lip with anxiety. 'Parliament still has the London militia,' he had reminded them, 'and the troops that have already said they'll go to Ireland.' Among which, they all knew, was a small contingent from Okey's dragoons, under a few Presbyterian officers, now stationed close to London. Their own Captain was one of them, which was how Samuel came to have temporary command, and Walter under him. 'Do you really think we'll get away with it?'

'That's why we have to stand united,' Walter had said.

'But what if the General refuses the rendezvous?' had been Roger's retort. 'Then we'll be done for.'

The messenger who had brought the letter, who was present at their meeting, had intervened. 'Black Tom won't let us down.

Most of the grandees are with us – there's your own Colonel, and Rich and Rainsborough and Lambert, and Major Harrison, of course. Then there's Colonel Lilburne, as you would expect, considering whose brother he is. They say Ireton and Cromwell will likely stand with us too, but they're still in London, in the Commons.'

Roger had not been reassured. 'To take our part, Black Tom would have to disobey Parliament. He's never done that yet, whatever the provocation.'

'He did over the petitioning, when they ordered us to do no more of it,' Walter had pointed out. 'He had the order read, but he let us go on as before.'

'That's hardly the same. And he's in worse health than he was then. If I was in his shoes I'd tell Parliament what they could do with their commission and take myself off to Bath or somewhere. Let someone else sort it out. And someone else might not care so much what becomes of us all.'

They had heard no further news since that day, and all that they saw here at Holdenby had only served to increase their anxiety. Roger was not the only one to be conscious of the danger that faced them. They knew well enough that once the army had been disbanded or sent overseas it would be easy for the Presbyterian faction to punish all those it saw as threatening its own attempts at a settlement – and the settlement Holles and his kind wanted was one that would take them back to the England of 1641, before the Irish rebellion had blown apart all hopes of bringing the King under Parliamentary control. Yet the years of war had given Walter and many of his comrades a vision of quite another England, unlike anything that had ever gone before. The hope was that it might be within their grasp at last; the fear that they faced ruin rather than victory.

'Have you sent word to Lieutenant Revol what's happening here?' Amias asked.

Walter shook his head. 'Until today I thought there might be nothing in it. I'll write as soon as we get back.'

For a time after that they rode in silence, on through the tangle of lanes towards Kislingbury, where General Fairfax had established his headquarters two days before the Naseby fight. Odd, Walter thought, how fate seemed to keep drawing him back to this countryside which, until two years ago, had meant nothing to him, yet which now he knew so well; a quiet, unremarkable landscape of gentle hills, small winding rivers, woods and pasture. Still sometimes as they patrolled they would come on the detritus of war, broken and abandoned weapons, a battered helmet, cannon-balls, once, the rotting corpse of a dead man. Walter had examined him as closely as the stench would allow, but the corpse had long since been stripped of everything that might identify it, and there was nothing to suggest it was the prisoner, so long sought and taken at last, whom Walter had so embarrassingly lost a year ago. In any case, though it had been only a few miles north of here that he had held Lord Milburn, it was unlikely he could have got so far as this, considering the condition he was in. He must have died in some other ditch, somewhere else. Not that the thought was really adequate consolation for having tied up a fair number of men for the best part of three days with nothing to show for it.

'Walter – sir!' Amias's low warning broke into Walter's thoughts. He looked up and glimpsed through the trees a small group of horsemen coming towards them. 'Our own men – or they seem so,' said Amias softly. But they knew well enough that, these days, there were men they could not trust wearing the uniform of the New Model. 'At least there are more of us.'

They drew rein and waited, barring the path. Then, as the riders came nearer, Walter gave a cry and spurred his horse forward. A moment after, he and Samuel met, dismounted, were laughing and clasping hands and slapping one another's backs. 'You never said you were coming!'

Amias broke in eagerly. 'What news? Do we get our rendezvous?'

Samuel looked round at him. 'It's to be at Newmarket, on the fourth. The regiments are marching already. But that's not why I'm here.' He turned back to Walter. 'Where's the King?'

'At Althorp, at bowls,' Walter said. Althorp's lands adjoined Holdenby's. 'He should have been riding out today. We were to escort him. Then this morning they cancelled the order.'

'Who's with him now?'

'The usual servants, Colonel Graves, an escort from Graves's regiment, not friends of ours. Samuel, I'm uneasy . . .'

One of Samuel's companions broke in: 'I'll ride on to Althorp.'

Walter realised then that the speaker was familiar to him, but before he could say anything the man had ridden away, with the rest of the group behind him.

Samuel, watching them go, said, 'You remember George Joyce, Cornet in his Excellency's lifeguard?'

'I thought I knew his face. What's he doing here?'

'He's come to secure the King. The agitators picked him. He had first to make sure of the artillery at Oxford, which he's done. I met up with him on my way from Bury yesterday. He has five hundred men at his back, who should be here by nightfall. We feared Graves and his crew might get wind of their coming, so rode on ahead to be sure nothing went wrong.'

'Does the General know?' Amias sounded awed, even afraid, as well he might.

'No. We thought safer not. He's done enough for now, agreeing to the rendezvous. We can't expect more. But Joyce has got Lieutenant-General Cromwell's authority.' He studied Walter's face. 'You said you were uneasy.'

'The change of plans today: they kept us hanging about at Holdenby most of the morning, with nothing to do, then sent us back to quarters. We didn't go. We thought it best to keep watch. It seemed to us they might be getting ready to send the King north, and didn't want us in the way.'

'One thing's sure,' said Amias, 'let the Presbyterians once get the King away to Scotland out of our reach and that'll be the signal for them to march in and crush us.'

'We have good information they're about to do that,' said Samuel. 'Which is why Joyce is here. And why I came back. Listen now, and then go and make sure all we can trust know what's planned. We want it done with the least trouble. When the men get here, Joyce is to arrest Colonel Graves.'

'That's mutiny!' exclaimed Roger.

'Not if we win. Anyway, we're in too deep to turn back now. We were finished long since, as far as the Presbyterians are concerned.'

The troops arrived quietly at dusk and had the house surrounded before its garrison knew what was happening. Then their friends inside opened the doors to them and, after the first joyful greetings, they were able, without opposition, to take control. Only one thing went wrong, for somehow, in the confusion and the darkness, Colonel Graves gave them the slip. 'No great loss,' said Amias, who was delighted by their success.

'It will be, if he comes back with reinforcements,' warned Samuel. Amias fell uncharacteristically silent. Soon afterwards,

Samuel left them, to return to Bury St Edmunds with news of what had been done.

Everything seemed quiet that night and the next day, but they were all on edge. 'One foot wrong, and we'll be hanged to the last man,' Roger had said gloomily at one point, at which Walter had grinned and said that there would not be rope enough in England to hang so many. But he knew Roger was largely right. What they had been a part of was a deliberate and calculated act against the ruling faction in Parliament and its friends. True, everything they had done since the war began could, if the wrong side won, have been called treason. But this time they – the common soldiers of the army and the agitators who represented them – had acted almost entirely on their own initiative. The fact that Lieutenant-General Cromwell was said to approve would not save them, for Joyce had nothing in writing.

Through the long hot day, Walter and his friends patrolled the lanes, watching for the least sign that they were about to be surprised. They thought Colonel Graves had gone to London, but they could not be sure. They knew for certain that there were troops loyal to Parliament stationed at Bromsgrove, only a long day's ride from Holdenby.

Late in the afternoon they passed through East Haddon, where they were quartered, and stopped there to eat. Several of the men who had ridden in yesterday were also lodged there now, so the women knew what was going on. Esther served Walter with unusual solicitude, and he thought it was the first time he had ever seen her frightened. 'Jane Sumpter was going to Daventry this morning,' Esther told them. 'But she saw a troop of soldiers coming this way, so she turned back. She said they were no men she knew, and they were taking care not to be seen.'

So Walter and his troop, with some of the new arrivals, rode afterwards towards Daventry, following every byway, and, though they saw no soldiers, there seemed to be more travellers than usual on the roads, in groups or riding singly, often in a south-westerly direction, like men making for a rendezvous.

'We should get the King away from here,' Amias said. 'If anyone comes against us with a large enough force, there'll be nothing we can do about it.'

'We should get him to Oxford,' one of Joyce's company said. 'We could keep him safe there.'

Walter rode back to Holdenby, to tell George Joyce what they had seen. 'I've sent to Cromwell for orders,' Joyce said. 'But if what you fear is true, then we've no time to wait for an answer.' Walter, conscious of how much the young man was taking on himself, felt sympathy for his predicament. They all knew that he was only acting on decisions made by the soldiers through their representatives, but that was not how outsiders would see it. In their eyes, he was in command and would be first to be called to account.

Joyce took Walter with him and did the rounds of the various places where his own men were quartered, in outbuildings and neighbouring houses. At each stop he explained what had happened and asked for the men's views as to what should be done, which, overwhelmingly, was that they should remove the King to Oxford, strongly garrisoned by troops sympathetic to them. Soberly, Joyce rode back to Holdenby and insisted on speaking to the King, who had already gone to bed. 'We can't wait till morning,' he had explained to Walter. 'We must be on the road in good time.'

'But what do we do with the King, when we have him safe away from here?' Amias wondered later, when they were back at East Haddon.

'If he'll make terms with us, then at the least it strengthens our hand,' said Walter.

'I thought you didn't want a settlement with the King,' Amias reminded him.

'No more I do. But it would maybe give us what we want the sooner, if he were to treat with us. Though it's my belief he never will. In any case, if he won't treat with us, then we have to be sure he doesn't treat with any other party.'

At six the next morning the King stepped out of the front door of the mansion. The early sun lit his tiny dignified figure, as neat and fresh-looking as if he rose so early every day, as if nothing last night had disturbed his rest. He paused first to take in the long ranks of troopers drawn up before him, and then he walked calmly towards Cornet Joyce, who sat waiting on his horse, equally calm. Joyce removed his hat and bowed from the waist.

The King looked up. 'What commission have you to secure my person?' he asked, in the haughty tone of one who knew quite well he was putting the other man in an awkward position. There was no trace of his customary stammer. 'Have you nothing in writing from Sir Thomas Fairfax?'

It was Joyce who stammered then, beginning a vague and rambling reply. The King broke impatiently into it, 'Tell me what commission you have!'

Joyce gulped, began to speak, fell silent again and then, in the manner of one suddenly inspired: 'Here is my commission, your Majesty.'

'Where, pray?' The King looked him over, as if expecting to see a paper half-concealed about his person.

Joyce turned and gestured towards the men behind him. 'These men, sire. They are my commission.'

For just an instant, the King looked puzzled. Then he realised what was implied. 'I see,' he said, and gave a sudden wry smile. 'As fair a commission and as well written as any I have seen in my life. We had better decide where we are to go, with the authority of this commission of yours.'

In the end, the King refused to go to Oxford, so they took him to Newmarket, where he was comfortably lodged and allowed at last to see those of his children who were in Parliamentary hands.

Joyce's company, with which Walter and his friends rode, reached army headquarters in time to hear the *Solemn Engagement of the Army* read to them by Sir Thomas Fairfax's orders, and to assent, with all their comrades, to its statement that they would not disband until their grievances were dealt with. To that end, a General Council of the Army was set up, in which elected agitators of however humble a rank were to play a part with the highest officers.

In the first days of August, Walter rode through the once familiar streets of London, in circumstances he would never have dreamed were possible even a few short weeks ago.

As he rode, he recalled the last time he had ridden through the capital, as they followed the Earl of Essex to the relief of Gloucester. The crowds had cheered them then, and they were cheering now, some of them, but he felt a lifetime removed from the excited, ignorant youth who had ridden out on that September day four years ago. Essex's army had been a rabble, he saw that now, held together only by a momentary enthusiasm. This army of which he was now a part was something quite different, something he thought perhaps had never existed before in all the long history of warfare.

Unity had brought them what they wanted, unity strengthened by the fact that the Presbyterian officers in the army had resigned. Since their captain was one of them, Samuel had been confirmed as captain in his place and Walter had become his lieutenant.

As for the rest of what they asked for, that had seemed about to fall to them too, until it all began to go wrong. Their Presbyterian enemies in the Commons had been driven out. But nothing was done to call them to account, and Parliament prevaricated, while the agitators called for action, even if it meant a march on London to force their will on the city. The grandees – Cromwell, Ireton, Fairfax himself – had put off that step, until the last few days, when the London mob rioting in the streets had burst into Parliament House and violently forced the return of the expelled Presbyterians. After that, Black Tom had hesitated no longer.

Steadily, day by day, the thing had been done. First, on Tuesday, they had reached Hounslow Heath – where, long ago, Esther had sought Walter out and they had been married. He was glad that another memory should be brought in to overlay that one, and one he could be proud of. There Fairfax had reviewed his army, in the presence of all the Independent Members of Parliament and the Speakers of both Houses, who had taken refuge with them from the wrath of the mob.

Then, selected regiments had been moved into Southwark, where the trained band welcomed them. The next step was across London Bridge, into the city. They had to put guns in place to force the raising of the portcullis, though there had been no need to fire them. All that was left after that was for troops to be dispersed to take over the city's outer defences.

That had all happened earlier in the week. George Joyce had told them what it had been like on Friday – yesterday – when Fairfax had led a small part of his army into the city streets. Joyce had been there, with the General's Life Guards. He had narrowly escaped court-martial for his action in taking the King from Holdenby, but in the end the King's evident liking for him had saved him. In the weeks since then the army leaders had made every effort to come to terms with their royal prisoner, putting to him a document drawn up by Ireton and Lambert and agreed by the new General Council of the army. The *Heads of the Proposals* called for limited Parliaments and the ending of tithes, yet allowed the King many things that the Scots or the English Presbyterians had refused him. They, for instance, had insisted that Presbyterianism must be imposed and the Covenant sworn by all, the King included. The Army wanted no one system to be established, but offered freedom of worship to all except Catholics. Yet the King had not been won over, and in the end it was without his authority – or any but that of a company of frightened MPs, backed by the power of the sword – that they had marched into London. 'Now we have to settle without him,' Samuel had said, with manifest satisfaction.

But before that could happen, order had to be brought to London. On that Friday, August the sixth, the soldiers had ridden into the city with sprigs of laurel in their hats, symbols of victory, and no hand had been raised against them. While the city rocked with the ringing of bells, even the staunchest Presbyterian dignitaries had scuttled out to bow before General Fairfax and stammer words of welcome, at Hyde Park and Charing Cross and New Palace Yard.

On Saturday, the entire army had its day of triumph. They gathered first to the west of the city, in Hyde Park, where they piled the greater part of their weapons into wagons, and the horse regiments dismounted. Then, to the beat of drums and the joyous blaring of trumpets, with regimental colours fluttering in the light summer wind, they began to march, in perfect order, through the main thoroughfares of the city towards Cheapside, with Cromwell at the head of the cavalry and Fairfax, exhausted by the strains of the past long weeks, riding in a coach with his own wife and Elizabeth Cromwell; and the artillery rattling in their rear. They passed very near the street where Walter had spent so much of his early life, but he only realised it afterwards, being too full of pride and triumph to think of anything but his good fortune at being a part of this day.

Once at Cheapside the regiments fanned out, leaving no street in the city's heart untouched by the tramp of their feet. For nine hours they marched, watched by admiring crowds who shouted and clapped, until at last, around nine at night, hot, exhausted, with aching feet but contented hearts, they marched in the dusk across London bridge and dispersed to their quarters.

Walter's troop was lodged near their Colonel at Fulham, not far from army headquarters at Putney. He was glad that they were well away from his old master's house. Esther, who seemed impervious to such uncomfortable sensations, began to make herself at home with all her usual vigour, setting out cooking pots, finding places for the surprising quantity of belongings they had accumulated during their years on the march, to the annoyance of the landlady, who objected to her own possessions being displaced to make room for others. 'Don't fall out with her if you can help it,' Walter said. 'We could be here a while yet.' He brushed his coat and combed his hair, and then reached for his hat. Esther watched him from where she knelt by the hearth.

'Are you going out again? What about supper?'

'I'll get something. Don't wait up.' He dropped a dutiful kiss on her upturned face and left her. No need to tell her he was to meet Samuel, who was quartered with the other agitators at Hammersmith, and who had promised to introduce him to some of his civilian friends, men from Lilburne's circle. That would only lead to more carping. Esther had no greater interest in politics than she had in religion, and had long resented his preoccupation with them both, for which she blamed Samuel, whom she had never liked. 'You were a better man before you met him,' she would say sometimes, which Walter knew was untrue.

As he made his way out of the house, Walter passed Corporal Harper on the stairs. 'There's only my wife up there,' he told him.

'She has been so good as to mend a shirt for me,' said the other man.

Walter felt a momentary surprise, but did not dwell on it, having more important things on his mind.

It was in those weeks in London, in hours of argument in the smoky rooms of the Mouth tavern in Aldersgate, with Samuel always there at his side, speaking his very thoughts more eloquently than ever he could, that Walter saw at last the new England they had dreamed of take definite and tangible shape, put into words and written down.

Yet the weeks passed, and no limit was set to the sitting of Parliament, nor were moves made to purge the Commons of Presbyterian members, or their sympathisers, and the new laws they hoped for were not passed, and their pay still only came in fitfully – and their arrears hardly at all. John Lilburne was not set free, and the grandees of the army continued to talk to the King, now moved to Hampton Court. They knew then that there was, after all, to be no quick and easy coming of God's kingdom to England, that there was still fighting to be done, of another kind.

Late in November, while the army was close to being wrenched apart by the passion of its diverse convictions, the King fled from Hampton Court. It was with the wavering Colonel Hammond, governor of the Isle of Wight, that he at last took refuge.

1648

CHAPTER THIRTY-FIVE

Elizabeth Liddell, standing gloomily at the parlour window look-ing out on the drenched May-time green of the garden, saw Dorothy – cloak pulled tight, head bent inside her hood – emerge from the sheltering belt of woodland that bordered their land, and then come running towards the house. Her mother knew quite well what she had been doing. Beyond the wood lay their neigh-bour's property, separated from it only by a low wall. In that wood, across that wall, was the one place where Dorothy might meet and talk with John Bolam unobserved. It was only too obvious that Dorothy was no more inclined than anyone else in this house to be obedient or reasonable.

Elizabeth sighed. In front of her, rain battered on the window, incessant rain, day after endless day. Behind her, clearly audible through the half-open door of the library, angry voices were raised in argument, flinging one hurt after another. Cuthbert this time, but it was just as likely to be Dorothy – and considering where she had been this afternoon, very likely soon would be.

Oh, she was tired of it all! She could hardly believe that there had ever been a time when the family at Widehope had been at peace. Yet when Ralph first came home, even the hardships of their life had seemed like play, so happy had they all been. But that had ended months ago. These days it seemed as if every one of them was at odds with everyone else – or at least, with Ralph, who seemed able to please nobody.

The worst of it was that Elizabeth could see both sides in the matter of Dorothy and John Bolam. Before the war, they had all looked on the Bolams, father and son, as the best of neighbours.

Even then, Elizabeth thought John had shown signs of a more than common liking for Dorothy, a hopeless enough matter, since Ralph had always aimed higher for her, even before her disastrous betrothal. But of course, since the war, the friendship with their neighbours had ended and they rarely had any contact with them, even when old Henry Bolam died and John was left alone to manage his newly inherited property. How long it had been going on, Elizabeth did not know, but it was only lately she had become aware that Dorothy was secretly meeting John Bolam. She had confronted her daughter about it, and Dorothy had admitted that she loved him and he loved her. Since he was a member of the very County Sequestration Committee that had imposed the most savage composition fines upon the family at Widehope, it was only natural that Sir Ralph should look unfavourably on his daughter's liking for young John.

'Time we found her a husband, before she does something foolish,' Ralph had said, more than once, but Elizabeth only asked him where he supposed he was going to find an eligible husband for his daughter, when so many young Royalists had been killed, and those who were left were either impoverished or in exile and both. 'Not,' she had added, loyally, 'that I want her wed to John Bolam. That's out of the question.' Secretly she thought that if the alternative was that Dorothy should not wed at all – as seemed only too likely, since she was already twenty-four – she might do worse than marry a kindly young man who loved her well, could afford to keep her, and might even prove a useful ally in the new order of things. But that was before it began to look as if there might after all be no new order of things.

As for Cuthbert, their hitherto dutiful elder son had his own quite different reasons for anger with his father. A few days ago Berwick had fallen to a small Royalist force under Sir Marmaduke Langdale, while Carlisle was also in Royalist hands, and the Scots were expected to march into England at any moment, in support of the King. There were risings, too, in Wales and Kent and Surrey and the south-west. Many of their Royalist friends and neighbours had unearthed old weapons and ridden at once to Berwick, to join Langdale's force. But not Ralph.

Elizabeth could hear Cuthbert now, arguing with his father in the bitterly indignant manner that had become only too familiar lately. 'You used to preach to us about honour. But it was from Mark I truly learned what honour was. He was proud to die for the King.'

A little pause, while Elizabeth shared the pain that had momentarily silenced her husband. 'As I would be,' Ralph replied at last, wearily, patiently, 'if I thought it would serve any useful purpose. But this poor land has had enough of war. There has been too much blood shed already, too much property destroyed, too many children made fatherless and wives widowed, too many sons . . .'

'Then if you've not the stomach to go yourself, at least let me go!'

'No, Cuthbert. One son lost is already more than I can easily bear.'

Elizabeth thought then that each one of their children had its own unique capacity to tear at the heart, and the more children there were, the greater was the likelihood of pain. That was one reason for her own resentment with Ralph, which was why she had put off telling him the news, until now. Only, when he emerged at last from his study beyond the library she had found that Cuthbert was there before her, bringing up yet again that endlessly repeated argument. Ralph spent a good deal of time in his study these days, since he had been forced to dispense with his steward and do all the administration himself. They were, Elizabeth thought, perilously close to becoming mere yeoman farmers. They employed many fewer servants now, and she and Dorothy, with the help of the younger girls, had to do all the dairy work themselves. There were few of the children who did not have some task to perform during the day; those, that is, who were not so young that they needed care themselves – of whom there would soon be yet one more, for which she blamed Ralph. She had borne him a son – their ninth child and sixth son – nine months after his return from Oxford. Now, while the babe was still with the wet nurse, she found herself pregnant again.

Once, she had been told that, to be able to conceive, a woman must take pleasure in the act of coition. Since she loved Ralph with a passion and tenderness that matched his own she had found that easy to believe. Desperate to avoid pregnancy, she had tried to force herself into coldness, to lie quiescent when he came to her, though it distressed him and spoiled the whole thing for both of them. And still she conceived. She wished there was someone whose advice she could seek, but it seemed disloyal to Ralph to turn to another person to find a way of preventing the children he welcomed so readily.

She wondered if he was beginning, now, to realise that those adored infants might one day grow into troublesome, opinionated young men and women. Like Cuthbert, who would not leave his argument alone. 'I don't understand you, sir. What better time will there ever be than this, to restore the King to his own? The whole country's crying out for it. How can Parliament prevail against such feeling?'

'As they have prevailed until now. By means of the Army.'

'But the Army's falling apart. It's been one mutiny after another since last year. It's finished.'

From somewhere upstairs came the enraged shrieks of children, and then a long anguished wail. Elizabeth thought it was small wonder that, in this house of anger, the little ones too should be at odds with one another. Her news would have to wait, while she went to see what the trouble was. On the stairs she met Dorothy, already changed into dry clothes, looking demure. Her cheeks were flushed – from the rain, Elizabeth hoped, but she feared it was more likely to be a direct result of what had passed between her and John in the wood. She knew she should have said something, but decided to leave it for now.

In the library, Ralph was still trying to win over his son. 'If the army had been left in idleness, then perhaps it might have destroyed itself. But war will only unite the soldiers, as nothing else can.'

'They're riddled with Levelling ideas. You said so yourself.' For some time the followers of John Lilburne had been known as 'Levellers'.

'Perhaps. But when it comes to it, the most hotheaded soldier puts his loyalty to the army first. Fairfax has always been able to depend on that. You couldn't have a more mutinous rabble than the one they had here in the north last year, before Fairfax gave the command to Major-General Lambert. Now, they're as settled and disciplined as he could wish. I've fought against both Fairfax and Lambert, and I'm convinced that if his Majesty had been blessed with more men of their quality we'd not be talking as we are now.' He paused, then said with a grim smile, 'I read that the senior officers at Windsor lately held a day of prayer and fasting. As they did before they took Bristol, and Dartmouth, and every other stronghold that's fallen to them. They're never more dangerous, or more united, than when they meet together in prayer.'

'Anyone would think you supposed God was on their side!'

'I do not believe God means us to win through yet more war, that's all. He has His own way, and we would do well to leave it to Him. And be sure of one thing, Cuthbert: when all this is over, there will be no mercy for those who broke the peace.'

'If that happens it'll be because men like you stayed at home, like cowards—' He broke off suddenly. His sister had come into the room. His eyes met his father's, saying as clearly as any words: We cannot talk of such things before her. Then he said, 'It's no use talking to you anyway,' and swung round and left the room, pushing roughly past Dorothy.

She stayed in the doorway. 'Sir, why does everyone always stop talking when I come into the room?'

'I think,' said Sir Ralph, a little absently, 'that Cuthbert feels you are not altogether to be trusted, from the company you keep.'

'That's unfair!' she retorted. 'I'm your daughter, sir. Can you really think I'd do you or Cuthbert any harm?'

'You do harm simply by persisting with a friendship I cannot approve. And do not deny that you still meet him. I'm not wholly blind. You will never marry him, you know.'

She came towards him, suddenly conciliatory. 'I know, dear father, that I need your consent, whoever I marry. But – well, this time I should like to choose for myself.'

'So you shall, within reason.' He reached out to take her arm in his, but at that she drew back.

'You mean, so long as I choose the man you want me to marry! Father, where will I find a husband if I don't have John? I don't want to grow old and shrivelled waiting for the wind to change and the King to enjoy his own again. John's just next door and he's everything I could ask for.' She thought, resentfully, of the bed still shared with her sisters; of the daily anxieties that pressed down on them all in this house, like a constant lowering storm cloud; of what it might be like to hold her own infant in her arms; of the way John kissed her and touched her at their meetings in the wood, and how she wished it could be without the cold safety of the wall between them.

'Except that he's a Roundhead and nowhere near good enough for you.'

'Times have changed, father. You have to realise that.'

'They have not changed so much that I wish to wed my daughter to a rabid sectary, just to keep in with the rising party. His father was a ploughboy, Dorothy!'

'You mean he sometimes hired out his labour to you, when times were hard or you were short of hands. He was a good honest hard-working farmer, who did well for himself.'

Ralph sighed, and put an arm about his daughter. 'Be patient, my chick. It may be the wind will change sooner than you think.'

'If you thought *that* you'd have gone to fight,' she pointed out sharply. She resorted then to what he could only regard as the most deplorably underhand argument. 'Don't you think, sir, that God has shown his displeasure with the King, by so often defeating him? Do you not think perhaps Parliament might be in the right of it?'

After that, Ralph went in search of his wife, to explode to her. 'That I should hear such treasonous logic from my own daughter! If any more were needed to prove his evil influence on her . . .!' Then, calming down, he asked, 'What is happening to us, Bess? Is there to be civil war at the very heart of this family?' He held her close, his cheek pressed to hers. 'Is Cuthbert right? Am I a coward not to go?'

'No, no,' she murmured. She could not remember that he had ever before openly admitted to self-doubt.

'I've given so much already. All those years away from you all. And Mark . . . To feel that this time it's the turn of others – is that wrong?'

'No, dear heart. You are right to stay.' She stroked his hair and said whatever soothing things she thought might help, hurt on his behalf and Dorothy's and Cuthbert's – hurt for all of them. Then, when he was calmer, she told him her news.

In the past she had resented the way Ralph always rejoiced at the coming of each child, seemingly unaware of the depth of her dismay at being pregnant yet again. This time, she watched his face as she talked, looking for the happy smile, the joyful exclamation.

They did not come. She even thought she saw a little furrow appear momentarily on his once serene brow. He said, almost in an undertone, 'Another mouth to feed.' Then he smiled and put his arm about her, 'God's will be done, my love.' He kissed her, and she felt no resentment after all, only sadness that it should have come to this.

The news trickled in through the spring and summer. In Wales, Cromwell easily crushed the uprising. In Kent, Lord Fairfax – as he was since the death of his father – routed the Royalists, who retreated across the Thames to Colchester. The Scots reached England, to join forces with Langdale and his northern Royalists. But Lambert and Cromwell combined to meet them in drenched and bloody conflict near Preston, and the defeat was wholesale. Few escaped, though Langdale was among them. They heard later that most of the captured Royalists were sold into slavery in Barbados, except their leaders, who were sent prisoner to London to stand trial. 'Thank God you were not there!' Elizabeth said to Ralph with a shudder. He simply held her tight, saying nothing.

The whole sorry business ended late in August, in the mud and blood and disease of Colchester's long and pitiless siege. When the town at last surrendered, Fairfax showed none of his usual clemency. By his orders the Royalist commanders, Sir George Lisle and Sir Charles Lucas, were condemned to death, and no one on his side questioned the justice of it.

Captain Walter Barras volunteered for the firing party that carried out the executions, and he did his duty with rage and grief at his heart, and a sense of being the instrument of God's inexorable judgement on two men who had once again plunged England into bloody civil strife. If it had not been for them, and others like them, he would not have lost the best friend any man ever had. For in the mass graves that bordered their camp lay Samuel Revol, cut down in the first savage assault on the town, more than two months before.

After that, there remained only one other to be brought to justice, the arch-criminal whose endless web of intrigue had entangled them all with such catastrophic results, that 'Man of Blood', Charles Stuart.

1649

1648

CHAPTER THIRTY-SIX

'When we set out upon this war, I never thought it would bring us to this,' Richard Metcalfe said to his mother, on the evening of his return home, early in January.

'To what, pray?' said his mother briskly. 'The King must surely now make terms. He cannot any longer close his eyes to the consequences of not doing so.'

Richard, who had been standing looking into the fire, sat down on a stool beside Dame Alice and took her hands. 'Madam, you must understand, it's long past that point. I think I guessed many months ago that the King would never treat with us, or not on any terms we could accept. Yet still I never thought—'

'But Tom Fairfax has stayed in London, and will sit with the Commission, so you say.'

'Tom's a fool – no, that's harsh perhaps. But he still thinks as you do, that there will be some last minute agreement, or at the very least that the court will find the King guiltless.'

'Perhaps he has reason.'

'No, madam. He was never a politician, and in this he is as much at sea as ever. They will find the King guilty and he will die.'

'You cannot bring a King to trial and execute him as if he were a common criminal! By whose authority could they do such a thing?'

'The authority of the sword, for that's the authority we're under now. They say – Cromwell and Ireton say – the power comes from the people, but I doubt the people want it done in their name.'

There was a little silence, before his mother said, 'Then it seems to me Tom was right to stay. If it turns out as you say, he can lead the army to rescue the King and restore order.'

'In this I believe they would, for once, not follow him. Or few would. It would be to divide them. I admit, the thought had come to me, and I talked of it with Tom, but I see now that in this at least he is right. He would not take a step that must plunge this poor land of ours into yet more bloodshed. God knows we need peace.'

Dame Alice stirred restlessly in her chair; it might have been due to the rheumatism that had become a permanent torment to her, it might have been rather from unease of mind at the picture Richard had been steadily putting before her since he returned home in such a state of unhappiness. 'That such a thing should happen – no, I'll not believe it even now. You must be mistaken.'

'I wish I were,' said Richard. Sometimes he found himself thinking perhaps it was all a nightmare from which he would suddenly awake, to find that none of it had happened: not the war; not the deaths of men he liked; not the hot troubled weeks of two summers ago, when the London mob had burst into the Commons to try and force a treaty with the King and a break with the army. The violence of that time had appalled and even frightened him. Not that he wanted to see the army ride roughshod over Parliament, as he knew some of the soldiers wanted it to do, but he had seen the justice of many of the men's demands, and had been sure there would not be peace until they had their due. He had been relieved when the army marched into the city to restore order. He had thought that would be the end of it. Looking back now, he wondered that he could have been so blind.

Last year's renewed war had changed everything, of course, turning many waverers against the King, making even Richard see that there was no making peace with him. After that, it had been inexcusable that a faction in Parliament had still tried to negotiate.

Even so, it had been a profound shock to come to the House of Commons one morning last December and find Colonel Pride at the door with redcoats in files behind him and a list in his hand, and to hear the army dictate who should and who should not have admission. He himself had been allowed to pass, but he had been tempted to say he wanted no more part in a house purged by the sword. He knew that Tom Fairfax had been deeply unhappy about the incident, as by so much that had happened since, though he had done nothing to prevent it. He was floundering, unable to see what he ought to do. When both their names had appeared on the list of those called to try the King, Richard had immediately pleaded his wife's indisposition as an excuse to absent himself. Others had acted similarly, in spite of pressure from their colleagues. Tom had said nothing. They needed his great name first on the list, to give legitimacy to what they were doing, but Tom in his bewildered modesty did not even see that. With all the evidence before him, he still seemed unable to believe that other men might have motives he would find abhorrent. The fiery, decisive soldier was another man away from the battlefield.

'What if you are right,' Dame Alice asked suddenly, her voice breaking into the quietness, which, in spite of the crackling of the logs in the hearth, the gentle ticking of the great clock, had a brooding oppressiveness about it, 'which God forbid. But if you are, what then? I know there was talk of making the Duke of York King, but he's got away now.'

'There will be no King. No King, no Lords, but a republic.' He could feel her sense of shock.

'Is that not to cut at the very foundation of property and authority and order?'

'I wish others might see as clearly as you do, madam. Pray that it may not come to that.'

He left her soon afterwards, making his way with some sense of reluctance to his room, where he knew that Barbara, dutiful as ever, would be waiting for him, even though she was in the last stages of pregnancy. He did not make love to her, not simply from consideration for her condition – though indeed he wanted to do nothing to jeopardise the safe arrival of a child who might be his longed-for son – but because he found it hard to feel any attraction for her. He would not have admitted it even under the most extreme torture, but he had been able to get her pregnant each time only by holding before his closed eyes a vision of Susannah Fawcett.

'Mistress Metcalfe must be very near her time,' Matthew Fawcett observed to his daughter, as they sat reading by candlelight that same evening. 'They'll call in Margery Nelson, I suppose.'

Susannah glanced sharply at her father, wondering if the remark was meant as an oblique rebuke for the sin which had deprived her of her most respected patient, along with all the others. But there was nothing in Matthew's expression to indicate that he was making more than a passing observation. 'I hope then she has an easy lying in,' she said. 'She's a timid lady.'

She was surprised at how genuinely concerned she felt for the well-being of Richard's young wife. This new ability to feel deeply for the troubles of others was yet another of the surprising consequences of Daniel's birth. She had never once guessed that so simple and everyday a thing as the birth of her child would have such an explosive effect on her emotions.

She had been prepared for the joys of motherhood, though she had neither sought nor wanted them. In fact, she had discovered that imagination had fallen far short of reality. She had not realised it was possible to love another human creature as she loved Daniel. She had loved his father, and the passion of their summer's meetings had seemed at the time to consume her to the exclusion of all else. Yet it was an insubstantial thing, scarcely remembered now, against what she felt for his child.

What she had not expected at all was the terror that from the moment of his birth had shadowed her every step. In his infancy, she used often to wake suddenly in the dark, listening for the sound of his breathing. Even when she heard it, she hardly dared to believe the evidence of her ears. She would get up and light a candle with shaking hands and peer into his cradle, terrified that he might somehow have ceased to live while she slept. Later, the terror drew back a little, but it was never very far away, stalking her until the moment came to fasten its claws in her, as savagely as ever. A cough, a sore throat, a slight rash, and she feared a consumption or a quinsy or (most dreaded of all, because most likely) the smallpox. When Daniel tottered on his unsteady legs too close to water or fire, she felt the terror cold on her skin as she rushed to make him safe. So many things, large and small, lay in wait to threaten his young life.

That Daniel might be snatched from her was her daily fear. From the very first, some cruel instinct had warned her that it might be by this means that God would punish her for the sin that had given him life – the more readily as she had never truly been able to feel that it was a sin. If anything could convince her of it, she knew that to lose Daniel would do so. There was no one she could speak to about her fear, because she knew quite well that those she might have confided in would look on such a punishment as simple justice, and would not see it as their duty to reassure her. Even her father, who adored his grandson, would have taken that view.

She learned to control the terror – she had to do so, or life would have been unendurable, for her son as much as for herself. He was upstairs now, nearly two years old, safe and well, asleep in her bed, where she would lie later beside his warm, immovable little body.

Now, for a few precious hours, she had time to herself. When Daniel was first born, she had felt neither need nor wish for any distraction. He had been her joy and her obsession. She had not minded that no one ever asked for her services at a birth or in sickness. But gradually, in spite of her love for him, and her fears, she felt a growing hunger for the work that, until his arrival, had been everything to her. Now, in these moments left at the end of the day, she had begun to study the notes so carefully made of each birth she had ever attended and to read everything she could on the subject. She wanted to try and reach some conclusions about questions which had concerned her in the past, when there had been no time to consider them. One day she hoped that she would be able to put her studies to good use, when her sin was forgotten.

'Hmm,' said her father. 'You think, then, that it was because she was afraid that Mistress Metcalfe had such a hard time?'

'There was no other complication. If she'd not dwelt on it so much beforehand, if she'd been too occupied to think about it, as most poor women are, then I think she'd have had an easier delivery.' This was something they had discussed many times lately: whether some women were, by their very station in life, inevitably doomed to more difficult labours. Her father took that view and so, up to a point, did Louise Bourgeois, that sensible French midwife. Gently-born women were more delicate, they asserted, and needed more – and different – care at every stage. Susannah respected their longer experience, but her own first-hand knowledge of giving birth only added to her growing conviction that, other things being equal, temperament, expectations and the attitude of the midwife might make all the difference. Her notes offered no obvious conclusion. There seemed to have been as many difficult labours, as many deaths of infants and mothers, among the poor as the well-to-do; perhaps even more. Yet on the whole poorer women took the whole business much more matter-of-factly. But then they did not expect to be able to lie in bed for days afterwards, their every need supplied by servants, as wealthy women did.

'Hmm. Did I tell you the tale I had once from Doctor Harvey?' said Matthew. 'He told of a camp follower in Ireland, wild Irish, and how on the march she turned aside to give birth in a ditch to twins, and afterwards walked barefoot for twelve miles, with her infants tied on her back, yet was none the worse for it. It's said that such women, in childbirth, have no need of midwives.'

Suddenly it seemed to Susannah that the room was full of the scent of damp grass, the rush of wind, the babble of water. And a voice, heavy with irony: *Wild Irish women are said to be good breeders*. She heard it as clearly, as distinctly, as if he had been in the room with her. It had been warm that afternoon, and they had stripped one another where they lay, stretched out on his cloak. She had traced the old scars on his back, asking what they were, and he had said, bitterly, 'My father's only lasting legacy.' Shocked, she had asked why his father had disliked him so much, which had led naturally to his mother and the reason why his father had married her. 'I'd heard that,' Susannah had said then, her interest caught in quite another way. She had plied him with questions, most of which he could not answer, until at last he had taken her face in his hands and said teasingly, 'Susannah, you're chasing a theory. Come back!' Then he had brought her back, in the surest way he knew. She could see his face now, close to hers, the smiling mouth, the blue eyes, and, almost, she felt the touch of his hands again. The unexpectedness of it, and the pain that came with it, made her catch her breath. In that moment she wanted him, hungrily, as she had not done for a very long time.

She forced her mind back to the present, to the candlelit room, her father's lined, thoughtful face at the other side of the hearth, the notebook open on her knee. 'I suppose,' she said, a little shakily, 'the Irish woman had no fear of giving birth. She was in good health too, used to simple food and country air.'

'Hmm, yes. There's another thing. She would, I suppose, have worn no stays. I understand the wild Irish dress often only in a plaid or some such loose garment.'

'That's a common difference between rich and poor. Rich women are more likely to have marred their bodies with too much tight-lacing.' She was silent for a moment. 'Yet if poor women give birth more easily – and I think I've not enough cases here to be sure of that. But if they do, then I'm sure too that their children more often die in infancy or childhood. Hunger and poverty don't make for healthy children.'

'Nor do slatternly wet nurses. The gentlewomen you've attended have taken care in choosing a wet nurse, but in London it wasn't always so. I've known of many a much-desired heir to a great estate lost by the carelessness of the wet nurse.'

'Yes. But then we agree that it's best for a mother to suckle her own child.' As she had done with Daniel, and wondered that any woman could ever wish to give up that arduous pleasure to another.

'As for your poor children – it may be that some die from deliberate neglect. Many a poor woman must regret the birth of yet another child.'

'Or is it that, being so burdened with work, they are not able to give so much care to their children as they would wish? There's so much we don't know. So much I want to learn. Yet—' She broke off, for she could not after all put into words what she had been about to say: 'How can I find out, if I have no patients any more?' To put that question would only be to bring discord between herself and her father, and she had no wish to do that.

'A lifetime is never long enough for all there is to learn,' said Matthew, more with relish than regret.

Barbara Metcalfe went into labour on the last Sunday in January, late in the evening. Richard hastily summoned his sister and his mother and several of the women servants, and then sent for Margery Nelson, who examined Barbara and declared that the birth was still some way off. It was only in the course of the next day that, called again, she admitted that the child was awkwardly positioned and it was not going to be an easy delivery. For most of that day and the next night Richard tried to find some part of the house where he was not haunted by his wife's moans and screams, so that he could concentrate on praying for her and their unborn child. Three times his sister came to find him, looking distraught, and begged him to send for Susannah. 'I know she's sinned, but Barbara's calling for her. There's no one can match her when a birth goes badly. Please, Richard!'

Three times, unhesitatingly, he refused her. Instead, late on the Monday, at the instigation of the midwife, he sent for a surgeon from Richmond, who was said to be skilled in such matters.

On Tuesday afternoon his longed-for son was born, but died at some time during the final stage of the labour.

'It's against nature, a day against nature,' Cecily Reynolds said to her husband, in the grey dawn of that same Tuesday, as they slipped shiveringly from the warmth of their bed and began to dress.

'Aye,' said Abel Reynolds. 'There's been no day like it in all of history.' He had said as much to her on Saturday, when they heard what the sentence was, explaining to her that English kings had been deposed and murdered often enough, but never before had an anointed monarch been openly judged and found guilty and condemned to death by his own subjects. 'To take arms against him, for God's cause, that was one thing,' he said now, 'but I never thought we'd come to this pass.'

Yet they had, and Abel Reynolds, unlike most London tradesmen, closed his workshop for the day and set out with his wife for Whitehall, to see a King done to death.

For the past two years London had been full of soldiers. Since last night, they were everywhere, in double lines along the main thoroughfares, their horses pushing through the crowds, more numerous even than the hundreds of people moving like a river along the streets, all going one way. Some of the citizens were in holiday mood and laughed and talked animatedly among themselves, as if this was any common execution. Others, like Cecily and Abel, hurried along in silence. Cecily was shocked to see that many of the soldiers, who had been standing about since before dawn, were smoking and telling coarse jokes. Had they not even the simplest human feeling for a man about to die? She wondered, uneasily, if Walter was somewhere among them, and tried not to look at them, in case she should see him. Yet if he was in London, Esther might be too . . .

At Whitehall Palace, overlooked by the windows of all the buildings that made up army headquarters, a platform had been built out from the wall of the royal Banqueting House. It was as if until she saw it, in spite of everything, Cecily had not really believed that the deed was truly to be done. Now, peering from a convenient step at the far side of the street, seeing that black-draped scaffold, the enlarged window that led on to it, the low block upon it, the mounted troops guarding it, she felt suddenly sick. She began to tremble and Abel, thinking she was cold, put out an arm to draw her to his side.

Near where they stood an old man had knelt down on the frozen ground, his head bent in prayer. 'Malignant dog!' snarled a bystander, giving the man a sharp kick. His wife rebuked him, softly: 'Have pity, Ned, we're all in need of prayer.' Cecily thought, with a tremor, that she was right. What punishment would God call down on England for this day's work?

Among the waiting throng, rumours and whispers spread: that the King had left St James's Palace; that he was already inside Whitehall, somewhere behind the long windows of the Banqueting House, most of them blocked up since the army came to London. But time passed: an hour, two hours, three. Midday came, and still nothing was happening. People said the commissioners had changed their minds, the army had decided after all to spare the King, the public executioners had refused to commit so gross a sacrilege. Then, early in the afternoon, a firmer rumour: 'They've been putting a bill through the Commons, so no one proclaims a new King.'

'Aye, that'll be it,' said Abel. 'You remember what's always been done, when a King dies? The Lord Mayor proclaims the new one right away, so there's no break in the succession. I'd guess Mayor Reynardson's standing ready to proclaim King Charles the Second even now. Once done, it's lawful. They can't risk that.'

It was nearly two in the afternoon when at last the excited stirring of the crowd told them that the time had come. The next moment, they saw a group of men assembling on the scaffold: army officers, guards, and two grotesquely disguised figures, who, Cecily realised after a moment of uneasy puzzlement, must be the executioner and his assistant.

Then, a sighing moan, half satisfaction after long waiting, half dismay, and the small, upright figure of King Charles, dressed all in black, stepped through the enlarged window on to the scaffold, with the Bishop of London, William Juxon, behind him. Looking calm and unafraid, the King exchanged a few words with the officers and then took a paper from inside his cloak and began to speak.

They could not make out what the King said, though he spoke at some length, and the crowd was hushed into silence. Even those at the front were too far off to hear, because of the ranks of soldiers in the way. After a time a woman nearby began to sob; Cecily felt close to tears herself. Then, quiet again. The King was pushing his hair into a cap, taking off his doublet. The crowd was still, utterly still, as if every man and woman and child in that confined space was holding its breath. There was no sound even from the horses.

From somewhere, silent words came into Cecily's head: 'Lord, have mercy!'

A new sound, sudden, sharp. Then, a terrible groan rose into the air, so great, so full of awe and agony that Cecily thought it must have been heard in every corner of the land. She herself had been a part of it, but she knew, somehow, that it was not made up of separate single voices, like her own and Abel's, but was rather the cry of a whole universe in its death throes, a groan that marked the end of time. Into its dying echoes the voice of the executioner cried, 'Behold the head of a traitor!' The words sounded, not awesome, but flat and mean.

Then came a clattering of hooves, at each end of the street. Shouts and screams. Mounted men riding fast into the mass of people from either side, scattering them. The crowd fled, running for their lives up alleys and lanes, wherever there was a way out, taking their terror into the still streets of the city. Abel pressed his wife back against the wall and they stayed there, watching the wave of horsemen pass. Within minutes, scarcely anyone was left in the place, though at the foot of the scaffold a last few struggled to dip handkerchiefs and scarves in the blood that lay spilt on the ground. Cecily pulled off her neckerchief and moved towards them.

Abel caught her arm. 'No, wife!' he said, his voice harsh. 'That's idolatry.' Then, more gently, 'Let's go home.'

At Widehope the news of the King's execution came like an earthquake, shaking the very foundation of their lives. Cuthbert, through choking sobs, raged at his father, 'You should have died sooner than let this happen!'

Ralph too was close to weeping, but he tried to answer calmly. 'No, Cuthbert. This happened, I believe, precisely because men went to fight, not because others stayed at home.'

For a moment Cuthbert looked as if he would strike his father. 'You disgust me – to blame the brave for what has happened, only to excuse your cowardice!'

When Cuthbert had gone to his room, Elizabeth put her arms about her husband. 'Grief has turned his mind – this, after so much else. He doesn't know what he's saying.'

'The worst of it is,' said Ralph, 'that I know he's right.'

He summoned the household to prayers, and earnestly asked for God's mercy on their sad and distressed nation. Then he prayed for the young King Charles, by the grace of God now King of England, if far from his country's shores; that he might one day be restored to his father's throne.

Susannah and her father had the news brought to them by Margaret, as they sat by the parlour fire, with Daniel drowsily content on his grandfather's knee. Matthew had been reading him the much-loved story of his biblical namesake, facing the lions in their den.

When Margaret had finished speaking, silence swelled into the room, to every corner. Daniel, conscious of profound adult emotions of a kind never experienced before, looked from one to another of the candlelit faces about him, but for a long time no one else moved and no one spoke. Then Matthew said. 'God have mercy on us all!'

'I'll say Amen to that, sir,' said Margaret.

When she had gone, Susannah said, 'I would wish for no man's death, but I can see why they did it.'

Her father looked at her in astonishment, though something long forgotten that she had once said suddenly came back to him, *For what he has permitted to happen in Ireland, and in this land too; for what he has done. Yes, I would do it . . .* But they had been talking then of a shot fired in battle, not a judicial killing. He was not sure if he thought that made any difference.

Then Susannah added, 'Surely the Lord has clearly shown that His hand was against him, in the victories we have won.'

Matthew, thinking that his daughter was no longer in any position to claim to know the Lord's mind in such matters, though he could not disagree with what she said, retorted, 'That does not give men the right to act as if they were gods themselves.'

When Richard Metcalfe heard the news, he felt as if a savage blow had struck him. He had expected it, yet it was still a shock, that it should at last have been done.

He saw something else too, with all the force of a revelation. The execution of the King had taken place at the very moment – two in the afternoon on the thirtieth of January – when his own infant son had died. With a sense of horror, whose rightness he yet acknowledged, he saw that the baby's death was his punishment. How could any child, born at that hour, be expected to thrive, still less one born to a man who had acquiesced, however unwillingly, in the slaughter of his King? For he had made no open protest against it, though he could have done, more readily than most of his compatriots. For that, his child – his heir – had inevitably died, as surely as if he, Richard Metcalfe, had murdered him.

He tried to explain something of this insight to his sister, but when he had finished he saw at once that she was unconvinced. She said nothing, but her expression told him as clearly as any words that she blamed, not the King's death, but his own obstinacy in not sending for Susannah Fawcett. He thought it a distressingly worldly view of the matter.

1650

CHAPTER THIRTY-SEVEN

At Kilkenny there was no slaughter after the town surrendered, not even of priests, though there were images and stained glass and other idolatrous objects to be smashed in pieces. For all its brave resistance, the garrison had not tried to hold out beyond a reasonable length of time, so the terms had been generous. It had been a different matter at Drogheda and Wexford last year, as Cromwell's army swept down the eastern coast of Ireland with its heavy guns and its well-paid troops, bringing the revenge of God's saints on the wicked population. Yet even the triumphant savagery of the taking of those towns had not driven out the simpler, two-year-old memory that still haunted Captain Walter Barras, gnawing at his conscience, haunting his dreams, as no killing of Papist Irish ever could.

In any case, it looked as though the massacres at Drogheda and Wexford acted as a salutary example to other Irish strongholds. The resistance that had seemed so strong, united as it had been by the execution of the King (even some of the Scottish troops under General Monro, formerly fighting the rebels, had changed sides), was now showing signs of crumbling to dust. Many of the Protestants among the rebel forces were fast returning to the fold, unable to stomach their priest-ridden allies any longer.

Cromwell did not linger in Kilkenny, which was just as well since the plague was raging there. Instead, the day after the town's fall he marched his army south-west, through the fertile green landscape towards County Tipperary. 'I think of all Ireland this is the part where I'd most like to settle down,' said Corporal Harper, when he found himself riding beside Walter.

Walter glanced at him. Esther had said something to him the other day about Corporal Harper's views on the land through which they had first marched last autumn. The Corporal was the younger son of a yeoman farmer from Hertfordshire, and was supposed to know about such things. Unlike most of his comrades, he also had some money, from an unknown source, over and above his army pay, and had more than once expressed an inclination to buy a piece of Irish land and settle down here – 'when all this is over'. He was probably the only man in Walter's troop to have a cheerful view of the present campaign.

The 'Cut Throat' expedition, the men had called it, when they knew they had been picked to go to Ireland. It was supposed to have been done fairly, with the drawing of lots, but many said it was all fixed by the grandees, to make sure the most troublesome units were sent to their deaths on Irish service. Walter did not believe that. After all, in their case, they knew from the outset that half Okey's dragoons were to go, with Daniel Abbott as their Colonel; and Daniel Abbott, who had been a friend of Samuel's, had seen the lots drawn himself, for the troops that would make up the new regiment. He had assured them it had been fairly done.

In any case, Walter had not been sorry to go. Esther wanted it and he did not greatly care either way. Now that Samuel was dead, all the fire had gone out of their troop. Walter, from love of his friend, had tried for a time to keep it alive, but he had lost heart himself, and now nothing seemed to matter very much – not even that Samuel had disapproved of the Irish expedition. It was one of the few things they had ever disagreed about. 'Why should the Irish not live at peace in their own land?' Samuel used to say, and Walter would argue, from long-held conviction, that for what they had done in the Rebellion, the Irish deserved to be punished. In any case, Esther wanted to go to Ireland. She was tired of England and looked forward to seeing more of the world. She had even, once or twice, hinted that she, like Corporal Harper, might like one day to settle here. Walter paid little attention to that. On the other hand Esther was still his wife and in a sense she was all he had left, so he supposed he owed it to her to try and make something of their marriage. Perhaps starting afresh in a new land would be what they both needed – except that he could not see how they would ever be able to afford it, unless he should one day be paid all the arrears due to him since the war began, which seemed most unlikely.

So in August last year they had set sail for Ireland, too large a fleet to be troubled by the small Royalist navy under their old enemy Prince Rupert, which had been harassing shipping for some weeks beforehand. Not even the seasickness he had suffered on the crossing had made Walter feel anything but relief that he was leaving England behind at last.

He had decided almost as soon as they landed that he did not like Ireland. It rained all the time, even more than at home. The population hated them and plotted secretly against them in a barbarous foreign tongue. To make matters worse, he had spent much of the past winter flat on his back with sickness, like many of his comrades, including Lieutenant-General Cromwell himself. Roger Tyler, one of the few who had been with the troop from the start, had died of it. Will Harper had remained heartily on his feet, and though Esther had nursed her husband with dutiful wifeliness, she had spent a good deal more of her time in the company of the Corporal, so Walter had learned as soon as he had recovered sufficiently to know what was going on. 'He's good company. He makes me laugh,' was Esther's excuse, when he had hinted that he did not much like it. She had seemed quite untroubled by any sense of guilt, and he had told himself firmly that it was because she had nothing to feel guilty about.

Yet on their first halt on the march from Kilkenny the unease came back to him. They were sitting about the camp-fire in the soft evening air – for once it was not raining – and Esther had just brought them the stew she had cooked, hot and savoury, and at that moment Corporal Harper repeated his approving remark about this part of Ireland – rather unnecessarily, Walter thought. Esther looked up from where she was ladling stew into bowls. 'It's good land,' she agreed enthusiastically. 'I'd like to have a little farm, somewhere like this.'

'We could be neighbours,' said the Corporal. Walter saw him exchange a look with Esther, a laughing secret look, as at some shared private joke. He felt suddenly sick with apprehension, knowing that there was something here that he could understand easily enough if he would only look into it a little further, yet not wanting to allow himself to know what it was. He realised that Amias Stephens, sitting on his other side, was unusually quiet. He glanced at him, and received a long, grave look, in which pity seemed disturbingly to play a part.

'You know General Cromwell's been recalled to England,' Walter said, trying to push the unease from his mind by changing the subject.

'They've been trying to get him back for months,' said Amias, rather too heartily.

'What should they want to do that for?' asked the Corporal. 'He's doing good work here.'

'Because Scotland's in uproar,' said Walter, with a gratifying sense of superiority, for once. Will Harper was not much interested in anything that did not directly affect his comfort. 'They couldn't stomach the King's execution. They proclaimed the pretender Charles the Second long since. Now they've invited him over. It's said there's likely to be an invasion.' He paused, then said, 'I've a good mind to ask for a transfer back to England. I'd sooner fight Scots than Irish any day. You know where you are with them.'

He saw Esther look at him with dismay and then exchange another look with the Corporal, which he could not decipher. He felt a rather mean sense of satisfaction, that he should have disturbed her complacency.

Often these days she came very late to join him in whatever bed they had been allocated. Tonight she was early, creeping under the blanket in which he was rolled in the corner of a great barn, putting her arms about him almost with something of her old coaxing tenderness. He lay very still, not giving in to her at all. 'Walter, you don't really mean that – about going back to England – do you?' She had her arms about him now, one hand caressing his neck, in the way he used to love; but not any more, not for a long time now.

'I might,' he said. 'I've not decided yet.' Then he turned his back to her and ignored all her further attempts to cajole a firm answer from him.

He fell asleep, and after a time he knew he was back in England. Over his head, the trees were heavy with new foliage, the sun warm on honey-coloured stone. He knew it was the wall of Burford church, though it did not look quite as it had in life, and he was facing it alone, preparing his musket to fire. But the three men were there, three soldiers in the uniform of the New Model Army. Once, he had laughed in a tavern with Cornet Thompson. Now, he saw the terror on the man's face as the shot exploded. Then, the other two, little more than boys, who looked him unafraid in the face. It was only at the last moment, when it was too late, that he saw that one of them was not an unknown corporal, but Samuel, his friend. He heard his own terrible cry of anguish as the men fell, as Samuel fell. It was Samuel's blood that burst in a great arc from the fallen body, drenching him from head to foot, so that he knew he would never be clean.

He woke, sick and shaking, and found it was still dark. But it was the darkness of an Irish night, and he was far from the Oxfordshire village where the mutineers had at last been hunted down, and in any case the dream had got it wrong, for by then Samuel had been in his grave for nearly a year. Yet if Samuel had lived, he might well have been one of them. Samuel too would have thought that the King's death and the declaration of the republic ought to have brought some change for the better, the ending of old evils . . .

No, he did not want to go back to England. He had only said what he did to annoy Esther. He had no intention of going back to the land where, two years ago, he had taken part in the judicial murder of men who had simply held firm to the Leveller principles that had been dear to Samuel; as they had been to him once, in the old days.

Here in Ireland perhaps he would be able to put that dreadful memory behind him. Here there were real enemies to be destroyed. Tomorrow (or was it today? Already it seemed a little lighter) they would be on the road once more, marching steadily nearer to the rebel-held stronghold of Clonmel. What he had heard about the garrison there made him eager to reach it.

Major-General Hugh O'Neill, born and tutored in war in the Spanish Netherlands, had taken up his post as governor of Clonmel in February, fortifying the place against the expected arrival of Cromwell's forces. With him were twelve hundred Ulster Catholic soldiers and his distant cousins Shane O'Neill and Ludovick Milburn, who had both fought under his command before, in Flanders.

Now, in mid May, the enemy was firmly entrenched about the town, and the entire garrison, along with many of the townsfolk, went to work as soon as day broke, at the point where yesterday's bombardment had almost made a breach in the walls. For the time being at least the guns were silent.

As the sun rose, Ludovick found a moment to look out from the walls, beyond the red dots of the enemy bustling to wakefulness, to the high green hills that stretched into the distance. He had brought with him no memory of the greenness of Ireland, yet the moment he saw it he had at once felt a sense of recognition. It was rest for the mind and heart and it still delighted him, even after all this time.

The return to the land of his birth had been an emotional one, but not quite in the way he had expected. The things he had remembered – which were few, and little more than impressions – seemed to bear no relation to what he found. He had somehow expected to feel an immediate sense of homecoming, and he had not done so. There had even been a certain strangeness in many things, to which he had taken time to become accustomed. He had realised to his surprise that, in spite of everything, he had begun to put down some kind of tentative roots during his time in England. Or perhaps it was simply that home was not after all a place, but a woman, without whom he could never find peace.

Yet he had found comrades and kinsmen, days of leisure spent hunting or hawking, hours of singing and the telling of tales, the free and open practice of his religion with those who shared his faith. And the company of women, had he wanted it.

Four years now he had been without a woman – he would not have thought it possible. Yet he had done it, not for lack of inclination or opportunity, but because he did not want to cloud a precious memory, nor give to any other woman even the smallest part of what in his heart he had long ago given to Susannah, wholly and for ever. Or if not for ever, then until such time as he knew for certain that there was no hope that they could ever be together again. Then perhaps he would be able to accept second best and find what happiness he could elsewhere.

He thought that time might not be long in coming. Since last year, when Cromwell's forces replaced the fragmentary, uncoordinated troops that had been trying to keep the Irish at bay, everything had changed. Now the enemy had a clear strategy, a well-paid, splendidly equipped army, however ravaged by disease. One after another the strongholds had fallen to the New Model Army, except at Waterford, where there was no dry solid ground for artillery. As for themselves here in Clonmel, supplies of everything had almost run out – food had never been plentiful, and now their ammunition was down to a few hours' supply. Enough, just, for this last thing they had to do; the thing that would snatch victory from Cromwell's grasp, just as he thought he had it safe.

Ludovick returned to work on building the long ramparts, constructed hastily from everything anyone could lay his hands on, which now ran back in two lines from the damaged portion of the walls, invisible from the outside. As he did so, the bombardment began again. The ground beneath their feet shuddered with the din.

He had been busy for some time when he felt a hand on his shoulder and looked round into the face of his cousin, who signalled to him to follow, and then led the way towards a nearby row of houses. 'Up here,' he said into a momentary interval of quiet. They went up to the top floor of one of the houses, where Shane indicated the window. 'Take a look out of there. Tell me what you think.'

The window looked out over the walls and, leaning out as far as he could, Ludovick saw that it was directly above the place where the breach was fast appearing; the point through which, presumably, the enemy planned to make their final assault.

'I know we'll have a warm welcome for them once they're through,' said Shane behind him. 'But—'

Ludovick straightened, grinning, 'Why make it any easier for them than need be? Two men to each window —' He leaned out again, looking along the row, counting the windows, estimating which gave the best access to the breach.

He never saw what hit him. There was a massive explosion, a brilliant light, a great blast of air that threw him violently backwards; thunder in his ears.

An interval, then thick smoke and dust, agitated voices coming and going, Shane's among them, not making sense, as if they were heard through water or from very far away. Pain beyond words. He tried to force his eyes open, but could not find the strength.

Then at last a voice very near, murmuring words he had heard so often before, but this time they were for him. He felt the touch of the priest's thumb on his closed lids. *Per istam unctionem* . . . And then Charles was there, his calm beloved voice echoing the words, and Ludovick felt a profound sense of peace and readiness.

CHAPTER THIRTY-EIGHT

Matthew Fawcett was not in church that Sunday morning, for he was still greatly weakened by the fever that had laid him low through much of the winter and spring. Margaret had stayed at home in case he needed anything and John was visiting his sister, so Susannah and Daniel sat alone in the Fawcett pew, Susannah only with difficulty keeping her attention on the service. It was a long time since she had felt that the worship that once had meant so much to her had anything at all to offer.

Even after three years, she had not been forgiven. It infuriated her that, in the eyes of the minister and his congregation, she was now like any other unregenerate parishioner, to be kept in order so as not to bring shame on the neighbourhood or to set a bad example. The humiliation forced upon her, and the continuing open disapproval, were, she knew, a means of assuring that the godly people of Thornside might lead orderly, tranquil lives, knowing that her kind were kept under control and could not seriously trouble their earthly journey. She knew that well enough, because she had been one of their number, not so long ago. Indeed, even now, she would not have conceded anything to Nathaniel Johnson's view that she was not, after all, among the Elect. So angered was she by their treatment of her that she thought she might by now have ceased to go to church at all if it had not been for Daniel. But it was one thing to make herself more of an outcast than she already was; it was quite another to expect her child to share that fate.

After the opening prayers and Bible reading, the minister told them of the safe return of Lieutenant-General Cromwell from

Ireland and announced that the ninth psalm was to be sung in gratitude for the victories that had manifested God's just judgement on the Irish.

> Thou dost rebuke the heathen folk,
> and wicked so confound,
> That afterwards the memory
> Of them cannot be found . . .

At Susannah's side, Daniel sang too, garbling the words, but following the tune with a sureness that she found astonishing in someone who was only three years old. 'Your mother had a fine voice,' Matthew had said, when once she had commented on it.

It was not the end of the news from Ireland. There was also a letter from the minister's brother, which Nathaniel Johnson read to them as soon as they sat down for the sermon. Jeremiah Johnson had followed the army to Ireland, so Susannah listened intently, hoping as always to hear that Ludovick was there, and alive; though for months now there had been regular letters, with never a word of Ludovick.

Lately we took the rebel stronghold of Clonmel, praise be to God. The assault was most fierce, for the rebels laid a trap for us and once in the town we found we could not advance without great hazard to our lives. One thousand five hundred of our number fell on that day. But the rebels did not await their judgement, for we next day entered the town on terms to discover that the bloody Papists who garrisoned it had fled, of whom that arch rebel Hugh O'Neill was the most notorious. I have never seen the Lieutenant-General in so great a rage as when he heard how he had been tricked. We pursued the rebels and killed about two hundred, many of them women and wounded who had fallen behind, but the greater number escaped us. We had one assurance of God's hand in the business, on learning that in the playing of our guns upon the town that great malignant Ludovick Milburn was slain . . .

Susannah sat very still. Ludovick's son lay propped against her, already on the edge of the drowsiness that always overcame him even during Master Johnson's most impassioned sermons. Alone of everyone in that place, she heard of that death with pain and grief, like a knife turning in her heart. Yet she could do and say nothing. He had gone and there was no one she could turn to for comfort, no one she could tell. Even his son did not know that anything had changed.

She had no idea how she managed to endure the rest of the service, though she supposed she must have stood and sat in the right places. Eventually, she found she was outside, but she felt dazed and unsure of herself, as if she could not quite recall what one was supposed to do next. As she hesitated near the door, Anne Greatorex passed her and then suddenly and unexpectedly glanced round to smile at her. It was an intimate, knowing smile, the smile of someone rejoicing in good news, wanting to share her satisfaction even with the friend she must no longer call a friend. Susannah walked quickly away.

In the sunlit churchyard, Daniel had run to play with the other children, who were jumping on the gravestones and running through the dandelions, with the noisy exuberance of young things released from long confinement. Susannah called him to her. It was not that she shared the only too common view that every bastard ought to be taught from his earliest years to know his place in the scheme of things; that he ought to be constantly reminded that he had been conceived and born in sin, lest he go the way of his parents; that he should be curbed more than most children, kept under strict control. She felt rather that in some way it was not fitting that her child should be playing so heedlessly when his father lay dead. Yet since she could not tell him of it, what was the point in spoiling his pleasure? She took his hand in hers and walked on.

Near the gate, in a favoured corner of the churchyard, a hawthorn was coming into bloom. Its heavy scent caught in her nostrils, with all the memories it woke of the summer of Daniel's conception. She almost choked on it, the pain was so sharp and sudden and without warning. She felt the rush of tears to her eyes, the ache in her throat where the sobs were held back. For she must not weep, not here, not anywhere that she might be seen and bring questions on herself. Never, ever, could she tell a soul what grief she felt, what loss she had suffered.

Daniel, impatient at her slowness, jumped and hopped beside her, tugging at her hand. Then he freed himself and ran a little way ahead, and almost at once stumbled and fell flat on his face. Jolted out of her thoughts, she darted towards him. He was already on his feet, surprised but not otherwise troubled – until he glanced down to rub the dirt from his muddy palms and saw blood on one of them, where the stones had grazed it. Blood meant hurt, so he began to howl. Susannah gathered him up in her arms and held him, comforting him more anxiously than ever the little scratch deserved, stroking and kissing him. He was quickly soothed, since there had been nothing much wrong, and then he grew impatient at the tightness of her clasp and wriggled to free himself. She let him go, but with an anguished sense of reluctance. She felt she wanted to hold him and hold him for ever, for fear that he should somehow be snatched from her too. She looked down at him, at the face bright again now, with no trace of distress. So few tears, so quickly over, and none for the father he would never know.

Once in the house, Daniel ran upstairs to see his grandfather, and Susannah, alone, went to her room and took from under the folded neckerchiefs in her chest the ring that Ludovick had given her. Just a device of metal and stone, something of no use at all. Yet it was all he had left her, in a material sense; their son's inheritance, if there were ever to come a day when it would be to his advantage to know who his father was. She turned it in her hand and then put it away, and then, suddenly apprehensive, went to make sure that Daniel and her father needed nothing.

She found the child perched on the edge of his grandfather's bed, singing his own nonsensical but tuneful version of this morning's psalm. So small and fragile a creature, her son, and any child's life could so easily be snuffed out by a sudden cold, an accident, so many small things . . . Not for years yet could she feel that he was safe; and even when he was grown, would the tug at her heart be any the less? She stood there in the doorway, tracing the likeness to his father, in the shape of his head, the soft curls of his hair, the fair freckled skin, the long nose, the proportion of his limbs. All that was left.

She came very close, during the following days and weeks, to telling her father everything. The pain was so great, and the need to keep it hidden so unbearably hard, that there were times when she felt she would go mad if she did not confide in someone – and her father was the only conceivable person in whom she could have confided. She could even have said to him, 'Now I know how you felt when my mother died. How you grieved for her, yet clung to me as her gift to you.' But then she would make herself face the stark truth of what her father's reaction would be, if she were to tell him. She had already hurt him almost beyond the point of forgiveness. For him to know that the man who had fathered Daniel was one so beyond all his mercy and compassion and tolerance would be to risk breaking everything again and returning them to the bleakness of those days before Daniel's birth. Besides, her father was still frail after the long sickness of the winter and to confide such things in him might be more than he could well bear.

She did, fleetingly, consider writing to Sir Ralph Liddell, or even going to see him. After all, he alone of her acquaintance had known and liked Ludovick. But there had been no communication between them in recent years, apart from the one letter telling them of young Mark's death, and Matthew's brief but sympathetic reply, and she could not be sure that he would take her disgrace less censoriously than others had done. He was, after all, a man of firm principles, with daughters whose morals he would be anxious to protect. More to the point, life must be hard enough for him, as a known Royalist, without having to shoulder her troubles too. She did not, after all, even know if he was still alive and living at Widehope.

So she fought her feelings, suppressed them, did all she could to occupy mind and body in a fierce round of activity in house and garden. She studied late into the night, when Daniel went to sleep and for hours afterwards, straining her eyes by candlelight as she read book after book, went over her notes, wrote down the conclusions she had drawn from them, and from past talk with her father. If ever tears came close to the surface she fought them with all her will-power, pushing grief and pain back out of reach, where they could not intrude. Most of the time she was able to live purely on the surface of her life, for it was safer that way.

It never seemed to get any better, yet she survived somehow through that joyless summer. Then in the heat of July her father suddenly grew very sick again, with a persistent feverishness that seemed to have no obvious cause but never left him. At the moment when she had begun to think he was at last recovering, having had two days of quiet rest, she went into his room one morning to find that he had died in his sleep.

She could have allowed herself to weep then, freely, openly, giving two griefs a voice at once, but somehow she seemed to have lost the power to grieve. It was as if she had been turned to stone, though beneath the surface the anguish was almost unendurable. Daniel did weep, for a long time, as if his heart was breaking, for the loss of the grandfather he had so dearly loved. As for Susannah, she knew she had lost not merely a father, an old man whose time had come, but a friend and companion who, even in the darker disappointed years at the end, had been constant in his love for her. While he lived, she had been to some extent protected from the knowledge of how very friendless she had become. Now she knew it with full force. Outside her household, where John and Margaret continued to serve her dutifully, there was no one. Within it, all her happiness now depended on a vulnerable three-year-old.

Matthew Fawcett was buried with the dignity he deserved, Nathaniel Johnson speaking at the graveside not only of his godliness, but of the warm friendship he had himself felt for the dead man. Then he spoiled it all, as far as Susannah was concerned, by fixing his penetrating gaze upon her as he declared roundly that the doctor's greatest grief had been his daughter's disgrace, which had destroyed his health and led directly to his death. Susannah, deeply hurt, fiercely angry, refused to speak to the Minister afterwards and hurried home with Daniel, thankful that he was too young to take in what, undoubtedly, others beside the Minister were saying of her. What made it worse was that she had a haunting sense that the Minister was right, and that his disappointment in her had aged and weakened her father.

On a wet Saturday night a month after her father's death Susannah was roused from her bed by Margaret, who told her that John Dowthwaite was at the door, begging that she would come to his sister-in-law.

She almost thought it was a dream, so long was it since any such summons had come, but – moving carefully, so as not to wake Daniel – she got up and dressed and found her medical bag, and kissed the sleeping child, and then went downstairs. John Dowthwaite, until recently a trooper in the New Model Army, lived at his brother Anthony's small hill farm near Marsett, across the dale beyond Semerwater. 'My sister's been in labour two days now and she's fast failing. They say you're the one knows best what to do, so I've come for you.'

She agreed to go with him, but she had a sense of foreboding. This had happened once before, that a desperate husband had sent for her, when all else had failed. By that time there had been nothing that she or anyone else could have done, and mother and child had both died. Afterwards, there had been mutterings that it was only what was to be expected, if you called so notorious a woman to the bedside.

Her unease was not lessened when she reached the farm and saw, after a swift examination, what the trouble was. The infant was badly positioned, with its back to the opening, the mother close to exhaustion, the contractions weakening almost to nothing. The most usual outcome in such a case was the loss of both mother and baby.

Yet in this moment of crisis she had no sense of panic. On her way to the farm she had been afraid that she would find that her skill had deserted her, that she no longer knew what to do or had confidence in herself. But now that she was here, in a room crowded with despairing friends and relatives, faced with what she herself knew to be almost certain failure, she did not hesitate. Her mind was suddenly cleared of any intrusive clutter. She knew what she had to do, and exactly how to do it. Louise Bourgeois had described the procedure to be followed in such cases, and her father had discussed his own experiences with her. Now, when she so badly needed him, she seemed to hear Matthew Fawcett's voice encouraging and guiding her.

She banished everyone from the room, except for the patient's sister, whom she knew to be a calm and practical woman. Then she spoke reassuringly to the exhausted mother and explained what she was about to do. She smeared fresh butter on her hands, waited for the last slight, ineffective contraction to fade, and then, carefully, gently, inserted her right hand into the mother's womb, while with the other she pressed on the abdomen where she knew the infant's head to be. With the fingers of her right hand she felt the curved back of the child, and then, further on, a small foot. Still talking softly to the mother, she reached for the baby's other foot, firmly clasped them both and eased them towards the cervix, while with her other hand she pressed on the abdomen to turn the child the way she wanted the feet to go. Thank God, she thought, that Ellinor Dowthwaite was broad-hipped, and not misshapen from too much tight lacing! She was brave too, and rarely did more than moan, when another woman would have screamed aloud. Susannah felt the infant move round, drew the feet into the passage, and then waited while the next contraction bore down. It was too weak to do very much, and she knew this child would have to be helped all the way.

It took what seemed hours of firm but gentle effort on her part, before the baby girl lay at last on the bed, as limp and almost lifeless as the mother now was. Quickly, Susannah cleared the child's airways and heard the first weak cry, and then left the infant to its aunt's care while she saw to the last stage of the labour. An hour later, and Ellinor Dowthwaite, drowsy with laudanum but already feeling better, was holding her newly washed and swaddled daughter in her arms, and Susannah sent for the father to come to the bedside, knowing that his wife and child had a reasonable chance of survival. 'This little lass of ours shall be called Susannah,' Anthony Dowthwaite declared. Susannah did not think she had ever felt such triumphant happiness as she did now, after so long when she had thought herself cast aside.

It was only when at last she made her way downstairs with the farmer, leaving mother and child peacefully sleeping, that Susannah realised what a strain the past few hours had put upon her. Now she felt, not triumphant, but trembling and shaken and exhausted. She had hoped to be able to find somewhere to sit down and rest before riding home. But the downstairs room was swirling with people, many more than she had banished from the bedroom last night, and they all seemed to close about her at once, asking questions that came so fast she could not take them in.

Anthony Dowthwaite did his best to answer for her, while she stood dazedly beside him. Then suddenly everyone began to move away and sit down, on the many benches and stools set out about the room. She found John Dowthwaite at her side. 'Each first day many of us gather here,' he said, 'to seek the Lord in our hearts. For that we call ourselves Seekers. You are welcome to join us, Susannah Fawcett.' She did not quite know what made her accept his invitation, unless it was the thought that if she were to go home now she would reach Thornside just in time to take Daniel to church, with all the strains that involved; or whether it was simply from an overwhelming desire to sit down on the one comfortable fireside chair, which the farmer's brother offered her.

It was the strangest act of worship she had ever experienced, for the men and women – most of them, like the Dowthwaites, from remote farms in the district – simply sat down and then remained where they were, quite still, heads bent, in complete silence. Susannah did as they did, but found it difficult to shake off the expectation that very soon she would hear something like Nathaniel Johnson's hard decisive tones leading them in prayer, as he used to do at the weekly prayer meetings on fast days – still did, presumably, except that she no longer attended them. She began to wonder if anyone would speak at all, or if they would all remain silent until hunger or the needs of the animals or some other necessity drove them to move.

Suddenly conscious of how weary she was – more weary even than her night's exertions warranted – she closed her eyes and allowed herself to relax. At first the quietness brought her a sense of relief. She became sharply conscious of the breathing of those around her, the ticking of the clock, the tiny shuffles and sighings of the peat fire in the hearth, the whistle of the wind through cracks in window and doors. Then she heard them no longer, for the silence pushed them out, and she no longer felt relieved or relaxed, but utterly alone. For weeks past, months even, she had shunned stillness and silence, avoided every opportunity to be alone with her thoughts. Now she was thrust into the most intense of silences, and suddenly everything she had tried to escape from began to crowd in on her.

There were other people in the room, it was packed to the doors, yet she had no sense of them, only of her isolation. She felt abandoned in a world that had lost all its boundaries, all its familiar outlines, and had become instead a strange shifting place, formless and unpredictable. She tried to reach out for the shadowy figures of lover and father that hovered always on the borders of her mind, tried to bring them clearly before her, but they slipped away and vanished.

She was afraid, and she was desperate with grief, and for the first time she faced the full horror of it. There was no one now to whom she could turn for support and comfort. Once, she had been sure that God was with her. Since her disgrace, she had tried not to look at the implications of it, to see what Nathaniel Johnson clearly saw, a woman who was not after all numbered among the Elect, but one of those rejected and cast aside, to eternity. Now, she felt that she was precisely what the minister believed her to be. She saw the truth in all its starkness, as she had never seen it before. Alone, rejected by God and man, bereft of two of the three people she loved most, with only a helpless child left in her care, perhaps soon to be snatched from her too . . .

She began to tremble, shuddering with terror and grief. She wanted to get up and hurry home, to assure herself that Daniel was still alive and well, but she had no strength in her limbs, only the trembling and the horror. She began to sob, desperate wrenching sobs that seemed to have a power and life of their own, as if they had taken her over and were tearing her apart.

From somewhere in that darkness of grief and loss she felt hands close about hers, voices murmur softly. She sobbed louder, all self-control gone, all the reserves that had so efficiently controlled her throughout her life drifting away from her. Then there were arms about her, someone was holding her and stroking her, as no one had ever done before, murmuring words that were part prayer and part consolation. The room grew noisy with loving, consoling sound. Someone began to sing, softly, and others joined in, uncertainly at first, then gaining in strength.

> *Hear thou my prayer, O Lord, and*
> *let my cry come unto thee,*
> *In time of trouble do not hide*
> *thy face away from me . . .*

She did not sing, for she could not, but though she wept still she had a sense of loving concern, which wrapped her round, without judgement or condemnation, such a sense as she had not felt for a long time, and this, now, from people who were near strangers to her.

Afterwards, tired yet relieved, and controlled after a fashion, though she felt just a little ashamed of such an uncharacteristic display of emotion, she went to take her leave of Anthony Dowthwaite. 'Come to us again, sister,' he said gently. 'We meet here each first day.'

She felt a tremor of fear. She knew that there was danger in coming here again, that the thing that had happened to her, though a release, was only a beginning. 'I shall give it some thought,' she said. 'Thank you.'

But she knew too that she would make that journey again, not simply to care for her patient, but for her own sake.

She was right to fear, for what happened the next Sunday morning was worse, far worse, than before, for it was more than just the release of grief and loneliness. At first there was the silence, the tiny sounds in the crowded room. Then she had the same sense of everything being shut out, of isolation within herself; just the silence and the darkness. Then patterns of red and white began to turn behind her closed lids, faster and faster, until they were spinning wildly, the colours merging, paling. They spun themselves at last into a white light that seemed to fill her head and spread on into her motionless body, right through her; a searing light, like a flash of lightning endlessly prolonged, a light that lit every corner of her self with a full and horrible intensity. For what she saw so ruthlessly illuminated was a mass of ugliness like nothing she could ever have imagined possible, an ugliness that she knew had lain hidden within her all her self-satisfied life. She saw deceit and spite and bitterness like maggots crawling inside her, she saw anger and lust and hatred.

Worst of all, she saw a supreme overbearing pride in herself, as great now as it had ever been, in spite of all that had happened; a pride that would not acknowledge that others had any equal place with herself. She saw that she had never known a sense of God's presence, for what she thought was such a sense was in fact only an unhesitating confidence in her own superiority; not God but self. She, who was no better than Jane Weatherald, the frightened girl who had aborted her unborn child, had yet despised her, regarding her without sympathy or understanding, while her own sin was the greater. Even Margery Nelson, the slatternly midwife she so looked down upon, had shown more true compassion. Meanwhile, she had talked of owing all her skills to God, of giving Him credit for all that was good in her life, while yet believing in her heart that everything she did was her own doing alone.

Slowly, she became aware again of the farmhouse kitchen and the other men and women in the room. She saw now, in the stark, unforgiving brilliance of the light that still filled her, that she was the least of the company, a horrible and corrupt thing, beneath contempt, for she had thought herself higher, been more sure of her own worth, than any of these others here with her today.

She tried haltingly to say something of what she had seen, not because she wanted so to expose herself, but because she knew she must; and the others listened. Today, as last week, hands clasped hers, voices murmured, and when she wept there were comforting arms. She knew the comfort was not a denial of what she had seen or what she had said, but rather an acceptance of her new self-knowledge and an encouragement to follow where it led.

Afterwards, she went home knowing that nothing would ever be the same again. Margaret opened the door to her. 'Master Johnson missed you this morning, mistress.'

Susannah halted just inside the door, looking at the angular weather-beaten face of the servant who had cared so quietly, so efficiently, for her father and herself through the years; an upright and godly woman who had threatened, in Susannah's moment of disgrace, to leave them, but had been persuaded by Matthew's pleading to stay; and who was still there, uncomplaining, uncritical. 'Not mistress,' Susannah said quietly. 'I am Susannah, and not worthy of any other title.' And then she kissed Margaret, who coloured bright red and looked as if she had no idea what to say.

1651

CHAPTER THIRTY-NINE

Lady Elizabeth Liddell first heard of the shattering defeat at Worcester from her son Cuthbert, who had been at their Tyneside coal pits that day. He had been given special permission to ride so far from home and had returned in the greatest distress. 'It was the most complete rout that ever there was, so they say. Oh, mother, what shall we do?'

'We shall wait for news of your father,' she had said, with a calmness that surprised her, for it bore little relation to what she felt. It was not until later, when she was alone, that she realised how much she was shaking, how frightened she was.

Ralph had been quite certain this time that he must go. He had even been cheerful about their prospects, but she knew him well enough to suspect that there was a kind of despair behind his apparent optimism. It stemmed partly from a sense of guilt that he had stayed at home last time, from the illogical thought that if he had acted differently then perhaps the King would not have died. Then, in recent years, there had been so many friends lost. At Drogheda, where the garrison had been largely English, many of his old wartime comrades had been slaughtered. Then there had been Ludovick's death at Clonmel. That had hit him very hard, surprisingly hard – though Elizabeth, who had never been able to rid herself of an irrational sense that Ludovick was somehow responsible for Mark's death, had not been able to share his grief. Yet even Dorothy had shed a tear for her former lover. And on top of it all had come the brief letter from Susannah telling them of Matthew Fawcett's death – not a death due to war, for he had been an old man dying peacefully, but it had only served to bring home to

Ralph what the war had cost, one way and another, in terms of broken friendships and lost hopes. All these things, Elizabeth knew, had driven him to join the young King Charles when in August news came that he had led an army into England. That it was a Scottish army had made Ralph hesitate a little, but at least the Covenanters under General Leslie had been roundly defeated last year at Dunbar and the King's army was now well filled out with Royalists. What was left of Leslie's army had wasted its life away in Durham cathedral, turned prison under the charge of Sir Arthur Hazelrigg, where hundreds upon hundreds of men had died in stinking squalor.

'Sir, you said yourself a Scottish army won't be welcome in England,' Cuthbert had objected when he heard what his father planned to do – or at least, when Sir Ralph made it plain that his son was not to be allowed to have any part in this dangerous enterprise.

'This army has our King at its head,' Ralph pointed out.

'And the New Model Army marching against them!'

'They haven't got Fairfax now, remember.'

The General had gone into honourable retirement just over a year ago, when the army had been ordered to march into Scotland. He had resigned on grounds of ill health, which had seemed plausible enough, except that it was rumoured his real reason was that he objected in principle to invading a foreign country and former ally, which had not then openly declared war on England.

'They've got Cromwell,' Cuthbert said next, 'and Lambert.'

'But they're in Scotland, with the cream of the army. The King has given them the slip. If he can get to London before they realise what's happened, then there's a good chance of success.'

'Then, sir, if you believe that, why may I not come with you?'

'Because you must remain here and take care of your mother and the little ones. You are a man now. As for what I have to do, its outcome is in God's hands. All I know is that this time I cannot stay at home.'

So he had gone, and since then Elizabeth had received no word from him, nothing at all, though the news of the defeat at Worcester haunted her, sleeping and waking. She could not rid her mind of the vision of the terrible slaughter they had heard about, of the bodies filling the streets, the hundreds of prisoners facing execution or transportation; the King himself on the run, pursued by his enemies. Only, there was no word at all of Ralph. She did not even know whether he was alive or dead, but in the absence of any other news she feared the worst.

Then, in the midst of all this terrible anxiety, she suddenly received a message from her cousin Isobel Fenwick. Cousin Isobel was a widow, elderly, devoutly Catholic, and for long estranged from her apostate cousin Elizabeth and her heretic husband. They had retained enough family feeling to exchange occasional letters, when there was a birth or a death to report, perhaps, but otherwise they had not seen one another for years. Now, suddenly there was this message, sent by the old woman's son, who lived with her, to say that Isobel Fenwick was very sick and anxious to see her dear cousin at once. Elizabeth was puzzled, and irritated too. As if she hadn't enough troubles already, with Ralph away and in danger and all the cares of the family on her shoulders! She almost sent word that she could not come, but thought better of it. If her cousin wanted to make her peace with her kin before she died, then she should be allowed to do so, and she lived only about twelve miles from Widehope, near the little town of Wolsingham. It was not so very much to ask.

So Elizabeth ignored Cuthbert's objections and set out, alone except for a servant, and the necessary pass, to ride to Heartwell along roads full of soldiers. It was an isolated house in the hills on the edge of Weardale, and she reached it at dusk. To her astonishment and anger, Cousin Isobel came to meet her at the door, but before she could exclaim, held a finger to her lips. 'Hush, ask no questions. Follow me.'

She led the puzzled Elizabeth inside, across the dark hallway, up the stairs, through rooms dimly remembered from childhood, to the attics, where she pulled a panel aside and revealed one of the mansion's many priest's holes. Then to Elizabeth's utter amazement Ralph stepped from it into the room – tired, dirty, dishevelled, unshaven, but her beloved all the same. Before she could find breath to speak, his arms were round her. They did not hear Cousin Isobel leave them, closing the door as she went.

Elizabeth's first overwhelming thought was that he was safe, and with her. She wanted only to hold him, to feel his body close to her own, to gaze into his face, kiss him, reassure herself by touch and look that he was unhurt and whole, snatched safe from the brink of death. There was for a long time no need at all for words. If there had been anything in the room but a bare floor they would have made love, there and then.

When at last the questions began to form in her brain, she still could not take her hands from Ralph, but stroked his face as she spoke. 'Why are you here? Why not come home?'

'Because that's where they'll look for me.'

She did not ask who 'they' were. She knew the King was not alone in being hunted, that every man who had fought in the royal cause at Worcester was an enemy of the English Commonwealth. 'Then what shall you do? Will Cousin Isobel let you stay here?'

He shook his head. 'It wouldn't be fair to ask, even if she was willing, and I think she was not truly content to have me land here like this. You see, my most dear heart, nowhere is safe for me now.' He paused, looking steadily at her, while she realised what he meant. 'I shall make my way to the coast, and hope to find passage on a ship.'

She seized on that like a drowning woman reaching for what she hoped was a rope flung her way. 'Then you must give me time to go home and pack what we shall need, and tell Cuthbert of course. Dorothy will—'

'No – no, dear heart! I would give anything to take you with me, but I must not weaken in this. It would be to put you in danger. I know you're not afraid. You have courage enough for two. But there is the other thing: if you stay safe at Widehope, then perhaps we may salvage something. And the children will grow up in their own home, under your tender care.'

'There will be another,' she broke in, though it seemed supremely irrelevant, 'in the winter.'

He held her more closely. She could feel his anxiety and his despair. 'Then take care, dear heart. I leave this new little one in your care too.'

'How can I go on without you?'

'You know you can.' It was only then that the full implication of this meeting was brought home to her; that it was also a parting, whose limits, if any, were hidden from them both. 'I shall write as soon as I have an address. Meanwhile, I leave everything in your hands, for you to decide what's best, for good or ill. Sometimes I think you've always known better than I what's right.' He gave her instructions about this and that, messages for the children and for friends, and at the end he said, 'Please God the day may come when we shall be together again,' and she knew he did not really hope for it any longer.

When she reached home, she found that soldiers had been there in her absence and had searched the house from top to bottom. Cuthbert had told them where she was, not suspecting that there was any reason to keep it from them. She could only pray that they had not thought to go and search there too, or that if they had Ralph had left before they got there. It was not until two months later that a brief letter from her husband announced his safe arrival in Paris. Soon afterwards they heard that the King too had reached safety.

By then they had already begun to feel the full force of the government's repression. In a way, Elizabeth knew they were lucky. Those Royalist soldiers who had not escaped faced trial and imprisonment, and many were executed. Every Royalist of any standing who had fought at Worcester was liable to confiscation of all his estates, but a wife was entitled to a fifth of the property, for her subsistence and that of her children, and even in these times there were sympathetic friends, who tried to shield them from the worst. It was not much comfort for Cuthbert, who saw his inheritance vanish before his eyes. Angry and resentful, he blamed his father. 'He wouldn't let me play any part, yet now I've got nothing, without having lifted a finger against the republic.'

In the end, against his mother's advice, he found a way to register his disapproval of the government, by refusing to take the Engagement, a new oath to which all adult males were obliged to subscribe, swearing loyalty to an England without King or House of Lords. The penalty for refusal was the denial of all rights to justice. In effect, that meant that debtors would avoid paying what they owed to him, rents might be refused, and he would have no legal recourse. 'I've got nothing anyway, so I don't see it matters,' he said bleakly, when his mother advised compliance.

The fifth of their estates left to them consisted of the house and the lands immediately adjoining it, no more than a small farmer might own for his basic subsistence. Everything else was confiscated and put up for sale. Some of the mines bordering the Tyne were bought for them by a friend, and leased back to them. They had hoped the same might be done with the rest of the lands in their own area, but they heard that their neighbour John Bolam had stepped in quickly – using the influence he had with the sellers, so they supposed – and bought them all. He then had the temerity to come round and ask openly for Dorothy's hand in marriage.

And, to Cuthbert's horror, Elizabeth declared that he could have it.

'You should have asked me, in my father's absence,' Cuthbert objected, in fury.

'You would have said no,' his mother pointed out.

'Of course I would, madam. And so should you. How can you? So soon after—'

'I think the time for being stiff-necked about our principles is over,' said Elizabeth sharply.

'But my father – he didn't want this match.'

'Your father has gone and God knows when we shall ever see him again – if we ever shall.' Then she burst into tears.

There was a small crumb of comfort in seeing how, at last, after all these years, Dorothy had found an uncomplicated happiness.

1652

CHAPTER FORTY

Susannah was astonished to see Anne Greatorex at the door, peering out from the hood of her cloak like a servant on some clandestine errand – which in fact it was, for Anne said, 'Susannah, my sister is brought to bed. Will you come to her?'

Susannah knew that Richard's wife was pregnant again, and near her time, but she had never supposed that would have any significance for her. During the past two years she had often been called out to the sick and to women in labour, but they had all been members of the group of Seekers to which she now belonged. As far as anyone else was concerned, she was still a source of contamination. She stared at Anne. 'I thought . . . Thy brother . . .'

'He's in London. He won't know till afterwards. It'll be too late then for him to forbid it. Please come.'

She did not hesitate after that, but sent Anne to sit in the parlour while she packed her bag. Then she remembered Daniel. He was playing quietly in the garden, but there was no one to watch him in her absence. Margaret was at market, and John with her, and to seek them out would take time. 'Bring him with you,' Anne said. 'Cook will look after him.'

In the kitchen where he belongs, thought Susannah ruefully, but she accepted the offer and called Daniel in from the garden. He was five now, a slender little boy with dark curls and an endless store of questions.

She took him up on the pony in front of her, and was reminded suddenly, forcefully, of her own small self riding in just this way with her father to call on his patients. She could feel again the firmness of Matthew Fawcett's arm about her, hear the creak of the

saddle, the clopping of the hooves against which his quiet voice
from somewhere above her head told her what he was going to do
today. When they reached the patient she would often watch him at
work, and ask eager questions and hear his explanations. Daniel
was full of childish curiosity too, but he had never before had the
opportunity to be involved in her work, even in a small way. More
than once she had found herself hoping that he might one day step
into his grandfather's shoes and become the fully qualified physician she had always wished she could have been. She thought
perhaps it was not quite suitable for an unrelated small boy to be
present at the birth of a child, and she was sure that Barbara
Metcalfe would not want it, but he would be close to what was happening, and even from that he might begin to learn. As they rode,
she told him something of what she would be doing today. He listened quietly, but made no comment at all and, for once, asked no
questions.

They reached the Hall and she told him he must go to the
kitchen. She waited for his protest. She would certainly have
protested, when she was his age. Instead, promised cakes, he went
happily away in the company of the footman, without a backward
glance.

Later, sated with cakes hot from the oven, and with not the
remotest thought in his head of what his mother was doing, Daniel
wandered at the heels of one of the gardeners out into the garden.
It was quiet and hot on this May morning, the air heavy with scents
reaching out unexpectedly from corners suddenly turned. He loved
gardens, loved the smells and colours even of their own neat and
useful garden. This one seemed a vast paradise, full of surprises and
hidden places.

There came a sound, quite without warning; the sweet soft
plucking of some stringed instrument, followed afterwards by a
slower and very much less tuneful noise which was like a sad par-
ody of the other. There were voices too. Fascinated, Daniel followed
them to their source. He stepped under an arch of yew and found
himself in a rose garden, and glimpsed on a bench at the far end of
one of the box-edged walks a man seated beside a fair boy very
much older than himself – he, it seemed, was the one making the
unappealing noise. Daniel crept along the grassy paths, round the
borders of the garden, until he found himself with a clear view of
the bench yet concealed from it by a large shrubby rose. By now the

man had taken up a pipe of some kind and put it to his lips and with skilful use of his fingers was drawing from it the sweetest and most haunting of sounds, sounds that reached out to Daniel and tugged him step by soft step nearer and nearer to the bench.

Then Daniel saw, close beside him on the grass, a pipe just like the one the man played. He had never before seen a musical instrument so very near. The temptation was too strong for him, and the sense of invisibility, for no one seemed to have noticed him. He crouched down and reached out a hand to take the instrument, and then put it to his lips, fingers experimentally closing some of the holes, and blew gently.

The noise sounded deafening, and master and pupil looked sharply round in astonishment. Since there seemed nothing else to be done, Daniel stood up and grinned. He did not wish them 'Goodday', as he might once have done, for the Seekers frowned on such usages: 'Is not every day good that the Lord has made?' they would say. Instead, he decided to get straight to the point. 'Show me how to do that.'

In the house Barbara Metcalfe gave birth without complications to a healthy boy.

Mother and aunt were full of gratitude. As so often before, Susannah said, 'It was not my doing, but the Lord's. To Him be the glory.' In the old days, she would have said that she spoke sincerely, but she knew now that in her heart she had always taken the whole credit for her own success. Since the momentous night at the Dowthwaites' farm she had come to feel, not self-satisfaction, but an overpowering sense of awe in the face of the everyday miracle of birth in which she was privileged to play a part. On this occasion she had, in truth, had little to do but allow nature to take its course, but she understood now, as once she had not, that even her skills, real though they might be, were not hers by merit, but as a gift, to be used to the best of her ability.

After that, things suddenly became difficult, in a way they had never been in the past. Once the infant was washed and swaddled and the mother rested, Dame Alice (now very infirm) was summoned, and little Grace, and the nearer neighbours and relatives who had called to offer help. 'There's wine for you in the parlour,' Anne said then, looking faintly embarrassed, and Susannah was reminded abruptly that, now her usefulness was over, toleration of her must be at an end. After Grace's birth, Susannah had remained in the room, to share the celebrations with everyone else. This time, she was whisked away before the company arrived in the bedroom, down a back stair to the little parlour behind the hall. Anne stayed with her, seeing that she had wine in her glass, and cakes to eat with it, but there was constraint in her manner. It was obvious that she did not quite know how to behave towards her former friend, once the practicalities of the birth were over. In the old days, she had looked on Susannah with unbounded admiration. As yet she did not seem to have replaced it with anything very definite, except a mixture of disapproval and curiosity.

'You've given up coming to church,' she said, after an awkward silence. Her manner was faintly accusatory. 'I hear you're frequenting those sectaries who meet at the Dowthwaites' place, you and the child, and Margaret too.' Susannah admitted it. Anne went on, warily, as if gathering courage to express a disagreeable truth, 'I hear you make your servants speak to you as equals. I know it's true, for I once heard Margaret Boulton say 'thou' to you, as if she were not a servant but a sister.' She studied Susannah's face. 'That's an unwise proceeding.'

'Unwise?' said Susannah. She smiled faintly. 'The wisdom of this world is foolishness with God.' It had taken a long time before Margaret and John had grown used to calling her 'Susannah', dispensing with the customary 'mistress' and learning to use the familiar, intimate 'thou' in place of the respectful 'you'. As they learned the new ways, almost imperceptibly the atmosphere in the house had changed. It was as if altering the way they spoke to one another had transformed a household of mistress and child and servants into one of four people simply sharing a house on equal terms, each carrying out his or her different tasks according to their various skills and needs.

Susannah tried to explain something of this to Anne, but she realised she was speaking a foreign language, meaningless to her companion, to whom a world in which servants could be anything but inferiors (however kindly used) was an alien one – terrifying, too, for, as she pointed out, she had seen in Ireland what could happen when the natural order of things was suddenly overturned. Susannah remembered the fears Richard had expressed to her long ago, when he saw that to encourage rebellion in poor men was to threaten the very foundations of society and property. But then to her such things no longer mattered very much. She was even a little surprised that Anne should think that the disgraced Susannah Fawcett ought to regard herself as superior to her blameless servants. But when she said so, Anne clearly found the very thought disturbing. 'All I can say is that I know this to be the way I must go,' Susannah said.

Anne shook her head. 'It seems to me there's no knowing where such things will end, if once you allow every man and woman and child to be free to follow whatever sect they choose. Have you heard of those preachers – Children of Light, some call them. They wander about the country, shouting insults and interrupting God's worship and speaking the most horrid blasphemy. Some have even claimed to be Christ himself. *That's* what happens when you have men without learning allowed to speak as freely as ordained ministers. There's one, a man called Nayler, from Wakefield. I heard he served under our cousin Tom, when the war started, though Richard has no recollection of him. Then he was in John Lambert's regiment, until he was sent home sick. His sickness seems to take strange forms, from what I hear. There's another was a weaver, before he thought he had a call to go preaching. He's from Leicestershire, I think. He would have done better to stay at his trade. I heard he's expected to come this way.'

'That's George Fox,' said Susannah. She knew that the Seekers were hoping he would visit them.

'The worst of blasphemers, from what I hear. I only hope he'll be stoned out of Thornside, as he deserves. The trouble is that in much of the dale there's no religion, no preaching to set against such men, only Popish superstition at best.'

'They're wrong to say he claims to be Christ. He's never said any such thing. But why not come and hear him, if he comes here, and judge for thyself?'

'It's people judging for themselves that's caused all this trouble,' said Anne. 'They'd have been wiser to leave the preaching to their betters, who are learned in theology.'

'Their betters, like Nathaniel Johnson?' Susannah asked. In the early days the Minister had more than once remonstrated with her for not coming to church on Sundays, and for encouraging her servants similarly to go astray. She set a shocking example, he had said, much as Anne, more kindly, was saying now. But there was nothing he could do to force her to conform. Two years ago Parliament had

repealed the recusancy laws, aimed originally at Catholics, which
once had laid down fines for those who did not attend their parish
church. Now, every man and woman was free to worship wherever
he or she chose, though the Mass was still forbidden. 'Dost thou not
see,' Susannah went on, 'learned men of all religions claim to have
authority under God, yet they don't all say the same thing. Isn't it
better to seek the clear light of the spirit in thine own heart?'

'How do you tell what is the spirit and what is self-will?' Anne
retorted. Then she said, 'I don't mean to quarrel with you,
Susannah. You may be sadly misguided, but I owe you too much to
want to condemn you.' She stood up. 'I must send word to Richard,
and then I must go and take Philip to see his new cousin. He's at his
music lesson, poor boy. He has no gift for music.'

Susannah, searching for Daniel, reached the rose garden at the
same moment as Anne. They both halted under the yew arch, staring at the little scene at the far end: the master, his pupil looking on,
and the small intruder playing with commendable enthusiasm and
even some accuracy on the recorder.

It was then that Susannah was reminded more forcibly than ever
that there were limits to Anne's toleration of herself and her child.
Anne gave a horrified exclamation and hurried across the garden.
'Master Lobley, this child has no business to keep company with my
son!'

Susannah, following her, called, 'Daniel!' and the little boy, with
reluctant obedience, laid the recorder aside and stood up. She saw
Philip stand up too – the child she had once nursed so tenderly, red-
faced now with shame and disgust. 'Ugh, Sukey Fawcett's bastard!
Get away from me!' He gave Daniel a shove and the little boy, bewildered and suddenly close to tears, ran to his mother. Susannah
decided that the wisest course was to leave as soon as possible, and,
without speaking to anyone, hurried to the stables, where their
pony was tethered. She thought it a bad sign that the child said
nothing as they went. There had already been several occasions in
his young life when his origins had been used against him. It was
not likely to get easier as he grew older.

They had just left the trees that sheltered the northern side of the
Hall and were turning on to the road leading back to Thornside
when Susannah heard someone call her name. She looked round
and saw the music master hurrying up the track towards them, so
she drew rein and waited for him to reach her. He took some time

to get his breath, and then glanced round, as if to make sure that they were not visible from the Hall. Then he said, 'Mistress, have you thought of engaging a music master for your son?'

It seemed so foolish a question that she almost laughed, but she did not want to hurt his feelings. 'Never, I must admit.'

'I'm convinced he has a rare talent, which if nurtured . . . I'm not seeking this for my own ends – except that I have few pupils of any skill at all, still less any who love to learn. To have so apt a pupil would be a pleasure. I could not, of course' – he coloured slightly – 'teach him at the Hall, and I think it would not be fitting for me to come to your house. But I have rooms of my own at Carperby. If you could arrange for the child to come there . . .'

'I'll think it over,' she said. But she had an uneasy sense that the decision was already made, for Daniel was incandescent with delight, and he pestered her all the way home. 'Please, mother – please!'

Susannah had a feeling that for a child in his position such frivolities as music lessons were unwise. Then she wondered if her unease stemmed more from her own ignorance of the subject than any objective sense of what was right. Then she thought: It can do no harm, to give it a try, at least.

She made a few discreet enquiries as to what manner of man the music master was, and was reassured to learn that Nicholas Lobley was a young man of great sweetness of character and known godliness, in spite of the fact that some of their Royalist neighbours also employed him. It seemed that he often attended Thornside church on Sundays, there being no suitable place of worship any nearer to his lodging.

So, not long afterwards, accompanied either by herself or by John, Daniel began to ride each week the three miles to the house where the master lodged, and each time came home full of happy chatter about all he had learned. She even went so far as to buy him a recorder and seek out from the loft the lute that had been her mother's, asking the master to see to having it restrung. As she did so, she had a wistful recollection of her own younger self, unconcerned about music, but eager to learn all she could of her father's craft. But there was still time, for Daniel was very young.

Two weeks later Susannah was returning on foot from attending a patient near Bainbridge, in the valley below Thornside. It was well into the afternoon and the market place was busy, for it was a Tuesday, though by now many buyers and sellers were beginning to pack up and go home. She pushed her way through the throng, up the hill, past the church, glancing over the wall as she did so. Then she stood still, astonished by what she saw.

Each market day Nathaniel Johnson preached at considerable length to as many as came to hear, which was a large proportion of his customary congregation but few others. Today something had evidently disturbed the usual orderly proceedings, for spilling out into the churchyard was a tangle of men and women, their shouts and jeers rising above the usual market day hubbub, which was stilled as everyone jostled towards the churchyard wall to watch what was going on. A man suddenly broke away from the crowd by the church. He was dishevelled and bloody, but he looked back to shout defiance as he ran. 'Woe to ye, hypocrites!' he cried, and something else that was lost in the angry roar. His pursuers picked up stones and earth to hurl at him. He backed towards the gate, continuing to shout, dodging the missiles. Then he darted through into the market-place, where others, not wanting to miss the fun, were already reaching for stones of their own.

Susannah, who remembered only too well what it felt like to be hounded by angry righteousness, caught his arm. 'Come with me!' She led him swiftly round the corner into the lane. They did not stop running until they were safely in the house with the door barred, though they heard the shouts of the pursuers continuing outside. Stones even hit the door. Halting to catch her breath, Susannah looked at the man; and then suddenly knew who he must be. 'Thou'rt George Fox.'

He stood facing her, a powerfully built young man in strange travel-stained leather clothes, with eyes that burned with a disconcerting fire. 'Aye,' he said.

He was also weary, battered, hungry, so she took him to the kitchen and put food before him, with Margaret's help. When he had eaten, she said, 'Someone told me thou claimed to be Christ.' She spoke a little nervously, for there was something about the man that awed her, though she could not have said precisely what it was.

'I claim only Christ's spirit within me, as in all people,' he said.

'In me too?' she asked, with a certain irony. 'Mother of a bastard child.'

He gazed at her for a time in silence, and she felt more uncomfortable than ever, as if he were seeing into her very soul. 'In thee too,' he said at last. 'Thou has only to turn thy face to it. But then,' he added, 'I think thou's already done that.'

As soon as it was dark, she saddled horses and led him out by the garden gate on to the hill and then by a long way round to the Dowthwaites' farm, where she knew he would be safe and sure of a warm welcome.

Next morning, so many came to hear him that they had to gather on the open hillside, since there was no room indoors. For all the numbers of people, a great silence fell as the young man raised a hand to indicate he was about to speak, and into it came only the sound of the curlews and the larks singing. And then his voice.

He was just an odd-looking young man standing in the wind under a grey sky, talking loudly in flat Midland vowels. He had not been speaking for long when it began to rain. It was all very ordinary. And yet it was not.

He spoke of the light in every human creature, the light that was judgement and vision and guidance in each moment of life, in each thought and action, without which no salvation was possible. From the moment he began to speak Susannah felt the whole world change.

She remembered the inward light, which, two years before, had shown her the ugliness of her pride. She knew it was the very same light that George Fox spoke of so passionately. Yet the light that was in each one of his hearers seemed, on this hillside, on this cheerless May morning, to manifest itself as a fierce and universal illumination, outside them as well as in, surrounding them, dazzling them. So all-encompassing was it that Susannah seemed to see the whole world laid out in its brilliance, so that it shone into every hidden corner, banished every shadow.

She saw first that the world was a fearful and terrible place, full of hate and anger and pride and tyranny, and suffering beyond imagining, and that its very foundations trembled with the uncertainty of the times. Yet she knew with sudden conviction that the power that moved it and tore it apart was not remote or random, but rather a massive creative force, like the savage pains of childbirth multiplied a thousand times, striving to bring forth some great and wonderful new order.

She felt the terror of it, and then in the next moment she saw that everything was alight with an intensity of colour which was like nothing she had ever seen before and yet was somehow the essence of every true colour: the green of grass and leaf more essentially green, the gold of dandelions more gold, the bronze of last year's bracken more deeply bronze than any green or gold or bronze that the human imagination could dream up. The air seemed sweeter and softer, the wind more fierce yet more invigorating, the rain tender and fruitful, the call of the birds sweeter than any music ever heard. It was as if all the true hidden loveliness of the earth, all that lay beneath the surface evil she had seen a moment ago, was at last visible to human kind, a vision of a perfection that was, in time, on this earth, somehow attainable after all. And she was one with it, a part of this glorious creation, not greater nor smaller than any other part, but in harmony with it, close to its heart, in touch with its secrets. She had felt judgement before; now she felt life in all its fullness, all its richness – life and love. She saw that every blade of grass was held cradled in God's hands, every flower and every single one of His creatures, large and small, that crawled or ran upon it, or flew above it, or swam in its depths. She saw that every one of His sons and daughters – alike a miraculous composition of interconnected bones and working organs and circulating blood – shone with the light He had given, there for every one to see, if only they chose to look. She saw the beauty, the possibilities for good, shining from every one of her companions. She saw suddenly that the healing power of her hands and her mind had always been a part of this glorious wholeness, only she had not seen it until now. She looked down at her hands, and they too seemed to shine, transformed to supernatural loveliness, as if the healing gift was made visible.

Later, she walked home with feet that wanted to dance, through the green and gold of the illuminated world, and at home found her beautiful child singing like an angel as he strummed on his lute, and she took him in her arms and held him and knew that she had never in all her life been as truly happy as she was now.

1653

CHAPTER FORTY-ONE

His part in the government of England was at an end. It was out of his hands, and Richard Metcalfe was deeply thankful.

He had in any case begun to think he ought to give up his seat, since Parliamentary business seemed lately to take so much time. Last winter his mother had died, so that her strong hand was no longer in control of his affairs in Thornside, as it had been even in her later years of increasing infirmity. Coming home, he missed her, yet he was surprised to find that he felt relieved too, as if an oppressive presence had gone from his life. He realised then that he had never ceased, in some degree, to fear her – to the extent, even, that he had been glad that his duties kept him so often away from home. Now, at long last, he was master in his own house. He looked forward to living quietly at home, among family and friends, far from the troubles of the capital; to ruling household and estate, instead of the troubled land that seemed to be spinning out of control. Here there was every chance of happiness. If his wife was not the woman he had once dreamed he might marry, at least she had given him young Thomas, his heir, who was a healthy thriving infant, his pride and joy; and she was both meek and dutiful.

He was rather touched at Barbara's indignation at his enforced return home, which seemed to stem from a wifely concern for any possible damage to his pride. 'How shameful it is that the army should presume to decide who governs us!' she exclaimed. He thought he had never before heard her express any interest in matters of state.

'I fear the army has long done that,' he told her. 'It is now out in the open, that's all.'

It had been no partial purge that Cromwell and his friends had conducted on the late April day two weeks ago, but a complete overturning. Every remaining member of the Parliament that first sat when Charles Stuart was still unchallenged King of England had been sent packing from the Chamber, and now only a Council of State ruled. 'Will there be new elections?' Anne asked her brother.

Richard gave a bitter little smile. 'Oh no. They are to nominate godly men to govern us. By which can only be meant a fanatic rabble. God help us!'

'You won't escape fanatics, even here,' his sister told him, and went on to enlarge on the subject in a way that most deeply disturbed him. 'They're spreading like the plague in this neighbourhood. Master Johnson has been forced to preach against them, every Sunday of late. Three weeks ago there was quite a disturbance about it.'

He should then have been forewarned, when, on his first Sunday at home, in the church where he expected to find his greatest solace, all his tranquillity was shattered. Everything seemed reassuringly familiar: the psalms, the readings, the prayers, the sermon which Nathaniel Johnson began in his sonorous, accusatory manner. That it concerned the troublesome people who called themselves Seekers, or Children of Light, or any manner of names, to hide the fact that they were simply manifestations of the Devil himself, that was unsurprising in view of what Anne had said, and Richard settled down to listen in the comfortable certainty that he would hear nothing with which he might even very slightly disagree. '. . . Quakers some have called them, for their trembling at the words of their preachers, though they reject the name. But Quakers they shall be indeed, at the Last Day when God shall call them to account for the stumbling block they have placed before His children!'

It was then that a woman came marching into the church and up the aisle to stand below the pulpit, facing the minister. Richard saw that she was shapely, upright, well-dressed. Though her spotless coif concealed her hair, and its lace-edged border hid her face from him, there was, he thought, something vaguely familiar about her.

There was a moment of tense silence, while minister and intruder stared at one another. Then Nathaniel Johnson cleared his throat and continued what he had been saying. 'Brothers and sisters, do not let yourselves be led astray by these false prophets who say that a woman can speak equally with a man; who say you have no need of minister or Bible, that your own will is enough—'

'Thou liest, Nathaniel Johnson!'

Richard felt himself go violently red. He knew that voice: clear, angry, sure of itself. He squirmed with inward embarrassment, as if by having loved it once he was somehow colluding in what it said.

'Thou knowest that was not what he claimed, for he spoke to thee in this very place,' the voice went on. 'Did he not tell thee, the Bible is God's own words?'

'But not the Word of God, Susannah Fawcett!' the minister retorted. 'Aye – that is what he said.'

'Because Christ alone is the Word of God!'

The Minister glanced at the pew where the churchwardens sat. 'Will no one get this woman out of here? If indeed she deserves the name of woman, who acts so contrary to her sex!'

Susannah heard the scuffling behind her, and said quickly, 'Thou dost hate the message of George Fox, for it shows thou art no more nor less than any other man. For thee – thou wilt not allow to all God's creatures the light that is their salvation. Thy message is despair, Nathaniel Johnson!'

She felt hands grab her, turn her, march her forcibly from the church. Then she was led, protesting all the way, jeered by some, cheered by others, to Thornside Hall, to be kept waiting there until Richard returned from church. As Justice of the Peace, he was responsible for dealing with any who broke the law by interrupting a minister in the midst of his preaching.

Richard felt as if he were in some kind of dreadful nightmare, to see the woman he had once loved so much hauled before him like any common criminal. First she went whoring with a nameless stranger, and now this! What was happening to this land, that even Susannah Fawcett should be driven mad?

'Do you know what these people do?' he demanded of her, dragging to the front of his mind all the dreadful stories his sister had told him. 'In one place I heard of, there was a follower of George Fox went naked through the streets. How can you ally yourself with such as these? That you of all people should disturb God's holy worship – I cannot understand it.'

'Why not, Richard? I'd have thought it easy to understand. What have I ever learned of God in that place, but that His judgement is harsh and I am outside His love and His mercy, like so many others?

From George Fox and the others so slightingly called Quakers, I learn a different message. I hear of a light in every person, that all are called to turn to it, that though there is judgement there is also hope, even the hope of perfection. Would thou turn aside from such a hope, if thou were such as I?'

'I don't know,' said Richard drily, 'for I cannot in truth imagine being such as you are now . . . If it were not that I owe you my son's life, then I should exact a harsh penalty for your interruption this day. As it is, take this as a warning, and walk in more peaceable ways. Next time I shall not be so tolerant. I do not think you would want your son to have a mother in gaol.'

'Better that than that I should turn from the light.' She looked at him with an earnest directness that seemed to dissolve his very bones. 'Richard, thou hast the light within thee too.'

He would not allow himself to be moved. 'Let this be, Susannah, or I shall be forced to silence you.' He stood up, ready to show her from the room. 'Once I thought I knew you,' he said. 'But you have long been a stranger.' To his relief she went with him to the door. She was just about to pass through it, away from him, when he heard himself ask suddenly, 'Who was the man – your bastard's father?' He knew that what he was really wanting to ask was, 'How could you love him, in preference to me?'

Susannah only smiled at him, and then turned and walked away without another word.

1654

CHAPTER FORTY-TWO

Four years Walter had been in Ireland, and all he wanted now was to get away. That soft and fertile loveliness, scarred by war but offering so much of hope, was now a devastated wilderness, not simply scarred but laid waste. Crops had been burned or trampled during the years of pacification, and in places people ate their plough horses, or even grass, for there was hunger everywhere. Wolves prowled right up to the fringes of towns, and the nights were broken by their howling. Hedgerows were lined with rotting corpses. Orphaned children wandered the roads, begging for food. Plague had followed hunger, spreading its horror over the land. And still, though the final stronghold had fallen, the last peace terms had been signed, marauding bands of savages – *tories* in the local language – swept down on unsuspecting troops of soldiers, slaughtering and maiming with sudden, terrifying rapidity. Those native Irish landowners who remained were stripped of their land and despatched to remote and desolate Connaught, to live apart from their conquerors. Only the poor and landless were left, to provide workers for the new masters, but the poor and landless were dying like flies. True, there were great swathes of empty land, waiting for cultivation, and every soldier had a right to his portion, in lieu of arrears of pay, but Walter had no wish to live in the midst of such misery.

The memories he had gathered during the past dreadful years were none of them good ones. Nearly all the men he had come over with were dead, of wounds or sickness – except Amias, who had lately succumbed to a graver disorder, the love of an Irish girl, something that was strictly against army discipline. They said, and

Walter had believed, that the Irish were an accursed people, to be wiped from the land because of their blood-guiltiness. But he thought now that it was almost as if the curse had been turned back on itself, as if every stroke of the sword against the Irish people brought disaster on the wielder of it. Walter could no longer even quite convince himself that what he was doing here was God's work, that he was an instrument of justice. He thought often of Samuel, and then something would stir uneasily in his mind: *This is what you did, for this you will be called to account.*

The days when Samuel had been his friend and comrade seemed a long way off now, virtually irrecoverable, even in memory. The excitement and vision that had fired him then were gone too. He felt dried up, spiritually barren. He wanted to stay with the army, because it gave him occupation and some kind of mundane purpose, but it was no longer the source of his strength and his happiness.

But if Esther had her way, he would lose even that last remaining security. She wanted – expected – him to leave the army, as soon as ever he could, and take up the offer of Irish land, so that they might settle there and begin a new life together. He was not sure why she was so enthusiastic about the prospect, for he knew she was as disenchanted with him as he was with her. Except when she babbled about their little Irish farm, she scarcely spoke to him, and then only in public, when there were others to hear. Months ago he had recognised that all affection between them was long dead. They might still, under law, be man and wife, but it was only in that coldly legalistic sense that Walter felt that they were married at all. The thought of being settled for ever in the hostile Irish countryside with only Esther for company was one he scarcely wanted even to allow into his mind.

For a long time Walter let Esther talk without contradiction of her plans – their plans – which included Corporal Harper owning land adjacent to their own, a proposal whose implications he knew perfectly well, but did not want to face. Month after month it went on, because for him to oppose her would force things to a conclusion, and that he was afraid to do. Yet he knew that in the end a decision would have to be made. The war was all but over, many soldiers had already left the army. His own troop had recently been sent to form part of the garrison of Limerick, on the west coast. It was not their first acquaintance with the city, whose long and bitter siege had cost General Ireton his life less than two years before, but it was a comfortable enough place to spend the winter months. It was while they were there, late in the December of 1653, that they heard that England was no longer a Republic but a Protectorate. Oliver Cromwell, backed by John Lambert and other senior officers, had driven out the short-lived nominated Parliament, on which such high hopes had been built, and Oliver was now established as Lord Protector of England.

'I'm not easy with it,' Walter said, as he sat with a number of others in the corner of an alehouse parlour, reading the latest news-sheets and studying the terms of the *Instrument of Government*, the new constitution drawn up by John Lambert. 'It's to put all the power in the hands of one man again. Why did we fight the King, if not to prevent that?'

'But the one man is General Cromwell,' said Amias, 'and he's elected, and he must have the agreement of his Parliament in all he does.'

'There's no Parliament yet,' one of the others pointed out. 'There's only his council.'

'Good men,' said Amias. 'Our best officers – Lambert, Fleetwood, Skippon, and the best of the old Parliament men. They'll get down to reforming tithes at last, and we shall have true freedom of religion—'

'Not for Papists, Amias,' said Corporal Harper, with a knowing grin. 'You'll have to get her to convert.'

'It wouldn't do any good,' said Walter, 'unless she could convince them it wasn't just for convenience.' He glanced at Amias, who had gone rather pink. Walter had no love at all for the Irish and – in theory at least – disapproved of Amias's love for one of them. It had put a barrier between them that hurt after all the years of comradeship, all they had shared. Yet at the same time he felt for his friend's predicament. All Amias wanted was to marry and settle in Ireland with his girl. But soldiers marrying Irish girls (unless they happened to be uncontrovertibly Protestant) faced dismissal and the loss of all rights to arrears of pay or to land in lieu of it. Yet without those things Amias could not marry his girl and settle down, for he had no other means of livelihood.

'It makes no difference anyway. She won't turn Protestant,' said Amias. Walter was astonished that he could continue to love in the face of such hardness of heart.

'Get your land first, leave the army, then wed her,' Will Harper suggested. 'Give it a decent interval and no one will be any the wiser.'

'She could live as our servant,' said Esther suddenly. 'Then you could get land near to us, and you could meet at our house.' For a moment, Walter thought that by *our* she meant herself and Will Harper, which was ridiculous, of course. Except . . . He realised that the talk was about to move on, and suddenly knew that he must speak now, if only because he did not want Amias to have his hopes unfairly raised.

'No, they couldn't,' he said. 'We're not staying in Ireland.'

There was a momentary silence, which had in it surprise, puzzlement, anger, embarrassment. Then Esther said, very clearly, 'You maybe aren't. I am.'

In that moment, in those few words, the depth of the rift between them was out in the open, acknowledged before everyone. Walter could no longer deny it, even to himself.

She did not come to lie beside him that night until very late, and it was only with difficulty that he had made himself stay awake so long. 'Where have you been?' he asked, routinely, not really expecting an informative answer.

'Doing things,' she said, and turned her back to him.

He moved closer. 'Esther, what I said today – I mean it. I hate Ireland. I'm not staying. I'm asking to be transferred back to England.'

'That's up to you. Only I'm not going with you.'

'You're my wife.'

'We both wish that wasn't true, I think.'

'But it is.'

A silence; then, coaxingly, as he had never heard her for a long time, 'Walter, no one would ever know, here in Ireland – whose wife I was, I mean. I could be Corporal Harper's for all anyone would know to the contrary.'

He suddenly realised, with a chill, what she was trying to say. 'You couldn't. That would be sinful—'

'Don't be so pious. We'd both be better off for it.'

'But the men know you're my wife.'

'And they know who I've been lying with lately.' Though he knew it too, he was shocked to hear her say it aloud. They had been discreet in their way; after all, neither she nor Will Harper wished to be charged with adultery, a crime that was not only against army discipline but also bore the death penalty. But it had been going on for a long time now, and those close to them could not fail to know what was happening. 'If there's any trouble when you've gone,' Esther persisted, in a way that showed how much thought she had already given the matter, 'then I'll go somewhere quiet and lie low a bit till it's blown over. When you've been gone three years, then they can't charge me with anything. That's right isn't it?'

He tried to know what he felt, faced with all this so suddenly. Pain, certainly, and a sense of failure and of waste; and yet there was, too, a certain relief, that there might be some end to the mockery of this marriage that once he had wanted so much.

Soon afterwards, before they had talked much more or come to any conclusion, Esther fell asleep. Walter did not sleep at all for the rest of the night, but by the time dawn came he had made a decision. He would go back to England, as he had always intended, and he would do so in the knowledge that Esther would remain here and, in due course, by some means, become as much the Corporal's wife as she could be, without any hope of making it legal.

He got his transfer easily enough. The bulk of his old regiment was now in Scotland, where the Royalists in the Highlands were proving troublesome, and good officers and men were in short supply. He had no particular wish to exchange service in one benighted land for that in another, but Scotland could not be worse than Ireland – after all, the Scots had once been their allies – and at least it would take him away from Esther, and keep him in the army.

He sold his share of Irish land to Will Harper, told him, sourly, he was welcome to Esther, and sailed back to England in the spring, through nightmarish storms which he thought would end his life and which made his first step on English soil seem like a miracle. Never had England seemed so tranquil and orderly and secure as it did now. He did not even regret the green softness of the early western spring which he had left behind.

He made his way north, staying one night with an old comrade, now an innkeeper in York. There was an itinerant preacher lodging there, an old soldier too, once quartermaster in Lambert's regiment. That night James Nayler – such was his name – preached in a packed upstairs room, and Walter joined the crowd to hear what he had to say.

Walter had heard many preachers in his life, some of them the very best in London, but he did not think any of them had ever matched this tall, graceful, mild-featured man for eloquence and passion. Certainly, none had ever struck him to the heart as James Nayler did. With his face alight, he told them not how few could be saved, how little hope there was, what terrible judgement awaited them, but spoke instead of the radiance of Christ's spirit, which could grow in each one of them and transform them all, if only they chose to seek it out.

It was water to Walter's barrenness, food to his hungry soul. He had not felt such joy and such refreshment since Samuel died, and perhaps not even before then. For the first time for many years he felt able to look to the future with hope in his heart.

1655

CHAPTER FORTY-THREE

Elizabeth Liddell missed Ralph dreadfully, with a consuming, comprehensive ache of heart and body that could not be assuaged. His absence took all the joy from her life. Their bed seemed one vast empty space, her daily tasks dreary in the extreme. The one small consolation was that, for four years now, she had not conceived a child, that their little Mary, born after Worcester, had no babies pressing at her stubborn little heels.

It was not much of a consolation. In every other way life was hard, even taking no account of Ralph's absence. All the burden of maintaining what was left of their estates fell on her. Cuthbert was no help at all. He was always out somewhere, though he never said where. ('I'm a man now, mother. It's none of your business what I do.') He was short with her when she exploded one day that if he was indeed a man then he should play his part in running things. 'What is there left to run?' he demanded bitterly, before going out again.

In a sense he was right, for the work his father used to do – overseeing their coal pits, supervising the farm, seeing that rents came in, inspecting damage to their property, ordering repairs, discussing flocks and herds and crops with his tenants, planning new projects – all those things had gone now, or almost gone. What was left was grinding, heavy, everyday farm work: milking, making cheese and butter, ploughing and sowing and weeding, mowing and reaping, herding beasts, lambing and shearing, an endless every-day, every-hour grind of hard, dirty, heavy work, not the work of a gentleman, but the work of a peasant, trying to scrape a living from the land. Elizabeth had even begun to go each week to market, with eggs and butter for sale, spreading her wares in Bishop Auckland market-place like the other countrywomen – though sometimes Betty, their one remaining maid, did that for her. All the graciousness of their past life, the music and singing and leisure to read and talk, had gone.

She supposed she had no real grounds for complaint about Cuthbert. On the whole he was no spendthrift, wasting money they did not have. But she could so have done with his support and help through these hard lonely years. Her son-in-law John Bolam was more than generous in the help he was ready to give them, but where her own pride did not hold her back from accepting it, Cuthbert's loathing for John kept her from doing so. Elizabeth understood her son's resentment and anger, and shared it too, to some extent. But life had to go on somehow, and to try and pretend nothing had changed helped none of them. She was troubled too because she knew it was time he married. He was already twenty-nine, a considerable age, and showed no inclination even to look for a wife. Not that she could think where he might begin to look, but so long as he was not choosy about fortune, then there were still eligible Royalist girls wanting husbands – except that their parents hoped for better prospects than Cuthbert could offer, and often preferred a well-to-do Roundhead; as indeed she could be said to have done for Dorothy.

If only she had Ralph to turn to for advice and comfort! She wrote to him, of course, but she knew that many of her letters went astray, for when she heard from him it was often in ignorance of things she had told him. That was hardly surprising, since the exiled Royalists were moved here and there, as their hosts in one place grew tired of them or their debts grew too great and others grudgingly gave them shelter. First, they had been in Paris, until King Louis recognised the English republic and drove out the exiles; then they moved by various stages to Cologne; and now Ralph was in Flanders (Spain was at war with the English republic). Letters had come from each place in turn, always when she had just sent a letter to Ralph's last address. If she had anything of great importance to tell him, she would repeat it in every letter, until she had some response from him. That was how she had let him know of Dorothy's marriage, waiting in dread for his reply. It had been gentler than she had feared, chiding but resigned, as if he understood the practicalities, while regretting them. He hoped that by the time he was again at Widehope there would no longer be cause for differences between neighbours, he had said. She longed for his letters, read and re-read them, yet in some ways they only made things worse. He scarcely ever told her anything about himself, how he was living, who he met, how he passed the time. She reflected that the old Ralph would have enlivened his letters with accounts of all he saw around him, the life of the people in the country concerned, its oddities, details of music he had heard, people he had met. As it was, she did not even know what other people shared his exile. Perhaps he simply thought it safer not to write of such things. They both knew that letters were often intercepted. Sometimes he gave her advice, but inevitably it would be on some matter now long settled. He spoke often of his desire to see her again and his love for her and the children, and asked endless questions, but when their correspondence was so disjointed and unconnected she only had a greater sense of loneliness. Yet it was better than it might have been. At least he was still alive, somewhere.

She longed to go to him, and at times seriously thought of doing so, but that would be to lose every last stake they had in Widehope, and besides she could not condemn her small children to a life in exile. Life might be hard here, but that would be worse. One day, perhaps, things might change, if only that Cuthbert might take on his responsibilities, so that when the little ones were grown she could leave Widehope and go to be with Ralph again.

Cuthbert had gone out early yesterday, as usual, though she had told him the night before that they must begin the sheep washing today – and finish it too, for they had only a small flock now. Cuthbert had even hinted that he might give a hand, so long as John Bolam was nowhere to be seen, so she had agreed not to ask for John's help. Then Cuthbert had stayed away all night and was still not home, which left her today with no one but the younger children and Betty, who had more than enough to do indoors. Dorothy, appealed to after all, had told her that John was bound for Durham today, on some state business, she thought.

Elizabeth was, then, surprised, when, standing up to her knees in the dub, forcing a sheep under water, splashed and muddied from head to foot, she suddenly found her son-in-law standing beside her. He gave her a hand with the sheep and helped her out of the water, without comment, then said abruptly, 'I saw Justice Pearson today . . .'

Elizabeth felt a tremor of fear. Before the war Anthony Pearson had been a mere schoolfellow of Cuthbert's, son of a neighbouring landowner of little consequence. He was now Justice of the Peace and secretary to the powerful governor of Newcastle, Sir Arthur Hazelrigg, who was steadily making a fortune from confiscated lands bought at rock bottom prices. Not that anyone had ever accused Pearson of corruption. The chief accusation against him now, and a potent one in Elizabeth's eyes, was that he had been seduced by the new and terrifyingly growing Quaker sect, which was responsible for the most alarming behaviour in its adherents. Many of their converts were women, whom they encouraged to wander the country and preach as if they were men. They were appallingly ill-mannered too, refusing to remove their hats before their betters, speaking to everyone as if they were equals. She could not help but think sometimes that, if things had turned out differently, Anthony Pearson would have remained in deserved obscurity and Cuthbert would have been the Justice, as his father once had been. That did not, of course, alter the fact that – for all his youth – Pearson was a man of considerable influence in the north of England, and one whose attention wise Royalists preferred not to draw upon themselves. She said nothing, since she did not know what to say, simply waiting for John to explain. Instead, he asked a question that might have had nothing to do with his previous remark; except that she knew instinctively that it had. 'Madam, where's Cuthbert?'

'He went off somewhere yesterday. I don't know where.' Then she dimly remembered some passing remark. 'A wedding, I think he said.' It sounded unlikely, even to her ears, for whose wedding would he be attending, that she did not know of? Except that she knew little of his life now, or his friends.

John frowned. 'You're sure you don't know where?'

'No . . . John, what is it? You know something.'

'Let's hope he comes home soon, that's all,' said John.

Cuthbert did come home, but not until the next day, a little after dawn. He was tired and sullen and refused to speak to her, still less to hear her rebuke at his neglect of his duties. When she said that John had seemed worried about his absence, he lost his temper and said some unpardonable things about his brother-in-law's interference. After that, he went to his room and stayed there until mid-morning, when he saddled up his horse again and rode away, without answering her questions as to where he was going.

The next day was Sunday. Cuthbert had neither returned home nor sent any message. Elizabeth went to church, the children with her. She loathed the man who had been forced upon the parish in place of the old Royalist vicar, but she continued to go to church out of habit, and because it gave her an excuse to sit still and do nothing – though that was difficult sometimes, when something said from the pulpit particularly enraged her.

It only gradually dawned on her that there was much excited whispering among the congregation, even before the service began, as if some startling news had just broken, though she had heard none. The Minister began his sermon, and she knew then what it was. He told them in the strongest and most condemnatory terms that a vile Royalist conspiracy had been uncovered, polluting every part of the land, though by God's mercy all had been thwarted. In Yorkshire, a gathering on Marston Moor had dispersed in panic. Nearest to home of all, many northern malignants had plotted together to take Newcastle, meeting for that purpose at Duddoe in Northumberland under the pretence of celebrating a wedding. Elizabeth felt cold, all over. It took a great effort on her part not to look round at Dorothy, who sat with her husband in the pew behind.

After the service, they went to dine at Dorothy's house, the more pleasurably since Cuthbert was not there to express his disapproval. 'You don't suppose it's to Duddoe that your brother went last Thursday?' Elizabeth asked her daughter, in the vain hope that Dorothy would dismiss the idea as ridiculous. It was, she thought, odd to find herself seeking from her young daughter the reassurance that she had so often given to her children. But then one of the few pleasures of her present existence was to discover in Dorothy, married and happy and a near neighbour, the most loyal and supportive of friends.

Dorothy, sitting comfortably at the fireside with her new baby at her breast while they waited for John to join them, was not reassuring. She hesitated for a moment before saying, 'I don't know. But I think John fears he may have done.'

Elizabeth suspected that Dorothy and her husband knew a good deal more about the business than they were prepared to say. 'Did you know about this beforehand?' she asked, though she was afraid of what the answer might be. What if she should find that her own daughter had allowed her brother to put his head into a noose, even if it was one of his own foolish making?

To her relief Dorothy shook her head. 'No. Though I think there were those who did. John says the Royalist groups are riddled with spies. And always falling out among themselves too.'

Elizabeth frowned, trying to gather together all the implications of what she had heard. 'Then where is Cuthbert now?'

'In hiding perhaps,' suggested Dorothy. 'Even overseas.' She smiled suddenly. 'The next thing you know you'll likely have a letter from him from wherever our father is now.'

'Antwerp,' said Elizabeth. 'At least, that's where he last wrote from.' She had brought the letter with her, since it had arrived only last night. She took it from her pocket and passed it to Dorothy, who began to read, as far as the demands of her child and her mother's talk would allow. 'You'll see your father thinks I should write to Susannah Fawcett to ask how she does,' said Elizabeth. 'You know he wrote when we heard of the Doctor's death, and she did not reply.'

'I don't know why he should be anxious about her,' said Dorothy crisply. 'She's not one who'd ever need looking after.'

Elizabeth's smile was, like her daughter's, laced with a little gentle malice. 'That's what I thought.' She felt again the unexpected pleasure of this equal and comfortable relationship with her daughter.

Then John came in and they saw at once that something was wrong. 'I've just heard,' he said gravely. 'Three of the Royalist conspirators were arrested last night at Jesmond. I'm afraid one of them was Cuthbert.'

Elizabeth had not thought things could get any worse than they already were. But they went on doing so, even after Cuthbert's arrest.

It was bad enough at first, for she would lie awake night after night, imagining Cuthbert transported to the West Indies, there like so many others to wear out his life in cruel slavery; or hanged at Tyburn; or shut up for life in some disease-ridden dungeon, worse even than the bleak cell where he was held in Newcastle. She longed for Ralph's comforting presence, his advice and his strength. As it was, she shrank even from telling him what had happened. Possibly he would hear soon enough anyway, by whatever means the Royalists used to communicate with the exiled court. But, in any case, there was nothing he could do to help her now, or to save his son. She thought, bitterly, that the royal cause had cost her family more than anyone had any right to ask.

At first, John was reassuring. Cuthbert was a very minor conspirator – a youngster led astray – and would quickly be released, once he had answered any questions they put to him.

But perhaps Cuthbert refused to answer them (he was certainly silent and sullen towards his mother on the few occasions when Elizabeth was allowed to visit him); perhaps the authorities thought him more important than he actually was; perhaps he had indeed been more deeply implicated than even John Bolam, with his inside knowledge of the situation, realised. Whatever the reason, months passed and Cuthbert remained in prison.

Meanwhile, even the most uninvolved Royalists realised that they were to be made to pay for the folly of the few. Twelve of Oliver's most trusted senior officers were promoted to the rank of Major-General and given a district to control. Major-General John Lambert was appointed to the northern counties, but being closely occupied in London delegated his duties in Northumberland to Colonel Charles Howard, and in Durham and Yorkshire to Colonel Robert Lilburne, who was already governor of York. It was to York that Cuthbert was transferred, some time in the autumn.

In each district the Major-Generals were to raise a new militia force, to keep the peace, and to pay for it the lands of active Royalists were confiscated and a ferocious new decimation tax was imposed on everyone of Royalist sympathies: ten per cent of everything they owned, whether land or personal possessions. The Liddells by now had nothing left to confiscate and were too poor to be liable for the tax, but they felt the repressive measures that came in with it as harshly as did everyone else. There seemed to be soldiers everywhere, and several times during the summer and autumn the house was thoroughly and ruthlessly searched. Even the smallest and most innocuous gathering with their friends was closely watched. They could travel no distance at all – not even to market – without permission from the authorities, which would often be refused for no very good reason. If it had not been for John's influence, Elizabeth would not even have been able to visit Cuthbert, just as it was John's money that paid her travelling expenses. Each time she visited Cuthbert, she herself was taken aside for half an hour or so of questioning, before being allowed to go home.

'I could bear anything, if only I could have just one letter from your father!' she said to Dorothy, one bitter day in December. It was in fact Christmas Day, but under the new régime celebration of a day so tainted with pagan associations was forbidden, so that it had become just another ordinary Tuesday. But that could not stop Elizabeth from knowing it was Christmas and from remembering past Christmases shared with friends and family, and so she had gone to call on Dorothy, in the hope that, without being told, her daughter would understand.

Dorothy hugged her. 'I expect his letters have just gone astray, the way they do sometimes,' she said.

By which she meant to imply that Ralph's letters must have fallen prey to the Lord Protector's efficient spy service, which was what Elizabeth told herself in her more rational moments. Unfortunately, she had no means of knowing that for certain, and could not help fearing that some harm might have befallen her husband. 'If I could only be sure . . .' She could not go on, for the constriction in her throat.

'I know he's well,' said Dorothy. 'I feel it in my bones.' She paused. 'One day, all this will be behind us. Even the hotheads among the Royalists will see they can't change things, and then they'll be reconciled, and father will be able to come home, and Cuthbert too. You'll see.'

'All I can say is, the Protector's going a strange way about it, if he wants reconciliation,' said Elizabeth drily.

'I didn't hear that,' said Dorothy with a smile. Elizabeth knew it was a gentle warning to be more careful what she said – not before her daughter, or John, who would never betray her, but in public, where any careless word might bring trouble on her head. 'Things will get better. I'm sure of it.' Then she said, with a casualness that, to her mother, seemed almost deliberate, 'I wonder if father did go and see Lady Milburn.' It was something he had mentioned in his last letter, which they had not discussed, because the news of Cuthbert's arrest had driven every other thought from their heads. *I remember that my Lady Milburn was said to have entered a convent in Antwerp*, Ralph had written. *I think to make enquiries and see if I might speak with her, if she is still living. She may be comforted to talk of her son.*

Elizabeth studied her daughter's face. 'You don't regret . . .?'

Dorothy caught the anxious note in her mother's voice, and smiled. 'That I didn't marry my Lord Milburn? Oh, that was a dream. My heart was never touched at all. I only thought it was. I didn't know him in the least. I think if I had I might not even have liked him.' She was silent for a moment, remembering those days that now seemed as remote as a fairy-tale, and as little to do with her life. 'I thought I was happy then, I suppose. Yet even if the war had never happened, even if I could have been sure of wealth and position and everything – no, I wouldn't change what I have now.' She smiled again, softly, her face a little pink. 'I wouldn't change John for anyone in all the world.'

Elizabeth put an arm about her. 'I never thought I'd ever say it, but I'm glad you wed him. He's a good man, and a kind one. He's the only one who's been able to make life bearable for us. He may be a Roundhead, but you couldn't have done better.' Then they went to dinner, which was more lavish than usual, almost worthy of Christmas Day.

1656

CHAPTER FORTY-FOUR

For the fifth time in a fortnight Daniel came home from school with visible bruises, a cut lip, torn clothes and an offhand explanation – a quarrel, a tumble, a rough game of football – that did not convince his mother at all.

He was silent through supper and went to his room straight afterwards. A few hours later he woke again with a nightmare, shouting into the July night until Susannah came to him. She sat on the side of the bed, holding him in her arms, murmuring the usual soothing words, trying to get him to tell her what he had dreamed. As usual, he would tell her nothing. This time, exasperated, she said, 'Daniel, this has gone on too long. I want the truth. Is it something at school?'

'I've told no lies,' he returned, with a hint of indignation.

'I know. But thou's said nothing at all, and I want to know. The other boys – they're setting on thee. That's it, isn't it?' He was silent. 'Daniel, is it because thou'rt a bastard?' Yet there never used to be trouble, as far as she knew, beyond the odd bit of name calling. She saw him shake his head. 'Daniel, tell me!'

When he spoke at last, what he said made her go cold. 'It's for being thy son – and thou a Quaker woman.' It all came out then, and she realised it was not after all a new thing, only grown worse lately. Since the moment he first went to school last March the other boys had picked on him, because of his mother's notoriety as a disturber of church services, a preacher in market-places, a vociferous publiciser of her new faith. There were other Quaker children in school, but their parents were rather more quiet about it, and securely married. Taken all together, the counts had mounted up against Daniel. She felt a horrible shame that her child should have suffered so long and she should not have known. 'Why did thou not tell me?'

'We should glory to suffer for the Lord's sake,' he said in a small voice.

She felt as if an icy hand had clutched at her heart. *It's not for the Lord's sake, but for mine*, said a small intrusive voice in her head. She held him close and kissed him. 'I shall seek the Lord in this, to know what I must do.' She had thought she knew. It had seemed clear to her that the spirit was sending her out to cry from the rooftops the truth that she had seen. Yet could it be right to be the cause of such misery to her child? Was it possible to look towards the light and yet be mistaken as to what it seemed to show her?

She knew she would not sleep again that night, so as soon as it began to grow light she walked up on to the fell, to the highest point where the whole dale was laid before her, grey and shadowed but for the gleam of the river. She stood with the wind catching at her skirt and her cloak, feeling a faint prickle of rain on her skin, and tried in the solitude to see what was right.

She knew that she was called, as was every human creature, to play a part in the Lamb's war, against the evil and corruption of the world. She knew, and thought she accepted, that to do so would inevitably bring suffering. Yet suffering for herself was one thing; for her child was quite another. Was that simply a mother's weakness, to be put aside?

She thought, I must not reason it out, I must not ask questions, just look and see what the spirit shows me. She closed her eyes, saw only the patterns of light and shade behind her eyelids, heard the roar of the wind, growing stronger as day broke, and then through it the long whirring call of a curlew. It was full of desolation, almost human in its loneliness and despair. Then she thought it was indeed a human voice, calling her name, calling and calling; then not one voice, but many, clamorous and insistent.

She felt as though she were in a great hall, bare of comforts, like so many she had worked in during the war, and around her, too many for the few beds, dumped just as they were in corners, passageways, anywhere there was the least space, lay wounded men, terribly wounded, their cries echoing in her ears. She saw them reach out bloody hands to her in supplication, begging for help; some clutched at her skirts, their grasping hands crooked in agony.

Then, instead, she was at the door of a farmhouse bedroom, where a woman was dying horribly from a difficult labour, while husband and children, gathered about her bed, turned mute, anguished faces towards the door. Worst of all, tearing at her heart, she saw Daniel bruised and bleeding in the midst of a crowd of boys, and they were hitting and kicking at him, their voices jeering, while he fought desperately, helplessly, and could not fend them off, and his voice cried to her: 'Mother! Mother!' and grew fainter and fainter until it faded to nothing and she could see him no more.

So much suffering, and none of it was her suffering, or even suffering that served any useful purpose that she could see. She opened her eyes and her gaze fell at once on her hands: small brown hands, strong and supple. Healing hands, Anne Greatorex had called them once, in awed tones. She had been right. In these hands, the hands of an ordinary human woman, lay the power to heal the suffering she had seen and much like it, a power given to her by the same spirit that was showing her these things. Christ was in that spirit, and in her, but she saw that He was not Christ the scourer of the Temple, Christ whose tongue lashed priests and hypocrites, Christ the judge. That Christ was for others to show to the world. For her, through her, Christ was the healer, the person who raised the sick and the dying, gave sight to the blind and made the lame walk.

He was the teacher, too. That also she saw, for she had a mind as well as hands. For months, years even, she had left her notes and her books untouched, neglecting her studies as things that were no longer important. But they were important, she saw that now, for she had experience and intelligence and understanding, which, put together, might one day help other healers in their work.

It seemed so obvious that she was astonished she could have been so blind. Once again her own pride, her desire to be first, had clouded her vision and caused her to neglect what was right. Now, looking clear-eyed at the light, she saw that it was for others, not herself, to seek deliberately to be sufferers and martyrs for the truth. She might have suffering thrust upon her, by chance, in the doing of a task set before her, but that would be incidental, and certainly not to be sought out. She had thought that because her life had been changed, then it must change in every detail, even to its central purpose. She knew that more than once she had been so concerned with bearing public witness to her new faith that she had neglected a patient, by putting off a necessary visit or giving too little time once she was there. It had taken her son's suffering to make her see what she was doing. She was not asked to make any kind of compromise; simply to walk back into the light.

She reached home just as Daniel, silent and heavy-eyed, came down for breakfast. 'Would thou rather leave school and have me teach thee at home, as I used to do?' she asked, and at once his relief seemed to fill the house.

She had meant it for the best, sending him to school as soon as he reached his eighth birthday, so that he should not be set apart from other children, so that he should learn to cope with the rough and tumble of everyday life. She knew that others would say she ought to teach him to stand up for himself, that if she were simply to take him away from school she would turn him into a milksop. But she was not prepared to go on living with his misery.

The next day was first day and the Quakers met as usual at the Dowthwaites' farm. Susannah told her companions what had happened and how she had seen that she ought to confine her activities to healing, and after some silent consideration of the matter they seemed to think she had come to the right decision. That was a relief, though she knew quite well that she would have acted no differently even in the face of their disapproval.

After that, one of the members told them how he had decided he must renounce music, though he had a fine voice and loved to sing. It was, he said, a vanity and a thing of darkness. That brought a murmur of approval too, and Susannah saw Daniel cast an anxious glance in her direction. He said nothing until they were on their way home, when he at once burst out, 'I can still have music lessons, can't I?'

Susannah hesitated. She suspected that Daniel felt about music much as she did about medicine, but that did not mean they could be looked at in the same way, for there was no sense in which music could be said to be useful to mankind. On the other hand, she could not bear to deprive him of something that meant so much to him, especially at the moment. In the end she said only, 'That must be for thy conscience.' He gave the matter a moment's thought, and then broke into a relieved grin, at which she had an uneasy sense that she was evading her responsibilities. He was, after all, only a child.

Daniel's nightmares ceased at once, and the next day Susannah began to teach him at home, as her father had taught her, and with as many interruptions for calls on patients, though Daniel never asked to go with her when she went out. He preferred to stay at home and practise his music, and the sound of his playing would greet her whenever she came home. Unmusical though she was, she found herself taking a certain guilty pleasure in it, which was, she supposed, a measure of how far he had already progressed.

For three weeks after leaving school Daniel, visibly happy, continued to ride each Thursday – fifth day – to his music lessons. Then on the fourth Thursday he suddenly returned home only two hours after leaving, with tears smudging his face. 'The soldiers came for Nicholas Lobley, mother, yesterday,' he said. 'They took him away.' He seemed to know nothing more about it, though he shed a few further tears, from disappointment. Susannah was glad she had not forbidden his lessons, but glad too that they had come to an end.

It did not take long to discover what had happened to the music master, for by next market day it was being talked of everywhere. Susannah broke the news to Daniel as gently as she could. 'He has deceived us all, most shamefully,' she said. 'All the time he was not a true music master, but a Royalist in disguise. It was a good disguise too, for he went from house to house and no one suspected he was carrying messages for Charles Stuart. Be comforted, my love. Thou'rt well rid of him.'

There was no display of indignation from Daniel, only a few moments of complete silence, while he looked profoundly thoughtful. Then he said, 'How did they find out?'

'I think Colonel Lilburne had it from questioning one of the Royalists they took last year.'

There was nothing unusual in the sight of soldiers riding or marching through Thornside. One morning in August Susannah heard them before she saw them, the hooves echoing between the houses as they came down the street from the north, harness jingling. It was scarcely light, but she had been up all night with a difficult labour and was just going upstairs to snatch a little sleep. She glanced out of the window as she went, expecting to see the soldiers ride on past the church and down the hill. Instead, they turned into the lane and came on just a few yards, and then halted noisily outside the house. She heard orders shouted, and a clatter of horses along the passage and then in the stable yard, though most of the troopers were still in the lane. They had surrounded the house, preventing escape – from what? There was no possible reason for unease, yet she felt her heart thud. Then there came a loud hammering on the front door. By the time she reached it, Margaret already had it open.

The Captain of the troop stepped into the hall and Susannah went to meet him, trying to hide her apprehension. 'Mistress Fawcett?' enquired the man. 'Mother of Daniel Fawcett?'

That did frighten her. She even found herself wondering if her son was, as she had supposed, still sleeping safely upstairs in his room. 'Yes,' she said, as calmly as she could.

'Then you're to come with us. The boy too.'

'He's only eight years old. What interest can you possibly have in him?'

'He's the one that's wanted. That's all I know.'

'Who wants him?'

'Colonel Lilburne. We're to take you to York.'

She had sometimes thought of going to York again, but not like this. Peered at by maliciously inquisitive neighbours, they were mounted together on one of their own horses and escorted through the wakening streets of Thornside, out on to the road past the Hall, eastward through the dale. That night they stayed at Boroughbridge, and the next morning were transferred to a coach for the rest of the journey.

Until she came to York, Susannah's main concern had been to reassure Daniel, who in any case seemed calm enough, and more anxious to care for her than to be cared for. Once in York, she almost forgot her son. Old memories swept over her. She peered from the coach at houses repaired and rebuilt and streets busy with the bustle occasioned by the elections to the second Parliament of the Protectorate. They entered the city by Micklegate Bar and she glimpsed Aunt Judith's house, no longer hers, for she had sold it last year. There were two soldiers standing talking on the steps. Then there was the house where Ralph had lodged and news had come of Marston Moor; and a man had faced her on the stairs, in the dark. Then on over the Ouse bridge, where she and Ludovick, exhausted, with chaos about them, had talked so strangely. And the river-bank, where they had first kissed. So many memories, suddenly more alive than they had been for years.

'Mother, thou's not listening!'

It was true enough. Daniel had been pointing eagerly to this and that as they went, and she had heard none of it. She had not even noticed that the coach had stopped and the soldier who had been seated inside had got out, to argue with a carter whose wagon was causing an obstruction in the street ahead of them. She looked down at Daniel, stroking his hair – dark silken curls, like his father's – and found herself saying suddenly, 'I first met thy father here.'

She had never spoken of him to Daniel before, beyond what was necessary to explain to him, in answer to a question asked long ago, what a bastard was. Now her son looked sharply up at her, the excitements of York driven from his head. She realised then that his silence on the subject of his father did not come from indifference. 'Who is he, mother?'

'A man I loved once, who is now dead,' she said. 'One day I'll tell thee about him, when thou'rt a man.' The soldier climbed back into the coach, so she put a finger to her lips, warning Daniel to ask no more questions. She supposed the man was there to listen to their conversation, in the hope of hearing something incriminating – and how was she to know what might be incriminating, when she had no idea at all why they had been brought here?

They were taken to the castle, to a room where they were to be lodged until such time as Colonel Lilburne was ready to see them. It was reasonably comfortable and a good supper was ready on the table, but the window was too high and too small for them to see out and the door was barred on the outside, and Susannah knew it was a prison. She reassured Daniel yet again. 'We have nothing to fear. We have done no wrong.' She wished she could as easily reassure herself.

They were taken before Colonel Lilburne the next morning. As they entered the room, the soldier by the door removed Daniel's hat, as a parent might do for a child forgetful of his manners. Daniel shot him a reproachful glance, snatched the hat and replaced it firmly on his head. Susannah was afraid there was going to be an unpleasant incident, but from behind a desk a man said good-humouredly, 'Let him be, Corporal.'

There were in fact two men behind the desk. Beside the sturdy russet-haired figure of the senior officer who was evidently Colonel Lilburne, sat the tall, elegant man who had spoken. He was about

Susannah's own age and she did not immediately recognise him, though something stirred in her mind. He seemed to be there simply to observe the proceedings, for it was the Colonel who spoke next. 'Please sit down, mistress. This is your son, then. Come here, child.' He beckoned to the boy to come closer to the table.

Susannah held Daniel where he was, just in front of her. 'What business hast thou with children, Robert Lilburne?'

'Sir – you call me sir.' He said it more as a matter of routine than as a rebuke.

'Thine own brother's turned Friend, Robert Lilburne. Thou should know we don't use worldly honours.' John Lilburne, from his latest prison in Dover castle, had recently published an account of his conversion to Quakerism.

Before the Colonel could say anything more, his companion had laid a hand on his arm. 'One moment, Robert – Mistress, I feel sure we have met somewhere before.'

'We have, John Lambert,' she said, for it had all come back to her now. 'I was with the northern army, in the first years of the war. With my father, Doctor Matthew Fawcett.'

'Of course – I remember well. You did good service for our wounded men. More than one owed his life to you.' He turned to look at Daniel. 'So this is Doctor Fawcett's grandson.' He paused. 'Are you a truthful child, Daniel Fawcett?' Daniel nodded so eagerly that his hat almost fell off.

Susannah wondered how much – if anything – the Major-General knew of her story. He had made no comment on the fact that her child bore her name, rather than that of a husband, and his manner towards them was quite without censure. All the same, his next question made her catch her breath from shock. 'Tell me, my child, do you hear from your father?'

'His father's dead!' She spoke sharply, from the sudden pain that shot through her.

She saw John Lambert look at her closely. 'Is that so? Yet in view of what we have heard . . . His father was kin to the Middletons of Ivelet, was he not?'

'Not at all. He has no living kin that I know of.' She felt as if she were feeling her way blindly through a mist, not knowing where she was going or why, not able to see what lay in the shadows, threatening her and Daniel. Ludovick had lodged with the Middletons that lovely summer. It seemed as if someone knew something, had even carried tales to the authorities. But what could that have to do with her son?

Lambert returned his attention to Daniel. 'You have been often at Ivelet?'

The child hesitated for long enough to allow Susannah to say, 'Indeed he has not! What possible reason could he have to go there?'

'That is what I hope to discover.' He smiled reassuringly at Daniel, who had gone fiery red. 'Well, child?'

'Yes, I went there sometimes.' He shot a swift, penitent glance at his mother, who stared at him in dismay. She felt as if the ground were cracking under her feet, as if she might at any moment find it had fallen away altogether.

Lambert reached for one of the papers in front of him and glanced at it. 'Three times in February and March last year. Twice in the autumn. Again five times this year. Is that right?'

Daniel nodded. 'Yes. I think so.' His voice came in a whisper. It was obvious to Susannah that he was frightened, as she was too by now.

'For what purpose were these visits made?'

'On a message for Nicholas Lobley.'

'And who is Nicholas Lobley?'

'My music master.'

So that was it! By some means the music master had entangled her innocent child in his plotting. Susannah felt a surge of fury. If the man had been there now she did not think she could have answered for her behaviour. Furious, half disbelieving, she heard the questioning continue. 'What were the messages about?'

'Music lessons. I think.' But it was obvious he knew now that they had been about nothing of the kind.

'Is that what Master Lobley told you?'

'He never said. I thought—' Daniel looked frozen, for young as he was he knew enough to understand the implications of what was being said.

Susannah broke in, 'Canst thou not see he knows nothing? If I'd known what that man was doing, I'd have sent word to thee at once, believe me!' Then she turned Daniel round to face her. 'Why did thou not tell me? How could thou keep it from me?'

He bent his head. 'He said I should not, for thou might not like it.'

'He was right about that!'

'I thought thou'd stop me going. I thought—' He began to cry. 'I'm sorry, truly I'm sorry!'

She held him, trying to console him. Over his head she looked at the two men. 'I beg you, let us go. He's answered your questions.'

'I'm sorry, mistress,' said Lambert, 'but we must ask a little further. It may be your son has not yet told us everything.' He came round the table and crouched beside Daniel, an arm about him. It was obvious, Susannah thought, feeling just a little reassured, that he had children of his own. 'Now, my child, we accuse thee of nothing, understand that. But you must do your best to help us. Will you do that?' Daniel nodded.

The questions seemed to go on for hours, again and again: What had Daniel done when he arrived at the house at Ivelet? Who had he spoken to? What form had the messages taken? Had he carried any answers back to the music master? Had there been other errands? His answers were innocent enough: there had been cakes from the old lady there, a large dog to fondle, and once he had been asked to sing for them and they had declared that he sang like an angel. Susannah thought, uneasily: Did they see the likeness to his father? But it did not seem that they had asked any pertinent questions or made any undue comment, so she thought that perhaps for those not expecting it, those who did not look every day for the traces of his father in his face, they would not be so obvious. In any case, perhaps it did not much matter now. What mattered was not the past but the present.

It ended at last. John Lambert patted the boy's shoulder and said, 'That's enough for now, young Daniel. But if you call to mind anything else, then you'll send word to us, won't you?' He glanced at Susannah, and she nodded her agreement. He walked with them to the door. 'Your good father – he is well? I seem to recall he was wounded at Bradford.'

'He died five years ago.'

'I'm sorry. He was a good man. He had a passion for tulips, I remember.'

'Yes.'

'I should have liked to call and talk of them with him one day. We tulipomaniacs are never lost for somewhat to say. I'm sorry that will never now be possible. I have a fine collection in my garden at Wimbledon.'

*

Soldiers came to Thornside again that year, towards the end of December, late one afternoon, three of them clattering over the frosty ground and dismounting in the lane before the house. Susannah, seeing them, drew a deep breath and waited for the knock, and, when it came, told Margaret she would answer it and walked as calmly as she could to the door.

'Mistress Fawcett?' Again! she thought. 'Letters for you from Colonel Lilburne.'

She felt a great sense of relief – for surely there could be no harm in a letter – and asked the men in. The senior of them, a corporal, handed her a package, neatly addressed to herself. She sent the men, in Margaret's care, to the kitchen to refresh themselves, and then carried her package to the stillroom, where she opened it. There were two letters inside, which Colonel Lilburne had forwarded to her. The first, to her astonishment, proved to come from Nicholas Lobley, written from his prison in York, and expressed his deep regret at having involved her innocent son in his schemes. He promised her that he had not taken on the child with that intention in mind, and hoped that the boy would continue to practise his music and take pleasure in it, in spite of everything. Susannah was not much mollified, and decided that she would say nothing of the letter to Daniel. She had half expected him, when they returned from York, to smash all his musical instruments in pieces and renounce any interest in music for ever, in view of its associations. But he had done nothing of the kind. It was clear that he loved it too much to be so easily put off.

The other communication, carefully wrapped, surprised her even more. It came from John Lambert, and was not a letter at all but a delicate and beautifully observed painting of a tulip, just such a one as her father had loved best, flame-red and white. A brief message came with it: *In memory of much past kindness and with regret that our last meeting was not of the happiest*. She gathered that the Major-General had painted it himself, and was greatly touched by the gesture, especially as he must have many other weightier matters on his mind.

She went to the kitchen then to see how the troopers were faring. She found them seated cheerfully about the table with Margaret's freshly baked bread in front of them, and her home-brewed ale, and a good piece of cheese. Susannah sat down too. 'Have you heard what's to become of James Nayler?' she asked, as soon as there was a break in the talk. It was a matter that had been in all their minds for many weeks now. The previous October James Nayler, perhaps the most loved Quaker preacher, had ridden in an ecstatic state into Bristol on a donkey, with a company of women strewing the road before him with palms and chanting 'Hosanna!' His fellow Quakers, however uneasy about the incident, saw in it a symbolic reenactment of Palm Sunday, a reminder that Christ's spirit dwelt in every human being. To nearly everyone else it was blasphemy of a terrible kind. He had instantly been hauled before Parliament and found guilty after a trial of dubious legality. The sentence was expected any day now.

The Corporal put down his tankard and looked troubled. 'Aye,' he said slowly, 'though the thought of it's cheerless seasoning for good food.'

'They've not condemned him to death?' Susannah felt herself go cold.

'No, he was spared that, though by just fourteen votes. Maybe death would have been more merciful. He's to be pilloried and whipped the first day, then two days later the same again, and branded and his tongue bored through with a hot iron. Then he's to be taken to Bristol and whipped again there.'

There was a silence. Susannah saw that Margaret, standing near the fire, had gone very pale. She was glad that Daniel was not there to hear. The sound of his lute came to them from somewhere upstairs, all sweet carefree innocence. 'That was Parliament's doing?' she said at last.

'Aye. That's the kind of Parliament we have ruling us, after all the years we fought for freedom. There were men spoke against it, a few – Lambert one of them, as you'd suppose. And they say Oliver told them they had no right to impose such a sentence. He's always hated persecution for religion's sake.'

'Aye. Ever a seeker after truth, Oliver,' said one of the other troopers. 'I reckon that's why he's letting the Jews back into England – so he can debate with them.'

'It's a pity his Parliament aren't of the same mind,' added the Corporal, 'but they paid no heed to him at all. And Nayler's not a strong man to begin with. God help him.'

'Maybe if Oliver had been King he could have stopped it,' said the third trooper, though a little warily, as if he knew he was expressing a dangerous opinion.

'We didn't take arms to make him King,' the Corporal retorted.

'I heard Lambert's opposed to him taking the crown,' said Susannah. 'But that he's on the way down, and it's men like Roger Boyle have Oliver's ear now.'

Roger Boyle, Lord Broghill, had begun his career in the King's service in his native Ireland, until Cromwell won him over.

'Aye. Old Cavaliers, all of them. Let's hope he sees sense.' The Corporal drank appreciatively from his tankard. 'Good ale this.'

In the spring the rule of the Major-Generals came to an end; and Oliver Cromwell refused the crown. His refusal brought relief to the Army, but made little difference otherwise. Dressed in purple and ermine, saluted by fanfares of trumpets, Oliver was ceremonially installed all over again as Lord Protector under the terms of a new constitution, which reinstated the House of Lords, after a fashion, and allowed him to choose his successor.

Once, everyone had thought that John Lambert, his most trusted second-in-command, would succeed him, when the time came. Now they knew he never would, for in the course of the long debate about the crown an unbridgeable gulf had opened between the two men. Lambert retired to his Wimbledon property, to cultivate his tulips in tranquillity.

1657

CHAPTER FORTY-FIVE

To have looked for the coming of the end of time, and then to see all their hopes shrivel away to nothing . . . It would have been a bitter thing, for one who did not know, as Walter Barras did, that God's spirit worked in all men; who did not know that struggle and pain were a part of the Lamb's War, which all, led by the spirit, were called to fight.

Yet the journey south in the summer rains tested him to the utmost. He had to struggle with every step he took not to question the way things had gone. There had been the exuberant growth of the past years, the fire spreading so fast, setting light to so many, until it had seemed as if the whole nation must be consumed by it. Day after day the numbers had grown, and day after day their enemies had dwindled. Even Oliver in his palace had heard Quakers with a kindly ear.

And then had come the step too far, the journey James Nayler made into Bristol, and the savage vengeance of Parliament seeking to hit at a power of which they were becoming terrified, as every hardened sinner must be in the face of God's imminent judgement.

Nayler's suffering ought to have made no difference – after all, to suffer for the Lord's sake was an intrinsic part of the Lamb's war – but every one of them had somehow found him or herself taking stock, standing back, trying to see if they might have been mistaken in the way they thought the light led them. Most scarcely faltered, except that the power in the land shifted firmly against them. Everywhere, justices sent Friends to gaol, where they were held in the most dreadful conditions. In villages and towns they were stoned and beaten. Even in the army the senior command turned on them, at least in Scotland.

So now Walter was leaving that country behind, turning his face to the south. It was a long way from Scotland to London, hundreds of miles, and with every step he was cutting himself off from the past, from all the years of soldiering, from the men who had for so long been his only family, his only friends. Except that those closest to him were leaving too, because they had no choice. Quakerism had swept through the army, in Scotland as elsewhere, given impetus by preachers who sought out the soldiers and declared their inspiring message. Walter's troop had, like others, quickly become a small nest of Quakerism. Though he was a captain, no mere trooper called him 'sir' or removed his hat or showed him any deference, and he did not expect it or ask it, for were they not all equal before God, in the light? They did their duty as soldiers, as before, with loyalty and courage and firmness, but only as the light allowed. They all knew that if once the spirit commanded otherwise, then no earthly order could be obeyed.

It was not perhaps much like the army discipline learned under Fairfax, but it had worked, and they had become a close-knit and fervent troop. Unfortunately, the army in Scotland was under the command of General Monck, a brusque practical soldier of Presbyterian sympathies and a dubious private life, who had no liking at all for Quakers. Exasperated by their growth, he had at last ordered the cashiering of all resolute Quakers in his army. Walter had been among those dismissed.

He had sought the guidance of the light, parted lovingly from his friends and set off towards London, which was the only home he knew, outside the army. He had a little money saved. He must make of it what he could.

Once across the border he followed a sudden impulse and turned aside from the road and made his way to Blackheugh. He had not seen that once-familiar countryside since he was a child of ten. It looked much as he remembered it – except for the house, that splendid mansion, so impressive in memory, now utterly decayed, the formal Italianate garden so overgrown that you could not tell it had ever been a garden, the stable yard knee-high with weeds. Whoever now owned the place clearly had no wish to live so remote from civilisation. They had even taken some of the stones of which the house was constructed for some other building project.

There were visible holes in the roof too. Walter looked at it all with a sense of triumph. In so short a time, all that splendour come to nothing, everything wiped out almost without trace! There was some justice after all. It was a slight compensation for the knowledge that after all the years of war very little else had really changed.

He reached London at evening on the last day of August and, seeking lodgings, made his way towards Aldersgate. The Mouth had been the meeting place of Levellers in the old days, and was now, he was told, a haunt of Quakers. If the inn could not give him a room, then someone there might know who would.

He had almost reached the inn when he found himself caught up in a crowd, sober enough, but determined. It carried him along a little way and then began to press against the houses on either side of the street, leaving the road clear. Just coming into sight at the end of the street, roughly from the direction of the Mouth, was a small procession. It was a moment more before Walter saw that it was a funeral cortège. The coffin was plain, a poor man's coffin, undraped by any pall, and the men carrying it and walking with it had their heads covered. There were no torches, no carriages, no mourning clothes, and no bell tolled. Yet it was this the crowd had come to see. 'Who's died?' he asked a young woman standing beside him.

'John Lilburne,' she said.

The years seemed to roll back, to a world long gone. That fiery spirit had been quenched at last, and somehow all Walter's youth had gone with it. He felt a terrible sadness, a sense of loss deeper than any he had felt before. The end of things – but the end he had dreamed of had been a time of fierce and noisy struggle, bringing about the destruction of evil and the coming of the Lord's day, not this sad dying of greatness and fire and youth.

'So plain a funeral.' There should have been grandeur, massive displays of ceremonial grief . . .

'Thou thinks him worthy of hat-honour then?'

He realised that, unthinkingly, instinctively, he had taken off his hat. He replaced it, blushing that he should so easily have returned to the old carnal ways – in his thoughts as well as his actions. Then he realised what her words implied. 'Thou's a Friend then?'

She nodded. 'Like Friend John himself. And thee?'

'Yes.' She was a small neat person, with gentle hazel eyes and a face that was comely without being beautiful. The sense of loss and bereavement faded. He was not alone, for his hero had died in the faith, and he had found one of his own kind here too. Past and present were linked in this moment. 'I'm just come back to London, from the army. I know no one here any more.'

She smiled. 'Thou has Friends.' She paused. 'I'm called Dorcas. And thee?'

He told her, while he wondered if she was married. Then he remembered that he still was himself. For the first time in many months he gave a fleeting thought to Esther, and wondered what she was doing now. Then he pushed her from his mind and went with Dorcas and the rest of the throng to watch the simple interment of the great Leveller.

1658

CHAPTER FORTY-SIX

Even though she did not then know what a difference it was to make to her, Elizabeth Liddell recognised that it was no ordinary storm. She lay all through the night of Friday September the third hearing the wind batter the house, the rain lash the windows, and knew that in the morning it would not be a question of whether any damage had been done, but how much, and what it would cost to put it right. That was the constant question these days – how much?

In fact, it was not as bad as she had feared. There was a tree down, but at least it could be used for firewood, and it had not fallen on anything that mattered, unlike a heavy branch near the orchard which had demolished a hen house. Then, part of the stable roof stood in need of repair, but when they had so few horses that did not matter so very much. Cuthbert even proved willing to tackle some of the work himself.

He had been released from prison early in July, returning home in much the same sullen frame of mind as he had left it, but at least he was safe. That had been the first clear sign that things were getting better, the first thing that gave Elizabeth hope that the years of loneliness and drudgery might after all be coming to an end. The Lord Protector did indeed seem to be working for conciliation with his old enemies, now that he had more power in his own hands. His former army friends seemed of little account these days: John Lambert, who had such strong support among those who wanted fundamental reform, was living in retirement, and other army leaders, while still within the government, had little influence any more. Oliver had even fallen out with Fairfax, though that was because his former commander had last year married his daughter Mary to the staunchly Royalist Duke of Buckingham, friend of the exiled Charles II. The Protector was so firmly established that Elizabeth sometimes found it hard to remember what it had been like when England had a King. Only a few hotheads, among whom even Cuthbert no longer counted himself, thought there was any point in Royalist plotting. Many exiled Royalists had come back to England, to live peacefully at home.

It was around the time of Cuthbert's release that Elizabeth received a letter from Ralph, the first for a long time. She had to read it through several times before she took in what he was telling her: that he was seriously considering returning home. Since then, she had lived in a state of hope, expectation and daily disappointment that left her constantly exhausted. Even without the storm, she would not have slept much that September night, for she never slept well. When Ralph's home, she thought, then I shall sleep again; once the first greetings are over. The thought of them set her trembling with anticipation.

Two days after the storm, the first whispers began to reach them – a rumour, passed on by Dorothy. Then, a day later, firm news that could not be denied. While the storm had been raging over England, Oliver Cromwell had died.

He was not young, and he had been unwell lately, but no one had expected this. Yet, for all the suddenness of it, there was little sign of any consternation in the country at large. Things went on much as they always had. 'Richard Cromwell is sworn in as Protector,' John Bolam told Elizabeth, the day after they heard of Oliver's death. Richard was Oliver's eldest son, a quiet country gentleman who was neither soldier nor statesman, which was a hopeful sign for the future. Things were not likely to change very much, Elizabeth thought. Ralph would still be able to come home.

Two weeks after the storm, she returned from market at Bishop Auckland to find Cuthbert watching for her outside the door, though it was raining and he was already soaked through. She thought that his eyes looked red, but it was hard to tell in the rain. He took her arm and steered her inside. 'Come and sit down, Mother,' he said, very gently. In the parlour, John Bolam was waiting, and Dorothy. Elizabeth felt her breath stop in her throat. Somehow she knew, even before Cuthbert tried to speak and then could not get out the words. John said, his voice very quiet in the silence, 'I fear there's bad news.'

'Ralph,' she whispered.

John nodded. 'He was on his way home, a fortnight since. The ship foundered. I'm sorry.'

She stood up and went to the window and looked out at the rain, and thought, 'He will never come back now. It was the last time, after Worcester, when we did not make love.' She had a sudden craving for sleep, deep dreamless sleep from which she would not wake, ever again; or only to find this was all a nightmare and Ralph was alive after all. But there was no time for sleep. There was more to be done than ever. 'I sold everything I took with me today. I must go and write up the accounts.'

'No, mother, not now,' said Cuthbert. 'There'll be time enough for that.' Then he hugged her, tenderly, warmly, as he had not done since he was a boy.

1659

CHAPTER FORTY-SEVEN

The snow rattled on the window, driven by a sudden fiercer gust of wind. Inside the house there was only silence, except for the sound of Daniel's laboured breathing, and the incongruously triumphant words running through her head: *The Lord Jesus Christ is come to reign; now shall the Lamb and Saints have victory . . .*

Susannah did not know why she should so suddenly have thought of them. They were George Fox's, from *The Lamb's Officer*, printed earlier this year, and John Dowthwaite had read them at Meeting in the farmhouse kitchen on a bright day last May. They had seemed to sum up all the hope of that time, a hope that, tempered a little by events, was there still, somewhere beyond the window, in the world from which she and her child were now excluded.

The whole of that long-ago morning came back to her now, as clearly as if she were there again, except that the sense of joy and hope remained far off, something recalled in her mind but not felt in her heart. Daniel had been sitting on the bench on one side of her. On her other side had been Ellinor Dowthwaite, who had murmured the words after her brother-in-law. Very likely she had been thinking, as many of them were, of her husband and the others in Richmond jail, where they had been for several months, for not paying their tithes. Now it looked as if very soon tithes would be abolished for ever and they would be free.

After all the years of struggle, after so many disappointments and betrayals, the time they had hoped and prayed for was close at hand. Richard Cromwell, floundering with the old problem of how to pay – and to control – the army, had been toppled by it, within

less than a year of his father's death. The remnant of the old parliament had been recalled, with doubtful members once more
excluded, and Oliver's son-in-law Charles Fleetwood had been
made Commander-in-Chief, though they all knew and rejoiced that
the real power lay in John Lambert's hands.

There had been little silence at that first Meeting of the new
order. When the reading was over, they had begun to talk of what
must be done, to organise petitions, to list men who would best
serve God's cause in the nation, men with God's spirit working in
them. 'Why not women too?' Ellinor Dowthwaite had asked, only
half jokingly. 'Can we not be justices as well as any man?'

In a gathering where the distinction between male and female
had never mattered, her point had not been ridiculed. 'That will
come, friend Ellinor,' Susannah had said. 'In Christ there is neither
male nor female.' She had felt Daniel nudge her then, and when she
looked round he had murmured with a grin, 'Thou'd be a good justice.' His eyes had been bright, reflecting the atmosphere of
excitement that had filled the room, like the electric tension before
a storm . . .

'Mother!' She went to the bedside. His eyes were bright now
too, looking up at her, as if begging her to ease his pain. She
brought him water, and bathed his marred skin.

. . . So beautiful, he had seemed to her, last summer. August, it
was, and they had been riding together towards Wether Fell, with
the silver expanse of Semerwater in the valley to their left, and
cloud wreathing the tops. She had been on her way to a patient;
Daniel had come with her for the ride. That day they had heard of
the Royalist risings that had suddenly erupted, most dangerously in
Cheshire, where Presbyterians once loyal to the Protectorate had
joined the Cavaliers. Lambert had marched out against them, and
many Quakers had joined him. That had caused some dissension,
for George Fox had spoken against the use of carnal weapons, saying that their only arms ought to be spiritual ones. John
Dowthwaite had been one of those who disagreed. Quarrelling over
the matter with his brother, he had ridden away to offer his services
to General Lambert, and had that very morning passed them on the
road, pausing just long enough to tell them where he was going.

'I wish I was a man and could go and fight the Royalists,' Daniel
had said, when he was out of sight.

He was only twelve and much too young; but Susannah had

remembered then what it said in the Bible, about the sword that had pierced Mary's heart, and she had felt she knew what it meant. Now she realised she had not known at all, only guessed; for now in truth she did know, with every successive twist of the blade in her heart.

Then, she had looked at her son and thought how beautiful he was, and, breathtakingly, how like his father. And how much she loved him.

Each year of his growing she had thought better than the last, bringing yet more joy and a lessening of the fear that had dogged her love of him from his birth. Lately the closeness between them had become open and conscious as it had not been before, at least not on his part. He would say small things – like the remark about her being a justice – that would make her realise suddenly how much he adored her. If anyone spoke or acted against her, he would rush to her defence, full of indignation. At the same time, she was the friend he turned to in any time of trouble, in whom he confided everything of importance, and she had begun to find herself doing the same, young though he was. The love between them seemed to be changing gradually into a tender comradeship that delighted her . . .

She looked round the room, shadowed, because the light hurt his aching head. The small bed, a chest, a chair and a table, a clothes press; and the musical instruments, recorder on the table, with a pile of sheet music under it, violin on the chair, lute propped in the corner. Silent now for so long. She who did not care for music ached to hear them played again, by the fingers that tore restlessly at the bed covers. Or his voice . . .

It must have been about two years ago, that day when she had gone into the garden, where he had been helping the lad who came in to do the weeding. She had found them singing, their voices echoing between the high walls in tuneful harmony, Daniel's clear sweet treble soaring above the vigorous but harsher notes of the other boy. Something Daniel had taught the lad, she had supposed, and then she had caught the words and realised it was nothing of the kind; or she hoped not, for she recognised it as one of the bawdy songs she had heard sung by the Cavaliers in York. She had been astonished and disturbed that something so profane should sound so heavenly. The next moment the singing had dissolved into giggles – and blushes from Daniel, when he looked round and saw that his mother had been listening. She had rebuked the two of them, and later told Daniel if that was what music meant to him, then it would be better for him to renounce it. He had been contrite, but had shown no inclination to give it up.

On the contrary, one day late in October, he had said, suddenly, without telling her how he knew, 'Philip Metcalfe's new music master's from Richmond. He's very good.'

It had been neither a question nor a request, but she had known quite well what was implied. She knew too what complications were involved in the whole subject. Daniel was nearly at an age when his future must seriously be considered, when if he was to follow a particular trade or calling he would need to begin on an apprenticeship or go away to university. She guessed – more than guessed – that if he had felt able to speak frankly about it he would have said he wanted to be a music master, since music was all he cared about. But he knew quite well that she believed, however reluctantly, that music was one of the carnal things that must be cast aside.

She had said nothing, not this time from unwillingness to hurt him, but because she had believed then that they were on the brink of a new age, when everything would be changed. If that was so, then all their old habits and ways of doing things – even such simple matters as apprenticeships, as they knew them – might very well be thrown aside. Except that the Parliament in which they had placed such trust was proving stubborn again, and resistant to change. It had released the dying James Nayler from prison, but there was little else to be said to its credit. Two days later, news reached Thornside that Lambert had sent Parliament packing and a Committee of Safety was to rule in its place . . .

Now, just a few days further on, it all seemed so trivial. The present had shrunk to this small room and the future was dark and terrifying and Susannah did not want to think of it at all. The light that had burned so clearly had gone. She did not know where to begin to look for it.

It had been extinguished on the day they heard the news of General Monck's refusal to accept the new government. He was in sole command in Scotland, with a large force under him, and he had declared himself in favour of the Rump, as they were calling the recently dissolved Parliament. 'That means war,' Margaret had said into the sudden silence that had filled the kitchen when John had told them the news, and Susannah had felt her heart beat faster. No sensible person had any fear of Royalists now; they had long been a spent force, easily crushed if ever they tried to rise. But if Monck were to march on London with his army, and Lambert to march against him – two of Oliver's most able generals, with Oliver's seasoned and disciplined troops under their command – then the outcome was not so certain, nor the future. Nor was their own safety, so near to whichever path Monck might take on his southward march. Susannah had not feared war in the old days, but she had not then been a mother.

'Please God they come to terms,' John had said, and Susannah had glanced at Daniel, who had just come downstairs and was sitting nearby. He was gazing into the fire with a distant expression and did not appear to have heard what was being said. She had realised then that he was very pale – he never had much colour, but now his fair skin had a greyish tint to it. He sat droopingly too, with none of his usual look of energy and vitality.

'What's up, lad?' Margaret had asked. 'Thou's no need to fear. We'll be safe enough.'

He had managed a wan smile. 'I'm not afraid,' he had said. But he had eaten little dinner and, when pressed, had complained that his head ached, and his back. Susannah had tried to remember if he had done anything that might have caused him to strain himself, but could think of nothing. She could only suggest he went early to bed, and tried to tell herself it was nothing to worry about.

Next morning – first day – he had felt rather worse, though he got up, intending to go to Meeting. But he was clearly so unwell that Susannah had sent him back to bed and had then spent the whole morning worrying about him, quite unable to centre her thoughts where they ought to be. She had come home to find that the pain in his limbs had grown and that he was in a high fever. It was then she had begun to be truly afraid. There had been an outbreak of smallpox in the town through the autumn, but there had been no new cases for some time. She had told herself Daniel mixed little with other children and it was probably just a feverish cold, but she knew she was fooling herself. The next day he complained of a stinging sensation on his skin. The morning after that the spots had come out, not many, but enough to leave her in no doubt what it was.

Full of dread, she steeled herself for what might come, while she

comforted and calmed him and bathed him with a soothing herbal
concoction, trying to remember what things had most helped her
when she'd had the disease, many years ago. There was, she knew,
little else that could be done, except to pray, which she did, endlessly, while she sat hour by hour at his bedside. In the grey hours
before dawn she sometimes found herself wondering how she could
bear to go on living if he died, but for the most part she tried not to
think of anything beyond the next few moments, beyond her son's
immediate needs. She was closed in by darkness, groping her way
blindly through it, not even daring to hope.

Once again Richard Metcalfe had been sent home at the behest of
the Army.

He had not minded being recalled to the Commons, though he
had heard of Richard Cromwell's fall with regret. He had seen hope
for the future in the young gentleman's lack of links with the army
and his essentially conservative temperament. But, failing that, he
had been confident that he and his colleagues in Parliament would
be able to agree on a settlement for the good order of the nation, so
long as the fanatics among them – Sir Henry Vane and his like – did
not gain the upper hand.

Yet within months here he was riding home again, with dismay
in his heart at the future prospects for peace and order. He felt a little more cheerful as he came within sight of the familiar grey towers
of his house, a safe stronghold against the world, which he had
made use of too little in the past troubled years. His small family
had gathered in the hall to greet him: a curtsey and a kiss from his
wife, a hug and kiss from his sister, a neat bow – hat removed –
from his nephew, and his own two little ones kneeling for his blessing. He felt their hair soft under his hand, warm, the bones of their
small fragile skulls alarmingly tangible. His heart seemed to melt
with tenderness. His children, his own flesh and blood: Grace and
little Thomas, sturdy and fair-haired, as he was. He bent towards
them, intending to take them in his arms, but they looked up at him
then and he saw no answering love in their faces, only an anxious
dutifulness. He straightened again, and told them they could stand
up. He knew he spoke brusquely, from hurt not anger, but it only
served to confirm them in their awe of him.

The next morning, at work in his study, he reflected gloomily on
his homecoming, and the strained and formal supper that had

followed it. He had looked forward so much to seeing his family again, imagining the joy and love that would enfold him the moment he stepped through the door. It was, he thought, another sad effect of these unsettled times that he was a stranger to his children. He prayed that now he was safe at home there would be leisure to put things to rights, that nothing would happen to drive him away again.

He was relieved to be interrupted by Nathaniel Johnson, who, hearing of his return, had called to see him. He was, like Richard, dismayed by the turn events had lately taken, and wanted to share his anxieties with the younger man. 'I ask myself if we can any of us desire a return to war,' he said. 'Yet without war what have we to look forward to – except to see God's will trampled underfoot, to have anarchy loosed upon us?'

'I fear you are right,' said Richard. 'The Quakers and other fanatics have grown and multiplied, while God's remnant has been rent asunder and cast into darkness. I ask myself what we have done to deserve such a punishment.'

'We are all mired with sin, however much the fanatics may deny it. All we have is God's grace, in which we must put our trust.'

'Sometimes,' said Richard hesitantly, 'I find it hard to keep a sense of His grace.' He saw that the Minister had not heard him, for he was turning over some of the papers piled on the desk, tracts and pamphlets advocating unthinkable changes that had been disgorged by the presses at an alarming rate since the spring and which, from a sense of duty, Richard had collected and read, as far as he had the stomach for it. 'I was trying to put some order into them,' he said apologetically, 'but I think they are incapable of being ordered, by their very nature.' He gave a wry smile.

The Minister did not smile, but not because he was out of sympathy with Richard. 'I can only pray that the Lord will be a refuge to His faithful people in this time of trial, and bring us safe through it.'

'Amen,' said Richard reverently.

'But, tell me, in worldly terms, do you think anything can be done? Anything is possible for God, of course, but . . .'

Richard shook his head. 'I don't know. The whole thing perplexes me.' Then, as if expressing a dangerous and heretical opinion, 'Sometimes, I find myself thinking the only way to restore order would be to call back Charles Stuart. On the right terms, of course.'

'I can see many dangers in that.'

'There are dangers in everything,' said Richard. 'But if the Quakers and the rest of them once rule over us, then that will be the end of order and property and good government, for ever.'

The Minister discarded one of the more violently worded pamphlets with a gesture of disgust. 'There's General Monck, of course. But does anyone know what he wants?'

'What we all want – an end to fanaticism and a return to order. Or so I suppose. He's a good soldier. But Lambert is a better, and his men would follow him to the ends of the earth. There's only one general who ever had a greater power to win the hearts of his men . . . and I don't mean Oliver.'

Next morning he rode to Nun Appleton, to see his cousin Tom Fairfax.

Walter wandered the steep, narrow streets that ran up from the Tyne and remembered how he had first walked there as a lonely thirteen-year-old orphan. He remembered how at night he had cowered in doorways, too weak to walk any further, trying to find a meagre shelter from the cold. It was in this place, from a doorway that he could not now recognise, that the Lord had first plucked him to safety.

The wind, spiked with snow, still cut through his clothes, though now they were not rags but the heavy red coat and sturdy breeches of a soldier, and there were boots on his feet; and the austere yet strengthening faith that had saved him then had grown into a burning light that warmed and cheered him even in this dark and bitter winter.

He was in Newcastle as a man and a soldier, preparing with his comrades-in-arms to defend England from invasion. That the enemy should be facing them from across the border was easy to accept, for that notion had been bred in him from infancy. What was harder to take in was the realisation that the enemy was made up not of Scots, not of Royalists, but of Englishmen of his own army, many of whom were his own old comrades.

General Monck was at Coldstream, looking across the Tweed into England, waiting. Walter's troop had been waiting in Newcastle too, for three weeks now; waiting for supplies to come from London, waiting for reinforcements, waiting to hear if Monck would, at this eleventh hour, draw back from the fatal step across the border into certain war.

The north was held securely for the Committee of Safety; for Lambert and the men who wanted the coming of Christ's kingdom. Long before Lambert's forces had reached it, Colonel Robert Lilburne had secured Newcastle, and Carlisle too and all the crossings to Scotland. Right from the start, men had flocked to him, deserting Monck, or driven out by him as he purged his now dutifully Presbyterian army of the last remaining Anabaptists and Fifth Monarchy men and Quakers.

Monck was playing for time, not being ready yet to fight, so the senior officers assured Walter and his friends. But until supplies came, they themselves were not ready to fight either, and meanwhile they were short of food and ammunition and shoes and pay, and it was bitterly cold.

Rounding a corner near his quarters, Walter met his lieutenant, his friend John Sawyer who, like him, had enlisted as soon as news came of Monck's defiance. 'I've been seeking thee everywhere,' John said. 'I've just had a letter from my wife. News from London.' He fell into step beside Walter. 'She tells me the apprentices have been rioting – for a free Parliament, they say. Some even call for Charles Stuart. They were fired upon, and several killed. Feelings are running high.'

Once, twenty years ago, Walter Barras had been like those young men, pouring into the streets full of youthful rage. In the end, he had found a home and a voice in the army. Yet these apprentices hated the army. They were too young to remember what England had been like under a King or to know what tyranny the army had freed them from. Walter felt a desperate sadness. For the first time he realised he was growing old.

Lieutenant Sawyer said, 'There's something else we've just heard. They're saying Black Tom's about to take the field.' Then, seeing the momentary brightness in his comrade's face, he added quickly, 'For Monck and the Rump, against us.'

Walter bit his lip. The shock and disappointment were profound. It hurt, to think that they might face their old commander in battle. For the first time his conviction that all would in the end come right began to falter. 'There are some would go over to him,' he said, quietly, in case to say it too loudly might make it certain.

His companion nodded, his face sombre. 'We're to march south, to be ready.' Then, more cheerfully, 'But first, tonight, we're bidden for supper with Friend John Turner.' He was a Newcastle Quaker, who had made his co-religionists in the army especially welcome. 'Will thou come?'

'I'll follow thee. Go ahead.' He stood on the river-bank, with the snow stinging his face, and he seemed then to see the future. He saw Lambert's army melt away, as the snowflakes were doing as they hit the grey ruffled surface of the water. He saw Monck march south, unopposed. He saw the old men take power in their hands again, the men who feared disorder and a threat to their own property more than they had ever wanted liberty, though once they had claimed to fight for it. He saw, joining them, the young men who had never known the tyranny of the old days. He saw a harsh revenge fall on John Lambert and Robert Lilburne and the others who had stayed true to their convictions, and on all who did not conform to whatever religious principles were held by the men in power. He saw himself back in London, a civilian once more, plying his trade in quietness, as the world moved on and passed him by.

As for the rest, the detail of it, he could see no further. But that was more than enough. It was not the future he had expected to see, nor one he wanted. His heart ached at the thought of it. But he knew he would have to accept it, when it came, because he realised now that he and his friends were too few to change the world, if the world did not want to be changed. There would have to be a different way. George Fox had been right. Their weapons were not after all of this world.

Susannah had not wanted to leave home, but the message had been pressing, and the snow had ceased falling half an hour before, so she could not say it was too dangerous to set out. Besides, the neighbour who came for her had himself risked his life by tramping through the blizzard from beyond Simonstone. Jane Pratt had gone into labour the night before, but they had all been prepared to let nature take its course, without outside help, until it became obvious that something was very wrong. 'We heard thy lad is sick of the smallpox,' said the neighbour. 'We'd not ask thee to come, but we fear Jane's like to die.'

Susannah went to pack her saddle-bag and then to say goodbye to Daniel, who gave her a wan smile. He was so thin, under the disfiguring, oozing blisters that scattered face and limbs. Sometimes there would seem to be a slight improvement – a lessening of fever, an hour or two of peaceful sleep – but always he would take a turn again for the worse, and she would know it was not over. Whenever he seemed a little better, she would wish she did not know only too well what complications might still arise, how close he still was to death.

She could hardly bear to leave him. Margaret clearly knew how she felt, for – undemonstrative though she generally was – she put an arm about her and said gruffly, 'I'll stay by him, thou knows that. And if owt goes wrong, I'll sharp send for thee.'

When Susannah reached the farm, soon after dark, she found that the baby had died in its mother's womb. She would have sent for a surgeon, but there was no one skilled enough within reach, so she had to do what she could herself. By morning the mother too had died.

It was a bright morning, the snow dazzling in its treacherous, beautiful whiteness. But Susannah felt as if she were riding home in the dark. She was desperately tired, not simply from the night's exertions and from her grief at losing a patient, but from the days and nights of watching and hoping and fearing at Daniel's bedside. As her pony struggled through the snow, skirting drifts, slipping on the thin frozen places where the wind had blown the path almost clear, she suddenly remembered the long ago winter when she had ridden with Richard and her father to Bradford. It had been just such a snow as this that year. Sixteen years past – in some ways it seemed no more than yesterday, in other ways it seemed centuries ago. She had been so young and vigorous then, and above all so sure of herself. At that time, she had supposed that with age came greater confidence and certainty. Yet here she was, middle-aged, afraid, and as full of doubt as she had been at the time of Daniel's birth; and terrified of what she might find waiting for her when she reached home.

She had thought when she heard George Fox that it was the end of her search, the beginning of certainty, that afterwards there would be no more doubt. She saw now that, on the contrary, the search was a lifelong thing, that certainty was never more than momentary, that there were many stumbling places in the path, many shadowed valleys from which she could not see a way out. She could only struggle to make out the light and do her best to follow it, rejoicing in the moments when all was clear, holding on desperately in the dark, trying to hope. It was just that at present she found it hard to believe she would ever see the light again.

By the time she reached Thornside it was snowing again and the streets were deserted. It should have been market day, but no one had come. As she neared the house something caught her ear, and she drew rein so as to hear better. There was a moment of sudden quiet, only the snow falling, and into it, faintly, distant, the sound of music, the soft plucking of a lute, a voice singing.

She had never stabled the pony so hastily, never moved so fast, running into the house. Just inside the door, she paused, listening again. Silence, a silence that seemed to shout at her. There was no one about. She dropped her bag in the passage and ran up the stairs.

The room was quiet, still, shadowed as ever. Margaret sat by the bed, in which Daniel lay unmoving. The recorder and the lute and the violin lay where they had always been, untouched. Susannah felt as if her heart had stopped.

Margaret turned her head, rose, came towards her. Was there some dreadful knowledge written on her face? 'I thought I heard music,' Susannah faltered.

Margaret smiled gently, 'He'll not be up to that for a bit yet. But he's had two bowls of broth and slept soundly since, for a good long time. I reckon he's on the mend.'

1660

CHAPTER FORTY-EIGHT

In London on the twenty-ninth of May, Walter Barras stood among the crowds thronging the Strand, hemmed in by a joy from which he was utterly shut out. He felt as if he were some alien being, a foreigner observing a ritual celebration that he could not begin to understand.

His head throbbed with the din of the bells and the roar of the people, ached with the brilliant colours of tapestries hung from house walls and flowers spread underfoot, the crushed perfumes heavy and sweet in his nostrils, overlaying the usual London stinks. But it was not the pain in his head that he minded, or the dazzling brightness that hurt his eyes. It was the sight that was the focus of so much joy, the sight that marked the very end of all his hopes: the passing ranks of soldiers, among whom he might once himself have marched, and in the midst of them, with his family and courtiers, the tall dark young man riding back to regain his throne.

Walter stood where he was until King Charles had disappeared from sight, his course marked by the spreading cheers of his subjects, and then he walked slowly back across the river to his little workshop in Southwark, through streets hot and smoky with bonfires, where men and women danced about flower-decked maypoles and fiddlers played till their arms ached. Everywhere was alive with the colours of flags and clothes and flowers, the laughter of children, the sound of triumphant singing.

He reached his house, and found that in his absence someone had smashed all his windows.

CHAPTER FORTY-NINE

Once, he would have made the journey from Widehope to Thornside in a day – not easily perhaps, but without thinking too much of it. This time, it had taken him three days, and they had all been difficult ones. He was unused to riding now, but there were few carriage roads in the dales. Exhaustion and pain had forced him to make more stops than he had intended, and even caused him to regret that he had so obstinately refused to bring a servant with him. But now at last, in the early afternoon of this September day, he was nearing the end of his journey.

It was hard to recall the vigorous man he had been when he last came this way, though the landscape tugged at his memory. Then he had been young and whole, not dragging with him the pain-racked encumbrance of a body that had clung to him against all expectation and all reason, for no possible useful purpose that he could see . . . No purpose, unless the outcome of this journey proved to be what he did not even dare to hope it might. Too long had passed, too much must have changed. But he had to know, and besides there was a ring to be reclaimed, which he had not expected ever to have need of again.

This had been a year of many surprises, though for him they had not been especially welcome. For the impoverished Royalist exiles the winter months had passed much as usual, avoiding creditors, idling the time away as best they could. For him, there had been the continuing struggle to return to some kind of normal life, once he left the hospital in Antwerp where he had been cared for since his cousin Shane had somehow managed to bring him from Ireland, safe from the savage revenge of Cromwell's troops.

No one had seriously expected him to survive the retreat from Clonmel, or the journey to the coast, or the sea voyage that followed, and he had still been close to death when he reached the hospital, which was attached to his mother's convent. No one had ever doubted that the wound sustained in Ireland was a mortal one. He was, they thought, just taking rather longer to die than had been anticipated. Lady Milburn had devoted herself to nursing him through his last days. Only, to everyone's astonishment, he had slowly regained some semblance of health, and it was she who had died, peacefully, in his arms. After that, he had left the hospital and moved into Ralph's lodgings, which were just round the corner from the convent. Ralph had been kind, but Ludovick had seen how deeply he missed his family. He had been on his way back to them when he had been lost at sea.

Then, in the spring, nearly two long grief-ridden years after Ralph's death, had come the news that the King was to return to England, and the exiles with him; against all expectations, with no help at all from Royalist plotters, almost without conditions. Ludovick had shared none of the jubilation of his fellow exiles. He only wondered yet again why he should be alive, when Ralph was not. In the past days, staying at Widehope, where his welcome was the warmer for Ralph's sake, he had been reminded more forcibly than ever how much Ralph had to live for. Ludovick had nothing, or nothing he cared about, though like all those whose property had been confiscated outright, he had his lands restored to him, more or less intact. He supposed that in returning them to something like their former prosperity he would find a purpose, of a kind. Certainly, he now had more than enough to keep him for what was left of his life – even to keep a wife, if she should say 'yes' to him. But he tried not to consider that possibility. He was weary of disappointment.

There was rain in the wind, faint spattering rain, short-lived and inoffensive. The light was clear, bright, the fells alive with cloud shadows scurrying over pale grass and dark sprawls of heather, and bracken turning to autumn bronze. Trees were browning in the gullies that pierced the slopes, their gold and copper branches tangled with the fiery berries of hawthorn and wild rose and rowan. Up here, not far from where he rode so slowly, a solitary tarn mirrored the blue of the sky in its ruffled surface. Above the gentle rhythmic thudding of his horse's hooves, there was little sound but the wind.

The track snaked over the hills, into shallow valleys, through the rocky beds of streams, up again, and brought him at last to where the land fell away and the whole dale lay before him, hazed, golden with autumn woods, the river laid out in shining loops. The road now wound steeply down to his right. He was almost there – and he was terrified. He remembered how it had felt waiting to go into battle, but this was worse.

A little further, and he glimpsed the clustered roofs of a small town, angled thatch and stone slabs, held in a sheltered crease in the slope of the dale. Thornside. The road twisted again, and the roofs were hidden from view. It was quiet here, out of the wind. Only the splashing of water could be heard, from somewhere out of sight to the right of the road.

Another sound. A bird? No, he thought not. Something else, less likely. He drew rein, straining to hear. The horse snorted, and it was a moment or two before there was quiet again. No, he had not been mistaken. But who on earth would be playing a lute in this isolated place on an autumn afternoon in uncertain weather? He would have suspected tinkers or gipsies, but he had never heard of lute-playing gipsies.

Possessed by curiosity, he dismounted and began slowly to lead his horse towards the source of the sound, which came from the same direction as the splashing water.

As he drew nearer he recognised the tune: Dowland's *Lachrimae Antiquae*, old-fashioned but with a melancholy beauty, and very familiar, for he had learned it as a boy. Whoever was playing it now was more than competent.

There was a small disused quarry, sheltered and sunny, at whose further end a stream splashed from a height to its bed below, and then ran on over rocks towards the road. Rowan and hawthorn had seeded themselves in its sides; and under one of the trees, not far away, the musician sat, a slight figure with his head bent so that the brim of his hat shaded his face. He had the music laid on the grass before him, held in place by four stones. At that moment the notes began suddenly to tumble one over another, falter, and then with a loud angry chord they came to an abrupt end. The musician looked up, saw that he was not alone, and blushed very red. He was surprisingly young, only a boy. 'I can't get that bit right,' he said, without preliminary. His eyes were clear and grey, very direct.

Perhaps it was the directness that drew Ludovick to him.

Whatever it was, unused though he was to children, uninterested on the whole, he warmed to this boy at once. He found himself saying, 'You took it a little too fast. Would you like me to show you?'

The boy held out the lute and the man sat down beside him and began to play. The boy watched him, intent on the movement of his fingers. At the end, Ludovick said, 'Now try again.'

He watched in his turn as the boy played, getting it right this time. 'That's it, isn't it?' he said, his face bright. 'It was my Grandmother's music, but there's no one to tell me how to play it.' Ludovick gathered then that it was some years since the boy had received any formal music teaching, which made his playing the more impressive.

They talked about other music, eagerly, openly, as if they had known one another all their lives, demonstrating a point now and then with the lute or a snatch of song: the boy's voice was sweet and pure and true. Ludovick had an odd feeling, as if everything had suddenly begun to happen very fast, too fast for him to grasp precisely what was happening. He had never warmed to anyone so quickly and so completely as he found himself doing to this child.

In fact there were, he realised after a time, things that he ought not to have liked about the boy. In all their talk, he had made no move either to remove his hat, as a well-brought-up boy ought to have done, nor to address him as 'sir'. It might have been absent-mindedness, for he did not otherwise seem ill-mannered. On the other hand, Elizabeth Liddell had told him the north was seething with Quakers, a new and terrifying sect, not even heard of when Ralph left England. Ludovick had found it odd that no one seemed to be in the least bit anxious about Catholics any more. The Quakers seemed to have dislodged them completely in the national demonology, which made him more than a little curious about them. What he did know was that they made no gestures of respect or deference by word or deed, and dressed plainly. This boy was plainly dressed.

'Do you live close by?'

'Thornside.'

For a moment Ludovick had almost forgotten what had brought him here; now it all came back, sharply, giving him a momentary sensation of sick apprehension. 'You've come a long way to play your music.'

'It's better to play where Mother can't hear.'

'Does she forbid you to play then?'

'No.' The boy hesitated, then said, 'She doesn't like it, but she says she has no liking for music anyway, so it would be easy for her. She says I must do as the light tells me.'

'The light?'

'That is in everyone,' said the boy solemnly. 'The spirit of Christ. As Friends teach.'

Friends were Quakers, so he had been right. 'What does the light say then? That you can play your lute?' He was faintly amused at so literal an attitude to spiritual things, but it was clearly of importance to the boy.

He had a look of concentration. 'Sometimes I see that it's a carnal thing that I ought to cast aside, that I only cling to it because I love it in the dark. Then I think I see that the spirit is in the music too and I must love it for that. I'm still seeking to know.'

The bewildering ethical complexities of the matter made Ludovick's head spin. When he was this lad's age, right and wrong had on the whole been clear-cut things set before him by others, to accept or reject as he chose and then take the consequences.

It began to rain again, rather more steadily, and he remembered that he had not come here to pass the time in conversation with a Quaker boy, however charming. He stood up, and the boy did too, saying, 'I'm going home now.'

'Then if I may I'll walk with you,' said Ludovick. 'I'm bound for Thornside too.' They set out, he leading his horse. Suddenly he heard himself asking, 'Do you know of a Mistress Susannah Fawcett?' He wished almost at once that he had not said it, for it brought nearer the moment when he would have to face the truth, whatever it was. But it was too late.

In fact the boy gave a crow of amused surprise. 'She's my mother!'

Ludovick halted. He could not at that moment have put one foot in front of another if he had tried. So she was married then, and this boy was her son. That explained the feelings he had, for they were Susannah's eyes that had looked at him. He realised the boy had halted too, and was staring at him in some concern. He tried to pull himself together, tried to say without bitterness, 'She's wed then.'

The boy coloured a little. 'No. I'm a bastard.'

Of course; stupid of him – after all, he had not said, 'She's not called Fawcett now.'

A bastard . . . He had taken a step more, then halted again. The world seemed to be spinning about him, though from somewhere he heard his voice say, 'How old are you?'

'Thirteen.'

He tried to do some kind of calculation, but his brain was working very slowly, struggling through a confusion of sensations. He thought it would be about right. Could there have been anyone else at that time? Surely not. 'Who was your father, do you know?'

'A Royalist, killed in the war. Mother says she will tell me the rest when I'm a man.'

So Ralph had not been the only one to hear that he was dead – or had she invented it to avoid awkward questions? He heard the boy's anxious voice, 'Thou's sick . . .'

'No – no.' He looked at the fair oval face, the long nose, the heavy brows. There was even, faintly, something of Charles there, he thought. His heart was thudding; anxiety, hope were fighting in him, and a tender, spreading joy that he tried to curb for fear that it might bring him to disaster. His son . . . What if he were to say it? But he must not, not until he was sure. 'I was . . . I've come to see your mother, that's all.' Somehow he struggled to stave off the boy's curiosity, encourage him to talk about himself.

The house, at the far end of the town, facing directly on to the street, was comfortable, simply furnished, spotlessly clean, the hallway dim and cool. A servant took the horse to the stables, unobtrusively, but without any mark of deference. Daniel – he had learned the boy's name – paused long enough to say, 'Wait there – I'll put this away, then I'll find Mother.' Then he ran upstairs with the lute.

Ludovick could not bear to stand there, waiting for the boy's return. He heard sounds from somewhere at the back of the house and made his way to a door, standing just open.

Inside, a stillroom, lined with shelves above a wide bench, full of shining flasks and bottles, and a woman in blue, with a spotless apron, pounding something in a mortar. A small woman, still slender, a white linen cap half-concealing her dark hair. Not a thread of grey that he could see . . . She paused, became aware that she was not alone, looked round. A brown face, scarcely lined, grey eyes as clear as ever. He saw surprise, the everyday surprise of someone suddenly interrupted while busy at some task; then a growing question; then, abruptly – with a rush of colour, a sharply indrawn breath – a mixture of recognition and doubt. 'Ludovick Milburn. I thought thou was dead.'

There was an intimacy in the way she said his name, without title or other embellishment, a woman speaking to a man on equal terms. Yet it was an intimacy that brought a little chill, for it made him realise as nothing else could have done that she was no longer the woman he had known and loved all those years ago, had loved so obstinately ever since, but someone different, older, changed by experiences he knew nothing of. Beautiful, scarcely touched by age, recognisably the Susannah he had known, she was yet a stranger, though one whom, in those few brief moments, he had already fallen in love with all over again. It was more of a beginning than an end, for he would now have to get to know her afresh, as if they had only just met for the first time.

'So did I, for a time,' he said, answering her at last. Then: 'The boy. Daniel.' He saw dismay in her face, then a question. He said, 'We met, out there. Is he . . .?' Suddenly his voice failed him.

'Yes,' she said. A little wry smile. 'Thou was wrong, when thou said thou couldn't.'

Again, that wild thudding of his heart . . . His son, to share things with, to teach and to learn from, to love, following not his own father's example, but the one Ralph had shown him, and Rob too . . . An heir to inherit the lands he was now glad he had regained; a hope and a purpose. He knew at last why he had lived.

If only he had known at the very first, then he would have made her marry him, stood by her as best he could – except that on reflection he could see that it would not greatly have helped her. He tried to imagine what it must have been like for her, bearing their son alone, but it was beyond his experience to do more than guess at it. 'It must have been hard.'

'Sometimes,' she said. 'Especially at first.' Then, her face suddenly transformed by the softest of smiles, 'I would not have had it otherwise, all things considered.'

Silence, while they stood gazing at one another. Susannah realised that she had kept her memory of Ludovick fresh by looking at his son, and it had now become so inextricably mixed with it that she had not realised how completely Daniel's image had replaced his father's in her memory. On first seeing him a moment ago she had not even recognised him. Now, minute by minute, she was seeing more in the figure before her of the man she had known.

He looked older than his forty-one years, his dark hair greying, his face lined and sharply angled, its colour unhealthy. The richness of his clothes could not disguise the fact that he was a sick man, and weary, one hand holding fast to the back of a nearby chair as if he could not have remained standing without its support. Yet the eyes were as she remembered them. He was not a stranger, for he had once been a part of her, and that could never be taken away.

Why had he come? To claim the ring he had given her? To claim her . . .? Could love survive so long, with so little to feed it? Hers had not, though something was left still, she supposed, a shadow cast by the past. But so much had happened since then. She had made so many discoveries, about other people, about herself. She had thought she saw with some clarity the path her life would take in the years to come. Not in every detail, of course, for nothing was ever certain. But she had seen that before long Daniel would have learned all he could from her and she would have to guide him towards the next stage of his life. After that, she would have more time to work at her studies and perhaps at last to write the book in which she would set down the fruits of her experience. Life would never be tranquil, of course. Ever since the King's return was first spoken of, persecution of Quakers had increased. She knew that in the years to come even the most unobtrusive of their number – those like herself – would be touched by the repression. She had been glad that Daniel would soon be an adult, beyond being hurt by her actions or what was done to her.

Now, suddenly, in a moment, everything had changed. Nothing was remotely certain any more, nothing mapped out, for she no longer saw clearly all the factors that must be taken into account. She supposed she could say to this man who had stepped into the stillroom like a sudden breath of icy air, 'Go away. I don't want thee to have any part in my life, or my son's.' In a sense she had that right, for she had borne all the hardship of Daniel's birth, raised him and loved him and brought him safe to where he was now. Yet she sensed that to do that would be to destroy Ludovick, and she had loved him once.

She heard Daniel coming down the stairs, crossing the hall. She had to decide: whether to shut this man out, close the door for ever on the past and by evasion and subterfuge exclude everything she did not deliberately choose to admit; or whether to allow him into their lives, even to welcome him, knowing that so much might then be taken from her hands, so much that was important to her threatened in ways she could not guess at.

Daniel stood in the doorway. She saw Ludovick turn to look at him, saw the boy's smile in return – warm, open, already looking at a friend.

'Come in, Daniel,' she said. And then, taking a deep breath: 'This is thy father.'